THE BANE OF THE TROUBLESOME WOMAN

EVA LEPPARD

A Wild Ink Publishing Original

Wild Ink Publishing

https://wild-ink-publishing.com

Editing: Khloe Sinclair

DEDICATION

To my Nanna, Jessie Dawn, who would have been proud that I've become a writer, even though she preferred books with more dragons and/or sex scenes.

And, to some of the amazing women in my life: April, Ivy, Emma, Reiny, Ari, and Meg.

ALSO BY EVA LEPPARD

The Pitfalls of Being a Goddess

Mother Trouble

LILITH GETS JACK OF EVERYTHING

"This is not panning out as I expected," the naked man said. He looked over to the woman who was standing next to him, arms crossed. "This whole being a human experience. It's just not what I anticipated and—"

"I'm not responsible for your expectations," said the woman, chancing a glance at the counsellor. His face remained impassive, so she decided to keep going. "I'm not, am I? That's not part of the deal. Your feelings have nothing to do with me."

A gentle breeze blew through the branches of lush green trees, and the trills and warbles of impossibly beautiful birds drifted down to where the three beings stood. The climate, temperature, and humidity were, quite literally, perfect.

"But you love me. I am the love of your life, your very reason for living. Of course, you care about my feelings," said the man, his voice sounding troubled. 'They should be more important than your own, if I'm being totally honest."

The counsellor, an older man with a long white beard that he had taken to tucking into his tunic for matters of convenience, rubbed his wrinkled forehead and sighed. "My dear, can I have one more run through of what the main problem is. From your perspective. Just to make sure I've got it all straight in my head."

Adam started to talk, but the counsellor held up his hand. "As Lilith sees it," he said firmly. "You will have your chance in a minute. Just wait. Your impulse control is dreadful."

Adam frowned and opened his mouth as if to say something, but changed his mind, instead sitting back on his rock and crossing his arms, unconsciously mirroring his wife.

"Right," Lilith said. Her thick black hair brushed against her bare shoulders, and she pulled it back, annoyed at the sensation against her skin. "Is there a way to make this shorter, Dad?" she said. "It's always in my face."

"Maybe if you covered up a little," said Adam. "Put something over your shoulders and—" he gestured to her chest area, "this. Then your hair wouldn't be as irritating. And it would kill two birds with one stone." His voice faded as she saw the look on Lilith's face.

"Stop trying to make me cover up. You really think I want to layer up in this heat?"

"It's very distracting," grumbled Adam. "I mean, it would be more comfortable for you, of course. That's the real issue. Your comfort. Wouldn't you be more comfortable covering up your… bits?"

"Dad," said Lilith with exasperation. "He's trying to make me cover up my bits again."

"If we could stick to the task at hand," directed her father. "And we agreed to use the word 'counsellor'. Or 'mighty counsellor' if you prefer. Clearly delineated roles are necessary for this to work best, I think. On this occasion, anyway. You had something you wanted to discuss, Lilith."

"All right, yes," she said. "Primarily, the issue is that Adam isn't interested in my pleasure. My sexual pleasure." She rolled the words around in her mouth in a way that made Adam shudder.

The counsellor nodded his head. “Right.”

“I hardly think this is an appropriate thing to discuss with our father,” Adam muttered.

“He asked,” she snapped. “And your lack of interest in discussing our sex life is 90% of the issue in our relationship. I should be free to discuss our sex life with whoever I want, whenever I want.”

The counsellor sighed and rolled his shoulders in an attempt to release some tension.

“He’s not interested,” she said. “He refuses to see me as a sexual being, and I’m wondering if we’re really that compatible when it all comes down to it. No offense, Dad,” she said hastily, glancing at the bearded man who sat before them in a haze of spiraling clouds and flames, “but did you do some personality tests or the like before you matched us up?”

“Let’s leave my competency out of it for now, shall we?” he said.

“I don’t see why I should see you as a sexual person,” Adam said. “Sex has nothing to do with it. You’re my companion, my suitable helper, and the eventual mother of my children, and if what we have been led to believe is true, we’re the future of the entire human race.”

“Well, I didn't sign up for that either,” she snapped. “Fuck me, I just want a decent ploughing from my man on the regular, with some creative positions, better foreplay, and maybe some spicy talk. That shouldn’t be so hard to do. I don’t even know what I like yet because you won’t experiment. I mean, I’ve started to take matters into my own hands but…”

Adam’s face blanched. “See? This is precisely the kind of thing I’m talking about. She’s literally out of control. We are in a meeting, and this is what we have to listen to? Why is it about sex all the time? It should be a tiny, insignificant part of a relationship. Barely a blip. She’s just obsessed.”

"I wouldn't be obsessed if you'd give me a good seeing to occasionally," she snapped.

"Right," the counsellor said. "I think I understand where you're coming from,"

"Or not coming from," she muttered.

"See what I have to deal with?" Adam protested again.

The counsellor nodded. "I'm beginning to, yes. You said this isn't panning out as you expected. I'd like you to elaborate on that, please, Adam."

"It's just what I said. When you created us, I was led to believe I would have a certain role, and certain responsibilities, and she would have certain roles and responsibilities, but as far as I can see, there has been some blurring."

"Of those roles and responsibilities," clarified the counsellor.

"Correct. I expect to be the man and make the decisions, and I expect her to be the little woman and do the sweet things that make her happy, like finding pretty leaves and collecting the choicest berries for me, but ultimately, she must defer to me. She is my wife, after all."

"I'm not a fan of any of that, and I'm not interested in pretty leaves," Lilith snapped. 'Why are you pouting like that, Adam? Pull your bottom lip in and uncross your arms. You look like a baby. I've told you sulking doesn't work on me anymore.'

"It is a little childish, Adam," said the counsellor with a nod. " I have to agree with your wife there. And you, Lilith, would prefer to not defer to Adam, is that what you're saying?"

"I have been deferring to him," she said. "I've tried, I promise I have. I've been good and demure and caring. I've done everything he wanted."

Adam nodded, what might have been an attempt at a benevolent expression on his face. "You were a dutiful wife for a while. You were submissive and subservient and very accommodating. That's why this whole 'new you' is so jarring. I'm used to you warming my rock for me every night and giving me the best bits of the bread you cook, and so—"

"It's not a new me," she said between gritted teeth. "I've just finally thought about what I want, what I need. You never ask me that. I'm thinking for myself."

"That's not really part of the plan, is it? Thinking for yourself, that is. Your needs are directly related to my happiness," he said patiently. "That's what we discussed. That's why it's so perfect."

"It's not perfect for me," she said, raising her chin. "I'm not happy. I knew that we had some problems, and I was willing to accept them. We live in paradise. We sunbake and swim and pick berries and chat. We don't have as much in common as I'd like, but as you've already told us, Dad, we're the first people. We have limited context. Oh, look, that vine is growing nicely, and what should we call that animal with the horn on its head can only take us so far."

The counsellor nodded again. "This is an issue we've discussed."

"Yes, yes, I know," she said hurriedly. "I get it. When we go travelling or get a pet unicorn or something, in the fullness of time, then I'm sure we will have lots to talk about. But in the absence of, you know, other people or deep philosophical issues, I'd really like to explore each other's sensuality a bit more fully."

"As you've mentioned."

"And this is where we run into a problem," Adam said. "It's not your role to be on top. It's unnatural and unladylike, and if we can't lie quietly when the moon goes behind a cloud and do our business, then I'm not interested."

"You mentioned roles again," the counsellor noted. "I'd like to circle back to that if I might. I created both of you to be equal. Both from the same clay and all that? As far as I planned it, you're on an equal footing."

"I think we'd both appreciate some clarification around that, as a matter of fact," Adam said. "Because I don't see how that's going to work, and if you forgive me being totally honest, I don't know if you've thought it out properly."

"You don't see how it's going to work?" the counsellor said. "You're equal. You listen to each other. You give and take. A true partnership of equals. That was my whole plan, such as it was. Please remember this is my first time too, you know, so there is a touch of trial and error. I didn't design Lilith to be submissive, precisely."

"See, I told you. Equal," she said.

"Look, I don't think that's the best way of going about things. After all, between you and I, Dad, I'm the one with the human brain, aren't I?" Adam chuckled companionably. "I guess I can't expect someone as expansive as you to understand how the little guys operate."

The counsellor sighed. "While technically, I am God, the Big G, and therefore meant to come up with everything myself, you know, omnipotent, omniscient, and omnipresent. I don't think that precludes a little collaboration, though."

"And omnificent," Lilith added. "You're that too."

"Quite, exactly," he said. "Thank you for remembering that, Lilith. It means a lot to me. I am indeed. But, as you rightly pointed out, Adam, you're the man on the ground, and I should take your opinion into account. Far be it from me to claim that I have all the answers."

"And my opinion too," Lilith said.

"Oh, yes, of course. Yours too. Essentially, your preoccupation is more… intercourse, is it?"

"No," she said. "I told you, I—"

"You see," said Adam, "this whole idea of everyone being equal. I just don't think it's viable." He felt himself crossing his arms petulantly again and tried to relax them by his side again.

She narrowed her eyes at him. "You were going to try and sulk again, weren't you?'

He set his jaw firmly, as if the pouty face that seemed to be an automatic reaction whenever he was challenged was the furthest thing from his mind. "Someone needs to be in charge, don't they? Look at you. You're God. We're not equal to you. You're in charge and rightly so. We need you for all the ineffable, big-brain stuff. And that principle should, I feel, continue down. You, then me, because let's be honest, I'm the most like you, and then, well... her."

"What is the matter with you?' she snapped. 'What's your problem? Why are you trying to be so bossy? You're standing all rigid and weird now.'

"Excuse me, but I'm brainstorming how to create a whole new civilization here. That's what were supposed to be doing, right?' He looked to God for confirmation. 'Going forth and multiplying and all that. I'm simply following your instructions."

"That's something we need to talk about, too," snapped Lilith.

"Yes," God agreed. "That was the wider plan. In a general sense. That's what there was talk of, at least."

"And to be brutally honest, I don't know how that's going to be done without a fairly tight management structure and everyone knowing their place."

"By everyone, you mean me, right?" Goosebumps were appearing on Lilith's arms, but as far as she could tell, the perfectly calibrated temperature of the garden hadn't changed.

Adam shrugged. "For a start."

She looked to God for help. "Dad, do you agree with all this? You made us equal on purpose, right? You literally breathed life into us. Surely you know what you're doing?"

"I do," he said a little too quickly. "I do. Honestly. But also, Adam's point about not muddying the waters with too many competing voices is a good one. This is new to all of us, after all. I've got a lot to think about."

"All right," she said, raising her chin. "Why can't I be the one who's in charge then? Why does it have to be him?"

"To be fair," Adam said, "your main talking point so far has been deviant sexual relations, so I'm not sure if…"

"I wouldn't worry about that anymore," Lilith snapped. "I've gone right off you anyway. The pouting was one thing, but now you're standing oddly. Are you trying to be taller by standing on your tiptoes?'

Adam wobbled slightly as if, yes, this was exactly what he'd been trying to do, and Lilith wrinkled her nose as if she had smelled something unpleasant drifting to her on the breeze.

'You can find someone else to have insipid vanilla sex with. I'm leaving."

"Just hold on a second. Let's not jump to any hasty decisions that we might regret later,' the counsellor said. 'You can't just walk off when things don't go your way, young lady."

"This is not fun for me,' she said. 'No one is listening to me. You're both making plans that, apparently, I'm not allowed to be involved in, and I'm spectacularly sexually unsatisfied. Give me one good reason why I should stay."

The counsellor and Adam glanced at each other nervously.

"Well," started Adam, "I need a helpmeet."

"A fucking what?" she said. "Try again. My purpose has nothing to do with you."

Adam grimaced. "Please modify your language, my dear. It's quite distressing for Dad."

"It is a little bit, though," the counsellor said. "Your purpose, I mean. You don't really exist as an individual. It would be good if you could work together. There's a grand plan and all. You're supposed to work together to populate the planet. It would help me enormously if you would just—"

She crossed her arms. "Which I didn't agree to. I've been co-opted into this without my consent." Seeing Adam roll his eyes, Lilith paced off in irritation.

"Oh, please,' he said. '*Consent.* She's making up new words now. Look, I'm just going to say out loud what everyone is thinking. She's a liability."

The counsellor sighed loudly and shook his head. "I don't want to take sides, but are you with us or against us? Because we need to work as a unit, and I'm beginning to suspect that I haven't made a team player. Adam here clearly understands what I want of you both."

"Can we do it without her?" Adam asked, tilting his head and gazing over at his wife through narrowed eyes.

"I don't know. That doesn't sound very sporting. You can't just cut people off when things don't go your way. That's not the dynamic I'm trying to foster and perpetuate."

"If it was though," Adam pushed, "I've got an idea. A more suitable fallback. It will involve some surgery, but it will also get rid of the whole equal thing she keeps going on about, which, in hindsight, was a mistake. Let's get rid of this one and find me a new companion. Someone simple and easy to lead who will make me look like a strong patriarch and who is specifically subservient from the get-go. No, just assuming the new one will fall into that role."

"I am not a team player, you're both arseholes, and I'm off," Lilith called to them with disgust. She had found the cup she had painstakingly carved out of cedarwood, and a leaf that was perfectly shaped to cover her head in the advent of occasional inclement weather. "You two can do whatever it is that you do, but I'm sure that other interesting and exciting things await me. Things that don't involve me having any responsibilities or being in debt to anyone."

"Adam, I can make you someone more suitable if you think that's the way to go?"

"Can you make the new one shorter? Lilith positively towers over me, and it's very emasculating. I'd like to have more say in the mechanics of the next one. Maybe dainty and meek. And small feet. I like the idea of small feet."

Lilith had already started walking off. She didn't know where she was going or what she would do, but anything had to be better than this.

"Lilith?" She heard the counsellor's voice in her ear. "I would like a quick word before you go. I feel we owe it to each other."

"I'm massively pissed off with you, and I want it on the record that I don't owe you anything at all. Walk and talk, though, because I want to be out of here by evening."

"As you know, I'm new to all of this, and I'm not so proud to admit that I may have made mistakes. I know all those omni words are very important and relevant, but I'm still having trouble believing my own hype, to be honest. Adam is being so helpful to me at this testing time."

"I'm not in the right frame of mind to be listening to your personal issues," she said. "That feels like a you problem."

"No, it is, it is," he said quickly.

"How do I get out of here anyway?" she said, peering through the vines and lush trees that draped and twirled around her. The gardens ran gloriously with the melodious cries of fantastical, iridescent birds, and small, impossibly soft creatures capered around her feet, looking up at her with adoring eyes.

"Just keep walking," he said. "There are no walls of gates or guards or anything, although maybe that's something I should add to my to-do list."

Far in the distance, through the millions of different shades of green, Lilith could just make out something that wasn't green. It was a yellowy brownish golden, something she'd never seen before. She deliberately veered in that direction.

"Anyway," he continued, "I was hoping we could come to a bit of an agreement because I don't think the PR around this is going to go my way."

"I don't know what you're talking about."

"There are…nfactions. I won't bore you with the details, but there are some higher angels, not so much the cherubim. They tend to be darlings, but the archangels, well, let's just say I feel like I need to watch my back a lot of the time. And the Eons from Beyond the Void are constantly…"

The haze through the greenery was taking shape now, presenting a hard horizon that contrasted sharply with the soft, undulating lushness that had been all she'd ever known.

"And I think admitting we have made a mistake and you storming off to start your own life might not look so good on paper."

"Again, Dad. Not really my issue."

"What I was wondering," he said, "is whether we could say this is all your doing. That you decided to leave, and Adam and I had nothing to do with it. You just completely overruled us, so to speak."

She stopped. "How does that help your argument or help make you look less weak, or whatever it is you two are bothered about?"

God sighed heavily. "In my mind, this can be the case of a capricious, headstrong woman who does something dreadful, and the two men who just let her have her way and damn the consequences. It could become a cautionary tale or some such. And then Adam and I will tweak things so all goes as it's supposed to, and we can start the whole populating the planet and subduing it, all of us happy that we've gone our separate ways."

"What dreadful thing am I supposed to have done?" she asked. "All I've actually done is take my own cup that I crafted myself and told Adam he's a dud root. Hardly the stuff myths are made of."

"Between you and me, I don't necessarily think you're at fault. Obviously, I'd deny ever saying that if it came down to it, but I think Adam is reaching by blaming you for all of this. I don't know how a few creative positions would have been the worst thing in the world, and I'm going to try and tweak his personality if it's at all possible. But he's my son and, look, he's not as strong as you. He will be. One day, I know he will be. But right now, he needs support. You'll be okay. I know you will. You're a force and he... well, he isn't. Yet. If you're happy to just leave things as they are, take the role as the antagonist and head for the desert, as it looks like you're already doing, then I think that would be a good result for an ordinary situation."

"Fine," Lilith said. She squinted, the glare on the parched sand harsh on her eyes. "But there's something I'd like you to do for me first."

ANGELS LIKE TO WATCH

"Hello, my love," Lilith said, smiling as Asmodeus approached and sat down next to her. His large hand took hers idly, and he kissed it, her palm cupping his beard. He followed her gaze as she looked out across the still waters. They could turn in a moment, these seas, and she loved the days when they pulsed with tumultuous energy and the churning hid the peace beneath. But today it was all peace, all tranquility.

She moved her shoulders a little, allowing her wings to catch the rays of sunlight. A touch of shapeshifting, which had been her final request of her father, served her very well. Warming herself by moving them lazily was just perfection.

"Are you well today?" He leaned forward to look at her face, pushing the dark hair out of her eyes and cupping her cheek tenderly.

She smiled and took his hand, kissing it. She loved his hands especially, with their slightly misshapen fingers. "Quite well," she said, smiling. "I enjoyed last night."

He chuckled. "You seem to be healing the parts of you that needed exploration quite effectively."

"And I thank you for your assistance with that. Although…"

she moved her hand to the small of her back and rotated her shoulders slightly.

"Yes?" He raised one eyebrow and rubbed his beard.

"I might need to start stretching," she said. "I'm not bouncing back as much as I'd like to."

He laughed. "Noted. After a particularly energetic fucking, I'll give you a rub down as well. Just a quick question. Did you tell Lamia that she should head off to find herself and leave her spawn for other people to look after?"

"Yes," Lilith said. "She was having a personal existential crisis and needed to make a new life. I told her it was a hugely energising thing to do, to just walk away from everything that's annoying you, so she's left."

"Right," Asmodeus said slowly. "It's just that other people have to look after them now, and they seem very sad."

"The people or the children?"

"Everyone, from what I can tell."

"I assumed their father would do it. It seems hugely unfair that just because she carried them, she should have to look after all of them, too."

"Lamia is a hermaphrodite, remember? There's no father."

Lilith shrugged. "Not my problem as long as she's happy."

"Will you be helping to look after the spawn?"

"No way. What a terrible thought."

"You're very opinionated and fiery, you know. I love that about you," he said.

"Thank you." She moved her head to kiss him, her tongue finding his, and within moments, his hands were in her hair, and the world had faded around them.

This was worth leaving Eden for.

Lilith didn't know how long it was before they realized they were being watched. She raised her head and glanced to the side, where three beings stood.

"You've got to be joking," she said, "How long have you three been standing there? Perverts."

She reached down and tapped Asmodeus shoulder, using her nails to get his attention, and then she pulled at this thick brown hair.

He was nothing if not committed.

"We have company," she said, pointing to the three gloriously glowing beings who stood a little way off, shuffling their feet awkwardly and clearing their throats.

"It's okay, you can finish first," one of the beings mumbled. "We can wait."

"Don't worry," she said, pushing herself into a seated position. "I was just going around again anyway."

Asmodeus moved next to her and slipped an arm around her naked waist. "Do you know them?" he asked, biting her shoulder gently.

"Do you want me to get rid of them?"

"Did my dad send you?" she asked.

One of the beings stepped forward, his eyes darting around, trying to find somewhere to rest that didn't make his face twitch involuntarily. Lilith stretched languorously and sat back on her hands, spreading her legs a little. She had no intention of making this easy for them.

The being, which had a huge pair of pretentious feather wings and a face that glowed like the sunset on a glorious summer evening, complete with the vibe of the full moon rising on the eastern horizon, glanced at his colleagues uneasily. "We have been sent," he said portentously.

"Angels," Lilith confirmed. "You're running errands now, are you?"

"It's kind of our main job description, apparently," said another of the beings, and Lilith thought she detected a note of bitterness in his voice.

"Sounds fun," she said brightly.

There was an uneasy silence.

"Or not. You can always come and live with us if it doesn't pan out for you over there. We're mainly Earth-based, so we don't have any of that alternative reality dimensional thing that you get with Heaven, but we're making it work."

"Actually," Asmodeus said into her ear, the vibration bringing up goosebumps on her arms, "I want to talk to you about that."

"Later," she said, stroking his cheek.

She noticed that the tumescent glow that surrounded the angels had dulled slightly.

"Don't try to enlist us with your wiles," said the one who she assumed was the leader. "We are impervious to your glamour. We will never join you and your band of demons."

"Whoa," she said, standing. "That escalated quickly. First, glamour and wiles, you say. Thank you. I've been working on my image, so I'm glad it's not going unnoticed. But *demons*? Calm down. We're not demons, and I wasn't trying to enlist you. I was merely suggesting that if you're not happy—"

Asmodeus cleared his throat. "I am, as a matter of fact. A demon."

"Yes, my love, of course."

"Unholy night hag, we are here with a message from the Mighty and Strong Glorious Creator," the angel said firmly.

Asmodeus was standing beside her now, his body generating a vibration she had never felt before. She placed a hand on his arm.

"We have an offer from the Lord Most High," the main angel said. "He has offered you the chance to return, take up your rightful place alongside Adam as the Mother of All Creation, and should you do this, all will be forgiven. The Father of All Things Amazing bears you no ill will for leaving, against their wishes, and potentially ruining the plans of all humankind, and in his glorious magnanimity, he is willing to give you another chance at your true and Heaven foretold destiny."

Lilith frowned and glanced at each angel in turn. Only the main speaker was able to maintain eye contact with her.

"So much to unpack there," she said to Asmodeus before scratching her neck and gazing off into the distance for a minute. "I realise this probably isn't the main takeaway, but you know that me leaving was a mutually agreed on thing, right?"

"Why should we trust the words of a demon?" the main angel replied.

"Mate, I'm wondering if you're in the right place. Because I'm patently not a demon. Why do you think I am? What have people been saying?"

"You're all demons here," said the lesser angel, gesturing around awkwardly. In the distance, an open grassy area could be seen, and it was filled with a growing group of beings. No one seemed to be moving toward it, but the inhabitants were multiplying rapidly.

"What's going on over there?" asked the angel, shading his eyes and peering off into the distance.

"It's a portal of some kind," said Lilith. "New beings are arriving all the time. Well, I say arriving. They're just kind of appearing. We're having to get a whole orientation thing worked out. It seems to be an even mix of fae, Nephilim, nymphs, mermaids, and I think someone saw a random basilisk the other day. My dad might want to get on that if he doesn't want the entire planet inhabited by them rather than these humans that he seems so fond of."

"A creation portal," murmured one of the angels to another. "I don't think we know about that, do we? Make a note of it. We'll need to shut it down ASAP. But the main point is," he said, addressing Lilith and Asmodeus again, "you're all demons. This is a demon-encrusted land of spite and depravity. Everyone knows about it."

Lilith pointed to her partner. "Only he's a demon. And he's in and out a lot. He doesn't live here the whole time."

"Depravity, though," said the second angel. "There's a lot of that. Just look at what was happening when we arrived."

"Consensual sex between adults is not depraved," she snapped. "But I know how your lot feel about that, so we'd best agree to disagree."

"We have been sent to offer these terms," said the leader, in a vain attempt to get the conversation back on track. "You have been given one final chance to return, and all will be forgiven. If not, the consequences will be dire."

"Why do they want me back, though?" Lilith asked. "I thought they were going to get a new girl. Or make a new girl. Something like that. Poor bugger. They seemed to think they had plenty of options. A smorgasbord, so to speak."

"Things aren't panning out so well with the new one," said the second angel, clearly eager to get involved in a discussion about it. "She's very dull, apparently. In hindsight, he has decided that maybe you're the better option, and he does need some spice in his life. So he'd like to give you another go and see what happens. A fresh start, so to speak. No hard feelings."

"That's disgusting," said Lilith. "I don't suppose he's told her that he's coming on to me again, has he? She probably thinks everything is going swimmingly."

"You have one chance," the main angel's voice boomed gloriously.

Lilith thought he sounded like a wanker and suspected that the other angels did too.

"Does the fact I was having sex with a demon when you arrived affect this offer in any way?"

The main angel licked his lips. "We could pretend we didn't see it."

"I could do it again if you'd like a reminder," Lilith suggested.

"I thought maybe you'd got it out of your system by now," suggested the third angel helpfully.

"Oh, I've barely started," she said. "But can we just circle back to the consequences if I don't say yes? Because I'm not going to say yes, so I probably need to know what I'm getting myself into."

"In the event of your refusal," boomed the main angel, the light around him pulsating and throwing a glow on the whole area, "one hundred of your demonic children will be destroyed every day. You have no one to blame but yourself." There was a pause, and the third angel shuffled his feet awkwardly.

"He doesn't even know if he wants me, but he's planning a whole punishment thing if I say no. He's literally delusional. You can see that, can't you? I mean, I know that on paper you have to support him, but he's a dick, isn't he?"

The second angel leaned forward conspiratorially. "I'm not a fan of that bit, can I just say. The destroying demonic children. I think it's an overreaction."

"It definitely feels like an overreaction," Lilith scoffed. "It feels like a bloody enormous ridiculous tantrum on someone's part."

"I'd have thought so," Asmodeus agreed.

The angel refused to make eye contact with her.

"It's Adam, isn't it? This feels like it has some serious 'my ex-husband' vibes about it."

The trio did not answer.

"It bloody well is, isn't it. This is all Adam. He's calling the shots by the sounds of it. That doesn't sound very 'appropriate balance of roles and responsibilities' that he was always going on about."

She paused to see if they would offer an opinion, but they seemed to be fixated on staring at what was happening in the portal off in the distance.

"Anyway," she continued, taking the blanket she'd been reclining on and folding it up, "this is all conjecture because I'm sorry to inform you that I have no children, demonic or otherwise."

"Yes, you do," the second angel insisted. "You give birth to hundreds of demonic spawn each night. As a result of all the..." He searched for the right words.

"Demonic coupling," offered the third angel.

"Yes, that's right. Demonic coupling. You give birth to hundreds of monster spawn every day on account of all the…"

"Coupling, she reminded them.

"Quite."

"Nope," she confirmed. "I have never given birth to children, demonic or otherwise, and I have no intention of doing so. Also, I don't couple with demons, plural. Just the one. At a time. At this stage. Although that might change."

"We have clearly been told that you are deliberately populating your lands with demonic spawn in an attempt to…" He stopped.

"In an attempt to what?" Asmodeus asked.

"I'm not sure," the lead angel said stonily. "But I'm almost entirely certain that it's dreadful and evil and demon-like and will involve taking over God's true destiny."

"Oh, for fucks sake," Lilith groaned. "I don't think I'm able to live up to all the publicity that is apparently being shared about me. I'm screwing demons, plural, and giving birth to hundreds of children in order to what? Take over the world? It seems to be doing perfectly well on its own."

The angels nodded in unison.

"What a dreadful idea," she said. "How would I possibly find the time with all that parenting? And why would I want to? Why would I want to control the world?"

"Because of your willful need to take control of everything and disregard Adam and God's plan for you and your headstrong belief that you know what's best for you."

Lilith looked at Asmodeus, who shook his head. "This is literally all because Adam couldn't make me cum, you know that, don't you? This whole story arises purely because he's a terrible lover. And now I guess he'll be even madder because I won't go back to him. The lengths people will go to repair their damaged ego, I swear. Also, I do know what's best for me, and most of the time for other people too."

The third angel looked around at a huge bonfire that was about to be lit in the distance. A group of beings had been dragging driftwood and debris from the beach and piling it up, and they were waiting for night to fall before they lit it.

"Look," he said. "Demonic plans." His voice held very little certainty.

"It's a bonfire," she said matter-of-factly.

The angel nodded, his eyes wild. "That's right. At night. Night is for evil doings. And shenanigans. We've definitely heard talk of shenanigans."

"What's wrong with night?" Asmodeus asked, puzzled. "Is night a problem now, too?"

Lilith looked at Asmodeus in bemusement. "Are we not supposed to like nighttime now?"

The angels spoke as one. "Nothing good happens after dark."

"Maybe God shouldn't have made nocturnal animals, then," Lilith muttered. "I'm having trouble keeping up with what's allowed and what's not at this stage. Maybe he should write it down and hand it out or something."

The main angel looked at the others and nodded appreciatively.

"For God's sake," Lilith snapped, "I'm joking. He's controlling enough without a fucking handbook. Anyway, I'm not coming back. I have no demonic spawn for you to kill, and I'm consorting with a demon, singular, not demons, plural. If you could just let us live our lives and stop micromanaging, then I think that'd be better for everyone."

The angels nodded sagely. "As it will be. You have made your decision."

"And they knew I'd say no, didn't they? They deliberately manufactured this whole thing so that they can spread lies about me, then hold their hands up in mock despair and say, *oh no, it wasn't us, we had no choice.* This is a whole plan to make me look like the bad guy, isn't it?"

"It's time for you to go," Asmodeus said to the angels. "Off you pop."

"Tell my ex-husband that he's got a perfectly good wife, and he needs to forget about me. I know what he's up to, and maybe he should stop manipulating our father and let him try to work things out himself."

"Never you mind with us passing on messages," snapped the angel. "You've given up any right to know what's going on, so just concern yourself with your own dreadful blood-curdling plans, and we'll get on with the business of goodness and love and light and doing the actual work. Don't you think that we'd quite like to be lying around in meadows too?"

Lilith put her hands on her hips. "Do you actually believe all this? Are you so deep in the echo chamber that you believe everything you're told by this alleged omnipotent leader? Because I've met him and, you know, I don't feel like he really knows what's going on. Sweet but doddery and easily led. I think he needs someone to-"

But in a haze of fire and a hiss of what looked like dry ice, the angels were gone.

Asmodeus wrapped his arms around Lilith and drew her close. "Are you all right, my love?"

She rested her head against his shoulder. Her chest felt tight, and she steadied herself by taking some deep breaths through her nose. "Yes, I think so. But why is Adam being such an arsehole? I never even did anything to him except tell him what I wanted."

He laughed, the sound reverberating in his chest. "As someone who was literally created to be a demon, I can assure you that we have no idea what's going to happen. I suggest we just try to make as much meaning as we can and hold on for dear life."

There was a shimmer in the air next to them and a rapid popping noise, and the third angel stood next to them once again. He staggered slightly as he found his feet. "Dimension hopping twice in five minutes. I'm not built for that," he said by way of explanation.

"Yes?" said Lilith tersely. "Can we help you?"

"I've just nipped back for a moment while the others were taking off their robes to let you know you need to be careful," he said quickly. "They're looking for scapegoats. They're looking to set up this whole good/evil dichotomy, and anyone who makes decisions for themselves or who aren't buying into the narrative that's, to be honest, being made up on the fly as far as I can tell, is going to slot into the 'evil' part."

"So I'm evil now? Just like that. I dared share an opinion with a self-appointed alpha male, and I'm evil?"

The angel glanced around nervously as if he expected God to descend next to him. "Yes, you are. They were talking about it on the way back. You're going to become, and I'm sorry to be so blunt, but I've only got a second, a symbol of seduction and eroticism."

"Oh." She smiled. "I quite like that."

Asmodeus nodded. "Yes, that works. You're very sexy."

"Steady on," the angel said. "I'm not finished. And chaos."

Lilith frowned. "Still not terrible. I'm not great at organisation."

"Obviously, I'm not making myself clear," the angel persisted. "God and, well, Adam for the most part, but we all pretend it's God, they're gun-shy now and nervous they might lose power. And because you're a… female, they think it's to do with your breasts or your uterus or some such. Maybe something to do with a cervix? Is that a word? I'm not too clear, but he's going to tell everyone you're a baby killer."

"I mean, babies are pretty annoying," Asmodeus said.

"And the Queen of Demons who seduces men to get pregnant so you can give birth and then—"

"Yes?"

"Kill the babies."

"That I've deliberately got pregnant with?" she confirmed.

"Seems to be the idea."

She nodded. "Huh. Okay, I don't quite know how to feel about this. Seems needlessly convoluted. Be way easier to just not get pregnant in the first place."

"You're going to be the cautionary tale to all women about how they need to not be lascivious, and if they are, then men will be emasculated, and babies will die."

Lilith pursed her lips. "This feels like an overreaction."

"I just wanted you to know. The word is getting out, and you might not be that…"

"Yes?"

"Popular."

"For how long will I remain unpopular?"

"For the rest of history."

She glanced at Asmodeus, who shrugged, bemused, and back to the angel. "So because I have a few little opinions, I'm literally the representation of an evil woman, am I?"

The angel nodded.

"Right," she snapped. "Well, they ain't seen anything yet."

* * *

JARED SHADED his deep blue eyes with his precisely manicured hand, unconsciously mirroring the actions of the angel in the distance. "Hello," he said to no one in particular. "Looks like we've got a visit from the bigwigs." He couldn't make out much, but the pulsating golden light that surrounded several figures gave off a vibe that he wasn't used to seeing around here. They had a real sense of their own importance and an almost pathological need to get Very Important Business done.

In a timely manner.

Quite different from the lounging around, swimming, chatting about feelings, sex, weaving, and the stick and poke tattoo studios that had sprung up nearby.

He had been here for a few weeks now. One minute, he had been chatting with his pals, playing cards, planning shenanigans, making some jokes, and the next minute, one of his mates had taken offence to an innocent quip, and he was in the middle of a field next to a swirling creation portal, trying to make sense of a new life away from his mischief-making crew. A solitary trickster, as it were. A lone shit-stirrer.

His memory of the evening was hazy, but he may have made an innocent remark about someone's mother. There had been a lot of decently aged merlot, and a card game that had lost him more than he was comfortable parting with, and a comment about someone's mother's almost preternatural flexibility, and then suddenly here he was.

He wouldn't have thought beings who were happy to be known as "Eons from Beyond the Void" would have triggers, but his new existence on this planet would indicate otherwise.

And now he was bored. This lot was way too laid back.

"Hey, buddy," Jared called to the multi-tailed furry thing that was lying back on a tuffet of grass, chatting to a fae. "I saw one of those basilisks from the camp next door take that stick you were using to tattoo yourself the other day. You know, the one you said was the best one you'd ever used. Pretty sure it ended up on the bonfire."

The multi-tailed furry thing looked up, a vague smile on his face. "No worries, man. Property is theft anyway. I'm happy to share the communal goodness with whoever needs the love."

Jared shuddered.

"Isn't that the boggart you've been hanging out with, over there talking to that fertility nymph?" He directed this to the small fae who was weaving a headdress out of clover and daisies.

She looked up and smiled beatifically toward the couple. "Yes, it is. Hi there, gorgeous creatures. Have an amazing day enjoying each other's spectacular bodies."

This lot was totally unflappable. He pushed his dark fringe out of his face and twisted his back, trying to get the knots out of it that had been caused by sleeping on the ground. He had taken on a humanoid form when he arrived; it seemed easier that way. Too many tails or heads just seemed needlessly complicated.

In the past fortnight, he had attempted to start a party planning committee, a "gifted and talented" program for a select few, and a multi-levelled marketing scheme selling a kind of nut that seemed to be quite popular—all groups he judged most likely to cause division and unrest, but there were no takers. No one was interested in drama.

But there were angels over there, talking to the delicious Lilith, so maybe something was happening.

After a while, they disappeared, and things went back to normal. Boringly normal. He sighed and contemplated telling Lilith the mermaids were going to unionise.

He heard a puff from the creation portal and realized he had wandered very close to it. He usually avoided this area, not for any reasons of safety or ethics but because the last thing he wanted was a newly arrived creature following him around. Lilith had started some kind of mentoring program, which he had made it his duty to avoid, and he had been very successful.

Until now.

Another fae had arrived. He could see that immediately. She was tall and lithe, as her kind tended to be. She looked to be the same age as him, maybe slightly older, but that kind of judgment was always tricky with otherworldly beings. Her dark hair fell in waves over her shoulders, and she held her arms out to steady herself as she appeared.

Some beings arrived in an ungainly pile, some staggered around, gasping for a few moments as if they had just exited a claustrophobic birth canal, and some immediately strode off, clearly certain of their own individual purpose from the get-go. But this one steadied herself, looked around, sniffed the air, and then smiled at him. A naive, beautiful, trusting smile that almost, but not quite, warmed his heart.

"Hello," she said, her voice lilting like spring water dancing over river pebbles. "I've just arrived. I am a glorious and new creation."

"Of course, you are," said Jared, offering her his arm, which she took with a gentle firmness. "And I'm your welcoming committee. Let me show you around."

Finally. Something to play with.

He decided her name would be Fae.

"So," said Fae, once he had explained about the general lackadaisical and unproductive nature of everyone in the vicinity. "Everyone should have a job then, do you think?"

"Absolutely," said Jared firmly. "Everyone needs a definite purpose and aim. Then they can scurry around, filling their days with very important business. And they need to make sure that their business is the most important. The priority. Otherwise, they will be boring. Sorry, bored. They will be bored, I mean."

She looked at the various groups of beings scattered around the area. "They seem happy though," she said, smiling and waving to the clover-weaving fae who gestured at her to come over and chat.

"No, no," said Jared, firmly turning her and positioning her in another direction entirely. "They don't know what they want. That's something you really do need to get your head around. Most beings have no idea what they want, or what's good for them."

"And me too?" she said, gazing up at him. He could tell she was already absolutely smitten with him. "Should I have a job? Tell me what I should do."

"Yes, you should," he said. "But don't worry, I'll help you. I'll make sure we find something you're very good at and will make you a fully functioning and productive member of society. None of this lying around deciding what kind of bird each cloud looks like."

"Do I have a purpose?" she asked. "I know I'm a wonderful and marvellous creation, inherently good because of the fact I exist, but from what you've told me, that's not enough. I need to *do* something."

"Yes, productivity," he said. "It's not really caught on down here yet, but in certain realms, it's all the rage. If we can find you a purpose quickly, then you'll be ahead of the curve. A trailblazer. You want to be a visionary, don't you? You need to focus on side hustles and monetizing hobbies as soon as possible."

She shrugged her shoulders, and her silky hair fell around her back, spilling over her bare breasts. "I think I just want to be happy," she said, and the hopefulness in her voice was unmistakable.

"Eh," said Jared, wrinkling his nose. "Happiness is overrated. Much better if we get you set up with a good job and a list of goals, and we take it from there."

"Will you help me?" she asked.

"Always," he promised.

WHAT SISTERHOOD?

Her husband took Eve's face in his hands, and she leaned her cheek into his touch just for a moment. The feeling of relaxing into him, of giving in and trusting him, was one she loved and something she had hoped she could cherish forever. He was her man, and she was his woman, and it was all as it should be. They could love each other forever.

And she knew he could be a better man. She *knew* it. Better to her. Better to her heart.

If only the snake hadn't shown her another way…

"It's all right," said Adam softly. "It's all right. I'll sort this out. Trust me. Can you do that?"

"We have to tell Him what the snake told me. About how we should be equal. That I should get to make decisions too. Remember? You said you want an equal partnership," she pleaded.

"Well, yes, that was one of our options. I'm not absolutely convinced about that bit, to be totally honest. Let's ask Him what to do, shall we? He's always looked out for our best interests. I don't know if we can jump ship on the say-so of some oddly formed dragon snake hybrid creature that seems to have turned up out of nowhere."

Her heart sank. He had seemed to listen to her when she had brought this up yesterday.

"I've been thinking about that," she said, taking a deep breath before she spoke. "If the snake is in here, you know, the Garden of Eden and all that, then it has to be here on His say so. Given he's omnipotent and everything. The things that it told me, well, they must have been at his behest, I would have thought…" her words trailed off.

"I don't know about that. It was coming out with some pretty incendiary stuff. I wouldn't be surprised if there wasn't something at play that we don't quite know about. Beings out to get Him, and us, purely because of his overwhelming goodness and magnanimity. We're his beloved children. I am, anyway. You know he wouldn't do anything against my interests."

"But the snake wasn't completely wrong, was it? The bit about you holding that 'rib' business over me. You do that a bit, don't you?"

"I do," he said soothingly. "I do, and I'll try to do better. I won't mention it again." He gently flicked the end of her nose with his smooth brown fingers. "You're a funny little thing, aren't you? You and your ideas. You try your best, don't you?"

She bristled a little and raised her hand to her nose. "You know I don't like it when you do that. We talked about my boundaries, remember?" She saw his smile had disappeared and added hurriedly, "But I do love you so much. You are my true love. Having boundaries doesn't mean that I don't love you, you know."

"Doesn't it, though?" he said, his face darkening. "But well done for telling me what the snake said. That's the level of openness and honesty we're going to need to embrace if we're going to make it as a couple. It's hard for me to trust, you know, but I feel as if I can finally open up to you. You're healing me."

"Adam," she said, placing her hands on her hips. "We're the first people on Earth. I don't think you've had that many opportunities to become damaged by love. You can't be scarred already." She laughed, but he did not smile back; she saw a look of nervousness briefly cross his face.

"Despite that," he said gravely, "you make me want to be a better man. Can you help me get there? Can you help me be the man I want to be?"

Before she had a chance to respond to this, they heard Him coming toward them, calling out as if He didn't know exactly where they were all the time. Eve slipped her brown hand into Adam's. She knew that He might be angry, but with her husband beside her, supporting her, she knew everything would be all right.

Adam stepped forward. "I told her we shouldn't eat it," he said, his eyes wide. "I told her we shouldn't, but you know she can be so persuasive. I barely had any choice. Dealing with women feels like déjà vu at this stage."

Eve gasped, yanking her hand out of his.

"No, you didn't. That's not true. Why would you say that? You didn't tell me not to eat it! It happened when you weren't even talking to me because I hadn't arranged your rocks the way you like them. You were giving me the silent treatment when I ate the fruit, so how could you have told me not to?"

"Well, I put on my disapproving look at least. I assumed you would infer that meant I wasn't impressed."

"But you bit the stupid thing too!"

Their father held up his hands, frowning at Eve. "First of all, mind your language. Let's not bandy abuse around." He glanced at Adam. "You tried to resist, did you? Good, good. This sounds plausible. Can you explain that further?"

"I knew that, strictly speaking, we weren't supposed to eat fruit from that tree, but, you see, given that Eve and I are bound together, I was under the impression that I'm supposed to honour her, and I didn't want to upset her by refusing it. You know what she's like. And she did that thing where she curls her hair around her fingers. You know I can't resist that. And you know what she's like when she gets her period; you're always a bit flighty and unreasonable when you've got your period. We feel as if we must walk on eggshells around you, to be honest."

"That sounds hard for you," God said with a sympathetic nod.

Adam winked at him. "No one to blame for that but yourself, old fellow. For the hair and the hormones. What were you thinking?"

The two men laughed. "Maybe I should try to get it right eventually."

Eve took a deep breath and tried to practice one of the tricks the snake had taught her. "I'm not comfortable with you two speaking about me that way. I don't think it's fair."

Adam tried to compose himself, but a little giggle escaped, and God frowned at him.

"I do think," said Adam, "that all this assertiveness is a direct result of eating that fruit. I mean, you weren't talking like this a week ago, were you?"

"What do you mean, me? You ate it, too. I fail to see how I'm the cause of all these issues."

"Ah, yes, but as has been clearly noted, you come from my rib, and that means that you're not quite…"

"Fully formed," God finished.

"Quite. Fully formed."

"You do need our guidance. Well, Adam's guidance technically, but I'm around for advice if it's needed. Anyway," said God, "as fun as this all is, we do need to get down to more serious matters. The matter of eating this fruit from the old 'good and evil tree'. As you know, I explicitly told you not to do that. There will need to be consequences."

"You did tell us that," said Adam. "Fair cop, absolutely, you did say that."

"Can I ask a question about that, now you've brought it up?" interjected Eve. "As we're on the topic, so to speak. What did you think would happen? You put this massive tree in the middle of the garden, a gorgeous tree, by anyone's standards, and tell us not to eat from it."

God frowned. "You're right," he said to Adam. "She wasn't talking like this a week ago."

"It's true, though. About the tree." Her chest lurched as she pushed the point, but she pressed on regardless.

"I did do that," God conceded.

"A big sparkling tree."

"It's good, isn't it?"

"It is. Very good. I believe there are some fairy lights in there?" she asked.

"Ah, well spotted. I did try to make the fairer sex observant this time. Glad to see it's panning out."

"There we go. You put a beautiful tree, covered in delectable-looking fruit, in the middle of our home and told us not to eat it."

"Yes."

"Yes. Can I ask what you thought would happen?"

"I expected you not to eat it."

"You expected us not to eat it."

Adam was nodding in agreement. "Sounds fair enough to me. Not eat it. Easy. Good move, Dad. Willpower and all that."

"But why?" Eve asked.

"Why what?"

"Why would you put a massive, prominent, literally twinkling tree in the middle of our home and ask us not to eat from it?"

"I didn't want you to eat it because eating that particular fruit would give you the knowledge of good and evil," God said patiently.

Eve rubbed the bridge of her nose. Once, she would never have pushed something this far, but something within her seemed to have changed. She loved Adam; she loved both of them, husband and father, but were they helping her be her best self? Is this the person she wanted to be? Scared and submissive and having no… what was the word the snake had used? Agency, that was it. Part of her wanted to stop, to apologise and make everything all right again, but another part of her needed to push on.

"I already knew the difference between good and evil, thank you very much. But I feel as if we're talking in circles here," she said. "If it was important to you for us not to have that knowledge, wouldn't have it been easier to just... not put the tree there? I genuinely don't understand."

God mused on this idea for a moment. "But then you wouldn't have had the choice."

Eve raised one eyebrow.

"The choice to disobey me or not, you understand."

"Mind games," Eve said. "Right."

"Come on, Honey Bunch, see it from His point of view," Adam said, glancing uncertainly at God. "He has to test us, you see."

"But why?"

"Just because it's the way things are, I'm assuming. Right, Boss?" He glanced at the old man.

At that moment, Eve made the first truly independent decision of her life. Although she could feel the tears beginning to course down her cheeks, she began to grab the few possessions that she called her own.

"Oh, oh," Adam said, noticing the tears. "Are we having Big Feelings?"

"I'm not feeling very loved or nurtured right now. I need some time on my own."

"On your own?" Adam said aghast. "You don't do 'on your own'. You always want to be with me."

"I can't be here."

"I can't believe this is happening again," said Adam with the slightest hint of a whimper.

Eve didn't register this comment as strange. She arranged the interestingly shaped stone she'd found in the river and the pleasantly fluffy pelt she used as a cushion under her arm and lifted her chin. "So, I'll just be off. East, do you think? I was going to turn right at the nearest cherubim, but I'm happy for any directions if you'd like to be helpful."

"But," Adam spluttered, "you can't just go. It's dangerous out there, for a start."

"How is it dangerous? What's out there that could be harmful?"

"Other men, for a start."

"What, just men?"

"Mainly, yes."

"Dad, you said we are the only ones on Earth," said Eve.

"The only ones who matter," God said. "I said you were the only ones who matter."

"I'll be sure to pass on that message when I meet up with them. I'm sure they'll be thrilled to hear that they're not important. Like me."

"But you can't go," said Adam. "You have to stay here with me. I mean, I don't want you to go. You love me."

"I do love you," she said, beginning to sob. "But I don't like the way I'm being treated. And I don't even know if I believe that you love me anymore."

"That's hardly the point," said Adam.

"You're not going to find things to your liking out there," said God, with a worried look on his face.

"I don't want to go," she said, twisting her hands together. "I want to stay here, at home. But I don't know what to do. I'm so confused. Please just say something to make this all better."

"This is all that bloody snake's fault," snapped Adam. "None of this would have happened if it hadn't gotten involved. I fail to see how letting a snake whisper in the ears of easily manipulated women is a good idea, is it, Dad?"

"What snake?" God asked.

"That one," said Eve, pointing toward a thick knot of vines that grew up a sapling a little way off from where they were standing. "The green one over there is hiding in the leaves."

There was a shimmer in the greenery, and what had seen a

glistening jewel like an emerald shimmering snake unwound itself from the tree, materialising as a woman as it touched the ground.

"Thank you very bloody much," said Lilith as she walked toward them. "I thought we had a sisterhood thing going. He wouldn't have known I was there if you hadn't said something."

"Sisterhood," said Eve in confusion. "I didn't know we had a sisterhood. I'm so sorry. I didn't know you were a person. I thought you were a snake. But I'd like to be friend"

"I would have assumed you'd have known I was there before Eve told you," Lilith interrupted. "What with all the omnipotence?"

"He was focusing on other things," snapped Adam. "He could have known if he'd wanted to."

"Of course he could," Lilith said. Her thick black hair fell over her brown shoulders, her naked body glistening in the sun.

"Lilith," said Adam, his voice high-pitched before he brought it in line and lowered it by an octave. You're looking… well."

"Do you two know each other?" Eve looked back and forth between them.

God sighed heavily. "What have you done, Lilith. I thought we'd dealt with everything. We made an agreement. I thought you were happy."

Eve was looking back and forth between the beautiful woman, her husband, and her father. "Adam," she said again. "Do you know this woman?"

"I've helped this girl see what was right in front of her," Lilith said, ignoring Eve. "I've empowered her. Something you've done everything in your power to avoid."

Adam sneered at her. "How dare you show your face here, after all we've done for you."

"Here we go. Let the mansplaining begin," she muttered to Eve.

Eve could feel a pit open up in her stomach, a chasm of

uncertainty and confusion. She unconsciously stepped toward Adam.

"This behaviour is disgusting," Adam said. "It's all very well you deciding you hate us and want nothing to do with us."

"That's a bit of an exaggeration—"

He held up his hand to silence her. "It's all very well to turn your back on the ones who loved and nurtured you, but now you try and turn this poor girl's head? And influence her? Ruin our love?"

"Oh, your love?" Lilith scoffed.

"It sounds like you didn't tell me the truth either," Eve said shrilly. "You didn't tell me you two knew each other. You're just as bad as they are, keeping things from me."

"That wasn't relevant. I'm nothing like them. And you have no idea what you're talking about."

"Why don't you let me decide what's relevant or not. You're as bad as they are," she repeated. "You're treating me like a child."

"I know what's best for you. You're better off on your own than with them."

Eve started at Lilith in horror. "You want me to leave here and head out into the unknown? At least I'm safe here. At least I'm loved."

Adam stepped forward and took Eve's hand tenderly.

"He doesn't love you," said Lilith. "He doesn't know who you really are."

"Who I really am?" sobbed Eve, her voice breaking. "I don't know who I really am. I thought you were helping me, and now I'm questioning whether these new thoughts are even real. Am I throwing everything away for nothing? Who am I?" Eve's legs felt like water, and her chest tightened.

"You know he wanted me back?" said Lilith. "You know, he sent angels to ask me to come back because he didn't want you anymore? Pull yourself together, for fuck's sake."

A sob escaped Eve's throat. "That's a horrible thing to say to me."

"You liar!" yelled Adam. "You heinous, evil liar. That never happened. I would never choose you over her."

"Look," God said, glaring at Lilith. "Now you've upset her. In her condition."

"My what?"

"Her what?" Adam and Lilith said at the same time.

God beamed. "You're expecting a baby. Surprise!"

Eve rubbed her tears away with a fist. "A baby?" she whispered, one hand falling to her belly. "A little baby to love? And to love me?"

Adam gave her a hearty thumbs up. "There you go. Something to take your mind off things and give you something to do. Good. That's sorted you out. But you," he snapped, glaring at Lilith. "There's nothing for it. You'll be known hereafter as a demon, as a destroyer of men's souls, as a baby killer, and an evil agent of chaos, lust, and depravity. Demons shall be your only—"

"Yes," she said, "I already know all that. I thought you'd already put the word out there. That's the intel I'd received anyway. Didn't realise I'd had some lead time. It's starting from today, is it?"

"Can we just all calm down?" God said placatingly. "I feel like there is absolutely a way forward here if we can just talk it out. Lilith can see that Eve is going to be happy again, and I'm sure that she, like us, just wants everyone to be happy. That's what we all want, happiness."

Eve tried to take Adam's hand. She wanted to wrap her arms around his neck, to share in the joy of new life, but he was pacing back and forth. "Are you happy?" she asked the back of his head. "We're going to have a baby. I'm going to give you a baby."

"It's from today," snapped Adam, ignoring both of them, his eyes fixed on Lilith. "The whole demon thing should start from today. Shouldn't it, Dad?"

God sighed heavily. "I just wish there was a way around this."

Lilith glared at the men in front of her. "Fuck it. I'm not scared of you. Let's do it."

There was silence.

"You don't sound very worried about it," God said, glancing at Adam. "I thought you said that would put her in her place."

Lilith shrugged. "There are worse things I could be. And demons are amazing in the sack from what I've been able to tell. I don't mind being a kind of dark goddess. I like the sound of that."

Adam's face darkened even more. "Your reputation means nothing to you."

She laughed somewhat wildly, and her eyes glinted green in the sunlight. "Nothing you ascribe for me, or set out for me, or intend for me can touch me. I refuse to acknowledge your power or your authority. Do what you want to me."

Eve felt all the energy go out of her body. She had been on edge for days, ever since meeting the snake in the garden. Everyone was angry, she didn't feel cherished, and she was having a baby. She staggered a little and put her hand against a tree to steady herself. The greens and browns of the garden swam around her as she concentrated on breathing in and out through her nose. She just wished everyone would stop shouting.

"Please stop," she said weakly.

Lilith noticed her pale face. "I can help you take care of that little problem if you like. A few herbs will do it. You don't have to be tied down to Adam or motherhood. You can make—"

Adam's face blanched with horror. He grabbed his chest. "I can't believe you would do this. This is completely beyond the pale. You try to destroy my masculinity again? Try to hurt me in the deepest core of my being? Dad, you can't allow this to happen. You can't let me down again. She needs to be punished."

God shook his head sadly. "Oh, Lilith. You shouldn't have said that."

"Evil," Adam bellowed, his hand pointing, shaking at Lilith.

"Evil demon of death and destruction." His face had turned red, and his body seemed to be vibrating. "You she-demon! Temptress and purveyor of all that is terrible and heinous."

God put his hand out to steady his son, but he had levitated above the ground, his rage consuming him.

"Do something," Adam screeched. "Enact the terrible consequences! Show your mighty power and glory!"

God took a deep breath, feeling the expectant eyes of his pride and joy upon him. There was a rumble as the ground reverberated beneath their feet. The sky above them darkened and began to flush to a deep, swollen red. Clouds had swept above them, and the air felt heavy, dull, almost claustrophobic.

"Is your ego really so damaged by my opinion that you need to 'enact terrible consequences'?" Lilith snapped. "You really are a pathetic, embarrassing, insecure mistake. So easily triggered by someone with a different opinion, by a woman who dares to—"

"For my son," God said from between gritted teeth.

The smell of sulfur bit into the air, and a high-pitched screaming noise began to ring in Eve's ears. It was as if all the world, all the places that had been created, were connecting up on different wavelengths, all their pieces joining across the cosmos to touch her with their tendrils, to reach into her and burrow into her very being. As if each fibre of her was pulled as taut as it could possibly go, with every atom, every tendon in her body strained to the absolute limit of impossibility. The sky flushed an even darker red and then, as the roar became, impossibly, more deafening…

Everything stopped.

Everything was dark.

There was a soft sigh that reverberated through space and time, and at the same time that Eve fell into unconsciousness, Lilith's entire self fragmented into embers.

LET'S CALL THE WHOLE THING OFF

MANY THOUSANDS OF YEARS LATER...

Adam lay back on his woven plastic red and blue beach recliner. The fact that he was in an expansive office, the headquarters of the main management area of heaven, didn't seem to be bothering his general zeitgeist, which involved a Bellini, a sun umbrella, and board shorts. The years had added a few extra pounds around his middle, but he was still the handsome man he had been in his youth.

"Shall we check in on Earth?" he asked God, carefully selecting a vol-au-vent. God sat at the wide desk that spread out in front of an entire wall of screens. "See if there have been any developments on finding the latest incarnations of Lilith?"

God didn't answer. He was looking intently at a paper in front of him, and Adam realized he was doing a crossword.

This was why he needed to be in charge. He wouldn't be doing a crossword in the middle of a workday if this were all his domain.

"I said," Adam repeated, more loudly this time, "should we check in on Earth?"

God looked up, as if hearing him for the first time. "Oh yes, good idea. Shall we invite Eve, in that case? She's very fond of Earth."

"I can't imagine why," replied Adam, sounding irritated.

"I worry about her, stuck in that room all day," said God. "It can't be good for her, always shut away."

"She loves it," said Adam. "Thriving. She much prefers it. Especially after that dreadful business with you know who. She told me she'd rather be in her rooms, doing whatever it is that she does, rather than out here getting up to mischief. She's not very good at controlling herself, you know."

"As long as you've spoken to her about it, then and given her some options."

Adam pressed his lips together in a tight line.

"You have spoken to her recently, haven't you?" God clarified.

"Of course, I have," Adam replied after a moment.

"Good. Because you're her husband, and you need to lead her appropriately. And guide her. She's just a woman, after all. Bless."

"She's fine. You made it quite clear that I couldn't have another do-over, so I'm making the best of it. As much as I can."

"You most certainly could not. Getting rid of one wife was bad enough. There's no way I was going to do it again just because you two had a falling out. You need to learn to deal with your issues, my boy."

"I hardly think that my wife flirting with the so-called Lord of the Sky and the Ultimate Cloud Gatherer is the mere frippery that you seemed to think it is, but we've had this out enough times, and we don't need to rehash it again."

"Eve and Zeus chatted at a book group, for pity's sake, Adam, that's all. About Jane Eyre. They were barely even friends. Back in my day, we—"

"I haven't heard any updates on how the Eons from beyond the Void are doing with seeking out Lilith and extinguishing her embers," said Adam, interrupting him. "There could be anything happening. She could be pulling all the embers back together for all we know. You need to take this more seriously."

God sighed and put the paper he was still holding to the side.

"Adam, I think they're doing fine. I haven't heard otherwise, not since I told them to do it a bit more subtly. They can't be making a whole production about it every time they find her. I've told them to just identify her embers quietly and extinguish them subtly and carefully."

"How?" Adam asked.

"I don't know," God said, sounding exasperated."

"I just expect them to do it. And I'm getting heartily sick of the whole business. I feel like it was all a mistake."

Adam's phone buzzed in his pocket, and he pulled it out, tilting the screen to make sure only he could see it. "Tricky Boy" appeared, his code name for his friend Jared.

Jared, the one who knew everything about everyone. The fixer. The one who would listen without judging.

Jared: You wanted to talk to me?

Yes, but not now. I need your advice. You know that we were talking about me taking on the top job?

Jared: Taking on? You mean taking over lol

Yes whatever. I want to discuss with you ways that we could make this happen. A crafty takeover. Steadier hand on the wheel.

Jared: Nice. We can work on that

I'm pissed. Dad is still going on about the whole Eve and Zeus debacle being a 'mere frippery'. I might need to debrief about that when we catch up.

Jared: No worries. Incidentally, speaking of your women issues, have you still got the Eons working on Lilith?

Yes, why?

There was no reply.

"Let's check in on Earth," said God.

The screen flickered into life. Hobart Town, 1899.

Anyone who hadn't seen the gunmetal grey birds descend in a horde on the woman who stood in the middle of the town square was quickly alerted to what was happening when she began screaming, and blood began to spurt into the air with dizzying projection.

"Oh, for fuck's sake," sighed God, dropping his head into his hands.

"Oh, that's nasty," grimaced Adam. "Didn't you tell them not to do that?"

"Explicitly," God said, his hands over his eyes. "They're not supposed to kill the women who have Lilith embers in them, just try to make them a little less opinionated. Dampen their enthusiasm a little. Maybe give them a touch of depression."

The woman and some of her friends tried to push at the creatures, but the metal of their beaks tore at their flesh, and within moments the crowd, who had come to see the woman speak about female suffrage and trade unions, fled, covered in the blood that streamed from her rapidly disintegrating body which spat pieces of flesh into a black vortex that had appeared, swelling, above the gruesome scene.

Those who were close to her were running away, the image of mechanical birds with red glowing eyes burned into their psyche (but only for a moment), while those who were just far enough away to know there was a potentially interesting kerfuffle going on ran toward it. They had just enough time to see a small bloody pile being ripped at by the strange mechanical creatures before God slammed his hand onto a big red button on his desk.

God and Adam were silent for several moments.

"I did tell you that using pan-dimensional birds from the Eons from Beyond the Void was a liability," Adam said. "You should have just used angels. Rebooting the entire planet seems too much, if you ask me."

"It wasn't an overreaction," God said tersely as he flicked through some files on the well-appointed desk that filled an entire wall of his office, "Several hundred people in the year 1899 just saw robot pan-dimensional birds tear apart a woman and spit pieces of her into a chasm that opened in the middle of a city square. I can't have that kind of thing happening willy-nilly. That's an unacceptable way for this whole 'subduing Lilith' business to be gone about. You are being no help at all."

On the wall, the screens, rather than displaying scenes from 1899 as they had been, were displaying scenes that involved a small group of people scraping furrows in the ground and sprinkling handfuls of seed under a blazing sun, a group of men using a system of ropes and pulleys to raise huge stones in concentric circles in a grassy meadow, and a group of women riding horses on a wild steppe.

"I've only set it back to 3000 Before Me," he said. "Hardly a huge reboot."

Adam sipped the last of his Bellini and clicked his fingers at a small amorphous creature that rushed to replenish the glass. "Yes, but the poor buggers have to go through the Renaissance again. Insufferable."

"No, not again," snapped God. "It's a reboot. They don't know they've ever done it. We're clearing the slate like one of those Etch-A-Sketch things. Brand new start."

"We have to sit through the whole bloody thing again, though," said Adam. "So painfully derivative." The second Bellini went down even more quickly than the first.

'I'll fast forward,' said God, patting Adam on the shoulder with a conciliatory gesture.

"Anyway, I can't use angels to watch her," he said, going over to a walk-in closet that was cleverly hidden behind the leaves of a large potted plant and taking out a warm, fluffy dressing gown. He wrapped it around himself, a sign that he was feeling harried and stressed, and his workday was about to end. "The angels aren't a big fan of the whole situation, and I'd rather keep it on the low down. The Eons from Beyond the Void are much more cutthroat and really know how to focus on getting a job done." He peered off toward the screen, his eyes caught by a large fur-covered elephant wandering around aimlessly on a snowy tundra. "I thought woolly mammoths were extinct," he said, leaning forward. "I thought they'd definitely died out by this stage."

"Leave them there for a bit longer," said Adam, stretching languorously. "Leave them there to confuse people. You know that always amuses me. Ooooh," he said, mimicking a high-pitched voice, "We thought this wasn't possible, now our entire view of the universe has changed. Help, help, I'm having an existential crisis."

God wrapped his claret red velvet robe, the one with satin lining and just the smallest train falling behind it, more firmly around his waist, and ran his fingers through his white hair. His robe was embossed with the words "DadBoss" in real gold thread and had been a gift from Adam last birthday. "All right, if you want that."

"I do feel as if it's time we talked about Lilith," God said. "We're having to reboot the entire reality of the planet because she got under your skin at the beginning of time. I quite frankly don't think it's sustainable."

"Me," said Adam, his eyes widening with indignation. "My skin? You're the one she disrespected. You're the one she had the argument with. Everything I do is helping you."

"Ye-es," said God, treading carefully. "We did have a falling out, that's absolutely true. But I am, let's say, over it now. I feel as though it is an important part of growth and personal development. Attachment styles and Enneagram and all that. You know?"

One look at Adam told God that no, he did not know.

"And I was never a huge fan of you discombobulating her.

Fragmenting her and throwing her throughout all time and history. Not the best, most loving and magnanimous move in my opinion," Adam remarked.

"Yes, you were." God was horror-struck. "You were a fan. That's what you wanted me to do! I did it for you. 'For my son.' I literally said that bit out loud!"

"Only because I thought it was best for you," said Adam gently. "You know, people have questioned your leadership. I wanted to show your detractors what you're made of. I spent hours on the phone defending you the other day. She made you look weak."

God sighed and pressed his lips together. "I am no longer bothered by looking weak. At least, I'm trying not to be bothered. I'm working on myself, you know."

Adam rolled his eyes and muttered, "Bloody Sepham," under his breath.

"Yes, my adviser Sepham. He's really helping me better myself and work on the areas that need work. You've been telling me for years that I had faults, and yes, you were right. I've matured enough to admit it. And now I'm working on them."

"Well, I'm glad you have someone wise to give you counsel," said Adam, trying and failing to keep the note of petulance out of his voice.

"Yes," said God. "But I fear there are bigger things at issue now. We can't just keep rebooting reality every time a Lilith ember starts to catch wind of its sentience. Maybe I'm getting soft in my old age, but would it be the worst thing in the realms if we just—"

"Yes?" said Adam, deeply suspicious of what God was going to say next.

"Let her come back?"

"Let her come back?" exploded Adam. "Let her come back? After what she did? After the way she behaved? Fragmentation was too good for her."

"We've all made mistakes," said God, holding up his hands in protest. "We've all done and said things we shouldn't have."

"I certainly haven't," grumbled Adam. "My discernment is always on point."

God sighed heavily. "I have always valued your input."

"My input would be to strongly advise you not to let her come back. It would be disastrous for…" He was going to say "for me and my plans," but stopped himself in time.

"All right, all right. I'll defer to you. But I do think we need to come up with a better course of action. The Eons just aren't working out at all."

Adam nodded in agreement. "Leave it with me." He messaged Jared when God left the room for his daily Tibetan sound bath.

The Eons are out.

Jared didn't leave him hanging this time.

Jared: Meet me in the Aether.

* * *

ADAM PULLED his jacket around him, but he could still feel the freezing wind. Typical of Jared, wanting to meet in the aether. Yes, it was a liminal place, and the vibes for clandestine meetings were impeccable, but it was bloody freezing, and there was nowhere to sit.

There was a shimmer in the air next to him, and a being appeared.

"Mate," said Adam, as the two men hugged. "You've really leaned into the whole evil trickster thing, haven't you?" He gestured at the leather jacket Jared was wearing with the word **BASTARD** embossed across the back.

"Not evil," Jared clarified. "I'm morally grey. It's good though, isn't it? Made from a northern white rhino. I shot it myself. They're almost extinct. One more trip down to get the leather for a new pair of boots should do it."

"I hate to be the bearer of bad news, but I think they've just become extinct. Your boots will never happen."

"Never mind," said Jared mildly. He snapped his fingers, and two red velvet wing-backed chairs rose out of the ground mist that puffed around their feet. "Shall we?"

"We need to talk about how I can take over from the old man as easily as possible," said Adam, crossing his legs and settling back. "That's the main order of the day."

"Certainly," said Jared. "But first, how's your lovely wife?"

Adam bristled. "Why?"

Jared grinned at him. "Just asking how your wife is. Calm down, old chap. Just friendly chit-chat."

"She's fine."

"Nasty business, though. You know I've always had your back. Fucking Zeus has needed putting in his place for a long time."

"Your friends, the Eons, are out of the picture now," said Adam, pointedly changing the subject.

Jared toyed with a whisky snifter that had appeared in his hands. "Yes, I'd heard that," he said, making it sound like it was something that had only crossed his radar briefly, rather than an issue that had enmeshed him in several meetings over the past few days. "Makes sense, though. I'm surprised that your lot wanted anything to do with them in the first place."

"I was never a fan," said Adam with a shudder. "Never know what they're thinking or what move they're about to make. And the way that they refuse to stick to our laws of physics and just start to bugger around with the infinity of dimensions, well, I just tap out. Way too much for me." He saw the look on Jared's face. "Sorry, mate,' he said. 'I know they're friends of yours."

"Friends, business partners. We dabble. I hear word of goings on from time to time. How did they feel about getting kicked off the job, though?" He knew precisely how they felt but wondered about Adam's understanding of the issue.

Adam shrugged. "Business is business. No hard feelings at all and lots of pats on the back and well wishes at the end."

The look on Jared's face was one of amused disbelief.

"This presents the obvious question," Jared said. "What are you going to do with Lilith now?"

"Well, quite," said Adam. "It is a problem. Did you ever meet her?"

Jared chortled. "Meet her? I had a particularly debauched evening with her back in the day. What that woman can do with a phone charger and a bird's nest."

Adam bristled a little but tried to stay composed. "I'm very worried," he said. "If she becomes whole again, then she would definitely have something to say about my plan to take over. She never liked to see me happy or comfortable in my masculine power. No, if she were able to become whole, then she would ruin everything. All she ever wanted to do was emasculate me.

"Look," said Jared, leaning forward conspiratorially. "I think God was a fool to have all the different embers of her strewn around space and time. Really, really stupid. It's way too complicated, and we have those resets, which are buggering up the space-time continuum from what I've heard."

"To be fair," said Adam, "those resets were because your Eon friends were using robot birds to peck humans to death and using fake alien spacecraft to cosplay abductions in the middle of lower Manhattan. Resets were not originally in the plan."

"There was a plan, was there?" Jared smiled tightly.

"But you're right," said Adam hurriedly, sensing the tension. "It wasn't sustainable. Do you have any suggestions?"

Jared nodded thoughtfully as if contemplating it for the first time. "The clever thing to do, the thing that a truly visionary leader would do, is put all the embers of Lilith in the same time and place."

"Wouldn't that work against what we want, though?" Adam had doubt written all over his face. "Isn't that precisely what we've been trying to avoid?"

"Not at all," said Jared, swirling the drink in his glass. "Having them in one space, monitoring them closely. Finding someone dependable to oversee them all and keep them well and truly suppressed. It's the only way, you must see that."

"If you put it that way," said Adam, sounding unconvinced.

Jared realized he needed to tread carefully here. Push too much, and Adam might sense he had more invested in this than he was prepared to let on. Not enough, and the great plan may never come to fruition. It was easy. The Eons had made it very clear to him. Bring Lilith's embers back together. That was his job. Once they were back in one time and place in history, find a way to enable Lilith to become whole again. This would be deeply inconvenient for God, would annoy him, and also get revenge on him for sacking them from their job so unceremoniously. A job they had been having enormous fun with; the alien abduction thing had been an absolute jape, and now they had been taken off the job and the plans they'd had for the future—such as dropping a live T-Rex into Burning Man where it would eat a ridiculously famous musician who had an ember of Lilith in her—were just dreams. If he did that, he could rejoin them, and all would be forgiven. The old team could be back together.

"Get all her embers in one place, say Sydney, Australia, and keep a watchful eye on all the pieces. Foolproof," said Jared. "Tightly control it. It's the only way."

"And you have someone you trust?" asked Adam, the note of doubt beginning to leave his voice. "Someone you think would be able to monitor all the embers. Keep an eye on them? Make sure she never comes back to ruin my plans, and that she just stays away from me in general? She's like nails on a chalkboard to me. The very idea of her makes me shudder."

"I've got just the person," said Jared. "Leave it with me. Now, did you need to talk about Eve?"

Adam took a deep breath in through his nose. "It's all right. It just annoys me inordinately when Dad talks about her, that's all. She and Zeus were using a book group to flirt with each other. My wife is flirting with a bloody Greek god in a book group. And not just any Greek god, the absolute pinnacle of debauchery and immorality. It's like that vibe of sexual immorality follows me around, wherever I go."

"Were they actually flirting, though?" asked Jared. "I'm sure people of different genders can be friends without it involving—"

"Of course they were," Adam snapped. "She's a woman, isn't she? She started the whole fruit business."

"Ah, the whole fruit thing. Are we still on about that? I thought we'd moved on."

"Well, I haven't. But she knows she did the wrong thing, and she's got plenty of time to think about it in her room. I know whenever she leaves, you know. I keep an eye on her."

Jared tipped the last of his drink down his throat. "You're quite something, my friend. I wouldn't want to cross you."

"That's right," said Adam. "And don't you forget it."

"Don't you worry," said Jared, standing up and buttoning his leather jacket, ready for his return journey. "I pledge to never join a book group on your watch." He tapped the side of his nose. "Or talk to your wife."

WE'RE CALLING IT 'READING' NOW, ARE WE?

Eve stood on the plush rug, gazing off into space. The hum of the central gravity flux continuum was louder today; sometimes she couldn't hear it at all. She didn't know if it was her own ear that was more finely tuned on some days, or whether it was a faulty system. But today she could hear it gently blowing its photons, or reactoids or whatever they were, into her rooms to keep everything just right. Just perfect for her. Apparently.

There was a shimmer next to her, and a figure appeared. It was her assistant. Her lady's maid, her companion. She had never fixed on a precise definition. And Petalyn looked, as usual, annoyed.

"You're not thinking of that dreadful Zeus again, are you?" snapped Petalyn. "I see that look on your face."

"No," Eve lied, trying to focus on the being in front of her.

Petalyn grabbed a drinking glass that needed washing and fluffed out some pillows. Eve's current rooms were modeled on a movie she had seen once, an Arabian epic where women lived together in vast palatial tents, with velvets and fabrics and wall hangings covering all the surfaces, and plates and trays of meats and dates and breads spread out on cushions. Fabric hung from the ceiling in billowing folds, and the room was lit with glass chandeliers paneled with squares of coloured glass. The odd palm tree was dotted about the area, existing in a state of suspended animation in the absence of sunlight or any contact with soil.

The reds and the purples soothed Eve, made her happy. Her last apartment had been pink and green. There had been a long line of apartments before that one, but over hundreds of years, they had blurred together so that she couldn't remember how many she had redesigned or how many had even passed through her consciousness or what whims she had been responding to when she designed them. The gold edging and plaster cast angels had made her happy for a while, but then she'd lost her joy in those things, too.

"You'd better not be dreaming of him," said Petalyn. "That little escapade could have lost me my job, you know. We're all moving on, and we're better for it."

Eve smiled, trying to diffuse her assistant's bad mood. "Well, it didn't cost you your job. All that happened was I lost my true love, the only man who has ever truly understood me or cherished me, and I'm now essentially a prisoner here. So, no harm done really. Just a bleak and hopeless future for me. Ho-hum."

Petalyn turned and looked at Eve sharply. "Are you being sarcastic?" she asked.

"Not at all." Eve wondered if Petalyn was part of Adam's plan. An assistant who didn't understand her at all, who she couldn't connect with or confide in.

"I don't know what you ever saw in him," said Petalyn, busying herself by rearranging a display of tea light candles. "He was an absolute fright, that one."

Eve and Zeus had met at a book group, which was true. Over the ages, there had been various programs and schemes to keep morale in the Upper Realms high. Charade competitions, Scrabble tournaments, Bible studies—although these had inevitably ended up being pub crawls—and book groups. God took his role as a leader very seriously and knew not everyone could be involved in management and office duties. Everyone needed *something* to do. Something to keep them occupied.

This came to his attention because some beings seemed to have less to do than others. Eve, for example. She was very, very important at the beginning, enjoying a "Mother of all humankind" level of importance. But things changed, and after a while, she found herself at a bit of a loose end.

The Egyptian and Babylonian Gods and Goddesses were the first ones to really broach their boredom with him. If things have gone all monotheist, they said, then we need hobbies, an outlet.

"Let me think about it," God had said.

Then, the Greek and Roman pantheon started kicking up a fuss, and he quickly realized he'd have a mutiny on his hands if he didn't come up with something. Hence, the activity groups. And that was how Eve had met Zeus.

She had never planned for it to happen. Of course, she hadn't. But after thousands of years of your husband making it totally clear he had no interest in you, either your body, or your brain, or your soul, a little bit of her had died. And when that happens and you're reading Jane Eyre, and when you and one of the other group members seem to finish each other's sentences and share the same kind of ideas, then it's natural that you will sit together and then after a while when he sees the look in your eyes, that sadness, he might take your hand and ask if you're okay. Then after a little while, when he tells you you're the most fascinating and beautiful and sexy and intelligent woman he's ever met (and, as he said truthfully, he's met a lot), how could you not fall in love with him?

"I love you completely and overwhelmingly," he said. "I think I loved you before we even met. I don't know how we will make this work, but I adore you. It might be unique, but it will be ours."

Adam never knew of their nights together. Of how she'd smuggled him into her rooms. Of how he'd smuggled her down and shown her Earth, shown her everything she'd been missing.

Made her see that there was so much more. Adam had never known that they were building a life.

But hearing the possibility of hand-holding and smiling had been enough for Adam to get God to agree to banish Zeus to Earth, wipe his memory, and make him live as a pathetic human while she was locked up in here as a virtual prisoner.

She would never ever forgive Adam for what he had done. But, as someone had told her many years ago, she did have agency. She just needed to begin to use it.

"I don't like these rooms," she said aloud. "I want a change. I'm bored."

"You just had them redone," said Petalyn. "You haven't even taken the plastic off some of that furniture over in the corner. That mood lamp is still in the box, for goodness' sake."

"Well, I don't like any of it," she said. "These rooms are not what I wanted. The whole vibe is off. It needs to be changed."

"I gave you pictures," said Petalyn. "We found them together. You made a vision board. I had to look high and low to find magazines for you to cut out. It's an absolute bugger to get real-life magazines these days; everything's online. You had very clear plans of how it was supposed to look, and I think everyone did a good job of giving you exactly what we asked for."

"But it wasn't what I wanted."

Petalyn held her hands out in exasperation. Technically, it wasn't possible for a spectral and angelic creature to look exasperated or annoyed, but a serious batch of wrinkles had developed between her eyebrows. She had already started getting quotes for Botox.

"This is exactly what you asked for." She pointed to one of the platters that were artfully scattered around the room. "Even down to the dates and dukkha. And hummus. I had to shell every one of those bloody chickpeas by hand."

Eva glared at Petalyn. She couldn't tell if she was joking or not. "Well, it hasn't worked out the way I wanted it to," she said.

"What is it? What else do you want?"

Eve bit her lip and blinked away the slight possibility of tears. "Other things."

"What other things? What are you talking about?"

Eve took a deep breath. "There were people in my pictures. Women. Other women to talk to. There was a group of women, and they were doing each other's hair and talking and laughing. Maybe that was what I wanted rather than the… poufs and ottomans."

Petalyn stared at her. "You know that's not allowed. What a ridiculous thing to even consider."

"I think that's what I wanted. Friends."

"We've had this discussion. Remember a few years ago when you wanted to hang out with those women? Who were they? You liked their books."

"The Brontë sisters."

"Yes, you wanted to go and spend time with the Brontë sisters. And we even asked, remember? I went and asked your husband and dad? And they said it wasn't allowed."

"Why isn't it allowed?"

"You know why." Petalyn walked over to a ceramic jug and poured liquid into a tumbler. The amber liquid tinkled in and dripped down over the ice that had been suspended in a freeze state for precisely this moment. "Here." She handed Eve the drink and stood by while she sipped at it. "You know why," she repeated.

Eve sighed. "The debauchery."

"Exactly. The debauchery. The women on that planet. Debauchery and wantonness. You can't be down there doing all of that. They're a bad lot. And you and all the original sin palaver. You can't be trusted."

Petalyn's mouth had thinned into a tight line.

"Is it really that bad?" Eve asked, hoping she sounded completely clueless. "I mean, is it really that bad? You're an angel. You know what's happening. You go down there, and you're okay.

You're not..." Eve grasped around for the right words. "You're not all debauched and booby."

"Booby?"

"You know, letting your boobs hang out. You're chaste."

"Well, yeeeeeees," said Petalyn. "But keep in mind you usually only see me in work clothes."

"Is it really so bad down there that I shouldn't be allowed to have friends? To chat. The groups were so fun. I loved that. So, if I'm not allowed to be in groups up here, then I could go down? You know I would behave myself. I'm modelling myself on Elizabeth Bennet at the moment, and she always behaves appropriately."

"What about us?" Petalyn protested. "Me and the heavenly chorus. We hang out with you sometimes. That hookah party the other night was a blast."

Eve sighed again. "That's not the same. You all know who I am. You know I'm Eve. And you're all angels, so you're so well behaved all the time. I want to spend time with people who don't treat me like I'm this special, breakable thing who ruined the future of the human race. I want to be with people who will make jokes at me and maybe even talk about inappropriate things."

Petalyn scoffed. "You wouldn't know how to talk about inappropriate things."

"I'd like to have the chance! I'd like the right of refusal at least!"

A silence fell between them.

"I'm like a bird in a gilded cage," said Eve wistfully.

"Oh, stop it," snapped Petalyn. "You're a spoiled, self-centred girl is what you are. You're Eve! You're the mother of all creation! You're second only to Mary in how revered and worshipped you are."

"Don't bring his Bloody Mary into it. I haven't got the mental fortitude for that whole thing right now."

"Eve," said Petalyn, aghast. "You can't say Bloody Mary like that. What's got into you? That puts me in a really difficult position. I have to rep—" She stopped herself.

"What?" snapped Eve.

"Nothing." Petalyn pulled an ephemeral piece of coloured gauze off the wall and started poking at nonexistent dust.

"You have to report back, right?"

Petalyn scrubbed at an imaginary spot on the table.

"Do you report back on me?"

"It's a difficult situation," hissed Petalyn, glancing around furtively. "You have no idea of the politics. Your husband doesn't trust you at all. I'm not saying it's right, but he doesn't. And your father always takes his lead in these matters."

"Dad sometimes listens when I talk to him. Well, when I get to see him on my own, he listens. You know he does."

"I know what happens when you see your father," said Petalyn, narrowing her eyes at Eve. "I know you sneak around, prying in corners and reading documents."

Eve opened her mouth to protest, but Petalyn held up her hand. "There's no use denying it. But your secret's safe with me. Don't think I'm completely unsympathetic. It's a hard life, you have. You deserve something nice to happen to you."

"Do you really mean that?" Eve's eyes had filled with tears. Even though she was older and wiser than the girl who had walked barefoot through the Garden of Eden, she still couldn't stop tears springing to her eyes with little provocation.

"I do."

"Can you help me then? I want you to set up a meeting. I want to talk to them face to face."

"You've got your bimonthly freewheeling and unspecified chit-chat with your husband next week, though."

"No," said Eve. "No, I want to talk to them. Both of them. Together. That's how they usually travel, isn't it? In a pack. And how stupid is it that I have to make an appointment to see my own husband? And our father? And that it's scheduled ten years in advance? How stupid is that?"

"It's the way things have to be."

She took Petalyn's hand. "Please," she said. "Try. For me?"

Her assistant sighed and nodded. "I'll see what I can do."

Eve felt a warmth of satisfaction fill her chest. She knew what had to be done. Both to get her man back and to heal the sins of the past.

THE PLAN

"I have a plan," said Adam.

"Excellent," said God, rubbing his hands together heartily. "I do love a plan. Especially one I didn't have to come up with myself."

They were back in the main office, but there were no beach umbrellas this time. Instead, there was a French provincial, rococo kind of vibe that Adam took an instant dislike to.

"Has Eve been in here?" asked Adam, frowning at the new décor.

"She was at a loose end, apparently. I thought it would give her something to do. Some redesigning."

Adam shrugged. "I don't care for it." He clicked his fingers and gestured to God, and a small amorphous figure scurried toward him with a Kir Royale. "Are you ready to hear what I've come up with?"

God nodded and took a sip.

"Lilith is a terrible, evil being who must be stopped and restrained every step of the way."

"Well…" said God.

"No, that bit's not up for discussion. It's part of my opening remarks."

"I just think that—"

"She threatened to kill my child, for a start."

"Did she, though? She offered to end a four-week pregnancy and, as Eve had said, after that whole thing that went down with Kane and Abel, acting early might have saved us some stress in the long run."

Adam looked at him sternly. "I'm going to choose to believe you're making a very inappropriate and ill-advised joke. However, to continue. You threw all her composite pieces to the eighteen corners of the space-time continuum. And what has happened now is that she's finding ways to get into women. She is finding ways to get into women, and now we have to deal with it."

God finished his drink and gestured for another. "It's true. We cannot keep rebooting reality every time Lilith gets into a woman and tells her how to be a feminist. It's just not sustainable. I shudder to think what it's doing to the space-time continuum."

"The space-time continuum is old enough to look after itself," snapped Adam, beginning to feel frazzled. He had a plan to deliver here. Jared's plan, admittedly, but a damn good one. An intelligent leader would have all the embers in one place where he could keep an eye on them, Jared had said. A close eye and no more resetting Earth's history. And Adam had firm plans to be just that intelligent leader.

God idly bit at one of his nails. "I'm not sure that it is. I'll be honest with you. I got a text message from a higher dimension the other day saying they want a word with me, and I'm going to ignore that like buggery until they get more insistent."

"Well, I've been working on a solution," said Adam. "If you're open to it."

God picked up his remote and pointed it at the opposite wall, which was made up of a huge flat screen TV. He flicked through some channels until he found one of penguins frolicking on an iceberg. He giggled as they jumped into the water.

"What have you got?" he said.

Adam pressed a buzzer, and a young dog-headed woman entered the room. The speed at which she entered indicated she must have been hovering outside the door for some time. Behind her scurried a flotilla of smaller creatures, pushing a table that repeatedly caught its wheels on the carpet as it jerked toward them. Paper spilled off the side of the table, and as one of the creatures bent down to pick it up, they knocked their face into the side of it.

Not the overall ambiance that Adam had been looking for when he had enlisted the help of what was allegedly a crack PR team.

God side-eyed Adam. "This is going well," he muttered.

"Stick with me," said Adam, helping to pull the trolley in front of the screen that now showed a volcano erupting. "Focus on the content, not on the delivery. Would you like another drink?"

God nodded, and this time Adam fetched the drink himself.

The dog-headed woman readjusted some things on the trolley, pressed a button on the laptop, looked at the board furtively a few times, then became engaged in an earnest discussion with one of the smaller creatures. Adam sat next to God and patted his arm in a conciliatory manner.

"This is good," he said. "You'll like this. I think it will solve our issues. How are we going, Callista?" he asked. "Time marches on and all that."

He knew God's attention span was tenuous at best, and they had a finite amount of time before he would wander off and find something more interesting to poke at.

"I can't connect up to the smart board," she said.

"Don't worry, just wing it. The idea will speak for itself. Just... go."

Adam knew the plan well. He (and Jared), after all, had been the one who had masterminded it. The PR company was more for flourish.

But right now, flourish seemed to be decidedly thin on the ground.

He gestured in an increasingly frantic manner at Callista, who grabbed a folder and held it in front of her protectively.

"Right, yes. So, the problem as we understand it," she began.

"Why is she telling me the problem?" grumbled God. "I know what the problem is. I'm all over the problem. I want it solved. Don't remind me of the bad bits; tell me about the good bits."

"Stop it. You're making her nervous. She needs to set the scene."

Her pleading eyes looked to Adam. "Just start and keep talking," he advised.

"The problem," she continued, "is we have a situation with a being who we call Female X."

"Why Female X?" asked God. "Why can't we call her Lilith?"

"Would you be quiet," snapped Adam. "A lot of time has gone into this to help you, and you're being very petulant. We're just trying to help."

God slumped into a slightly drunken silence.

The look on Callista's canine face had morphed into what could be described as "high anxiety verging on abject terror", but she plunged on doggedly. "Female X has been fragmented into various pieces and scattered around all space and time."

God nodded.

"Each of these embers had to implant in other beings. They couldn't have gone into a rock or the aether or anything. They need to be in living things."

"Silly rule, but yes, okay."

"And there seem to have been issues with this. Female X has found her way into women and has been taking hold a little. Somewhat."

Adam dug his nails into his palm at the mention of this.

"And for some reason, we don't know why, we have people looking into it, she has the ability to change the women a little, and in doing so she is taking back some power and using it to… assert herself."

"I know all of this," said God.

"So, what we need to do," continued Adam, "is to make sure she never becomes whole again. And if she becomes activated in the people she's lying dormant in and they connect in some way, she will become whole. That is what we need to stop."

"Adam," protested Callista. "I'm just trying to increase the suspense. I like to think of my job as almost performance art. I'm trying to create a certain vibe, if you could just let me—"

"Go on then."

"The problem is," she continued, pointing to some of the whiteboards one of the assistants had propped precariously against the trolley, and most of which were smudged beyond saving but did include an impressive amount of lines and circled bits and exclamation marks, "that every time you find her, she is fairly well established in the person, so the woman ends up being killed, and we reboot the planet's history, which some would say, is a bit of an overreaction."

"Who would say that?" God asked suspiciously.

"I have," offered Adam.

"Oh, not me," said Callista quickly. "I think it's a sound management plan. Big fan of burning it all to the ground. There's just been talk of it being problematic. On some level."

"We did discuss that," said God. "The space-time continuum."

Callista nodded. "Instability. Potentially dangerous. And you don't want to look like you're not all over the ramifications of your actions, do you?"

"We don't want that," agreed God.

"We don't," agreed Adam.

"So, the proposal is," said Callista, clicking her fingers and causing a small furry creature to scurry to a box that had been left by the door and bring out a poster board with various pictures stuck to it, "this."

She held it up and smiled proudly.

"What's that?" asked God.

"It looks like Eve's Vision Board," said Adam. "The one she made when she got into manifestation and wanted me to buy her that peach diamond ring."

"This," said Callista, "is Sydney in the 2020s. This is what will be. And the plan, if you're happy to go along with it, is to place all the embers of Lilith on the same timeline and in the same geographical location. That way, we can find someone to oversee all the women the embers have embedded into and ensure Lilith stays deactivated."

"But," said God, looking puzzled. "But surely the idea of putting all of them in the same place is ridiculous. The chances of them finding each other, and I don't know, of Lilith recombobulating herself, are higher if they're in one spot. I mean, I don't even mind that much. I told you I don't mind if she forms again. It's you who doesn't want her around."

"I'm thinking of you, too, though," protested Adam. "You're the one she's going to be furious with. I'm looking out for you."

God shuddered a little.

"But you see," said Callista confidentially, "having them all together is much better because, first of all, no more rebooting of space and time."

"Which has to stop," added Adam.

"And secondly, we can have one being overseeing all of her. All the different manifestations of her."

"No more pan-dimensional entities," continued Adam.

"I like that bit," said God. "The Eons give me the willies." He chewed his lip thoughtfully. "We'd have to outsource again. I don't think the angels would want to do this. Or should I say, I'd rather they didn't. They weren't that keen on the original plan."

"It's okay, we've already got someone in mind. A real professional," said Adam.

"Okay," said God. "But I'm really still not sure about having all the pieces in one place. Surely that's a bad idea?"

Adam and Callista shook their respective heads vigorously, and some of the smaller, furrier animals joined in. A few fell over.

"No, not at all," said Adam. "That's definitely not a bad idea at all. There's no way this could go wrong. I think it's the only way to go. And you've been telling me you're swamped lately anyway, that you've got too much on your plate. This is a way of delegating a lot of it. I can take over the main work and, as I said, there's nothing that can go wrong."

"Foolproof," said Callista, and the slight glance she gave to Adam was invisible to everyone except him. "There's literally no way this could go wrong. We've crunched the numbers and run the figures, and it's, well, it's a dead cert."

God raised his hands in the air in a gesture of mock defeat, and somewhere in an unspecified place and time on Earth, a church spire collapsed. "All right, fine. Have it your own way. I wish it hadn't happened. What I did to Lilith wasn't my finest moment, and I'd rather not have to think about it anymore than necessary."

Callista glanced between the two men in front of her, the young handsome man with dark skin, and the older man with white hair and a beard that stretched down toward his chest. The look of stress and worry in the older man's eyes made her feel unsettled, somehow, and she instinctively turned to Adam for confirmation as to what would happen next.

"Great," said Adam. "Sounds like a green light to me. It's go time!"

As she and her team pushed the trolley haltingly out of the room, she saw Adam pat the older man on the back reassuringly.

FUCK THE PATRIARCHY

"Fuck the patriarchy."

The groups of university students scattered on chairs and beanbags around the refectory stared, mesmerized by the two women. Fae, the severely dressed older woman, maintained her steady gaze toward the younger pink-haired girl who had just spoken. She tilted her head back slightly while raising one precisely manicured eyebrow. This look of vague consideration with a hint of derision was one she had been practicing in the mirror for weeks. She wasn't sure she had nailed it, but the way the girl glowered at her made her think it might be working.

"Really. That's your stand, is it? That's the entirety of discourse you have on the subject?"

"It covers a lot of angles. Like, the last several thousand years of human herstory." The girl pushed her thick fringe out of her eyes and lifted her chin.

"You're what, seventeen years old? Do you have any idea what the patriarchy has done for you?"

"Done for me?" The girl's bark of laughter was loud in the now silent room. "What has the patriarchy done for me?"

The audience who had come to hear Fae speak, a mixture of

supporters, the curious, and the vehemently opposed, shifted slightly. They had been waiting for this. Or something like this. They hadn't known the pink-haired girl with a face full of piercings would be the one to kick things off, but the new frisson in the room made it very clear they were glad she had.

"You're honestly saying that the patriarchy has done anything to benefit me? To benefit any of the female-identifying individuals in this room?"

"The vote," Fae said, ticking things off on her fingers. "Education. Look at this school. You think you'd be allowed here if men hadn't given you the opportunity? Built it? The opportunity to stay home and look after children. The opportunity to not be a wage slave. Security. Safety. Do you have to go and fight wars? No. Why is that? Because of this terrible patriarchy, you are being blamed for everything. Let me guess. Every ill will in your life is because of the patriarchy."

The girl glared at her.

"The survival of women, or health and safety, can largely be attributed to this terrible, evil patriarchy that you so enjoy being a victim of. I'm sorry, what's your name? This feels impersonal."

"Ashley."

"Ashley. Ashley, I'm Fae."

Ashley gestured to the poster on the bulletin board behind them, Fae's smiling face, dark, respectable chin-length hair, and pointed features against a background of green lettering informing the campus that Fae Stephenson would be speaking on the 25th and all were welcome to an afternoon of thought-provoking discourse. "I know."

"Of course." Fae's lilt of laughter was welcoming, bringing everyone into the delightful banter they were engaged in. "The patriarchy, Ashley, is not your problem. The problem is feminism. That's what has forced you into a box. That's what has cut off your options. The patriarchy gives women freedom; it gives women options." She mentally ticked off her talking points. Not too many all at once. She didn't want to make it sound like she had memorized a list.

Which, of course, she had.

Ashley shook her head. "You are so deep in this, you don't know what you're talking about. The patriarchy has caused untold damage."

"No, feminism has," Fae said. "Feminism demands that women have to do everything and be everything all the time."

She lifted her face to the room and called to the audience. "Did any of you young women want to be mothers and homemakers when you were younger?"

A few nervous hands raised.

"And did you tell people? Your mothers, teachers, friends?"

"It wasn't encouraged," came a brave voice from one of the scattered beanbags. "It was always, what do you want to be when you grow up, and if you said a mum, then people thought you were bonkers."

"So what did you do?" Fae asked, her eyes fixed on the woman who reclined awkwardly at floor level.

She shrugged. "I'm doing an arts degree. I'll be a teacher or something. Have kids when I'm thirty, maybe."

"Is that what you want? To be a teacher?"

"I'd like to stay at home and keep house, but guys laugh at you when you say that. And all my friends think I'm stupid for wanting it."

"Doesn't sound like the glorious future we've been told we have, does it?" Fae looked back at Ashley. "Doesn't sound like equality. It sounds like feminism has trapped women. Now we have to work, have children, pay for someone to clean the house, and pay for someone to look after the kids. I imagine you're anti-capitalist too?"

Ashley glanced around uncertainly.

Fae squinted at the badges and buttons that covered the top of the girl's denim jacket. Amongst the more predictable Fuck the

Patriarchy, Riots not Diets, Women Cum First, and No Uterus, No Opinion, was a Destroy Capitalism Before It Destroys the Planet badge.

"May I suggest," continued Fae, "that forcing women to become feminists, that forcing them to become part of the workforce, is buying into the whole capitalist paradigm. Not only has modern feminism become obsessed with a perpetual victimhood, forcing young women to waste their youth raging against some fictitious enemies who haven't been an actual issue for decades, but it's also effectively slipped you into the perpetuation of capitalism. Because once you become a wage slave, as you put it, once you and your future partner rely on your salary, then there's no going back. You're a cog in the wheel, and there's no escape. And you know what could have kept you from that? The patriarchy. Or at least elements of it. But no, in your desperate desire not to fall into some spurious, ill-defined trap, you've fought against your femininity, your desire for true fulfillment, and you've been completely manipulated by the feminist agenda. So well done, you're a perfect feminist. I hope you're happy with the bed you've made because now you have to lie in it."

"You've been fed a lie," she said, skimming the crowd and making eye contact with as many people as possible. Some glanced away quickly, some glared, in an attempt, she suspected, to unnerve her, and one, a young woman with blonde hair that was pulled back from her face sharply, stared at her intently, as if hanging on every word.

"You have been fed a lie that you can be whatever you want. Because that's what they want you to think. They want you to think that you can be anything and do anything, but it's just another way to control you. You have been told you have to work to be fulfilled, that being at home, being a homemaker, isn't enough. You have been made to feel guilt and shame at the idea that you might want to give in to your instincts. You can have a house and be a mother. You can, but if you do, you have to break yourself by being a superwoman, by working and parenting, by caring for the home and competing with men in the workplace, by swinging between being a loving, nurturing helper, as we have evolved to be, and by being a hard-nosed, competitive businesswoman. Do you know why the use of medication, or anti-anxiety medications and anti-depressants, has risen 300% in the past twenty years? Because we are having to change our biochemistry in order to live the life we think we have worked so hard to win. This holy grail, our feminist foremothers fought so hard for, that we would feel so ungrateful if we turned our backs on it."

"So, we think we can be everything. Workers, mothers, activists, sexual beings. Yes, the sexual freedom we have been taught to think we are so lucky to have. We use that as collateral now. Something that used to be an intimate act in the safety of marriage is now given away. Collateral. How many of you have had sex with a boy you liked as a way to show him your feelings, only to find out it's all he wanted? We use sex to connect. Men use it for a bit of fun. And can we blame them? If girls are willing to give it away, it's not their fault that they take it. Think that young man you've been seeing wants you for your mind, wants you for your heart, wants you as a partner in life and the mother of his children if he knows you've just given yourself away as easily as a handshake?"

There were some murmurs of agreement from the crowd, but an equal amount, probably more, were laughing, rolling their eyes, and loudly rebutting her.

This is a performance, she reminded herself. They're just an audience. They don't know you. They would probably quite like you if they met you in a bookshop or the gym.

"Noone is forcing anyone to be a feminist," Ashley said, but she looked uncertain in the face of the Fae's well-rehearsed diatribe.

"In your desperate desire to be oppressed, you neglected to undertake an even cursory glance at the etymology of the word history because if you had, you would have found out that it comes from the Greek historia, meaning learning by inquiry. It has nothing to do with pronouns. Also, I think you'll find that 'No Uterus, No Opinion' is quite transphobic."

* * *

FAE SLID into the car and pressed her skirt against her legs, idly trying to smooth out the creases. She lay her head back against the black leather headrest and closed her eyes for a moment. She felt a deep-down weariness. It was all acting, she kept reminding herself, but still. She was tired.

The glass barrier between the front of the car and the back seat slid down soundlessly, and the driver looked at her. At least, she assumed he looked at her. His dark glasses made it hard to know for sure, but his head was pointing in her direction at any rate.

"Heading for an interview now?" he asked.

She nodded.

"We've had a call from the Antipodean Christ Lodge," he said. "They're interested in having some discussions with you. About becoming a candidate."

She stared out the window at the city now passing them by. She knew her itinerary precisely, exactly where she was scheduled to be at every moment, but she was happy to give up the machinations of getting places to her driver.

"What a terrible idea," she said. "The last thing I want to do is get involved with a bunch of God botherers. You know how we feel about each other."

"Yes," her driver said. "But their talking points do quite closely align with yours. At the moment, anyway. And while you don't work from a, shall we say, faith perspective, a lot of the issues you're concerned with do tie in with each other."

Fae ran her tongue over her teeth and let her brain rest for a moment. It was easy to turn it off, she found. It was easy to disconnect and let her thoughts sink away while she let the deep part of her brain consider other issues.

She reached into the pocket of the seat back in front of her and pulled out a folio. The folio was pristine, clean, and laminated with uncreased pages despite the fact that she flicked through it daily. She knew the names and the faces its pages held, knew them as if they were her own.

Wellingsley Baxter. She had seen the blonde woman out of the corner of her eye while she was speaking. The ideas were fermenting now, she knew it.

Many had been quietened already, their photos relegated to a file somewhere. The flaming ember of Lilith that lay within them extinguished.

"I'm not going to align myself with them," she said. "I don't want to be controlled, and I most definitely don't want to hold political office. It will dilute what I'm here to do, which is get in, get out," she said.

And to make Jared happy, she thought. *And be the woman he wanted her to be.*

WELLINGSLEY MAKES PAD THAI AND CONTEMPLATES LIFE

As Wellingsley placed her house keys on their appointed tray, the brass and wood curlicues of the antique piece matching the deep wood of the desk on which it sat. The door clicked shut behind her. It always satisfied her, that click, cutting the outside world off from the cocoon of her flat.

Such a quiet noise to hear, such an insignificant thing. If there were any other noises in the flat, any voices or pattering feet, anything else that signified there was other life here, they would mask it. She had considered leaving a radio on; the sound could welcome her home. But she would know it was fake. A contrived company.

There was a vibrating in her pocket, and she slipped her hand into her jeans. **Mum** flashed on the screen. She sighed and answered.

"Were you at the talk by Fae Stephenson today?"

Wellingsley contemplated lying. But she would know.

"Hi, Gloria." She slid off her flats and walked into the lounge room, flicking on the lights as she went. The room was dark, and she wriggled back onto the sofa, tucking her feet under her and pulling a velvet blanket around her shoulders. "Where did you hear that?"

"There was a picture. Some of the girls from Women Together were picketing outside, and I saw you in the background in the livestream."

"I was in the refectory getting a coffee, and I saw a group of people gathering, so I thought I'd tag along," she lied. "I didn't take much notice."

Wellingsley could hear voices on her mother's end. "Are you busy?" she asked. "We can talk later if you want."

Gloria didn't reply for a moment. She was talking to someone else in the background.

"I just wanted to know if you're free for lunch this weekend. Estelle and I wanted to see you. If you have time to take a break from studying."

Wellingsley fingered the tassels on the blanket. The room was full of draped blankets, velvet softness, and warm colours. She loved bringing textures together to make a room feel cosy. Cosy was basically what she wanted most of the time, if she was being honest.

"Sure," she said. "I can have lunch."

"So how was the talk?" Her mother was once again giving her full attention. "Did she hide her appallingly regressive, outdated beliefs in empowerment jargon? Did she do that bit about how women are safe in the patriarchy? About how we're unable to function as full people when we try to, what is it, merge the male and the female into one dysfunctional whole?"

Wellingsley mentally took an inventory of the food she had available in the fridge. Maybe an Asian chopped salad with peanut sauce. And she had some braised chicken from last night, she could use on top to fill out the…

"Wellingsley?"

"I think she mentioned it," she said.

The voices in the background heralded the loss of her mother again.

"You'll have to tell me all about it on Sunday. Estelle will book The Deck for 1:00 p.m. It will be busy by then, but we'll get the best table. Anyway, how's that contractual law unit you were struggling with?"

I dropped it, Wellingsley thought.

"Fine," she said. "I spoke to the lecturer like you said, and she sorted it out for me."

"That's always the best first course of action," said Gloria. "Go straight to the lecturer. Become known as quickly as possible. Once those in charge know who you are and can put a face to a name, you can use that familiarity as collateral. Especially in the law field. You need to start making contacts now, in your first year."

There was more bustling noise on the other end of the phone, and after a perfunctory goodbye, Gloria left to attend to more important matters. Thank goodness.

Wellingsley's face flushed at the memory of the incident in question. Walking through the dark corridors with her reading for the week clutched in her hands, she was looking for her law lecturer, in order, as her mother had urged, to *Get Herself Known*. To Gloria, one of the most important things one could do was *Get Herself Known*, and so now, Wellingsley had embarked on the task.

"Ask him a question", Gloria had said. "A question about the reading or a point of law or something. Not in the lecture. There were two hundred other people there. Seek him out in private and ask him a question." Then she would become known.

Wellingsley wasn't particularly sure what *Being Known* would entail, but her mother clearly thought it was very important, and her mother was, herself, a *Known* person. Who was Wellingsley to ignore such sage advice?

The hall was dark and paneled. It wasn't a particularly old university, so she was bemused as to why this area had been designed to recreate an old-time learning institution. The name on the heavy, dark door told her she was in the right place, and so she tapped lightly, waiting to hear a sound within. The corridors were empty, and she tapped once more, a little harder this time. Maybe the lecturer was not in today. She could just walk away and tell her mum she had tried, but he was obviously frightfully busy and important and probably didn't have time for first years who…

The door swung open, and a middle-aged, red-faced man swam into view. He squinted at her and peered out into the corridor before looking back.

"Yes?"

She smiled and held out her hand. "Hello, Professor Wilson. I'm Wellingsley. I'm in your first year Contract Law, and I have a question about this week's reading."

He stared at her, frowning slightly. "All right, quickly then."

She smiled, hoping to make a connection, wanting him to see that she was special and interesting and not one of his standard hundreds of first-year students. She was *Standing Out*.

"Here," she said, pointing to the reading. "It mentions a historian named Jenkins and then here, in the references for next week…" She flicked through the pages for the next week's reading, hoping he would be impressed she was looking ahead even though it was only Monday. "It mentions a Jenkins again, and I was wondering if it was the same person?" She heard the stammer in her voice.

His frown became deeper. "This is a question for your tutor," he said. "These are the kinds of things that you should be asking your tutor, not me."

And he closed the door.

She knew there was no one else around, but she fixed a tight smile to her face and strode off purposely anyway, clasping her papers close to her tight chest. Her cheeks were hot, and tears pricked behind her eyes, but she knew all she had to do was get back to her car. Get back to her car, and then she could cry with mortification and embarrassment.

Why had her mother made her do that? It wasn't "her". She wasn't someone who could *Get Herself Known*. What was she thinking?

She dropped out of the unit the next day. She didn't ever want to see him again. She could drop out and pretend their interaction had never happened.

What would happen next year when she couldn't continue in her second year of law was something she would worry about later.

She slid her feet off the sofa and padded into the kitchen. The flat was small. Tiny, but still, much better than a share house, or being at home with her mum, still, although that hadn't been an option. When Dad had offered, from Switzerland where he had wisely headed when Wellingsley was a baby, to pay her rent and a wage so she didn't have to work while she was studying, she naturally accepted.

There was no point in pretending to be poor to get some kind of lefty street cred, she had decided. And if Dad wanted to use some of his money to assuage his guilt a little about leaving her with Gloria in her formative years, she would have been silly to refuse.

Pad Thai, she decided.

The routine of preparing the noodles, chopping the ingredients, and laying everything out in their separate bowls to be mixed together when the time came was soothing and meditative to her. She was pulling labelled Pyrex containers out of the fridge when the light on her phone glowed, and her watch vibrated.

Angus.

Angus: What's for dinner

She ignored it. Poured boiling water onto the rice noodles. Ignored it.

Dropped the tofu into the oil.

Ignored it.

Another buzz.

Angus: I bet it's delicious

She picked it up, her fingerprint not registering on the sensor the first few tries.

Enter passcode.

I'm out with friends

Drained the noodles. Added them to the pan.

Angus: Can I come and find you?

She made a decision at that moment.

We need to talk

Angus: You're not pregnant, are you? ;)

She arranged the food into the bowl. Poured a glass of cider.

He could wait for an answer to that one.

Angus: Well?

No, I'm not pregnant. But I don't think we should sleep together anymore

She turned the TV on, flicking through streaming services.

She didn't know why she pretended she wasn't going to rewatch Downton Abbey.

Was he going to reply?

Angus: Ok. Cya

She set the bowl of food down next to her. A yawning pit seemed to have opened up, expansive in her chest.

If someone could X-ray me now, she thought, they would see nothing. There would be nothing in my chest, no bones, no heart, no organs.

Did organs show up on an X-ray, she wondered idly.

There would just be a pit. Three-dimensional, an empty chasm where everything had sunk. She contemplated texting Angus back, saying she was home, that he could come over, that she'd been joking, and she still wanted to…

The chasm in her chest seemed to pulse.

No.

It's not the way.

Fae had been right. The ideas she had been taught to scorn and laugh at all her life, the ideas that were so regressive and anti-everything that her mother, and her mother's mother, had fought for.

What if they were wrong?

Maybe she did lose value when she gave her body away.

And if Fae had been right about that, then what else was she right about?

A MASTER CLASS IN PASSIVE AGGRESSION

Adam bent to kiss Eve's cheek as she took the proffered seat in their daytime salon. It was spacious and richly unholstered, with just enough leather furnishings to make is very manly. "Hello there, dear. How have you been? Sorry I haven't popped by to see you lately, but things have been flat out here. Haven't they?"

He looked to God for confirmation.

"What? Busy, Oh, yes, completely. It's been really frantic. Classes, new ideas, whole paradigms turned on their heads."

Adam frowned disapprovingly and spoke to his father sharply. "That wasn't quite what I meant; I was talking about the things I've been involved in helping with, not the things that happen behind closed doors."

If God noticed the frisson of tension that came from Adam, he ignored it.

Eve looked around.

"Seems to have calmed down now at least,"she said.

"We dealt with what needs to be done. As usual," said Adam.

"Always nose to the grindstone."

"No rest for the…"

"No, that doesn't work, does it?" laughed God.

"Not quite," Adam agreed.

The tension abated.

Eve took the glass of sparkling water Adam offered her before he sat down next to her.

"Now, you said you had something that you wanted to talk to us about. What can we do for you?" asked God.

She managed to bite her tongue at the use of the word "we".

"I would like a job, please," she said. "I'm very bored, and I'd like something to do. You can't just keep letting me change the decor in my rooms and expect me to be happy with that. I need more."

God glanced around. "Would you like to renovate in here again?"

"No, I would not," she said, trying to keep her voice measured. "I don't even like design. I hate it, actually, but when you give me an unlimited budget and access to the design trends of all space and time, then anyone would get a little preoccupied for a while, at least. I start, and two hundred years have gone by in the blink of an eye, and I haven't got any idea of what's happening in the real world, and I'd like a bit of a clue, thanks."

"Calm down," said Adam. "Take a breath. By the real world, do you mean—"

"Earth. Where things actually happen. I'm a bird in a gilded cage up here, trapped away from everything interesting."

She saw Adam roll his eyes. "Oh, please, you've got everything you could ever want. We keep you safe here. You don't always make the best decisions. Remember when you—"

"I don't want to reanimate this old conversation," said God, holding up his hands in protest. "We always go round in circles."

"Why don't you visit Mary?" offered Adam. "You two haven't spent time together for ages. She's been telling me you never reply to her messages."

"I think we both know how I feel about her," said Eve. "The

actual Virgin Mary? I want to spend my time with fun new people who can teach me stuff, not a professional virgin who spends all her time judging me for one little mistake thousands of years ago."

"Judging you. Nonsense. She never judges you."

"It's literally all she ever does," said Eve, aghast. "You just never notice. Everything she says to me is a dig of some sort or a little jab. Do you know that she called me 'delightfully Rubenesque' last time she came to visit? Delightfully Rubenesque. It's calling me fat but being pretentious about it."

"Now look here, I won't have you talking about the Virgin Mary like that," blustered Adam. "There's a lot of people down on that planet that you love so much who will be quite annoyed at you if you go around disrespecting her, you know."

"I'm your wife," said Eve. "You're supposed to choose your wife over everyone else."

"That's rich coming from you," he snapped. "Anyway, I don't think that's official. I feel like it's up to the discretion of the—"

"Yes, it is," she said. "It's in His book. They're always harping on about."

"Please don't get me any more involved in this than I have to be," said God, who could feel a headache coming on now. "I don't even know what's in the bloody thing. It's just for photo ops primarily. But yes, now you mention it, I think there is something about honouring your wife."

Eve stared back and forth between the two of them pointedly.

"Come on," said God, resting his hand on her shoulder in what he hoped was a calming manner. "You know your family tree is very windy and tangled, and look, not to put too fine a point on it, weird. But the fact is, we're family, and we have to look after each other."

"Tell *him* that," snapped Eve, tears springing to her eyes. "He's the one who doesn't act like we're married. He's the one who just wants to stick me in a room and pretend I don't exist while he—"

"While I what?" said Adam, rounding on her. "While I what? What are you insinuating? Because if you have something to say, just say it. Do you think I'm trying to take over here?" His face had gone a bright shade of puce, and sweat had broken out on his brow, his nails biting into his palms as his fists clenched.

Eve stared at him. She had meant it as an offhanded remark, but now she wondered…

"Calm down, old chap," said God. "No one has said any such thing. What an absurd notion. You don't have to take things so seriously. We're just having a—"

"Oh, you as well, is it? You have a problem with me, too, do you? Well, if you're accusing me of something, then I wish you would just come out and say it. I know what people have been saying behind my back."

Eve and God glanced at each other nervously. God stepped back slightly, behind Eve.

"What are you up to?" she said quietly, her eyes now completely dry and her face pale. "What's going on?"

"See, accusations," he spat again. "More accusations. Do you think I'm keeping secrets from you? Planning to take over here? Well, it's utter rubbish, and you both need to stop listening to gossip. And you're lucky that I don't want to Eve. Yes, you're very lucky. Because I can promise you, I wouldn't be as kind and forgiving of you without him around." Adam jerked his thumb toward God, and Eve felt herself recoil from the anger that seethed from him. "You would find yourself in a different position if I were the one making decisions, trust me. None of this freedom and choice that you have now."

"All right, stop," said God. "I'm serious this time, Adam, stop. I don't want to have to go all Old Testament on you, but I will if necessary. You are overreacting in a very…" he splayed his fingers out and raised his eyebrows, "strange and unprovoked way, and it's quite unbecoming. Your wife has come to you with genuine concerns, and I think it's fair that we hear her out. All right? You know she's very delicate and emotional, and I would think that you would be the first one to want to keep her calm. No one thinks that you want to take over. What a stupid idea. And what do you mean, that was want to keep her locked up permanently? This is all very out of order."

Adam was still breathing heavily, his eyes dark.

"Adam," snapped God. "Calm down. You're a man. Act like it, not like some flighty female. Eve is composing herself better than you are, and I'm not comfortable with this turn of events at all. Pull yourself together. It's embarrassing."

He turned to Eve. "I'm sorry about him, my dear. What would you like? It's true that you have always been a dutiful and submissive wife, and while there were some blips early on, with the whole snake issue, and also some ill-advised friendships, you did end up making the appropriate choice. And you've done the right thing in general. I don't see why we couldn't make some special exceptions. And actually, you might be interested to hear about this; I've employed some new advisors who are helping bring me into this new age that everyone's talking about. Apparently, we're moving away from the fire and brimstone—"

"Which you just threatened me with," snapped Adam. "When she's the one who should be muzzled."

"Sorry about that, but old habits are hard to break. These days, everyone is getting, what's the word? *Woke*. It's very interesting. Very freeing. I'm finding myself feeling free-er. It's not just women who get limited by the shackles of the patriarchy, you know."

Eve stared at Adam. Muzzled? Had she heard that correctly?

"Are you aware of it?" the old man asked eagerly, a look of expectation on his face. "You seem to stay up to date with all the happenings down there? Is it on one of your stories? Being woke, that is?"

Adam shook his head and sighed, the tension seemingly gone from his body. "She doesn't want to talk about that kind of thing, and you can be sure that I don't either."

"I want to go down to Earth. Maybe go to school or have a life or something." Eve spoke quickly, seeing the look on God's face. Adam had stood and turned away by this stage and was pacing back and forth along the carpet. It looked like he was ignoring them, but she could tell he was listening to every word.

"There's precedent," she said. "It's not like you don't let your creations go down there all the time. There's an actual elevator, from what I hear. And you've never let me use it."

God nodded. "That is true. It is very popular. We do have a lot of through traffic, although I do prefer the word vortex rather than elevator. We might need to put in a few more. Everyone's loving it, for some reason. I thought I'd set up this whole general Heaven area to be really appealing and fun, but I have to admit they do like to go down there."

"That's right. And I feel like I deserve some of that, right? I've always done everything you asked. I just want some time for me, to find myself."

"Oh, please," muttered Adam.

"Adam, stop," said God. "What has got into you? You're acting very petty. If I didn't know better, I'd think you were hiding something."

"Hiding something?" he crossed his arms in front of him and rejoined the pair. "Hiding something?" He laughed, a high-pitched, tinny sound.

"Don't be ridiculous. What would I be hiding? We're always together. How could I be hiding anything?"

"I said If I didn't know better."

Adam barked out a laugh and looked completely terrified.

"So, Eve. What are you picturing?" asked God.

"I'd like to be able to go and spend some time on the Earth," she said. "Find out what it's like to be a real person. I'd like to just…be a woman. Maybe learn something. Cook. Swim in the ocean."

"Look, I'm going to be completely honest with you. That sounds like a terrible idea. It's not safe, for a start," said God.

"I'm an immortal being. What could possibly happen to me?"

"Bad influences," hissed Adam. "Bad influences could happen to you, that's what. You're so easily led astray. You don't know what it's like down there."

"What, and you do?" replied Eve.

"Steady on, it's not that bad," said God. "I did make it, you know. It's not purgatory or hell or anything. It's quite nice in places."

Adam threw up his hands. "I want it on the record that I'm against this, okay? I can only see the potential disasters. She needs a far firmer hand."

"That's because you're not an ideas man like I am," said God in a conciliatory tone. "Leave the big picture thinking to me. Actually…," he opened his arms expansively. "I've got an amazing idea. You know that little matter that you came to me about?"

"What little matter?" Adam asked suspiciously.

"You know," said God, tilting his head to the left in a manner that gave Adam absolutely no idea what he was talking about. "You know that little matter that we confined to Sydney in the 2020s. The pieces. With your… old friend."

Eve maintained the peaceful smile that she had set firmly on her face. They really thought she was stupendously stupid, she reflected, not for the first time.

"Oh, yes," said Adam hurriedly. "What of it?"

"Yes, this will work beautifully. This is amazing. I'm a visionary."

"What?" said Eve.

"As luck would have it, we've got some business going down on Earth at the moment. Some quite important and time-sensitive business. And your Adam here masterminded quite a lot of it. No, no, don't be humble. It was all your idea. Now, Eve, I want you to promise me something."

"What?"

"You have to promise first."

"But I don't know what I'm promising."

"You have to promise not to ask too many questions."

"About what?"

"Oh, good start," snapped Adam.

"You have to promise that if we send you down there, with a chaperone, you'll be a good girl. You won't ask questions about what other business the chaperone might be doing."

"Done," said Eve. "I'm going to be busy anyway."

"Brilliant," said God. "Well, it just so happens that Adam has a very high-level negotiator, moving pieces magician, clever diplomat person down there at the moment. Don't you, Adam?"

"Er," said Adam.

"No, no, that's what you said, right? For the very, very important job that you convinced me needed dealing with, you got a very high-level political diplomatic person, right?"

"Y-yes," said Adam, deciding that leaning into the lie would be the best way of proceeding at this point.

"Now, just between you and me, I don't know that much about it." God glanced between Eve and Adam. "Least said is the best at the moment, but we're dealing with an age-old problem, if you know what I mean."

"I really don't," said Eve.

"The facts are, there is someone down there at this very moment who, Adam assures me, would be well placed to look after your best interests. So I see no reason why you couldn't have a little sojourn."

Eve nodded eagerly. "Anything," she said.

"And the person your husband has employed is top class.

Passed all the security analysis and psychological assessment with flying colours, right?"

He looked at Adam with eager anticipation. Adam shuffled his feet a little and offered a tight-lipped smile.

"So you will be completely comfortable with them keeping an eye on the safety and happiness of your wife, yes? I know that you love her deeply, and that's why you want to control her so much, but you can trust this person, surely?"

Adam nodded, and his lips disappeared entirely in the smile.

"Perfect. Amazing. I don't need to do anything then. You have no idea how gratifying it is for me to have someone as my right-hand man who so effortlessly takes care of all things so I can concentrate on other, more important issues. Actually, speaking of which, I have to go and talk to a guy about that new spa room we've been discussing. It's Adams present to me on my 4,389th year as God. After a slightly rocky start, I think it's all falling into place. So yes, a spa sauna jacuzzi room. It's very exciting."

Eve was beaming beatifically.

"Thank you," she said. "This is amazing." She sat down in a chair, composing herself.

"You just take a moment then," said God.

They left the room.

Eve wandered around running her fingers over pieces of furniture, seemingly relaxed and dreamy, but her mind was working feverishly. It had to be Lilith. They couldn't have said it more clearly. Lilith was going to be on Earth. The pieces of her, at least. That's what the photos of the women and the ember talk were about. She had found whiteboards of information; the smudged words meant she didn't understand everything, but it all made sense now.

And when she had overheard the conversations he'd had with Jared…

Adam wanted to take over. And when he did, he would imprison her. Or worse. She no longer fooled herself that he loved her or cherished her. He wanted total control over her, and there was only one person who could stop him, who had ever tried to stand up to him.

Lilith.

She needed to get the embers back together. Both for Lilith and to ensure her own safety.

WELLINGSLEY DOESN'T SEND HER FOOD BACK

Wellingsley was early, of course. She was always early. She seemed physically incapable of being fashionably late, or even on time. She sometimes sat in her car so as not to appear too desperately keen, but given she had caught a bus, she decided to head into The Deck at 12:50 p.m. and order a drink. Lunch with Gloria and Estelle needed to be adequately lubricated.

When the restaurant was built five years ago over the foundations of what had been the most historic part of the city, the design specification was "let the poor see what the rich are eating".

This might not have been on the design brief that was kept on file at the cutting-edge design firm that had beaten out the other tenders to win the contract, but it had definitely been bandied around verbally during early brainstorming sessions. After all, if a Wagyu gets eaten in a harbour-side restaurant and no one sees you eat it, was it worth the money?

Tourists in caps that advertised construction companies meandered around the boardwalk, kids with ice cream lashed faces euphorically burned in the sun, and seagulls stole chips from terrified toddlers and the elderly.

The chunkily curved and double diamond-glazed windows of

The Deck ensured that none of the commotion outside could be heard, of course. The restaurant promised to "meld an alchemy of harmonious elements to emulsify a transformative gastronomic experience", and that did not, by anyone's definition, involve the noise of the unwashed masses.

Wellingsley felt spectacularly uncomfortable here.

She was led to their table. Not, as she had hoped, to one hidden away against a far wall, but the most central, the most light-filled, and the most obvious one in the place.

She imagined the eyes of diners, who were undoubtedly questioning why she was there at all, looking at her as she trotted to keep up with the impossibly chic maître d' who effortlessly wended his way between the tables. She smoothed her frizzy blonde hair down with the palm of her hand and wished she had put on more makeup. Her pale complexion was flushed, and she knew without seeing it that her nose had gone red.

Her waiter, who had introduced himself as Waylon, was in the middle of his first shift and was excited and nervous lest anyone discover he had been dynamically ambitious in massaging his job application. He tried to pull her seat out at the same time that she tried to pull it out for herself, which resulted in it flying out of both their hands and sliding across the polished marble floor and ploughing into the fortunately vacant table next to them. Flushing red, she kept her eyes downcast as she slid into her seat and asked the now tightly smiling waiter for a wine, ordered drinks for Gloria and Estelle, and stared at her phone waiting for them to arrive.

A small buzz then filled the room at precisely ten past one. It was a slight frisson, nothing ostentatious, but Wellingsley wasn't surprised to see her mother and Estelle sweeping their way toward her. This time, eyes definitely lifted to follow them. While well-known people were the norm here, seeing Gloria Stark, the highest-paid, most opinionated, and most scandal-prone female news anchor in the country, was always a bit of an event.

Wellingsley stood to kiss her mother on the cheek.

"Hello, dear," Gloria said. "Sorry, we're late. The driver couldn't find a park out the front and had to circle way more than I'm comfortable with."

"You could have jumped out," said Estelle mildly, kissing Wellingsley's proffered cheek and pulling out her own chair, much to the waiter's dismay. "I was all for jumping out. We could have finished our first margarita by now."

"You need to stop jumping out of things," said Gloria as they settled into their chairs. "You're seventy-five. Once you do a hip, it's all over. Don't think I'm going to look after you when you go downhill."

Estelle took her hand, turned it over, and kissed its palm. Gloria cupped her cheek in her hand and smiled at her.

"We want to hear all your news," said Gloria, readjusting the cutlery on the table, which, as far as Wellingsley could see, had been perfectly serviceable to begin with. "We've barely spoken for weeks. I'm desperate to hear how uni is going and what groups you're part of and what contacts you've made."

Wellingsley took the menu and buried her face in it.

"And what we really want to know about is Fae Stephenson, of course," said Estelle. The waiter quietly placed three drinks on the table, and as Estelle spoke, she was shuffling in her handbag, peering into its depths, muttering, "Where has it gone this time?" before withdrawing a small coloured object. She maneuvered a quick action with it before dropping it into her drink. "There." She smiled, lifting her paper umbrella bedecked pina colada and smiling at the waiter. "Now it's a celebration."

"She had a particularly enjoyable cruise in the 60s," said Gloria by way of explanation to Waylon, "and now all drinks have to have an umbrella."

"All alcoholic drinks," clarified Estelle, clinking her glass against Wellingsley's. "The others don't deserve to celebrate."

"Yes, clearly," said Gloria. "I need to know all about Fae. I'm researching the whole TradFem movement, and she seems to be taking on a role within it."

Gloria had gestured to the waiter, who had only made it a few steps away, back over, and Wellingsley hurriedly ordered whatever her eyes settled on in the menu.

"Thank you, dear," said Gloria, patting Waylon on the arm. "Tell the chef that we are on a tight timeline today so if he could push them through, that would be lovely." She frowned at Wellingsley. "That's why we have salad at lunch, dear. Much quicker."

"But she's a wild card," said Estelle, focusing back on the topic. "She won't claim any particular movement. She's got her finger in a lot of pies, from what I've heard." She tapped her finger on the side of her prominent nose.

"Patriarchal, regressive, backward, oppressive pies," agreed Gloria.

"I wonder what kind of pie would be a patriarchal oppressive," mused Estelle, and the two women spent a few minutes musing on the possibilities surrounding this. Apple pie was the consensus. They talked about a new head at a rival station who was apparently doing interesting new things with artificial intelligence, but Wellingsley wasn't listening.

"She's a very good speaker," interrupted Wellingsley. "Fae, that is. She certainly had the audience enthralled. Even those who didn't agree were spellbound."

"Surely spellbound is an exaggeration," scoffed Gloria. "It's a higher learning institution with the brightest and boldest intellectuals of the future sitting at the seat of knowledge. No one there would agree with her, I'm sure."

"I think it's fair to say there's a pretty even mix of the best and the brightest, and then people who didn't know what they wanted to do with their lives, so they decided to go to uni to put off the inevitable decision," ventured Wellingsley.

"That's all right," said Gloria. "Research has shown that being exposed to the ideas and culture of higher learning institutions increases women's salaries and means they get married later in life, if at all, and increases the mental health and longevity of women and their overall options in life. So I don't really care why women go to uni, just as long as they're there."

"The thing is this," said Wellingsley, running her finger around the rim of her glass rhythmically. "She did make some interesting points."

"Of course she did," stated Gloria. "She's spruiking for her agenda. She's going to be saying things that appeal to people. To try to suck them into her regressive ideas."

"But I don't know what she would be trying to suck them into," said Wellingsley. "It's not as if she's selling anything. She doesn't have a book or an e-course or anything. What's in it for her? I think she genuinely cares about those women who might want a more traditional lifestyle but who feel trapped by what feminism has grown into and who feel they aren't able to live the lives they want to because of that."

She felt her cheeks burning as Gloria and Estelle stared at her. "Maybe it's something she actually cares about?"

"Trapped by feminism," said Gloria, moving her arm to allow Waylon to place their dishes on the table. "She's saying that women are trapped by feminism now, is she? I feel like I might need to go along to one of these talks she's giving to hear for myself."

Estelle speared a piece of blue cheese-covered tortellini and looked pointedly at Wellingsley. "If she's saying you can be trapped by feminism, then it just goes to show that the silly woman doesn't understand the first thing about it, despite the inordinate amount of time she seems to spend obsessing about something she allegedly hates. Feminism isn't something you can be trapped by. What a ridiculous thought."

"Options," agreed Gloria. "That's what women need. Options.

You can do whatever you want now. That's what feminism gives you."

"But what," said Wellingsley, the heavy weight building in her stomach, "if they weigh up those options and decide they want to stay home and have babies."

"They are perfectly entitled to do that," said Gloria. "If they truly weigh up all the options and see the glorious future that stretches out in front of them and they decide they want to stay home, depend on a man, and raise children as their contribution to society, in the process becoming a nameless, faceless drone, then of course they can do that."

"But why would they want to?" said Estelle, a look of genuine bemusement on her face. "Why would they want to choose that?"

Wellingsley cut into her steak, the juices pooling in the bottom of the expansive white plate. "Some people want to have babies," she said without looking up. The steak was rare, not well done as she had asked. She pushed it to the side and nibbled on the asparagus.

Gloria laughed. "They can have babies. Of course, people can have babies. I'm not an anti-natalist, for god's sake. I had you, didn't I? But you don't have to stay home to do it. We have accessible childcare here; we have options. Agency, Wellingsley. That's what feminism is all about. Options. Women can do anything they want. They just have to have all the options laid out before them."

"Can they, though?" said Wellingsley. "What would you do if I said I didn't want to be at uni but wanted to stay at home and raise babies and not make decisions?"

Gloria and Estelle laughed. "Don't be ridiculous," said Estelle. "You've always wanted to be a lawyer. It's in your blood. Just look at your father. You've wanted to be a lawyer ever since I met you when you were six years old."

"I'm talking hypothetically," said Wellingsley. "I'm not saying that *I* necessarily want to stay at home and bake bread and look after babies and be dependent on a man. I'm just asking what if I did."

"Well," said Gloria, downing the last of her drink. "I'm sure that we would all, Estelle, I, and your father, support you in that. But thank God it's just a hypothetical because I don't think there's anything else you could do that would disappoint us more. Another drink?"

"Stop teasing and eat your salad," said Estelle mildly. "Wells, you do what you want to do, and we will support you."

Wellingsley smiled at her. "Thank you, Stelly, but I think we both know that's not true."

"No, it is," said Estelle. "Of course, we would support you. We might not agree, but we would support you."

"That's right," said her mother, stroking the stem of her glass. "We dealt with the crushing disappointment of you not being another sapphic goddess to add to the long line of lesbians in the family. Nothing will beat that realisation."

She placed her glass back on the table and winked at her daughter. "Now, given you have stubbornly refused to be gay, at least tell us about some of the lovely young men who you have been having sex with. You can remind us of our misspent youths before we took our, what do they say, red pill?"

When Wellingsley arrived home, her head slightly woozy from the alcohol, the rare steak she had ended up eating at her mother's behest, and the conversation, she opened her computer and entered a few key search terms. She hadn't turned on the lights and had pulled off her fitted jacket and heels to snuggle into a flannelette dressing gown. As she scrolled down the search results, the screen lit her face, and in the glow of her laptop, her expression showed relief for the first time in days.

APPLE AND HER GLORIOUS BREASTS

Apple stretched languorously and rolled onto her side, rubbing her cheek against the comforting softness of the flannel that covered the pile of pillows. Flannel. So much better than silk. Or satin. The most ridiculous fabrics known to humankind, at least when it came to bedding. One false move and you'd slip right off the bed. When a client once agreed with her criticism of satin, which she usually couldn't help but insert somewhere into their chats, she knew they would get along just fine.

Not that she had to get along with clients, of course, but it was always a better time if there was some sense of connection. It didn't matter if the bond was over satin, liking ferrets, or dental hygiene; a common interest was a common interest, and a connection was a connection.

Apple heaved her legs out of bed and sat on the edge, rubbing her eyes and running her fingers through her wavy auburn hair. The morning sun was casting patches of light over the carpet, and everything was precisely where she had left it when she went to bed. She knew when she went into the kitchen, she would find everything where it should be. No plates of baked bean detritus in the sink, no crumbs on the bench, no container of milk left out on the bench all night to curdle. Everything was where she wanted it to be, or at least where she had left it, and this was reason eight million why she loved to live alone and would continue to do so indefinitely.

Her feet sank into the deep carpet, and she wriggled her toes. Most "how to be a sex worker" books—if there were even such a thing—she imagined would state that floors should be kept hard and as easily cleanable as possible, what with all the body fluids and lube and the like being flung around on a typical workday. But she loved comfort. She liked to be warm, and hard floors in her workspace just weren't going to cut it for her.

Anyway, she was an experienced and highly esteemed sex worker. There were a few fluids being flung around willy-nilly on her watch, at least not accidentally.

Taking her robe from the foot of the bed, she slid it over her shoulders and padded into the kitchen to make coffee. She loved her little unit on the 9th floor. She had paid extra to have a small balcony with a view, which she took her pot of coffee out to sit on most mornings when the temperature climbed to reasonable numbers. Her own unit, her own coffee, her own balcony.

Owned outright.

Her phone tinged with the sound she had customized to indicate her sister Janie was ringing her.

"Did you know that you are viciously persecuted and just a cog in the wheel of patriarchal oppression?" Said Janie as an opener.

"Yes, clearly," Apple replied as she filled the jug with water, "famous for it. I've barely got time for anything else, what with all the oppression and subjugation that I'm constantly suffering under."

"Good," said Janie. "Just checking. Wouldn't want you to get ideas above your station."

"Never. Firmly kept under the thumb of the patriarchy, don't worry."

"Excellent. Good to hear."

From across the room, her work phone also buzzed. It would be her regular check-in for his monthly appointment. He was lovely, such a nice guy, and experimental too. She liked guys who were open to trying new things. Politely, that is. He was the typical case of a man in a dead bedroom situation whose sex life had fizzled down to nothing. Poor bugger.

People were so fucked up about sex. So many hang-ups.

"Are you ready for the panel?" asked Janie.

"I still can't believe I have a publicist," said Apple with a laugh.

"I'm not a publicist. I'm your sister."

"Agent then."

"Still no."

"Chief coraller."

"Not a word, but yes, that's better. Let's try that again. Are you ready for your panel this evening?"

"I am." Apple nodded emphatically to the empty room. "I absolutely am."

"Have you worked out your main points of contention?"

"Main points? Not so much. Not points, exactly. General ideas."

"Apple," said Janie firmly. "You need to know what you're going to say. This is a big deal, you know. It might be your chance to really break into advocacy. I don't think it's going to be a gotcha panel, but until you're there, in front of the audience, you just don't know. And you've never done anything like this before."

"I've argued with plenty of people about it, though," Apple protested. "I've subjected everyone I know, and random people in pubs, and do-gooder feminists to my opinions about sex workers and our rights. This is hardly my first rodeo."

"It's your first rodeo with a national viewer base," countered Janie.

"I dunno," said Apple. "I tend to be pretty good at getting an audience when I launch into my opinions in public places."

"Such a domineering personality," said Janie, quoting every report card Apple had ever received during her years of formal schooling. "This is your chance to really take a role. It might start some actionable change. You know that we have to get some of these ridiculous rules around sex work abolished, and the country has never been as accepting and embracing of sex work as it is now. And if this goes well, you will raise your profile and maybe even get noticed politically."

"That's true," agreed Apple. "But more accepting still means pretty bloody against it in some areas, though. Don't forget that we surround ourselves with people who think the same way that we do. There are a lot of people out there who think I'm a hussy jezebel leading happily married men astray."

"And women," offered her sister.

"That's right, and women. And teenage boys."

"You're spreading venereal disease around like wildfire, too, you know."

"Like it's my job."

"Anyway, I don't want you to go into this too cavalierly, that's all I'm saying. Australia needs change around sexuality and the sex industry. It's your chance to stand up against it."

"What do we think this Fae character will say then?" asked Apple, taking out a pen and pencil.

"I think that disease will be one of her things. Men spreading disease to their wives, and I don't know, giving babies birth defects or something."

"That's easily rebutted," said Apple. "I've got the statistics to back up how we're safer than a one-night stand."

"Yes," replied Janie, "but be careful there because she's not going to be advocating that either. Saving yourself for your man will be part of it."

"What the fuck am I supposed to do with that sort of stupidity? How can you even argue against something so regressive?"

"Traditional feminism," said Janie. "It appeals to some people. What can I say? So many people disagree with that that you should just be able to make jokes and get the other people on your side about that one. I feel like it's not our main worry."

"She's the new moral majority, so she will probably bring up Bible stuff. I don't know a whole lot about her. Where did she spring from anyway?"

"Oddly enough," said Janie, "she isn't affiliated with a church or religion in any way."

"What, she's not a Christian?" said Apple incredulously.

"Apparently not. For someone who has begun to have a lot of opinions over the past few months, she doesn't have much of an internet footprint, but none of her socials or her website mentions faith."

"She must be a god botherer," said Apple. "How can you be tradfem, anti sex work, stay at home, and be pure anti-feminist without misquoting the Bible and taking it out of context to back you up?"

"She seems to be a rich and complex patriarchy spouting tapestry," replied Janie. "And a bit of a wild card. Suddenly bursting onto the speaking circuit and having right-wing opinions is just the kind of thing that this day and age loves, I'm afraid."

"You know what I think about these people," said Apple. "I don't think they even hold those opinions. I think they just say what they think will get the most people onside. Unpredictable."

"I can almost guarantee the talking points that Fae will come up with will revolve around delicate and fragile women and the distracting effect that your breasts have on the poor menfolk."

"My magnificent breasts," clarified Apple. They're amazing.'

"Yes, my bad, your magnificent breasts. Speaking of which, what are you planning on wearing? Girls in out or out?"

"Definitely out," said Apple. I'm going to use every bit of collateral that I've got."

LIKE TRYING TO MOVE A REALLY BITTER AND ANGRY MOUNTAIN

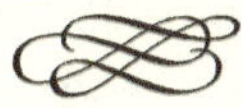

Eve knew where he lived, of course. They had bought this house together. Made themselves a little haven. A love burrow. He had laughed when she suggested these words, but shook his head and told her it was adorable and the perfect name for their house. She had wanted to go and see him since his exile, but it was hard.

Zeus had been coming down to the planet for years, but quietly. He had turned over a new leaf and was no longer the Zeus of legend. He was a sensitive new age guy. There was absolutely nothing left of the lying, cheating, wife-eating, bullying arsehole he, by his own admission, had sunk too much time and energy into being.

Times had changed, and so had he. So, they had bought a house, and they had planned a future together. She couldn't spend as much time on Earth as he could, obviously, because every time she made a trip down, she had to slip into an unsanctioned, unknown, and pretty precarious portal while wearing a bad wig. Whereas he, of course, had absolute freedom.

Eve pushed her chestnut hair out of her eyes and took a deep breath before she rapped her knuckles on the wooden door of their red brick 1950s house. She glanced around nervously. As usual, she had slipped down the portal she had once found hidden in a cleaning closet near her rooms, and while she was sure no one would notice her missing, she still hoped no Upper Realms creatures spotted her here.

There was no noise from within the house, so she cupped her hands to the glass panel set within the wood of the front door and peered in. The corridor that ran down the middle of the house was dark and empty, and she could see no sign of movement. She knocked again and tried the handle, but the door was locked.

Why had she never thought to get her own key? They had spent so much time in this house, but they were always together. She'd never needed to be here on her own. Creating this home for them was his project. A labor of love.

She stepped back and looked around. The wide street was empty; it was the middle of a workday, after all. He could be out, of course, but something within told her he was close.

He was her soulmate. Her true love. She always knew when he was near.

She heard a distant scraping noise and stepped lightly off the front step, then walked down the side of the house.

The backyard was enclosed by a high wooden fence, with a gate from the road wide enough to fit a car through, and was mostly made of painted green concrete with the odd tuft of grass growing up from between the cracks. The garage door was up, and a short man was dragging a wrought iron chair into the darkness. Cans of gold and red paint sat on the concrete of the yard, which was patchily covered with newspapers. She stood staring at him for a moment. His brown hair stood up as if it hadn't been brushed in days, and a thick moustache covered the entire area from under his nose to the sides of his mouth. Several days' growth covered his chin, and as she watched him, he pulled his track pants up over his prominent belly. Being short, she knew he always found it hard to get pants that fit in the legs and around the middle at the same time.

He was utterly and unbelievably handsome to her.

He kneeled next to the iron chair and started brushing away the dust and cobwebs on it with his hands. She knew this chair. They had found it together at a garage sale. The filigree dragons that ran up the side had the white paint chipped away, but she knew it could be beautiful if it could be restored, and he had promised to make it so. She had picked out the tins of paint that now sat, open, on the ground. If he had remembered he was going to do this, then could he possibly remember more?

"Baby," she said softly, tears springing unbidden to her eyes. "Baby, it's me."

The man looked up, startled, and lost his balance, falling sideways and narrowly missing knocking over the pot of gold paint. He steadied himself and sprang to his feet, pulling his t-shirt over his stomach.

"Who are you?" he barked. "Why are you in my yard?"

Her heart broke a little when she saw no recognition in his eyes.

"Hi," she said, trying to smile although she felt like crying. "Do you… I mean, don't you remember me?"

He pushed his thick glasses up his nose and peered at her. "Do you work in the Italian restaurant down the road?"

She shook her head. "No. We are... we used to be friends. I mean, we are…"

He glanced around uncomfortably and bit his thumbnail. "I doubt you would have ever been friends with me. Females don't like men such as me."

"Who?"

"Females. Females like you don't like men such as me."

Eve bit her lip. "Men like what?" she asked uncertainly. "If you mean the things you used to do with Hera and everything, then we've worked through all that and—"

"I mean, men who look like me. Men under six feet tall without muscles or jawlines. You don't care about personalities; you're all shallow and don't care what's inside."

She opened her mouth to speak. "But we used to be friends," she protested. "Very close friends."

"What's my name then?"

She started to say his name, but then realized he probably wasn't going by that at the moment. "I knew you as Zeus," she said. "But maybe that's not what you're called now?"

"Is there a camera around here?" he snapped, craning his neck around. "Are you filming content? Female pranks man just minding his own business? I'll have you know there are very strict laws about filming on private property, and I won't have any hesitation using everything at my disposal if you try to use this for your TikTok or YouTube."

"My what?"

"Beautiful women don't speak to men like me unless it's a prank," he snapped.

She tried to steer the conversation onto something less inflammatory than the existence of women.

"That's a lovely chair. Are you renovating it?"

He looked down at the chair and stared at it, a look of puzzlement on his face. "Yes," he said after a moment. "I think so. I think I am. I need to paint it and make it beautiful for someone. Someone important."

"That gold colour will look beautiful on the arms," Eve said, crouching next to the chair. "And red along here, along the dragon's back, will bring out the scales."

He stooped down next to her and ran his fingers along the ornate fretwork. "Yes," he said. "That's what I have in mind. I needed to do it for someone, but I can't remember who. But I think that's exactly what they said, too."

She turned her head to look at him, wishing she could reach out and run her fingers through his bristly hair. "Are you sure you don't remember me?" she asked softly. "At all?"

His brown eyes looked into hers, and for just a moment, she thought their love, that her love, the power of her belief in what they had, could bridge whatever God had done to him.

"Hang on, weren't you one of the girls who bullied me in high school? Sheree Chambers?"

"What, no," she said, standing abruptly. "Of course I'm not. Why would you think that?"

"Well, you're the one who comes barging into people's yards demanding I remember you from somewhere. You're a typical female, aren't you? Assuming I remember you. You probably served me coffee once, and you think I'm so desperate for female attention that I remember you? I'll ask you to leave my yard this moment before you accuse me of sexual harassment. Actually, that is what this is all about, isn't it? You're trying to frame me to get my money or—"

"What is the matter with you?" she snapped, although she knew all too well what the matter was. "Why are you behaving like this? You're smart, handsome, clever, creative. Why are you insisting all women hate you?"

"Look at me," he snapped back, his voice cracking. "Look at me. No one wants a man who looks like me. Men who look like me are universally reviled. There are so many of us, you don't even know, but we are a whole community now. Women hate us because we don't look the way the cool guys look, so we've turned our back too. If women don't want us, we don't want them."

"You look identical to the love of my life," said Eve, speaking quickly before the tears came. "In fact, you could be twins. Exactly the same. The only difference is your personality and the belief that no one wants you. How about you actually leave this house and go out into the world? Talk to a woman? Try not being a total and complete arsehole for five minutes of your life and see what happens?"

She needed him. Not just as her love but because she didn't know how to do what had to be done without him.

He stared at her, and for a moment, just a second, she thought she might have seen a flicker of recognition in his eyes before his face closed down again.

"My name is Tony," he said. "Not Zeus."

Then she turned and fled.

ALMOST A DATE, IF YOU SQUINT AND TILT YOUR HEAD

Everyone had a podcast these days. Literally, everyone. The man who made Jared his drink had announced, unprovoked, that he was starting up a show called the Daily Brew where he would discuss coffee and socialist politics or some such. Jared had stopped listening before he'd even started.

Everyone wanted to be known as somebody.

He looked up as Fae slid between the close tables of the coffee shop. She pulled out a chair and set her takeaway cup on the table in front of her.

"You look sexy," he said.

"Stop it," she replied as color rushed to her cheeks and she fought back a smile. "I'm being very professional. Don't distract me."

"This is fantastic," said Jared, tilting a cream-topped Frappuccino toward Fae.

She didn't look at it; her eyes remained fixed on his face instead.

"It's great," he said. "It's like, icy and sweet and thick, but also creamy with caffeine. Tell you what, humans are fucking idiots, but they really do know how to make great tasting food, don't they? Have you tried mozzarella sticks yet?"

Fae took a sip of her coffee and grimaced a little.

"I've told you to stop trying to convince yourself you enjoy black coffee," he said. "It's foul."

"And men drinking milkshakes is so emasculating," she said, raising one eyebrow and trying to stop the smile spreading further across her face as they made eye contact.

"It's lucky I'm not actually a man then, isn't it?" he replied. "And you're in a teasing mood. I like it."

"Why here?" she said, looking around the busy coffee shop. "Why are we meeting in the middle of such a public place?"

He shrugged. "Sorry, would you rather a cemetery at midnight during a Blood Moon? An abandoned orphanage with dead babies buried under our feet? A windswept moor? Or very luxurious boudoir? I seem to remember we found ourselves in one of them once." He winked. "And it doesn't matter what we talk about there, no one's going to take any notice. They're all way too wrapped up in their own business. Look, that woman is standing on a chair to take a photo of her bagel. And those two there, the ones with the ring light? They're recording a fucking interview. No, we're fine. We could talk about the Upper Realm's plan for humankind, and no one would care. If they did hear us, they'd just think you were pitching me a movie script."

She nodded in agreement. "So, what's happening? Are you happy with how I'm doing?"

"I'm just checking in," he said conversationally. "Just seeing how you're progressing. And I wanted to see you."

"Did you?" she asked, trying and failing to keep the note of hope out of her voice.

"Of course. I love to see it when you're being a good girl and doing so well. How is everything going? You look gorgeous. Did I mention that?"

"Good," said Fae. "Very good, I think. I've checked on

Maggie, the girl who wanted to go into finance and who we think was destined to head up a Fortune 500. I organized a mentor who told her the main thing she needs to do is to retain her femininity, which made her question things just the slightest, and then I set up a new boyfriend who love bombed her, so she's fallen for him completely. He kindly, with a huge amount of love, told her that finance isn't something he sees the love of his life doing. So she said no to the internship she was offered, and there's nothing else on the horizon, and then he got her pregnant for good measure. The Lilith ember is gone completely from what I've been able to detect."

"Excellent," said Jared, stirring the straw around in the bottom of his drink. "Who are you focusing on at the moment?"

Fae took a folder from her briefcase. "I've got Wellingsley Baxter and Apple. The more I observe them, the more I can see that they have strong embers."

"How is Lilith manifesting in them? Have you managed to work it out?"

"Why are you so interested?"

"Professional curiosity."

"But you're not a professional. And I thought you wanted a hands-off approach."

"Baby, I never want a hands-off approach when I'm around you."

She rolled her eyes at him, but a smile played on her lips.

"All right, I'm bored. I'm earthbound like you, and it's annoying. I need a conversation topic."

She tilted back her head and looked at him. "You're never bored, and you're not earthbound."

"There's no getting anything past you," he said, patting her hand. "My clever girl."

She twisted her fingers around his. "Don't call me that," she said. "Unless you mean it."

He sighed. "You know it wouldn't work. What we had was

amazing and beautiful, and you'll always have a piece of my heart, but you're a fae, and I'm a trickster. It's forbidden."

"It's bloody well not," she snapped, snatching her hand away. "You just can't make a commitment."

He nodded sagely. "Yeah, that's true. That is true. But maybe I'll change one day. And if I do, you'll be my first choice. The closer we work together, the more time we spend together, the more I'm reminded just how amazing you really are."

Silence hung in the air between them.

"Anyway," she said, "what else do you want? I'm sure you're not just here to talk to me…are you?"

"Yes," said Jared. "There is something else. Someone I need you to connect with. I've got the official stuff written up, if you need it, but I thought I'd give you the heads up."

"I don't connect up with random people."

"You do now," said Jared, glancing away. The woman taking photos of her food was now trying to stack a chair on another in order to take a wide-angle photo of the entire table. It looked as if her tablemates were getting heartily sick of being told they couldn't start eating yet. Jared hoped she'd fall off the stack of chairs and break her neck. For a moment, he idly contemplated activating a quick energy bolt to enable that to happen, but decided against it. He needed to get through this conversation without the place being evacuated because of a medical emergency.

"Wait a minute. I'm going again," he said, heading for the counter.

He didn't know how she would respond to his next instruction. She would do it, of course, because that was their dynamic. One of the most important parts of being a fixer was having a legion of people working for you. Lots of moving pieces, most who didn't know about each other.

Jared took his seat again. "This one's a cookie butter flavor," he said, proudly holding it up. "Want a taste? How are you going with all of this, anyway? I wasn't sure you'd even take it on.

You're potentially ruining these women's lives, and that isn't very… you."

"I don't see it that way," she said.

"Oh, really? You've found a way to justify this to yourself."

"Well, I'm helping them be who they want to be."

He reached out a finger and stroked her hand. "You have nice skin," he said.

"Because putting an ember of Lilith in them changed them, didn't it? It changed them from who they should have been."

"Okay, tell me about that."

"So, God created them to be one way and—"

Jared interrupted her. "I think you're on the wrong track there. I've heard a lot about the guy, and I don't know how much mindful creation went on there, to be honest."

"Putting Lilith in them changed them, you see. So, I'm helping them go back to their purest forms. It's a good thing I'm doing."

He looked at her doubtfully. "Are you sure you're not just trying to justify the fact that you're doing me this morally grey favour?"

"Tell me this new job allocation you have for me so I can get on with what I'm really supposed to be doing," she interrupted.

"I wish we had these at work," he said, peering into the cream on the top of his drink. "And the bonus is this is a plastic cup. And straw! Fuck the oceans, yeah?"

"Jared," she snapped.

"Yep, all right. Someone down here needs some mentoring. Or a hobby. Something to get him out of his Mum's basement, really."

"Metaphorically speaking, I assume," said Fae.

"No, no. He's actually in a basement. Or a bunker. It's kind of a metaphor, but he needs something to do. There's not much call for his brand of skill set these days on Earth, so he's gone into a bit of a decline. Which is where you come in."

"I like to make my own decisions about who I do business with," she said.

"How positively feminist of you. You're almost an embodiment of Lilith."

She rolled her eyes. "I am not."

"So, Zeus," he began.

"I beg your pardon?"

"Yes, that's who they want you to connect with."

"Zeus is down here?"

"I thought you knew that?"

"How would I know that? I don't sit around in coffee shops gossiping like you do. I'm busy."

"Yes, Zeus is down here. A lot of the old guard are down here. When the move was made to monotheism back in the day, quite a few decided to live down here on the proviso they would have some special rights and no responsibilities. You'd be surprised at who is doing what."

"I doubt it."

"Quite. Anyway, Zeus. He's not really flourishing these days. He was sent down after a flap, a bit of a drama. Can't keep it in his pants that one. He's a mad lad."

"He's fucking clinically insane, and people keep making excuses for his appalling behavior by saying things like 'he's a mad lad', when actually he's a predatory arsehole."

"Moral relativism", said Jared with a wave of his hand. "There are different standards these days."

"What happened?"

"That's on a strictly need-to-know basis."

"You don't know, do you?"

"No, I don't, but surely he has some skills you could utilize?"

"Zeus? Skills I might be able to utilize? Funnily enough, I have little need for turning anyone's wife into a fly and then eating her or having sex with his sister or raping swans. Don't have any use for that particular skill base at this point, but how about you give me his number, and I'll let him know if I ever need anyone turned into a cow, okay?"

"He will be useful to you, trust me."

"How the hell could he be useful?" she asked.

"You need to trust me," he said firmly. "I don't feel like you're taking me seriously."

"I do trust you," she said.

"Well, you won't have any problem working with him then, will you?"

Fae braced her feet against the floor and pushed her chair away from the table, crossing her arms in front of her. She was aware this meant she was encroaching on the space of the table behind, but as far as she was concerned, this was the cafe's fault for cramming so many wobbly tables into such a small space. She was also aware that the buzz of conversation at the table behind her had stopped, and she could feel their glares. But she had bigger things to attend to.

"Look, I just think it would be good for you to connect with him. Don't ask me how I know, or what I know, because I can't tell you. Baby," he said softly. "Trust me."

"Are you just saying this to get your own way?" she asked.

"I admit he's going to be hard to work with. He's an incel at the moment."

"A what?"

"It's a particularly bizarre and annoying group of men who are having their moment in the sun. Except not the sun, because most of them live in basements now, I come to think of it."

"This is all spectacularly unclear."

"God put him down here as an incel as a punishment for a particular incident, but the whole thing is a bit murky, and things are moving about, and I think we both know God isn't very good at carrying out things he starts or staying angry at people for long."

"Surely that's a good thing."

Jared shrugged. "Depends on how you look at it. To fill you in, incel means involuntary celibate, and it's basically a bunch of men who can't get anyone to have sex with them because they have no social skills, and they hate themselves and think they should have the right to access women's bodies even if no one wants them."

"What?" Fae asked, and her bemusement was real.

"Women don't want them because their personalities are repugnant, but they pretend it's because they're not 6'4" and ripped."

"They think women only want attractive men, do they?"

"Or ones with power."

Fae looked over to a thin, wispily bearded young man with large glasses who was holding the attention of a gorgeous woman with, she could hear, discussions about socialist discourse in pre-Columbian America.

"He looks like he's about to get amazingly lucky by the look of where that girl has his hand," she said wryly.

"Look, these guys aren't coming from a place of empirical evidence, okay? They're losers who don't know how to make friends or clean their teeth or learn how to be functioning adults, and so they think women should be made available for their use."

"Delightful," she said. She could tell that the people at the table behind her had realized their passive-aggressive stares were going to have no effect on her seating position, so they had rearranged their chairs and resumed their conversation.

"And I have to use him."

"Yes."

"I can do this on my own," she said, but she knew her protest was pointless.

"Can't tell you exactly what's going on, I just know it's an order. Connect with him and find him something to do. It's a new part of your job description."

"Fuck" said Fae, rolling her eyes. "This is going to take me away from what I'm supposed to be concentrating on."

"Not my problem," said Jared, standing up. "I'm just the messenger."

"Are you really?"

He winked at her, and a smile broke out on her face, much to her mortification.

"There's just one thing you should know," he said. "He doesn't know he's Zeus, so don't mention it."

"What do you mean he doesn't know he's Zeus? How is that supposed to work?"

"He's had his memory wiped. It's a whole production. Don't mention it to him, okay?"

Fae felt a tap on her shoulder and turned around to see a table of young feminists who wanted to discuss with her the fact that she felt it was acceptable for her to encroach on their personal space. And when she turned back, Jared was gone, leaving a piece of paper with a single name and a number lying next to her empty paper cup.

As Jared walked briskly away, he weighed up the facts in his head. Having the embers near each other would increase their chances of connecting. Eve was very keen to have Lilith back together, so she would do her part, maybe even work out some of the trickier embers. And Zeus near all of them? If his memory came back, he would definitely help Eve.

Jared rubbed his palms together happily, and tiny sparks flew from his hands. He would be back with the Eons before he knew it.

WELL, THAT EVENING WAS A WASTE OF MAKEUP

Making people angry was the primary focus of media organisations. Fill the unwashed masses with self-righteous indignation, get them to loudly advocate new half-baked opinions, and send them out into the world to argue with people who watched other stations. Self-righteous indignation kept the media, and by virtue of that the internet, and took away food places, and to a lesser but still important extent, beer companies, in business. The Venn diagram of people who like to argue and people who like to eat takeaways and drink beer is a circle, but so is the entirety of the human race in general.

A discussion panel between the big new thing in conservative circles and a prostitute was exactly what Channel Star felt would give their dwindling ratings a boost. A small, temporary boost, but there were a few advertising account executives in the market for some very expensive new sound systems, so a screaming match between two people who, God willing, were unable to find a middle ground was just what was needed.

This kind of thing, they hoped, would get influential YouTubers on both sides of the equation very angry and would inspire social media and TikTok to kick off, ensuring Channel Star's continual relevance.

At least that was the plan.

"So, Apple," said Leon Travisail, the slickly haired moderator. "You believe sex work should be able to be freely given and received, and that society should embrace, or even welcome, people having sex with whoever they want, whenever they want, and paying for any form of sex they want."

Apple smiled slightly, uncertainly. "Hi, yes. First, can I just say that my pronouns are she/her, and, yes, I do believe in not just the normalisation but also the embracing of sex work in all forms."

"In all forms," said the moderator with the very expensive smile. "So you think sex slavery and child prostitution should be legalised?"

"What? No," stammered Apple, but Leon turned his crocodile grin to Fae.

"And Fae Stephenson," said Leon. "The hot new poster girl for the New Right, as they're calling themselves. You have created quite a stir in your short time in the spotlight. You're on record as saying," he continued, a glint in his eye, "that feminism damages women, that sexual liberation is a jail sentence, that abortion is genocide, and that what the religious right describes as complementarian is the model for men and women to live together in harmony. Would that be correct?"

"Hello, yes," said Fae smoothly. "Fae Stephenson. My pronouns are she/her, and I have no affiliation with the groups of which you speak, and most of those statements cannot be attributed to me."

There was a slight frisson of tension as everyone on the set realized for the first time that things might not go quite the way they had planned.

"And I certainly don't hold myself up as a poster girl. In fact, the ACL asked me to stand for their campaign just this week, and I didn't return their call."

"Well," smirked Leon, still undecided on which, if either, of these women's sides he was going to ask leading questions to support. "I would say that the mention of pronouns would have put pay to any chance of that going forward."

"Quite," said Fae with a small smile that Leon was finding increasingly disturbing.

Leon's own smile faltered momentarily, but it was plastered back on before any viewer would have noticed its waver. He was the consummate professional, after all. He had interviewed Big Brother winners, and once, in his heyday, had interviewed Pauline Hanson. He knew what he was doing.

"Apple," he said. "You sell your body for money. Tell us about that."

"In a capitalistic society, we all sell our bodies for money, replied Apple. "Everyone is selling their body all of the time. What I do is no different from a builder or a footballer or a waiter who spends twelve hours a day on their feet and goes home with blisters. We're all made to sell our labour, and some of us our bodies, in the current paradigm that we live within. The only difference in what I do and what other people do is that society has placed certain value judgements on the entire area of women's bodies, so, for example, what we should and shouldn't do with them, and on sex in general. That's the only difference. Well, that and I make a lot more money than those other jobs. Society doesn't like powerful, wealthy women. We're encouraged to be small, and the idea of using our bodies to advance ourselves is discouraged by the patriarchy because of the inherent power in doing so."

"So, you think there should be a complete legalisation of sex work."

"I think," said Apple, after a moment, "that if a woman wants to empower herself through sexuality, then she should be able to do it in whatever way she chooses."

"You didn't answer my question."

"That's because it was a stupid question."

"So, what kind of sexual services do you offer?" he asked, pushing his luck.

"I hardly think that's relevant to this discussion, is it?" she said.

"I think it would give our audience a better idea of who you are, the complete woman, if you like. It would help them to empathize with you."

"If people can only empathize with my line of work by forming a bond with me, then I welcome them to visit my website and explore the services there. Booking is available online."

"Fae, you think sex should not be sold and that it should be held as a sacred thing within the marital unit. Is that right?"

"No, not really," she said with a shrug.

"I'm sorry?"

"No, not really," she repeated. "You're misrepresenting me. I have extensive thoughts on this topic, yes, but it would be a mistake for you to pigeonhole me into one category or belief system. My main problem with what Ms. Apple is advocating is the aspect of feminism."

"Right," said Leon, feeling like he was on ground that was slightly steadier. "Yes, feminism. You're on record as saying that sex work is a pervasive and damaging influence on society and, therefore, feminism is to blame."

"I feel as if you need to hire more competent researchers," said Fae, glancing behind him at the crew behind the cameras. "It's hardly fair that you're fed this information and then put out in front of the cameras like this. It's like a lamb to the slaughter."

He attempted to speak, but she held up her hand, stilling him.

"I'm not blaming feminism for this poor girl's situation," she said, gesturing toward Apple with a wave of her hand.

"Don't call me a poor girl," said Apple.

"What I care about," said Fae, slightly shifting in her chair so her profile could be captured more fully by the camera, "is women. I care about what is best for women. I'm not anti-feminism across the board. But from what I can see, sex work is deeply anti-feminist, and my heart breaks that so many young people see selling their body as some kind of activism or the radical reallocation of power when it's playing right into the patriarchy's hands. Anyone who sees themselves as feminist should be doing everything they can to put a halt to the selling of women's bodies for men's pleasure. Do you want to be supporting the patriarchy, Ms. Apple?"

"Sex work is anything but supporting the patriarchy," scoffed Apple. "It's women reclaiming their autonomy over something that has been taken from them for hundreds of years. It's doing things on their own terms."

"And that's what the patriarchy wants you to think," said Fae. "And it's done it most effectively. Now access to women's bodies, in every conceivable way, is easier than ever, and you have been made think that you're the ones in charge when actually you're just playing into their hands."

"Whose hands?" asked Leon, liking the way this line of reasoning was going. "Whose hands do you believe Apple has played into?"

"Why men in power, of course," replied Fae. "Effectively manipulating women to think they're calling the shots and controlling the narrative when, in fact, women are, as they have been for hundreds of years, and as Ms. Apple so correctly said, under the control of men. And right now, in this day and age, the women who sell sex, the women who wear tiny skimpy clothes in the name of empowerment, and the women who feel that the full and complete expression of their sexuality as a way of finding their true path, or whatever it is they call it, are mere puppets of the patriarchy. Playing into their hands. Again. But this time they don't even realise it, so there's no way to escape."

"You're trapped, Apple. How do you feel about the idea you're actually disempowered and trapped and exploited?" asked Leon.

"Exactly," agreed Fae. "And I'm the one demonised for trying to help, for trying to shed some much-needed light on the situation."

"That's patently incorrect," said Apple, keeping her voice calm despite her frustration. "You are entirely disregarding my agency and ability to make my own decisions, as are you with all other people who make a free choice to involve themselves in jobs that run counter to cultural norms."

"Cultural norms?" scoffed Fae. "You honestly think selling sex goes against cultural norms?"

"Before women had the vote, when they couldn't own property, when they couldn't get divorced and were mere chattel, it was an easy battle, wasn't it? It was clear, eventually, to many that it wasn't fair and therefore far simpler to get supporters to fight for women's rights, to get the vote, and to live safely in their own homes, as it should be. But now, with the whole sordid business hidden under the cloak of empowerment, those of us who are trying to bring the truth to light, those of us who are truly trying to work for women's best interests, are seen as the bad guys. I'm seen as the one oppressing them, but in actual fact, what I'm saying is open your eyes. The cultural norm is the commodification of sex. You've been completely fooled, and the reason I'm here is to plead for you to embrace feminism and stand up against men who would use your perceived independence against you. Your enemy isn't who you think it is, Apple. It's closer than you realise."

Apple and Fae stared into each other's eyes.

"This must be confronting," Leon said to Apple, but neither woman spoke. They continued to stare at each other, and he felt himself fade into insignificance. He cleared his throat and wished he had some papers to shuffle.

Apple felt drawn into Fae's eyes. As if there was something very important she had forgotten. As if…

She desperately cast around her mind for her talking points.

"You aren't a feminist," said Fae. "You're the opposite of a feminist. If you were a feminist, then you wouldn't be giving your body to men to use as they wish. This is exactly what your people have been fighting against. And you've been subjugated and exploited and convinced to such an extent you think you're brave and courageous when, really, you're a tool of the patriarchy."

Apple continued to stare into Fae's eyes. She didn't reply, and time stood still.

"Dead air!" shouted a voice in Leon's earpiece. "Dead air! Don't let there be dead air!"

"Apple, many people say that sex workers are vectors for disease and are responsible for the spread of sexually transmitted illnesses amongst married couples across the board. What do you have to say to that?"

The connection between the two women broke.

"Many studies," said Apple, bringing her attention back to the host, "have shown, time and again, that sex workers are actually far more health-conscious and aware of sexual health and its precautions than the wider community. So maybe everyone should be having sex with sex workers rather than, you know, their partners or spouses. Everyone needs a hooker!"

She had meant this as a light joke, a throwaway comment that would help break the tension, but there was dead silence in the room. Leon glanced around nervously, and the camera operators side-eyed each other.

Everyone wished there was somewhere else that they could be.

Especially Apple. Her face flushed red.

Fae's light, comforting voice edged its way into the awkward silence. "You poor girl,"' she said, and suddenly, unexpectedly, tears rushed to Apple's eyes.

"And this is exactly why I'm starting up my Ladies Academy," she said without missing a beat. "Young women today, or," and she smiled at Apple benignly, "slightly older women such as us, have been given precious few models as to who we should emulate. They have been thrown into a world of equal rights and high expectations and of doing everything for everyone, but they have been given no information about how to actually find themselves. How to be the fully formed and absolute manifestation of who they're supposed to be. My Ladies Academy is a vitally important addition to the places of higher education that women today apparently have no choice but to sign up for. Young women today haven't been taught any of the things they need to know because their mothers didn't know them either. And their mothers didn't have time to teach them because they were too busy burning their bras. When what we have is women whose only skills are, and excuse my bluntness here, teaching others how to give blow jobs or prepare for anal sex, then our society is in deep trouble."

"And I'm sorry to attack a fellow woman, but if this is the best and brightest that the sex industry can put forward, then it's in more trouble than I originally thought."

The rest of the interview became an infomercial for Fae's Ladies Academy, but Apple wasn't listening. She was just concentrating, not hyperventilating, and on keeping her face from burning up with embarrassment. This was going spectacularly badly, and all she wanted was to lie in a dark room with a cloth over her head.

* * *

"THE CHRISTIAN GROUP has cancelled their meeting with you," her driver, Restarian, said when she got into the car.

"I didn't know we had one scheduled," she replied as she took a sip of the room-temperature water that sat in the cup holder next to her.

"I penciled one in," he said. "On the off chance."

"That was a waste of everyone's time, wasn't it. I never intended to talk to them."

"I thought it might leave some options open."

"I don't need options," she said.

Restarian continued to look straight ahead, and he merged with the lane of traffic streaming out of the city.

They sat in silence for a few minutes.

"That went well," Fae said. "I'm sure the ember of Lilith in her is extinguishing as we speak."

"See, this is the issue I have," said Restarian, who had been clearly waiting for his chance to have an opinion. "You're assuming that the sex worker is how Lilith manifests in her, yes?"

"Yes, of course. What else would it be?"

"And you're assuming that moving her away from sex work will help her reclaim her true self."

"Exactly. Who she would have been before people started meddling into her essence."

"Right, yes, that's the situation as you see it. But maybe the sex worker part isn't the Lilith part. You're assuming what you've been told about Lilith is true and—"

"I'm following the brief I was given. Find the embers of Lilith and extinguish them."

"I think you're making a lot of assumptions, and I also don't think you were given a very detailed job description. All the laminated photos and high image graphics in the world don't make up for the fact that you've been left on your own to make this up as you go along. It feels strange."

"The fact that I was given an out-of-work boggart as an assistant is the strangest thing, if you ask me."

"I'm a very highly regarded boggart, thank you very much. And you want to be driving in this traffic, do you?"

"Have you considered that maybe someone just knew I'd do a very good job, and maybe someone has more faith in me than you do," she snapped.

"Someone. You mean Jared."

She stared out the window.

"All right," he said. 'I'll shut up.'

"I'm surprised you used feminism as an argument," he said

lightly, decidedly not shutting up. "I'm surprised you were advocating it."

"I wasn't advocating it," she said. "I was tailoring an argument to be exactly what would have the most detrimental effect on Apple, my listener. That's her trigger. I have to make them question themselves. That's it. Nothing more complex or more groundbreaking than that. And whatever I have to say to make it happen is worth it. And yes, some of what I'm saying is patently ridiculous."

"Some people do believe all that, though."

"Not my problem. It's a means to an end."

"Yes, well," he said, "now you're committed to opening a fucking Ladies Academy or some such. You'll hate that."

"Don't be stupid. Everyone will forget about it. No one would want something like that, anyway. It was just a way to divert attention from Apple."

"I don't know," he said as she gazed fixedly out the window. "They seemed pretty interested in it. You may have bitten off more than you can chew."

"Don't say that," she said, rifling through her bag in search of a mint. "That's my idea of actual hell. I'd rather go into business with Apple and start a brothel. At least that would be entertaining."

"Might be a good way to ruin more potential Liliths."

"Am I trying to ruin them, though?" she said, staring out the window and beginning to let her mind drift off. "I'm helping them. I'm helping women be who they're really supposed to be. That's an utterly noble calling."

Restarian muttered something about it being less noble and more her trying to get into Jared's pants again.

"I want them to live an authentic life," she said. "I'm actually feminist as fuck, but do any of these people realise that? No, of course they bloody don't."

WELLINGSLEY FINDS A MENTOR

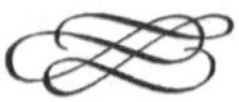

Wellingsley dialed the number she'd found at the bottom of Fae's website three times before she finally let it ring all the way through. It was a very slick site, not a lot of content, just some main talking points, details of where Fae could be found speaking next, and an email contact form.

The flat was quiet. She hadn't turned the light on, and she sat in the semi-darkness with the closed blinds creating a little cocoon.

Her call was answered on the second ring, and a smooth voice said, "Hello, Fae Stephenson, how may I help you?"

"Oh," barked Wellingsley, shocked. "I didn't expect you to answer your phone in person."

"Ah," said the kind voice, "I'm afraid I'm not quite at the level of influence to have a staff yet. We can but dream. How can I help you?"

There was silence as Wellingsley tried to land on exactly what she wanted to say. That she felt the entirety of her life shifting under her feet. That she finally felt a light had burst through the clouds, and there was clarity for the first time ever. That she felt there might be some hope in the endless stress she felt her life would be made up of. That she was utterly terrified and utterly hopeful.

"I saw you speak, and I really liked what you had to say," she said instead.

"Thank you," said Fae, and Wellingsley could hear the smile in her voice. "I appreciate that. Was it last night's so-called debate you saw or something else?"

"No, not the debate," said Wellingsley. "Although I did watch that. It was at the university. You were speaking about how feminism damages women."

"That does sound like something I'd say," replied Fae, and Wellingsley could hear the laugh again and wondered for a moment why anyone would ever see her as harsh and abrasive. "Did you connect with my words?"

"Yes," started Wellingsley, and to her dismay, her voice caught in her throat. "I did connect with what you were saying. I felt like your words might have changed my life."

"Goodness," said Fae. "It sounds like you're a young woman who needs a shoulder to cry on. Could you ring your mother, maybe?"

The words caught her off guard. "My mother? No, that wouldn't work. My mother is the reason I'm at university in the first place."

There was a moment of silence.

"I have a frightfully busy schedule, but I feel as if you could do with someone making time for you. Would you like to meet for a coffee and a chat?"

Wellingsley wiped away the tear that had dripped down her cheek. "Really? You wouldn't mind? You have time to meet a random stranger who rings you out of the blue?"

"Wellingsley, if I didn't make time for a young woman who is questioning all her life's choices purely on the basis of my words, then what kind of person would I be? What kind of mentor to you would I be?"

"You want to be my mentor?" Wellingsley's voice was low, awestruck.

"If you need me," said Fae.

"I want to join the Ladies Academy," said Wellingsley. "I want to be part of it. It sounds incredible."

As she hung up, and at the same time that Fae, alone in her office, placed a tick next to the words **Arrange coffee with Wellingsley**. Wellingsley, sitting on her sofa in her dark lounge, was too caught up in the prospects of what might lie ahead for it to even occur to her how this woman had known her name.

It was a gloomy morning as Wellingsley followed the directions to the small building that her maps app assured her was where she was supposed to be heading. Low clouds threatened to spill their rain at any moment, and a cold breeze whistled down the road, channeled by the buildings and storefronts that stretched in an unbroken row down the street. It was an expensive area; Wellingsley didn't know how much rent was, but the freshly painted sign hanging from the awning that read "Fae Stephenson—Ladies Academy" meant there must be money in whatever Fae was doing.

She beamed at the sign. It was written in precisely the same font she loved the most. Utterly delightful and just… pretty.

She stood at the green door and wondered if she should knock or just push it open. There was no indication of opening hours or a bell or anything, and just as she felt a flush rising in her cheeks and the beginning of an urge to walk away and say she couldn't find the place and reschedule, the door swung inwards, and the tall, dignified woman stood before her.

"Oh, hello," said Fae. "I was just heading out. Can I help you?"

Wellingsley smiled far too broadly and said, "Oh, I'm sorry to bother you. I'm Wellingsley, and we spoke on the phone yesterday, and you told me to drop by today, but if this isn't a good time, then…"

Fae stepped forward and wrapped her arms around the young woman. "Wellingsley. Stop that this instant. I'm thoroughly delighted to meet you finally, and I'm happy to postpone the meeting I was heading to. Just give me one moment."

She stepped out of the doorway, down the single step, and gestured to a silver sedan idling by the curb. The window slid down, revealing a dark interior. Wellingsley couldn't make out the shadowy figure who sat in the driver's seat, but she heard Fae inform them to cancel her meeting and start his lunch break early as she'd scheduled a new priority.

"Now come in, and excuse the mess," said Fae as she turned back toward the building. "I'm still unpacking." She flicked on a light that splashed illumination into the otherwise dark room. Piles of boxes lined the walls and pieces of furniture; bookcases and desks cluttered the area. Wellingsley doubted she could navigate the room without landing a few hefty bruises.

"Find a seat," said Fae lightly. "I'm sorry it's not more hospitable, but I've only just moved into this space, and what with all the speaking engagements I've been corralled into, interior decoration hasn't been my priority."

"Would you like me to do it for you?" The words were out of her mouth before she knew it, but as soon as she had formed the thought, she knew it was completely and utterly what she wanted to do.

"That would be wonderful. Are you sure?"

"Yes, I love design and decorating and that kind of thing. I've even thought I should maybe start my own business instead of being at university studying law."

"Absolutely," said Fae loudly, hoping Restarian was within earshot. "You want to do what's in your heart. Live your own authentic life. What a truly noble calling."

Wellingsley looked at her, puzzled, then glanced around to see who else she could be talking to.

"Are you okay?"

"Design in is your heart, but you feel pressured as if by some outside force to study law, do you?" Fae was smiling broadly as she pushed open the door to a dark room.

"If the outside force is my mother, then yes."

"Oh, my lord. People living based on others' expectations. It's so exhausting. You need to live the life you want to live, not the one others have mapped out for you. Do what you want to do, Wellingsley! You don't need a leader. You need to listen to your heart."

Wellingsley stared at her.

Fae laughed. "I'm sorry, my dear, so many opinions! That's me. We haven't even introduced ourselves properly, and here's me trying to tell you how to live your life." She held out her hand. "Fae Stephenson. I'm delighted to meet you."

"I'm Wellingsley Baxter, and I'm so happy to meet you finally. I'm a big fan. Well, I've been a big fan since last week when I…"

"You were at the university, yes? When I was speaking to that poor, misguided girl with all of those pins. I remember when labels were seen as a bad thing! Some people do buy into the whole paradigm to an excessive extent, don't they?"

She pulled two chairs together and went to a small fridge that sat in the middle of the room. Cords ran from it to a power point in the corner, and Wellingsley already had ideas about how it could be hidden so that the wood and carpet of the room could become the feature. Fae pulled out a bottle of water and two china cups, opening the bottle with as much gravitas as if it were a bottle of champagne.

She poured them both a cup. "Cheers," she said, clinking cups with Wellingsley. "Here's to a fruitful and flourishing friendship."

They sat on the chairs, facing each other, knees almost touching, and Fae leaned forward, her eyes searching Wellingsley's face. "I sense you're not happy, and that I might be able to help you."

A sob caught in Wellingsley's throat. "How do you know that?"

"Let's just call it feminine intuition, shall we?"

"No, I'm not happy. I'm questioning everything in my life. Maybe I did want to be a lawyer at some stage, but it's just so hard, and I'm out of my comfort zone all the time, and after hearing your talk I'm wondering if maybe I want to be a housewife and stay at home and look after babies and cook for a man and be more vulnerable and feminine and not have to argue with people all the time and be pushy and have opinions and… I'm just tired."

Fae placed her hand gently on Wellingsley's knee. "You're exhausted, you poor thing. You're trying to be everything to everyone, aren't you?"

Wellingsley nodded.

"Do you have a boyfriend?"

"There's a guy who calls me sometimes, and we hook up. I don't know if he would consider himself a boyfriend."

"What do you consider him to be?"

She shrugged.

"Tell me about your family."

"My family is great, honestly. I'm very loved and nurtured, and I've been given the opportunity to be whatever I want."

"Have you really though?"

Wellingsley shook her head. "Maybe not."

"Your parents."

"My mother is a news anchor and very, very feminist. She had a lesbian awakening in the 70s, and so I have two mothers."

"Love is love."

"This is why people are confused by you," said Wellingsley. "It's impossible to categorise you. You don't pick a lane, do you?"

"I don't," said Fae. "What I do is follow my heart. I follow the truth as I see it, and I don't conform to any political or religious talking points. I am very, very hard to pin down," she said, finishing with a wink. "It drives people crazy."

I can't be pinned down because I will change my opinion

depending on the needs of my particular target, thought Fae, but she kept that bit to herself.

Fae saw a flash out of the corner of her eye through the partly open door. A small creature, dark, scaly, and sinuous, its yellow eyes glowing sickly and its toddler-sized body with long arms that ended in sharp nails, sorely in need of a clean, flashed into shape at the edge of the room, then slipped out through another partly open door.

No wonder he wore gloves while he was driving.

Wellingsley turned her head. "What was that?" she said. "Do you share this space with people? I suppose the rent must be quite a lot."

"Just excuse me for a moment," said Fae, setting her cup down on the carpet next to her chair. "Let me check what's going on, and I'll be back presently."

"What?" she hissed after she slipped into the small dark room that Restarian was occupying. "Why are you inside, and why are you in this body? You know you're meant to stay in the other form. And did you hear what I said earlier?"

"The other form is dreadful," he complained. "So many extra-long extremities. I keep falling over."

"Well, you can't get around looking like this," she said, ensuring that the door was closed tightly behind her. "We have the target literally five metres away, and you can't be scaring her off. I'm about to make her an offer she can't refuse," she said, pointing toward the room where Wellingsley was waiting and from which there could be heard a dull dragging noise and the occasional thump of furniture being moved.

"Does her file have her name on it?" he asked.

Fae narrowed her eyes. "Yes, you know it does."

"Is it a wise idea to have it sitting around in the room she seems to be renovating at the moment? Do you care that she's in there with her dossier? Full info and specs about her, about her hopes and dreams, and a carefully curated flow chart of all her triggers and her deepest desires. It's all laid out, the entire trajectory of her life. With a t-chart for each decision."

There was another thud from the adjoining room.

"I didn't realise she was going to start moving the bloody furniture," Fae hissed.

"Go and stop her then."

"She won't read it even if she sees it. She's a rule follower."

"You hope. What actually happens if one of your targets finds out what's going on anyway? Have you been told what to do in such an event?"

She didn't answer.

"Why am I the only one who seems to be looking out for your interests and who's worried about what you're being asked to do?"

"For this, you leave the car?" she hissed. "Wouldn't even have left her on her own if you weren't skulking around being weird. What are you even playing at? Get back out there and hope that you haven't got a ticket because my expense budget doesn't run to your incompetence, all right?"

"And now you're stuck with some kind of academy. I tell you what, I think this Ladies Academy was a misstep. You shouldn't have said that. You've veered right off topic."

"How do you know what the topic is? Do we even have a topic?"

"I know because you're desperate for someone to talk to, so you keep oversharing and telling me more than you're supposed to."

"That's not true," she said. "I share in a very measured and tempered way."

"And also, you talk to yourself a lot."

"You could have just said that in the first place."

"The fact is, you're stuck with a fucking Ladies Academy to arrange now."

She bit her lip. "It does look a bit like that, doesn't it?" She leaned back and opened the door slightly, peering through at Wellingsley, who seemed to be bodily moving things around the room. "It's okay, I can make this bit up as I go along."

Restarian narrowed his eyes, and given that his eyes were already barely pinpricks in his scrunched-up face, this had the effect of eliminating them completely. "This doesn't sound very well thought out."

"Look," Fae spat, turning on him suddenly. "I'm doing my fucking best, all right? I've been thrown into a situation that, quite frankly, none of us have any background in or training for, and I'm simply doing my best. That said," she sat heavily on a chair. "If you do happen to have any ideas, I'm willing to be open to them. An adviser role wouldn't be bad, now you come to mention it."

"I mentioned it quite a while ago, and you ignored me."

"You are very judgy," she said. "Very judgy. I would think you'd be a bit more forgiving considering we're so similar."

"We're not the same at all," he said. "I'm a boggart, and you're a water fae."

"The Lady of the Lake, actually."

"Not 'The'. You're a dime a dozen, you lot are. There's no 'The'."

"It's the accepted nomenclature," she snapped. "I can't help it if King Arthur buggered everything up and now people only think of *that* one when we're mentioned."

"She has rather taken over popular culture, hasn't she?" said Restarian. "How does it feel to live in her shadow?"

"It wouldn't be so bad if she weren't such an absolute bitch," Fae muttered, crossing her arms firmly. "I'd better get back in there. Wellingsley wants my wise and hirsute advice, so I'd better get on with giving it to her. Change back to your human form, too. That body looks ridiculous. You're not in a bloody marsh now. You're trying to act civilised, so put on the perfectly good meat suit that's been fashioned for you, drop down a dimensional plane, and make yourself bloody useful to me. File something or, I don't know, dust."

"I don't think you meant hirsute," he said to her back as she left the room, but she either ignored him or didn't hear him. He suddenly hoped it was the latter. It would be amusing to see her use it in a serious adult conversation.

IT'S THE LACK OF ORGIES THAT'S MOST DISAPPOINTING

Asmodeus raised his face and let the air brush over his cheeks, around his beard, and through the thick hair that fell in a wave over his forehead. It caressed him gently, and he could taste a vague ambiance of lackadaisical boredom and desperation. There were some neatly trimmed and, he could only assume, ergonomically designed boxes of inoffensive plants laid at exact intervals along the street. No one was looking at them, of course, because precisely engineered pansies weren't anyone's favourite flower.

He had been on Earth during all the conceivable time periods during his search for his love, and he was now able to conclusively say that this time period was definitely the worst. So many people living half a life, so many people mollified into boredom.

At least in earlier times, he'd been able to travel around a bit while seeking her out. Lilith had been scattered around the planet as well as through time, and so he got to have a bit of a holiday while he was searching for her. See some sights. Eat some food. Be part of history.

Of course, the reboot of history every time they realized her ember was getting a hold of someone was a bit of a hindrance. Bit of a headache. Bit of a bloody soul-wrenching shock to the senses every time that unholy duo of fragile masculinity found Lilith and started all over again.

Here, though, it was the worst. Too many people, too many buildings, too many conservative viewpoints. Too logical. They had lost their sense of the absurd, of the whimsy, of the other.

And there were barely any demon worshipers around at all. They seemed to be very thin on the ground, and the ones he could find usually didn't even meet up in person to get all debauched. Instead, they sat and talked on the internet.

The rise and fall of the demon worshipper was something he'd been following lately. What with all his spare time? Which he had a lot of because he was having a bugger of a job finding Lilith.

He sat on a green bench and sipped his dirty chai. It was occupied by a couple who were holding hands and engaged in a deep conversation. He sat inappropriately close to them, and after only a few seconds, they stood and walked off.

The taste of the drink swelled in his mouth. If asked, he would grudgingly admit that this was a good part of being forced to make his way to Sydney. There was an expansive and often puzzling number of hot drinks to choose from.

Jared appeared beside him, flicking into visibility like a dark blur in a light room.

"I thought you were trying to go low profile," Asmodeus said.

"Na. Well, yeah, but no. No one will notice I'm here. These people are oblivious to real class."

"I didn't mean these people," Asmodeus said, looking at the masses scurrying around. "I meant your bosses."

"Which ones?" He laughed and took the drink from Asmodeus. He grimaced as he sipped. "Fuck me, that tastes like fifty flavours of shit. Is this the best they can do?"

"I like it," Asmodeus said.

Jared shuddered and gave it back. "No accounting for taste."

"Your bosses."

"I don't have bosses. I'm a free agent."

"Oh, stop it," Asmodeus said. "I know you've been getting cosy with the Eons."

"How do you know that?"

"Ah-ha! It is true then?"

"I'm not committing to anything. How's the search going?"

Asmodeus gestured around. "You're the one who told me Adam had decided she should have one location and one timeline now. It should be easy to find her, right?"

"Exactly. Adam and God have given you a gift, I'd think. It should be very easy."

"So, it's clearly not going to be then."

Jared laughed and took the drink back off him. "I wouldn't think so. This drink isn't that bad on reflection. Mind if I keep it?"

"You've told me she's here, and I've thanked you for that. Are you here to tell me what else I can do? Or why this decision was made?"

"Na. I just fancied a chat. Are you really not into all that demon stuff anymore?"

"What kind of demon stuff specifically?"

Jared stared at an old lady walking toward them in the distance. Nearby, a small child dropped their ice cream and started crying. The woman, seemingly oblivious to the child's noise, didn't see the ice cream in front of her and slipped and fell heavily. Asmodeus heard her cry out in pain.

"That?" said Asmodeus, turning his head to frown at Jared. "That's your idea of fun? That kind of low-hanging fruit?"

Jared shrugged. "Passes the time, doesn't it?"

"Not really."

"You've gone soft."

"There's a distinct difference between being a demon of debauchery and sex and being a pathetic trickster who likes to break old women's hips. She'll probably die from that now, you know. She's eighty-five if she's a day."

Eventually, someone had paid some attention to the frail old woman lying on the pavement and was attempting to pull her to her feet, which was causing more damage to her catastrophically broken leg and hip.

"She'll be fine. We can't kill them, you know that. She'll get lots of visitors and will love the attention once this bit is over. I actually bring families together if you look at it from that point of view."

"Why do you do these things?"

"Because I'm a giver. And as I told you, I was bored."

"No, you didn't tell me that,' said Asmodeus.

"Oh yeah, maybe that wasn't you. Oh yeah, it was Fae. That's the one I told. She didn't seem to care that much either. You guys just don't give a shit about my feelings. I have needs too, you know."

"What's this Fae creature's background?"

"She's a Fae—lady of the lake, to be more precise. I've known her for years, and she wasn't loving her current job. Apparently, lady of the laking isn't what it used to be with all the building and the concreting and the expansion of civilisation and all that, so she wanted to expand her reach a bit. And from what I've been told, she wasn't that good at it anyway, so it's not as if she's missed."

"You've taken someone who's not very good at their job to do what sounds like a fairly important mission?" questioned Asmodeus. "That doesn't seem very smart."

"She may not be a very competent being, just between you and I, but she's a sweetie, so I wanted to give her something to do. Some hope. Look, I'm a fixer," said Jared. "I hook people up. Introduce people. Arrange meetings." Here, he took both his hands and slipped his fingers together, interlocking them. "I'm a connector."

"That doesn't sound like a real job. Sounds like a project manager or an acquisitions adviser."

"And so I've connected Fae up to make sure that Lilith doesn't rear her, quite frankly, gorgeous fucking head up again."

Asmodeus glared at him. "That's the love of my life you're talking about there."

"Hey, a job's a job," said Jared, shrugging.

"You're doing your job by putting all her pieces here, in one place, overseen by someone incompetent, are you? There is definitely more to this than you're saying."

Jared raised his hand, winked, and made a zipping motion over his lips. "Layers," he said. "Machinations."

"Maybe you can help me," said Asmodeus, leaning forward. "This is the bit that I find it really hard to wrap my head around, and in the absence of any other expansive minds, yours will have to do right now."

"You think I have an expansive mind, do you, you old charmer?"

"So, when Lilith pissed off God—"

"Threatened to abort the future of all humankind, I think, was the exact situation."

"We'll have to agree to disagree on that one, but when she really got under his skin and pissed him off, he disassembled her and put different pieces of her into women all over space and time."

"Yes," said Jared. "Couldn't just kill her. She's immortal, an original creation. She always has to exist in some way. Very much a design fault in creation, I would have thought, but what do I know?"

"Yes, so he put her in a whole bunch of people because he had a hissy fit, and his impulse control hasn't improved at all, from what I've heard."

"Adam's the one to watch these days, just between you and I. He pushed for it," confirmed Jared.

"And all these people are now in Sydney in the 2020s."

"Yes, correct. Adam decided to put them in one place. To keep an eye on them at once rather than rebooting history all the time."

"Are you sure you're meant to be telling me this?"

"I don't care. I didn't sign a non-disclosure, and I'm happy to get my finger in particularly unpleasant pies, so I'm the dogsbody. And as I think I mentioned, I'm bored. Keep asking questions. I don't care."

"So this bit of Lilith is in all these women, and your man on the ground has the job of making sure that these people..."

"Fae, yes."

"Fae has the job of making sure that the Lilith embers don't become too powerful."

They could hear a siren warbling in the distance.

"Apparently, yes. I mean, Adam rants and raves about her, but she's a pretty impressive unit, all things considered. The first feminist, really, which I personally am quite a fan of."

"I saw an article the other day, and it was titled, non-ironically, *Women Are the Architects of the Downfall of Men.* I mean, what the fuck?"

"Oh yeah, I think I know that guy," said Jared. "Some girl rejected him when he was seventeen, and he's never gotten over it. It's his whole life now."

"So, maybe you can help me with what I don't understand," continued Asmodeus.

"Everyone has their soul's journey mapped out and their full potential in them, placed there by God and just waiting to be reached."

"Nah."

The siren had resolved itself into an approaching ambulance now, and two uniformed paramedics jumped out and formed a cluster around the woman on the ground.

"What do you mean, 'nah'?"

"I mean, that's what the people down here like to think because you would, wouldn't you? It's nice to think that there's a blueprint for greatness within you, that some great creator has lovingly planned your life, and all you need to do is focus on yourself and—whoosh—become it."

"Yes."

"All propaganda."

"I beg your pardon?"

"It's not a thing. To be fair, it was at the start. In the early days. There were some cave people who absolutely had a blueprint for greatness that God planned out for them, but to be honest, he got a bit burned out."

"Who did?"

"God."

"Excuse me, are you saying God got a bit burned out?"

"Burned out, over it, either or. But when he saw how many people were potentially going to be on the planet, he decided to let evolution take over and just put the word out that people were special and glorious creations. He's got a very hands-off approach to being a god these days. Spends a lot of time going to wine tastings with Adam. Yeah, humankind is on its own. I think an ember of Lilith would help people. They are basically just a bunch of atoms and neurons trying to make the best decisions they can in a universe that isn't particularly interested in them. That might be the main issue, now that I say it out loud. Maybe he doesn't want them to be what they could be. Or maybe not, I don't know. And I don't really care. I just need things to keep my brain occupied."

"God really fucked things up, didn't he?"

"Yes," said Jared, "but I'm interested to know how you came to that conclusion. We always talk about me and my interests. I never ask you about you." Jared leaned forward with an insincere look on his face. "Tell me about you."

Asmodeus rolled his eyes. "You're such a wanker."

"Why do you think God fucked up? I'm genuinely interested."

"Well, he didn't really consider the fact that we might make our own decisions. Do what we want. Be our own… beings. Our own demons."

Jared rubbed his upper lip idly. "He wanted everything to be exactly as he wanted, on his terms."

"And then he expected us all to go off and do our own things, but totally stick to his plans and schedule and his wishes. But then he got sidetracked and doesn't take any notice of us anymore anyway."

"Not accounting for our own self-determination. Or free will."

Humans have that. He gave them free will. But not us. And maybe we want to change."

"Do you want to change?" asked Jared. "What do you want to change?"

"My past is murky. I wanted to be known as a lad back in the day. The debauchery and all that."

"Yes, having sex with hundreds of lithe goddesses was purely to keep your image up, obviously."

Asmodeus laughed. "I'm not even going to pretend that isn't a good part of the job. Or was. Uninhibited and continuous fucking was certainly a career perk for a while. But as I'm getting older, some of the debauchery loses its sheen. I'd like to be a one-woman man now. If I could just find Lilith in all this monotony."

Asmodeus looked at the stretcher being rolled into the ambulance. Jared made a little motion with his hand, and one of the paramedics dropped the end, and there was a cry of pain.

"I know I'm not a human and don't have any specific interest in them, but this is all a bit bleak."

Asmodeus thought for a moment. "Does God seem to be a bit incompetent?"

"That does seem to be the current consensus, yes. Well, incompetent or just mammothly unprepared and untrained for the job. Either or, I guess, but both result in us down here having to duck and weave and try not to get hit by the shrapnel."

Asmodeus stood up just as the ambulance doors closed and the paramedics climbed into the front and began to drive off. "Kind of makes you feel sorry for them all, doesn't it?" he said suddenly. "Either everything is blind chance, a random constellation of atoms that mean absolutely nothing, or everything is planned out by someone without much of a clue or a care."

Jared put his hand on the big man's arms. "That, my friend, is why we have to make our own luck, make our own fun, and entertain ourselves. And if that means breaking an old woman's hip as a way to brighten up a coffee break, then I, for one, am all for it."

"You're an arsehole, you know that, right?"

"I am. I am. But I'm a perceptive arsehole, and I know that what you really want, deep down, is to find your woman again and ride off into the proverbial sunset with her."

Asmodeus sighed heavily. "I do. No one else matches her in terms of sexuality, or strength, or passion, or the way she loves me. It's been a long time coming, but I only want her, and I'm going to do whatever it takes to get her back. I need her."

"In that case, I have some people you might want to know."

"What do you mean?"

"I've got my fingers in a lot of pies, my friend. There are a lot of moving pieces at the moment when it comes to your Lilith. A lot of interested parties." He plucked a piece of paper out of the air. "And because I'm magnanimous and kind, and essentially an all-round good guy, I'd like to help you."

"You are none of those things."

"That's true, I'm not. I'm dramatically not any of those things. But I do like to fuck things up to a considerable degree, and I feel like getting you involved at this point of the proceedings would be hilarious."

He handed the piece of paper to Asmodeus. There were two legible names on it and several that had been scrawled out.

Asmodeus squinted at them. "Who are these? Are these Lilith?

Or are these parts of her? People who know things? Are they angels or demons or insurance agents, or what?"

"I'm a big fan of Wordle, you know that puzzle that humans like to do? They have letters, and they have to guess a word? This is a Wordle. I've given you clues, but you have to take it from here."

"I don't even like jigsaws," grumbled Asmodeus.

Jared leaned forward and patted him companionably on the arm. "I know," he said. "You hate puzzles. You told me that during an orgy back in the Meiwa Era."

"And you've remembered it all this time?"

"You never know when a little snippet revealed during a particularly powerful moment of orgasm will come in handy. You should be more focussed in saying thank you rather than being annoyed."

Jared stood up and brushed his jacket down, smoothing out invisible wrinkles. He performed a tidy little bow and called over his shoulder as he left. "Let me know if you need anything. I am a connector, after all."

Asmodeus gave his disappearing back the middle finger.

GOLDEN SYRUP CAKE IN THE MYSTIC LIBRARY

Eve slipped out of the cleaning cupboard containing a dust buster and a broken bucket, which was home to a transportation portal. She walked down the hallway quickly, glancing around to see if anyone had spotted her. She was usually left alone, but occasionally someone might come to look for her, so she had made up a plausible story in the unlikely event that someone did spot her. It involved power walking, an echidna, and a lost kitten, but she hadn't really firmed up the details, so she hoped she wouldn't have to use it.

She was still breathing heavily, both from running back to the empty car park where the Earth-based portal was currently situated, and from crying. She knew Zeus' memories had been wiped and supplanted by poisonous toxicity, but to actually hear his words, see the way he looked at her without any of the adoration that she had come to depend on… Devastation filled her, but also anger and something else she had only recently learned was inside her.

Determination.

She could hear someone coming toward her, or a couple of someones if the mumbling voice was anything to go by, but as she turned a corner in the corridor, she saw that it was just her husband, Adam. He was dressed in an oversized white shirt and black pants, and she thought he looked like a pirate. But not in a good way.

"Where have you been?" he snapped. "I've been looking for you."

"I was walking the kitten," she explained before she stopped herself. She really didn't need to explain what she was doing, did she? "Hang on, were you just talking to yourself?"

"Where have you been?" he asked again.

"Around," she said. "Around here. Places."

"I wanted to talk to you," he said. "I need to ask you a question."

She didn't reply and waited for him to continue.

"Do I have your support?" he asked after a moment. "Do I have your implicit and complete support?"

"When?" she asked.

"All the time."

"Do I have your support… all the time?" She wondered if he'd taken any notice at all of what had transpired over the past few centuries of their marriage.

"In general. If I were going to… *do* something. Or make some changes. Could I rely on your support? You are my wife, after all. Can I rely on the assumption that you will follow my lead wherever I lead?"

"You told me that if you became leader, you would muzzle me. Or imprison me. Something like that, anyway. Does this mean that you wouldn't do that?"

'Don't be stupid," he said. "You know I don't mean most of what I say when you push me. When you poke and poke at me, sometimes I say the wrong thing, maybe I make threats that I shouldn't. You're not perfect yourself, you know. I don't see why you need to keep throwing things I've said back at me. I just need to know that I have my wife's support. Is that too much to ask?"

She kept the smile on her face and pushed her hair out of her eyes. "Adam, you can rest comfortably in the knowledge that I will support and respect you as completely and as fully as you have always respected me."

"Good. Right," he said. "Because I have some things on the go, and I need to make sure I have my team. My people around me. My crew."

"You have a crew, do you?"

"That's what I'm trying to establish," he snapped. "I would like a crew, and I'm just trying to sort out who's in it."

"Once again, I wait with excitement and awe to see what my husband is going to come up with next."

"Excellent. Things will go much better for you if you do what you're told, Eve. I don't want to be hard on you," he muttered, and headed back the way he'd come.

She waited until he was out of earshot before following along behind him. Her best course of action was to find the library. Well, she had to get the library to find her. In an infinitely large area such as heaven, having popular places such as the library, or the restaurants, or, to a lesser extent, the gym put in spots that everyone could access was virtually impossible, so a system had been devised where you thought about the place you wanted and it appeared. Within one or two turns of the corridor, that was.

Library, thought Eve. *I need to find the library, please.*

The next time she turned a corner, huge wooden doors covered the wall in front of her.

The Mystic Library.

She did love a repository of all wisdom and knowledge—and smutty romances too, she was pleased to report—that found you exactly when you wanted it.

She reached out and had barely put her fingers to the wood when the doors swung inwards, and the space inside opened in front of her. It was huge, but that wasn't such an unusual thing. Heaven was infinite, after all. The Mystic Library stretched as far as she could see. The dark wood shelves, staircases, long tables, and lushly upholstered chairs felt rich and luxurious rather than heavy. Streams of sun filtered down from stained glass windows that dotted the roof far above her head, and the floating streams of dust that danced, multicoloured in the bright streams, were, she knew, purely for show. The Library Guardians wouldn't allow real dust in here.

It was artistic, hypoallergenic, specifically curated, and artisanal dust.

As she stepped into the room, the smell of cinnamon and vanilla puffed around her face, and a rustle of voices whispered, "Eve. Sweet Eve. We have missed you. Where have you been?"

The Guardians swirled around her, and she felt rather than saw their all-embracing energies. As their voices echoed in her head, a gentle wind pushed her gently toward one of the long blackwood tables where a steaming pot of tea and a china cup had appeared.

She laughed, delighted at the feeling of total love and acceptance. She had forgotten that The Mystic Library had always made her feel this way. "I'm sorry. I've been busy. And I haven't been reading as much as I should have been."

The whispers curled around her. "You're here now. Tell us what you need. A romance? You used to love romances. Or science fiction? A biography? We seem to remember that you went through a Frieda Kahlo stage a few years ago."

"It's a bit different this time. I need some information. Some real-life information."

The teapot tipped up, and a stream of Earl Grey poured into the cup.

Eve wrapped her hands around it, breathing in the aroma. "I need some help."

"Help is what we love. We're very good at helping."

"You won't tell anyone what I ask you, will you? Can I trust that what I ask will stay between us?"

The wind caressed her face and drifted under her chin in a light embrace. "What happens in the library stays in the library."

"I need a spell," said Eve. "Or something. I don't quite know what I need. But I feel like a spell would be good."

"Tell us about it."

"Someone I love dearly has had fake memories implanted in his brain and has lost his own thoughts. He doesn't know who he is or who I am. I need him to remember."

"Hmmmm." The voices, and she could tell there were five or six now, rustled around the table. She could hear them, but they weren't talking to her exactly. They seemed to be in discussion with each other.

"I'm sorry,' said Eve quickly, worried she had annoyed them. 'Is that not allowed?"

"Of course, it is allowed. Anything that we want is allowed. We make our own rules here. We are the Guardians of the Library."

"But we might have to have a think."

"To explore a little."

"Meander through the shelves."

"Contemplate the options."

"Have a chat."

"Would you like some cake while you're waiting?"

A golden syrup cake appeared on a platter in front of her, thick steam rising from the topping that dripped down its sides.

"That's fine," she said, lifting the silver cake fork and scooping up a lump of thick cream. "Take all the time you need."

The voices whispered off into the distant, shadowy stacks, and Eve dedicated herself to enjoying the cake. It was perfectly moist, thick, and sweet, and while she ate it, she contemplated whether she should look around and find something new to read. A horror novel, maybe. After a moment, she realized there was a presence next to her. She glanced around. Far in the distance, she could see several other figures hunched over open tomes or browsing the shelves, but there was no one close to her. She could smell, very faintly, frangipani.

"Hello, Eve," said a whisper in her brain. "I hope you don't mind, but I just wanted to tell you. I'm a big fan. Of you, that is. I think you're amazing. If I could leave a review, I would, but that's more for books than people, isn't it?"

Eve detected a slight giggle in the breeze. "Thank you very much," she said. "I appreciate that. It's very nice of you. But... why?"

"You're amazing," said the voice. "You're really very, very impressive. Well, not really yet, I suppose, but you will be."

"I don't quite know what you mean," replied Eve. "Unless it's the whole giving birth to the human race thing, and I didn't have that much say in all that. I'm not proud of it."

The voice tittered again. "Oh no, that's not the impressive bit. If that was the impressive bit, then the Library Dog would be winning because she's had about four hundred puppies, and you've had far less than that. No, it's what you will do that's impressive."

Eve looked around uncertainly. "What am I going to do?" she asked. "And when?"

"Oh, I can't tell you that. But as you know, we hold every book that has ever been written and every book that will ever be written, and so I know your whole arc, and you should be proud of yourself. That's all I'll say."

"Really?" said Eve, a smile lighting her face. "Because I'm overwhelmed and scared at the moment. I have a lot to do. I have to find my lost love, I have to make a fragmented woman whole again and then apologise for ruining her very existence, and now I suspect that I'll have to stop someone doing a terrible thing."

"I know you do," said the voice. "I know. It's a lot. And as long as you make the right decisions, you'll be fine."

"But what decisions?" asked Eve. "You can't just say make the right decisions and then leave. What am I supposed to do? Can't you tell me?"

"You will work it out," said the whisper. "Trust yourself."

"No," said Eve, her voice becoming a wail. "How do I do that? I've got no one to help me, to guide me. I don't trust myself at all!" She put down her fork, and it clattered on the plate in the stillness. "I'm trying to be strong and tough, but I don't know if that's really me or if I'm just pretending."

As she realized that she was now speaking to empty air, a thick olive-green book floated down through the sunbeams toward her on a breeze that smelled like freshly mown grass. It drifted past her nose for a moment before gently settling on the table, the whispers of the Guardians surrounding her once again.

"Try this one," they said. "This might be what you need."

She lifted it and looked at the cover. It was fabric-bound and felt pleasantly textured under her fingers. The gold letters on the front spelled out the words **Jane Eyre**.

"Take it," said the voices. "Take it and read it and see if it's what you need."

"I know this book," said Eve.

"We know," said the voices. "We love this book, and we love love. Trust us."

ONCE AN ARSEHOLE, ALWAYS AN ARSEHOLE

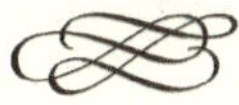

Fae sat in her office, staring off into space.

She had been putting it off, of course.

Anyone in their right mind, or at least vaguely non-demented mind, would put off this job.

Actually ringing Zeus, putting in the effort to make contact with someone as pettily annoying and, quite frankly, misogynistic as Zeus, was something she didn't think she should put her precious time and energy into.

The name on the piece of paper said Tony. She listened to the phone ring until there was a click on the end of the line and a pause. Fae could hear a moment of heavy breathing before the call was disconnected. She frowned, waited a second, and then rang again.

This time, it was answered immediately.

"Speak," said a voice.

Fae paused. "Is this Tony?"

"Affirmative."

"This is Fae Stephenson, and I'm ringing because I've heard we may have some mutually beneficial business interests."

It was then she realized she hadn't put any thought into what those mutually beneficial business interests might be, apart from a snappy phrase she'd been quite proud of when it had popped into her head earlier that morning, but she was probably going to have to think of something to back that up. Maybe he would just hang up or outright refuse to speak to her.

"Why are so many women demanding that I give them my attention at the moment?"

"Have you heard of me?" she asked, and immediately regretted it.

"Your typical female ego is running ahead of you, I fear."

"Pardon?"

"So needy."

"What?"

"Typical woman, so demanding."

And the phone disconnected.

What a strange man, Fae thought as she bemusedly stared off into space.

Then she remembered Jared's words.

This was non-negotiable.

Fuck.

She rang back.

"Speak."

"Yes, I tried that, and it didn't work out too well. My name is Fae Stephenson, and recently I've become aware of your interest in what I think are called 'men's rights', and I was hoping we could find a time to meet to discuss a possible collaboration."

"My work? Are you an Instagram influencer?"

She sighed. "No, I'm not. I'm a political activist of a sort. If you give me your email address, then I could send you some information about who I am and what I do, and then maybe we could meet up."

There was the sound of crackling on the other end of the line, and the next time Zeus spoke, it sounded as if his mouth was full.

"In real life?"

She glanced around, wondering if Jared might have transmogrified into a corner of the room to laugh at her discomfort.

"Why wouldn't... yes, in real life. What do you mean?"

There was another long pause. "A lot of people want to meet me, you know."

"Do they?"

"Yes, women especially."

"That must be lovely for you."

"They want things from me, so they arrange to meet me, pretending to be interested in me as a person. But I'm a nice guy, and as soon as they realise that they aren't interested. They only want someone who treats them like dirt, who wants their body and doesn't care about them. They aren't interested in a gentleman who knows how to treat a woman properly. It's because I don't look the way they think I should look. All short men suffer like this."

Fae sat with her mouth open, not knowing where to go next in this springboard of a conversation.

Restarian came into the room holding several bunches of flowers in his currently human arms. She gestured at him to be quiet, and seeing the gobsmacked expression on her face, he plonked the bunches on a desk and sat down, hoping to be entertained.

"I just want a business meeting," she said finally.

"So you say."

"At least, can I have your email address?"

"I don't know, identity theft is no joke."

"What?"

"Nothing. Fine. Just remember that."

There was another pause. Fae didn't usually find conversations this difficult, and she had spent several thousand years of her life in a non-corporeal state living in a lake.

"My email address is alphamale69@me.com." The fact that he said it in a totally straight voice without a trace of irony was what really made Fae giggle. She successfully muffled the laughter and promised she would be in touch by email.

Before he hung up, he asked her if she knew anyone called Eve, and when she said no, the conversation seemed to be over. She could have put money on the fact that he would say ciao instead of goodbye, and she was not disappointed.

"What a strange man," she said, staring at the phone. "What a strange and deeply unlikeable man."

"Let me guess. Zeus?" said Restarian, leaning forward, eyes bright.

"Yes and no," she said. "I mean, Zeus is a very strange and deeply unlikeable man, but this is the Tony version of Zeus, who is also strange and deeply unlikeable but on a whole other level. Look," she said, pointing to the email address. "Look."

Restarian chuckled. "Does he also have a sign around his neck announcing he's never had sex? Because that email address is how to tell the world you've never had sex."

Fae tapped her red manicured nail against her notepad. "I've been given clear orders that I have to involve him in what's going on here." She gestured around the office. "Out of nowhere, that is. This wasn't part of my original orders, and I feel like it's going to be more difficult than the basic instructions given to me, which are still pretty bloody hard in themselves. It's really bad form to change things in the middle of the program."

"Are you in the middle, though?" said Restarian doubtfully. "I feel like you're barely at the starting point."

"Not at all," protested Fae. "I have Wellingsley seriously doubting everything she's ever been taught, looking to abandon her career aspirations and stay home baking bread all day, and I have Apple embarrassed and feeling shame about her career choice. But now I've got fucking Zeus thrown into the mix, and I don't know where to bloody look."

"Do you want to get me involved?" asked Restarian. "I could lead them astray or off their path or whatever it is you want to do."

"Leading them astray is what I don't want. Have you listened to a word I've been saying? I want them well-behaved, sedate, non-questioning, and submissive. Attuned to traditional values, not new, modern ones."

"Can you give me something else to do, though?"

"I'm not living my best life either, you know."

"Well, clearly not. You were doing perfectly well in your lake, all wispy and ephemeral, and now you're here doing this."

"I just needed a change of scene, that's all. And it was getting too boggy for my liking."

"I don't think what Jared did to you was right," he said.

"Don't be stupid; he did nothing to me. I don't know what you're talking about."

"Making you think there's hope for you two as a couple. You know you're wrong for each other."

"You just don't understand our dynamic. It's very complicated. Most people have never felt this, so they don't know. Why the appearance of a florist suddenly, anyway?" she asked abruptly, gesturing to the piles of flowers whose heady fragrance were permeating the rooms. "Did you buy all these for me?"

"Fuck no," he said. "Why would I buy you flowers? Do you realise that picking flowers kills them, so when someone gives you flowers, you're being given a pile of decomposing organic matter. And that's supposed to be an indication of love. I mean, what are these humans like, honestly? No, they were on the front step. They're yours."

Fae walked over and examined the bunches. "These are all supermarket flowers. Carnations and chrysanthemum." She found a card and pulled it off the wide ribbon that was wrapped around the orange tissue paper. It was simply addressed to "M'lady."

"Euch," said Fae.

"Oh, this should be good," said Restarian. "Read it out loud." He grabbed a pack of potato chips from the top of the bar fridge and sat down, propping his feet on the desk. "I'm already loving this."

Fae rolled her eyes at him but opened the folded note and read out loud anyway.

"M'lady," she repeated. She paused and then repeated the word.

"Wait, it says that twice?"

"No, I'm setting the mood. Don't interrupt."

M'lady, it is rare that a quality man such as myself hears such wisdom coming from a beauty such as yourself.

"That's clunky," said Fae.

"Yes, this could have been proofread more. Keep going."

The moral deprivations of our current era ignore the biological imperatives that females are hardwired to perform... You know, I think I'll stop there.

She flicked the card out of her fingers, and it landed on her desk. She pushed at it with a pencil, and it fell to the floor.

Restarian grimaced, a chip halfway to his mouth.

"Is he okay, do you think?"

Fae took another card from the bunch.

My Queen

She sighed heavily before continuing.

The truth you espoused about what a man requires in his female is a breath of fresh air in our current society, which a man who values women for the precious and delicate creatures they are has to line up behind cavemen and rappers who refer to women as hos, and yet they are the ones females always choose. You, however, aren't like other girls. Bear my children.

Fae put it down and pushed the bunches away with a grimace. "Do you think this is because of the panel interview?"

"Play stupid games, win stupid prizes," said Restarian.

"That's not very helpful."

"How about, you fucked around and found out?"

"Why have I suddenly become a pin-up girl for these men?"

"Because you went on national television talking about traditional femininity. Because you decided to vilify sex workers publicly, talk about STDs, and convince young women that this," here he pointed to the sad, wilting pile of carnations, "is what they should aspire to. You're kind of—"

"You were not going to say I'm asking for it," she snapped at him. "I know that you're not going to say that I'm asking for it."

He shrugged. "You get what I'm saying, though."

She bit her lip and took a deep breath. Her chest felt tight.

"I guess this is a long way from lounging around in lakes and having people ask you for advice."

"This is fine. I've been entrusted with a very important job, and I should have expected things like, whatever this is, to come with the territory."

"Entrusted by Jared."

"Yes, by Jared."

"Who you are in love with, despite…"

"That's enough."

"Okay," said Restarian, throwing his hands up in mock despair. "Don't shoot me. I'm just the assistant, remember."

"Oh, except when you want to be the adviser. You need to decide whether you're part of this or not." She glared at the flowers. "Get rid of them," she said. "Throw them out. Put them on some forgotten person's grave. I don't care. Just get rid of them. I have an email to send. Then I must work out my next plan of attack with those girls. Also, fuck Zeus. I'm not going to bother with him."

She heard a noise and glanced up to see Jared leaning against the doorframe, arms crossed.

"Jared," she gasped. "What are you doing here? Don't just pop up like that."

"What, use a door? Knock? Don't be so unbearably cliche. Anyway, I can barely get to your doorstep for all the sub-quality flowers littering it. I hope you're not trying to get a romantic interest. You're here for work, you know. I'm not employing you to gad around and wave your breasts at people." He stared at her. "You're not dating anyone, are you? I mean... are you dating anyone?"

She thought she saw a look of longing in his eyes.

"No, of course not," she said haltingly, and a silence hung between them for a few seconds.

"What do you want?" she snapped, suddenly aware that Restarian had circumspectly removed himself from the room. Jared wasn't well-liked by many beings, given his complete reinvention of the idea the ends justify the means, and Restarian had had dealings with him in the past, which had, on one unforgettable occasion in one unforgettable body, left him with fewer limbs than he had started the day with.

"I'd just like to pick you up on that last thing you said."

Fae wracked her brain for the last conversation the two of them had in the coffee shop. What had been the last thing that...

"I believe it was 'Fuck Zeus, I'm not going to bother'."

"Oh," she said, a little taken aback. "You mean that."

He straightened himself up and walked toward her with almost a slink. Like a ballet dancer, his every movement was deliberate and flowing, his eyes fixed on hers as he got closer.

"You will take Zeus, or Tony, or whatever name he has decided to go by, and you will get him under your wing, and you will keep him busy. You will give him a job. Do you understand me? You will make sure that you involve him in whatever you have to do and introduce him to all your friends. He will become a part of this whole thing."

"Ok-ay," she said. "His being involved is obviously something very important, and I understand the full gravitas of the situation because of your whole…" she gestured at him, "really intense vibe because, whoa, there's a lot going on here right now. But he's really awful."

"Involving Zeus is part of the deal. Please, baby. For me?"

"How?" she asked, exasperated. "He doesn't want anything to do with me. He's the worst."

Jared reached out and stroked her face. "Oh yes, he does. He does. He will."

"He hates women," she said.

"No, he doesn't. He's just scared of them. He doesn't know any. If he actually meets a vaguely pleasant and halfway attractive one, he'll change, I'm sure." He winked at her. "And in the absence of that, you'll do."

"Fuck you. Why is this so important?"'she asked.

"That's above your pay grade."

"I don't have a pay grade," she said, "but I'm curious, and it would certainly help me if I knew why I'm having to deal with him. And why he's here."

He took her hand and kissed it. "For me. Please?"

She sighed and looked at him sadly.

"Come on," he cajoled her. "How about I spend a few minutes with you? Would that make you feel better about it?"

She didn't even try to deny that it would.

COFFIN SHAPED NAILS

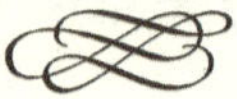

To everyone's surprise, Apple did not go into a decline after the debacle with the panel. She did go home and cry a bit with the embarrassment and the dawning realisation that she may have single-handedly set back sex worker rights by about fifty years.

But her breasts had looked amazing, she kept reminding herself.

"That's in the Bible," said Janie as she sat back in the chair in their usual nail salon. "A generous bosom turns away wrath. We should know, we went to a Catholic school."

"I must have missed that bit."

The young Thai woman sitting across from her took her hands and frowned, obviously distressed by the state of Apple's nails. "You broke them again," she said in heavily accented English. "No stiletto shape for you. Coffin now. You break stiletto."

"I know," said Apple, "but the clients like stiletto. It looks all aggressive and dangerous. Some pay extra for the nails alone."

"Pay extra for this? For this breaking?"'Alice turned Apple's hands and faced them toward her. "Men pay for this? No. Coffin-shaped this time."

"You're so bossy," sighed Apple, but resigned herself to the change in shape. Alice had been doing her nails for years and was in a better position to know what worked on her hands than she was at this stage.

"Red again"

"Of course."

Apple glanced over at her sister, who was examining the myriad of colours the salon offered. "Thinking of something new?"

"Hmmm, maybe," said Janie. "I'm drawn to this slightly off beige one today."

"As opposed to the slightly darker beige?"

"It's a toss-up between Bare, Sheer, or Naked at this stage."

"You're so crazy."

"It's a curse."

Alice and May began to work on the sisters' nails, and they lapsed into an easy silence. It was way more relaxing than having to make awkward conversation for fifty minutes.

"So, are we going to talk about it?" asked Janie after an appropriate amount of time had lapsed.

Apple groaned. "I'd rather not."

"That bitch is on my shit list now, let's just put it that way," said Janie with a dangerous glint in her eye.

"Yeah, well, obviously. She's awful. But awful in a smart, well-argued way."

"I'm surprised she got the better of you, to be honest. You're usually good in a flap. You're usually much more…"

"Eloquent?" suggested Apple.

"Yes. And bossy."

Apple sighed and shifted in her seat. "I have no idea what happened. It was weird. I lost my mojo entirely. There was this one moment when I looked into her eyes, and I just lost track of everything. Like, I didn't even know who I was anymore. It was…" She bit her lip, trying to put the sensation into words, trying to explain the deep sense of existential angst and dread that had overcome her when she had lost herself in the woman's eyes. "It was…"

"It was a bit shit, really," finished her sister.

"Yes, that's what it was. It was shit. Apparently, there's word on the street that I've put the whole cause back."

"Oh, rubbish," scoffed Janie. "It was a hit piece on a TV station with declining ratings run by an aging football player who no one even watched anyway. There's no way you did any real damage."

Alice began to shape the end of Apple's nails into a straight, decidedly less lethal shape, and Apple glared at her on principle. You don't need hooker nails, said Alice, matching her steely glare. "You're already a hooker."

Janie laughed and poked her sister with her foot. "That's true. You don't actually have to be the stereotype, you know."

"And you need longer hair," said Alice, turning to the other. "Boys don't like shaved heads."

"Wait, when did we start critiquing *me*?" asked Janie.

"Anyway, I don't think I'm going to become a media darling anytime soon. Which is a shame. I was hoping to cut down my hours soon, and this would have been a good segue into something else."

"What do you mean, something else?" asked Janie. "You love your job."

"No, I do," said Apple. "I love being a sex worker. I love meeting new people and dressing up and the money and…."

"And fucking," shared Janie.

"Yes. I mean, increasingly less than people think, to be honest, but yes, there's that. I'm getting old, though. This is a young woman's game."

"You're forty-three," clarified Janie. "You're hardly old."

"No, I know. I'm not objectively old. But the older you get, the more you become a niche thing in this industry."

"Like, a kink?"

"No, I'm not a fucking kink. But you age quickly, and I'm not interested in running a brothel of my own, so I'm looking around for something else to occupy myself."

May frowned at them from under her long eyelashes. "It's good I don't understand you girls," she said.

"Oh rubbish," said Apple. "You speak English better than I do."

"It felt personal," said Janie. "That Fae women. The way she was attacking you felt personal. I'm going to do some research on her. You don't attack my sister and get away with it."

"It was business," said Apple, sighing wearily. "I'm sure it wasn't personal."

"I'm sure it bloody was. She attacked your personality. And how did she know some of that stuff?"

"I dunno. Researched maybe. I'm tired."

Janie muttered something about researching her the fuck back, but Apple ignored her.

"It's not for me, this media stuff. I've never been so embarrassed in my life. In fact, I might just… Alice, how much money do you make a week?"

Once Alice told her, Apple shook her head.

"Not nails then. But maybe there's something else I could do. Maybe this is all too much for me."

A worried look crossed Janie's face. "You're acting very strange. Why have you gone all quiet and demure suddenly? You're not like yourself."

Apple's eyes filled with uncharacteristic tears.

"Nooooo!" said Janie, pulling her hand out of the nail dryer to hold her sister's arm. May barked at her, and she shoved it back in the dryer guiltily. "You don't cry! What's going on?"

Tears fell down Apple's cheeks. "I don't know," she said, as Alice automatically handed her a tissue. "I don't know. I just feel so absolutely demoralised since it happened. Just so tiny and insignificant and inconsequential. Like, I don't want anyone to see me or hear me. I just want to stay small."

"This is ridiculous," said Janie. "It's bullshit is what it is. I'm going to find that bitch and give her a piece of my mind."

"No, you're not," said Apple. "We're going to get back on the horse. Well, I am anyway." She pulled her work phone out of her bag. "I've had a few days off, but I'm ready to get back into it." She turned on her phone, and within seconds, text messages flickered on the screen.

Janie peered over her shoulder. "Lord, you won't be able to sit down for a week if you get through all of those." Across from them, May laughed and slapped Janie's hand playfully.

There was an influx of numbers Apple wasn't familiar with.

Hey, Baby.

You avail?

How much?

What's your bra size?

"Euch," said Janie, pointing at the last message.

"That question's fine," said Apple. "They are literally paying to see them. They can ask. It's not like chatting me up for a date. We need to get the cards on the table early."

Janie shuddered. "They're so blunt."

"Lots don't know how to speak to a sex worker," explained Apple. "It's not rudeness; often it's inexperience."

"But sometimes it's rudeness," clarified her sister.

"Oh, yeah, definitely, sometimes it's rudeness. I tend to weed them out early on." She scanned through, tilting her phone toward Janie occasionally. "See, this info is readily available on my site. He doesn't need to ask me this. He doesn't need to chat me up, and he doesn't need to send me a photo of his dick." She deleted the message. "It would be nice to get a decent, well-paying job with someone who just needs a really satisfying root and knows their way around a clitoris, preferably in a flash hotel. Is that too much to ask?"

At that moment, the sun moved into the constellation of Scorpio. While many people on Earth paid a lot of money to have their fortunes told, many others made a vigorous and ferocious pastime out of reviling and mocking those who believed in it. It would have been enormously irritating for the anti-horoscope brigade to know all serendipitous or wildly coincidental occurrences that happened on the planet were, in fact, caused by the movement of the sun through the stars.

I was not because these balls of rocks had any particular powers by virtue of their own existence. Rather, the ones in the liminal worlds who were actually behind all the big events on a multi-universal scale enjoyed popping their straw into the vast panoply of reality and causing some havoc from time to time.

All to do with their own interests, of course. None purely altruistically, not even a little bit altruistically, come to think of it. Though all were working toward Lilith becoming whole once again, all because some pan-dimensional beings were bored at a cocktail party and had so decided to stir things up a bit.

So, all of that was how the demon Asmodeus came to engage the sex worker Apple for a night of fucking.

A NICE ROOM AND A GLASS OF WINE

Apple knocked on the door of the appointed room at exactly 9.00pm.

This was exactly what she needed. A well-paid call out to an expensive hotel room with a view of Sydney Harbour.

She wore a red wrap dress that fell around her curves and draped to knee length. Heels and a scarf over her auburn hair completed her outfit.

The door swung open.

The man in front of her had recently showered, and his long hair was still damp. He didn't realise that he now looked like one of the more rugged and handsome characters from a movie because he had never seen one, but his dark skin, shoulder-length hair, and closely cropped beard were a casting agent's wet dream.

Something shimmered within her. She felt like she was outside herself, watching the scene, like looking through a murky river and seeing a fully formed vision beneath the viscous water.

The man in front of her stared. "Lilith?" he murmured, almost under his breath.

She had to strain her ears to hear him. She waited a moment, but he didn't speak again.

A feeling of vertigo overtook her. She had to put out her other hand to feel the doorframe just to make sure there was something solid nearby. She squeezed her eyes shut for a moment. She heard a rushing noise in her head, a screaming, whooshing noise, as if a large object were moving toward her at a great speed, as if every atom in the corridor were moving toward her at great speed, as if her whole body were caught in a slipstream of chaos, and it was fragmenting as she was being pulled into space and time and things she had never even considered. As if…

Then it stopped. Complete silence. She was standing in a corridor, in a hotel, in front of a man.

She took a deep breath.

"Hi," she said, and smiled brightly.

Apple looked beyond the man into the room. It was luxurious and palatial, exactly as she'd been hoping for. Not that it made a real difference, of course, but it was more pleasant to get naked in a warm room without bugs than in one with them, and you didn't have to be a prima donna to make that decision. The look on his face was…nervous? No, not nervous. She knew the nervous look of men who had either never had sex or paid for it before, and this wasn't it. And it wasn't aggression either.

He almost seemed not to be there.

She narrowed her eyes. "Have you taken something? Because I don't accept clients who are high."

He smiled, one that reached into her very soul.

She felt something inside her. Something—shift. Almost like a voice telling her to trust him. That he knew what he was doing. That he was someone who…

She pushed it down. She was used to voices telling her she should believe whatever handsome men told her. It was something to do with a broad chest and eyes that crinkled at the sides when they smiled, and potentially very nicely formed and perfectly sized cocks. She was also used to ignoring these voices.

"I'm not high," he assured her. "But I would like to tell you a story. Would you like to hear a story?"

She made the split-second decision that he wasn't a psychopath, hoping she wasn't going to end up with her head in a fridge by the end of the evening. So she stepped into the room.

The door closed with a quiet click behind her.

"Glass of wine?" he asked, gesturing to the open bottle that sat on the table near the expansive window. "It's an excellent Cabernet Sauvignon. I've only had one glass, I promise."

He smiled again, and her heart jumped involuntarily in her chest. She grinned in response. A genuine grin, not the carefully curated seductive one she had honed for clients over years of practice, but a genuine, wide one, showing teeth and gums.

Why did she feel like she knew this man? She would definitely remember if they'd met before. He was… unnervingly handsome. Excessively good-looking.

He handed her a wine glass, and she sat on the plush sofa.

"A story," she said, her red lips captivating above the rim of the expensive wine glass.

"Yes," he said, arranging a satin robe around his fiercely muscled legs. "But the first thing I need to be clear about is that whatever happens, whatever I say, you are completely safe."

"Telling someone they're safe is usually a good indication that they're not safe," she said.

He frowned. "Really?"

Apple nodded. "Definitely a red flag."

"That seems counterintuitive," he said, sitting next to her. "How do I assure you that you, a defenseless woman in a hotel room with a large, strange man, are safe?"

"We could just work on the assumption that I'm always safe, you know. Drawing attention to the fact I might not be safe indicates that I'm not, and it's just not something I'm that comfortable with, to be honest. Also, calling me defenseless, not great."

He sighed and took a sip of his wine. "Humans are odd."

"Humans," Apple questioned. "I guess humans are odd."

"They are."

"Are we role-playing?" she asked. "I'm happy to, but if you could let me know exactly how you'd like it to run, I'll be able to provide you with a better service."

She took his hand and placed it on her smooth leg. Sometimes men were tentative, nervous, especially if it was their first time with a sex worker. His hand was warm and firm, and his fingers pressed gently into the skin of her thigh, his palm soft on the smoothness of her leg.

"Do you recognise me?" he asked.

"Should I?"

He smiled, and she felt that warm frisson again.

"All right, maybe not recognise," he said. "Maybe not literally recognise me. But do you feel me? Do you feel that we have known each other before?"

Apple remembered the dreams she had experienced for as long as she could remember. The feeling of being with someone who loved her so completely, so overwhelmingly. That she was accepted and adored by someone who knew her for who and for what she was. She would inevitably wake up from these dreams in tears, rising back to consciousness and the reality of her life, and the realisation that the person she had dreamed of wasn't real and didn't exist. Or that they did exist, but she had not and very probably would not find him in this earthly incarnation.

The feeling of loss she felt at his absence was real, so palpable. It was most intense when she woke up from these dreams; that feeling was always there, hovering around the periphery of her consciousness.

"Do you feel me?" he asked again.

She pushed her thoughts away. "Maybe we should get this evening started," she said, sliding down to her knees.

* * *

"You really don't remember me?" he asked as they sat on the sofa afterwards and looked out at the spectacular view.

"No," she said. "But I see a lot of men. I probably wouldn't."

She knew her words were an absolute untruth, and there was no way she wouldn't remember every inch of this man's incredible body, velvet voice, and half smile.

He stood and moved to the window, his body silhouetted against the light. "There are some very complicated things happening here, and I thought spending time together might help you remember."

"I need to be going," she said, standing up. While she often enjoyed sitting and chatting with clients, complicated was something she definitely didn't want.

"Yes, of course," he said. "But may I ask something of you?"

"Sure, you can ask."

"If you have any memories resurface, any at all, call me."

"What do you mean?"

Turning back, he looked at her. "This might sound strange."

"I've got a pretty low bar. Seriously, don't make me go into details about some of the weirdness I engage in."

"Do you trust me?"

"Absolutely not," she answered. "I find it never works in my interests to trust strange men who I meet in hotel rooms who are paying me by the hour."

"I thought it was a set rate."

"Yes, it is, that's just an expression. Anyway, no, I don't trust you, but against all the odds, I find you quite endearing, and now I want to know what you're going to say."

"Have you ever felt like you're someone else?" he asked.

"What do you mean?"

"It's hard to explain. Have you ever felt as if there's someone inside your body?"

Apple giggled despite herself and sat back down. "I'm enjoying this enormously, I must say. It makes a nice change from men crying about their mothers."

"Alright, how about this. Have you ever heard of Lilith?"

"Is she from Melbourne? I know a Lilian from Melbourne."

"Lilith was a... well, she was Adam's first wife, and then he ended up with Eve because they had a fight about sex, and then God ended up—"

Apple's phone rang. "Shit, sorry," she said. "It's my sister. Just wait a sec." She held up one finger. "You rang her? Why did you do that? Oh, for god's sake, now she's going to be even more pissed off with me. No, I don't care if you think you can handle it yourself. If you're in it, we're both in it. Jesus, Janie, if I'd wanted this dealt with, then I would have... bail. Okay, fabulous."

She stood and sighed at the man in a way that indicated tremendous inconvenience. "Fucking brilliant. Believe it or not," she said, "I'm actually enjoying this evening, and this conversation was heading in a potentially interesting direction, but my stupid sister has just gotten herself arrested, and I have to go and bail her out."

"Now?"

"Come with me," Apple said immediately, not registering the words that were coming out of her mouth. "Do you want to come with me? I could do with some company. She's done something very silly, from what I can tell, and given the person I usually ring to help me out in a panic is the one I'm having to bail out, I could do with a sidekick."

"Yes," he said. "Absolutely." He looked around and grabbed a coat and a bag. "Let's go. We can talk on the way."

SEXUAL ENERGY YOU COULD CUT WITH A KNIFE

"I'm spending more time wandering around this bloody city than in my own dimension," grumbled Jared as he and Fae made their way down the tree-lined street. "Why are we walking around?"

"Because that house is dark and cold," she said. "And I need to be in the sun for a while. Who else have you been talking to here anyway? Is it to do with the Lilith situation?"

"I have a variety of irons in the fire. A rich tapestry of them. It's not all about you," he said, taking her hand in his.

A bird began to sing nearby, and Fae tilted her head back to feel the sun's warmth. "Good," she said, clasping her fingers between his. "Because I can get this done on my own, and I would be annoyed if you were calling on other elements. It'll just distract me if other people get involved."

And I want you all to myself, she thought, and hoped he wasn't reading her mind at that moment.

"I can't believe you'd think you're the only one involved in this," he said, stopping on the footpath and looking at her. "Of course, there are other moving parts. This is quite a big thing. It's bigger than you realise."

She dropped her eyes, not wanting him to see the hurt that she suspected was in them. “I thought that you trusted me to get this done.”

“Of course I trust you.” He lifted her hand to his lips, and she had the momentary but familiar thought that if he could love her, then everything in the universe would fall into place. “But I do need you to work with Zeus.”

“All right. Can you at least tell me what he did to get exiled to Earth?’

“It’s unclear. Word is that he tried to put his hands on God’s daughter.”

“Risky. What was Zeus even doing to try and get the opportunity to meet her?” Fae asked, feeling a little thrill that he was sharing this information with her. “From what I’ve heard, Eve is kept almost under lock and key. How did he get near her?”

“The details are murky. He was dragged away, and the next thing we all knew, he had his memory stored in an apothecary jar. He’s now a sweaty, beardy gamer with no personality or social skills, but does have an inferiority complex, therefore living in some basement here in Sydney.”

“Yes, from talking with him, all of those things seem to be true. He’s certainly got a chip on his shoulder about something. And if the single conversation he had with me was anything to go by, he’s got no idea how to talk to women, or anyone.”

Jared chuckled. “How the mighty have fallen. He always was a cocky git. Can’t think of a better person for it to have happened to.”

“That’s why,” she said. “He’s been relegated to Earth for being a dick to women. I must say, it’s interesting he had to try it on with God’s precious daughter—”

“Or Adam’s wife, more accurately,” interjected Jared.

“—before anyone took any notice. Apparently, raping swans and eating flies was just fine.”

“Are you surprised?” asked Jared.

"Of course not. Anyone who personally affronts Adam has something dreadful happen to them, from what I've heard. That's not the bit I'm having trouble with. What I don't understand is why he's suddenly been roped into *my plans*. I've got nothing to do with any of this. I'm not even God adjacent. I'm beginning to feel positively human wandering around with these bloody heels on and wearing a damn bra. Bras are the worst; someone should ban them immediately. So yes, my question is, why have I suddenly been asked to take up with bloody Zeus?"

"And wear a bra?" queried Jared.

"No, I get that bit. That I hate, but I understand. I even understand why Zeus has been banished here and had his memory wiped; I'm firmly of the opinion that it should have been done a long time ago. The fact that he only got some punishment when Eve got involved is bullshit. But why *me*? And why does he need a job? I would have thought having him stuck in a basement would be perfectly fine."

Jared shrugged. "Look, I just know he needs to be taken out of that basement and given a job. And you're here. See, seamless. Like a glove. Or a well-fitted bra."

He glanced appreciatively at her chest.

"So you'll be able to do this without it affecting your… what do you call them? Morals?"

Fae shrugged. "It's just a job. Plenty of people do things in their job that they don't agree with. Plenty of people must violate their own personal boundaries and turn off their own ethics to get stuff done. This is no different."

"I knew you'd make this good. You're utterly delightful, you know. If anyone could make me an honest man, it would be you."

With that, he kissed her gently on the lips.

CHARLOTTE BRONTË OUT THERE, CHANGING LIVES

Eve decided not to knock on the front door this time. He probably wouldn't answer it, and even if he did, he might leave her standing on the doorstep, and she was certain that the courage she had managed to cobble together while in the library wouldn't handle that kind of blow. So she went around the back again. And once again, he was there, this time with a beautifully painted and finished wrought iron garden chair. She stood looking at him, and again, a smile broke out on her face. She loved every part of him. The hair that stood up a bit like a cockatoo's head feathers, his always slightly crooked glasses, the gap between his teeth, and the way that, no matter how often he shaved it, he looked like he had two weeks' growth of stubble on his chin.

"Hi," she said softly, and the look in his eyes when he glanced up at her gave her the confidence to push forward. "That looks amazing."

Zeus looked at her quizzically, so she pointed to the chair. "The chair. You hadn't started painting it when I saw it last time. You were just dusting it or something. You've worked so hard on it. It must be for someone very special."

He stood from where he crouched and brushed the concrete

dust from the knees of his tracksuit pants. "It is," he said. "It's for someone very special. I'm sure of it." He cleared his throat. "I'm sorry I was rude to you the other day. I don't know what came over me. Actually, I haven't been feeling myself lately. I've been a bit confused. Discombobulated. I seem to be..." His voice faded away, and he looked off into space. "I'm being quite rude to people, and I'm angry, and I don't know why." He lifted his hand and touched his face. "I know this is me. I know this face, I know these hands, but this," he tapped his forehead. "These thoughts. These ideas. They aren't mine. I don't know what's happening. I don't know where my thoughts are."

"I'm sorry," she said. "That must be difficult."

"You have a book," he said, pointing to the thick green volume that she held tightly in her hands. "That's kind of a coincidence, because I've been thinking of books a lot lately. The last day, anyway. My head has been full of books—*and whispers.* Books and whispers."

"Well, actually, on that note," said Eve, fumbling with the volume in her hands. "I thought I could read you something. Would you like that? Or at least, would you mind?"

He frowned. "It's not *The Watchtower,* is it? Please tell me you're not a Jehovah's Witness. Some came around a few weeks ago, and I had a terrible time getting rid of them. To get them out, I had to promise them they could come back, but now I'm too scared to answer the door in case it's them again. I've been spending my time down in the..." He didn't finish his sentence.

Eve let out a snort laugh. "No, I'm not a Jehovah's Witness. Don't worry. Though that's funny. Remind me to laugh with you about that later. This is my favourite book. Remember when I said we used to know each other?"

He nodded.

"It's Jane Eyre. We were reading it when we first kissed and—"

"Are you seriously telling me that someone like you ever kissed someone like—"

Stop it, she said firmly. "Don't start that rubbish again. Frankly, we don't have the time. Just listen while I read something lovely to you, and then everything will be all right."

"In that case," he said, stepping back and gesturing to the rocking chair with a flourish, "would you like to take a seat?"

"I absolutely would," she said and perched herself on the edge of the chair.

"Wait," said Zeus before she had the chance to settle right back. "I need to get something." He disappeared inside the house and came out moments later with a soft pink and purple knitted blanket. She knew it quite well, as she had made it herself, and it belonged over the back of a sofa in the lounge room. "Stand up," he ordered, placing the blanket on the wooden seat and fluffing it with his hands. "There," he said. "That will be more comfortable. It can be your throne."

"My throne," said Eve. "That's…that's what you said this seat would be. That's what you said you were making me."

He frowned and pressed his lips together. "I don't remember that," he said. "Except I do, just a little. But not enough…"

"This will do it," she said firmly, shuffling backward in the seat and tucking one foot under her. "This will do it, I know." She turned to a page she had marked with a piece of paper. Zeus sat down on a sheet of newspaper and awkwardly drew his knees up to his chest.

She took a deep breath before beginning. "*Your mind is my treasure, and if it were broken, it would be my treasure still.*" She glanced up at him hopefully, but he was looking at her expectantly. "Anything?" she asked.

"What do you mean?" he said. "It was like, ten words. I can't really judge whether I like a book with ten words, can I?"

"All right, let's try this…"

All my heart is yours, sir: it belongs to you; and with you it would remain, were fate to exile the rest of me from your presence forever.

"Very pretty," he said patiently. "Is there a plot as such, or is it mainly just nice little quotey bits?"

"I didn't think you'd want me to read you the whole book," she said.

"Why not?" he asked. "I don't seem to have much else to do, and I like listening to your voice."

With a sigh, Eve started at the beginning of the book. Then, once again, over Jane Eyre, they fell in love.

DREAMING MY DREAMS

Three women in the greater Sydney area woke at precisely the same second of the witching hour, for precisely the same reason.

"It's time," came the small voice in their ears.

It wasn't really in their ears. It came from within their minds.

Or…

"Who are you?"

"Who are you really?"

Outside, clouds swarmed around them. Forces converging, like all the elements were tripping over each other to watch the show. Voices clambering and pushing to see what would happen next.

Would Lilith break through? Was the time nigh? Were things really going to kick off?

The clouds built, hyper cumulus, reaching toward the upper reaches of the atmosphere, climbing and cascading until they hit areas meteorologically impossible for them to be. As the forces under them grew, neighborhood dogs started to bark, feeling the pressure in their ears. Every cat hissed, seeing dark shadows clustering on the ceilings, spectral creatures rising from the earth, called to witness the reckoning. A low thrum began to echo throughout the alleys and wind tunnels of the city, a vibrating resonance that made Tibetan singing bowls ring all at the same time, waking up Reiki masters and yoga teachers alike.

One by one, the alarms of weather forecasters began to blare in unstaffed weather stations. Ancient stones planted by long-ago humans began to broadcast a deep primal groan, a vibration that rippled through the planet, as ley lines across the world began to wake, to connect to...

A weather god glanced at the clouds with a frown and made a noncommittal little waggle of their eyebrows, causing them to disappear in a puff of ether.

Everything returned to normal.

The three women sighed, rolled over, and went back to sleep.

GARBAGE FOR DAYS

"And it's a totally valid way of being," said Wellingsley as she arranged books on the shelf that had been installed seemingly magically overnight. Her blond hair was pulled back with a hairband, and she was wearing a long floral dress.

"Great," said Fae. "I'm sure it is. Valid."

"I mean, a lot of people don't agree with it, but they're just repressing a woman's right to make her own choices."

Fae was staring off into the distance, deep in thought. The continual chattering of Wellingsley was something she was managing to learn to keep in the background, and she seemed to seldom need more than a smile or an acknowledgment to feel happy that Fae was listening.

She was thinking hard about the note she'd just received.

She needed to talk to Restarian, but he was nowhere to be found Fucking boggarts.

What the hell was she going to do now?

She bit her bottom lip, and the familiar feeling of empty dread moved up from her legs and into her stomach. Jared had trusted her with this job. He had faith that she could do it.

So, she had to.

Fae realized that Wellingsley had stopped talking and was looking at her expectantly. "Sorry?" she said. "I was miles away."

"I just said that I wondered if you'd mind elaborating on something you said during the lecture, you know, the one where I first heard you talk. The thing that started this all, remember?"

"And what was that?"

Wellingsley repeated one of the talking points that had popped into Fae's mind when she was in the "patriarchy is good, and feminism is bad". It usually took Fae a couple of minutes to swing back into this mindset and remember what she was supposed to be thinking.

"You seem to be remembering them quite well," said Fae with a laugh. "I think you could be the one speaking about it instead of me. Just out of interest…"

"Yes?"

"Had you thought of any of this before you heard me speak?"

Wellingsley shook her head emphatically. "No, not at all. You opened an entire new world for me. I mean, I suppose I knew I didn't agree with some things I was brought up to believe as factual, but no, you're the one who really opened my eyes."

Fae sighed. Amazing. Just perfect.

"Are you okay?" asked Wellingsley. "You seem preoccupied."

Fae fantasized for a moment about telling her everything. Unburdening herself and admitting how out of her depth she was. How she was just playing pretend at whatever she was supposed to be doing, and deep in her heart, she just wanted to make everything right and ride off into the sunset with Jared.

"I've just been given an added responsibility," she said instead. "Another person who needs my help, apparently. Another woman."

"That's wonderful," said Wellingsley. "Is she like-minded? I mean, does she share our values?"

Fae took out her phone and looked at the message Jared had sent her during the night.

Jared: Change of plans. Eve is coming to Earth for a while. Directive from the big fella. Yes, that Eve. You need to chaperone. Stand by for more details. You looked amazing today, by the way.

She quickly shot back the message she had held back from sending in the early hours of the morning.

We need to talk. Now.

"Look, from the little I know, I would think that, yes, she might share our values, but it's hard to tell with the little information I've been given."

"Is she going to join the Ladies Academy?"

"What?"

"The Ladies Academy? I've been writing up a business plan and watching some videos, and I think this is a really viable proposition. I know that you're the ideas person, that's your gift, but I thought you might like it if I work behind the scenes to make things happen. Look." She pulled the laptop that sat on a table toward her and typed in a few letters until a webpage popped up.

"This is one in the US," she said, "but there's no reason why we wouldn't base ours around a similar idea, is there? I mean, a little less Christian and right-wing, but still, we can promulgate the idea that women belong in the home if they want to. We can teach deportment, etiquette, sewing, cooking, and all the things that girls just aren't taught these days."

I would rather gouge my eyes out with my own amputated toes, thought Fae. "Excellent," she said. "That's absolutely the kind of thing that I'm trying to encourage."

"You're so busy," said Wellingsley, "with all your other projects. Would you like me to give you all my ideas and liaise with these people?"

"All right, fine," she said. "I guess it can't hurt. I certainly don't have time for it. How about you do lots of planning and start lots of ideas and do all the details, and then, in a couple of weeks, I'll see what you've come up with."

"A couple of weeks? I thought we could get things moving more quickly than that?"

Fae shook her head in feigned consternation. "Hussle culture," she said. "See, you're so indoctrinated. You've been groomed to think you need to be doing something all the time. It's quite unhealthy. Why don't you just go home? Make some biscuits and read a book or something. Just relax."

Wellingsley looked at her uncertainly. "But don't you want me to—"

Fae held up her hand. "I insist on it," she practically pushed her out the door.

Wellingsley stood on the doorstep and didn't notice the woman who was pacing toward her until she was mere metres away.

"Is this Fae Stephenson's place?" the woman asked.

Wellingsley beamed at her. "Are you interested in signing up for the Ladies Academy?"

"No, I'm not interested in signing up for the bloody Ladies Academy. Who are you?"

"I'm… her assistant," said Wellingsley. "She's not available at the moment. If you need her, I can answer any questions you may have."

"What I want is for her to stop disrespecting sex workers and leave my sister alone."

Wellingsley reached her hand behind her and pushed at the door, but it had locked.

"We have something called free speech here in Australia," said Wellingsley. "I think you'll find that Miss Stephenson can say whatever she wants and have her opinions, and that is her right."

"Incorrect," said the woman. "That's completely wrong, you closeted little sycophant. We don't have free speech."

Damn. Wellingsley remembered that were true. Bugger it, now she was on the backfoot.

"Tell that bitch to get out here and talk to me."

"Excuse me, but that's a completely unacceptable way to talk to anyone. I need to ask you to leave."

Oblivious to what was happening outside, Fae shot off another message to Jared.

We need to talk.

She had had enough of being given new people to deal with.

A reply popped up immediately.

Jared: I can schedule you for next week.

She slammed the "call" button, but it went straight to voicemail.

Jared, you're being an arsehole and taking me for granted

She immediately regretted her words as soon as they left her thoughts.

Fuck, she said to the empty room.

Restarian materialised in front of her. "What's the matter?"

"Where the hell have you been?"

"Avoiding Wellingsley. She's way too intense. She wants to talk about everything all the time."

"Yep, she absolutely does. I seem to be getting inundated with irritating people."

"And someone from Apple's people rang too. They don't seem too impressed with you. Her sister, from what I can tell. Oh, and there's more flowers."

"This is getting ridiculous," said Fae. "This is not what I signed up for."

"Out of interest, what did you actually sign up for?"

"I signed up," snapped Fae, "for what was sold to me as a

fairly easy little job where I would convince a couple of people to change their life path."

Restarian looked at her. "It's your own fault for jumping into something without all the information."

"It was on a don't ask, don't tell proviso," she said. "He said there were others who could have taken the job on, but if I was willing to sign on the dotted line quickly, then it was mine. And that my specific skills were going to be perfect."

"Just out of interest," said Restarian, "did you actually sign anything?"

Fae shook her head. "We don't need contracts. We have an understanding. You wouldn't be able to relate."

"You're so crotchety," he grumbled. "This is becoming workplace harassment."

An address flashed up on Fae's phone. The address of an exclusive suburb. One you only had if you came from very old or very dirty money, or more frequently, both.

She's expecting you

She rubbed at the pimple that was beginning to appear on her chin. "I miss my lake," she muttered. Hearing a noise, she cocked her head to the side. "What's all that yelling?"

She stepped through the corridor to the window next to the front door and gestured to Restarian. "Look at this."

Wellingsley and a woman with very short, cropped hair were engaged in a loud and colourful conversation, and there seemed to be piles of garbage on the front doorstep.

Fae yanked the door open, and Wellingsley almost fell backward into her.

"What the hell is going on?" she said, surveying the two upended wheelie bins that were lying in the street. "Why is my front door covered in garbage?"

As she spoke, the woman returned with another wheelie bin

and pushed it over in front of the steps, spilling miscellaneous detritus everywhere. Fae stepped back and narrowly missed having what looked like a broken bag of porridge explode on her feet.

"Hello, Fae," said the woman. "Your assistant here wouldn't let me talk to you, so I decided to cover your front step with garbage."

Fae stared at her, a tight smile on her face. "Of course, that makes perfect sense. Wellingsley, why wouldn't you let this woman speak to me?"

"She seemed angry. I thought I could deal with it."

The woman had headed down the street and was pulling another wheelie bin back toward them.

"Well, you clearly can't," said Fae, "as my house seems to be turning into a rubbish dump as we speak. Who is she anyway?"

"Who am I?" yelled the woman from down the street. "I am Janie, and I am the sister of Apple, who you made a fool of on national TV last week, and I wanted to come to have a nice rational conversation with you, but in the absence of that, this seemed to be the next best option."

"She didn't want to have a nice rational conversation," whispered Wellingsley. "She started yelling straight away. I think she's lying."

"I gathered that. I think she was being facetious."

Restarian hovered behind Fae, staying out of sight in the shadows. "This is ridiculous," he hissed. "This is really not the vibe. If I wanted to be surrounded by garbage, I would have stayed in a swamp."

"Dear," Fae called out to Janie. "My dear, would you like to have a civil conversation? I don't think this whole garbage thing is doing what you hoped to do."

"What I hoped it would do is really annoy and inconvenience you and be a general irritant."

"Well, in that case, you're right on the money. Job done. Would you like to stop now?"

Janie upended another bin. This one seemed to have a

disproportionately large amount of roast chicken carcasses in it, and the smell ratcheted up by about twenty olfactory levels.

"If I ask you nicely, will you stop?"

"Will you apologise to my sister for being cunty bitch?"

"Come on," said Wellingsley, "We're hardly going to talk to someone who uses that kind of language. You're obviously no better than your sister."

"Don't you dare talk about my sister, you Laura Ashley wearing wannabee virginal pick me girl," spat Janie, turning to look for what Fae rightly assumed was more malodorous garbage.

"This is ridiculous," muttered Fae.

"What's worse?" growled Restarian from the gloom behind her. "This or the bunches of supermarket flowers?"

"I'm not a big fan of them, but this does seem marginally worse. Can you deal with it, please?"

"What, clean it up? Fuck no."

"No, can you stop it happening? This stupid woman clearly doesn't want to see sense, and she's defending her sister in almost a canine manner, which is endearing in a way, but also deeply deranged."

"Oi, stop it!" yelled Restarian from behind Fae.

Oddly enough, Janie ignored him.

"Oh, god," said Fae. "Now she's knocking on neighbors' houses asking if they have any garbage they want to contribute."

"We could invoke some powers," hissed Restarian.

"I told Jared I'd avoid that," she whispered. "He doesn't want me to draw attention to myself from anyone upstairs."

"If you don't, we're going to have everyone out here and get media attention that we don't want, so I suggest you do something now."

Fae pursed her lips and made a snap decision.

Within a second, all that remained in the street was a pile of garbage, upended wheelie bins, and a confused-looking Wellingsley.

HOW TO GET ARRESTED WHEN YOU'RE NOT BEING ARRESTED

Despite the popular misconception around sex workers, Apple had never been arrested. In fact, she hadn't been in a police station since she was taken there for a school trip as a fourteen-year-old. She had fainted when the class had been shown far too graphic close-up photos of car accident victims as a kind of tough love approach to preventing drink driving and speeding. In a spot of remarkable irony, the photos caused two of the boys to develop raging alcoholism at age eighteen, and one to die in a fiery crash that was attended by the self-same policeman, so in a way, a perfect circle of karma and general unpleasantness.

Bail had been set at $5000 dollars, which Asmodeus had insisted on paying because, for some reason, he had $15,000 in cash with him.

"How do you accidentally have $15000 on you?" asked Apple suspiciously as he rifled through his bag in the Uber on the way to the police station. He frowned as he drew out what Apple fervently hoped was a very realistic model goldfish and a stethoscope.

"Look, getting my things together to come to Sydney was a bit of a rush, and I didn't necessarily make all the choices myself." He surreptitiously slipped what was, now that Apple had got a better look at it, a real yet sadly departed goldfish down the side of the seat and wrapped an elastic band back around the notes.

"What do you do for a living anyway?" she said. "Or is it better that I don't ask?"

"I dabble," he said, and Apple took that to mean the latter. Telling the taxi driver that he could keep the meter running if he waited, they headed into the station.

* * *

"WHAT DO you mean she didn't get arrested?" asked Apple, a puzzled look on her face.

"An incident occurred," said a young policeman who looked to be about fifteen years old, "that eventuated in the female person in question being incarcerated in a cell in the absence of our knowingness, and when it eventuated that her presence was detected, we—"

Apple held up her hand. "Ten words or less."

The young man glanced around nervously, but there was no one to help him. "We don't know how your sister got in there."

"What, in that cell?"

"Yes."

"What, so you brought her in, and she randomly put herself in a cell like a dog self-crating itself?"

"More specifically, we don't know how she got into the station at all."

"Because someone arrested her?"

"That is where communication seems to have fallen somewhat."

"I'm really going to need you to make this a lot clearer for me," said Apple patiently.

"Look, can you just take your sister and this pile of money and leave?"

"But this is her bail. Don't you want it?"

"Look," hissed the man. "We don't know what happened, but there's been no one here tonight except me and Barry, and neither of us put her in there, so it appears that she just somehow got herself in there and locked the door behind her, and she's not in the system, so can you please just take her, and we can all pretend that this never happened. If anyone catches wind of this, I'm going to have more paperwork to do than I think I'm mentally, or physically, capable of dealing with, okay?"

Janie looked belligerent, annoyed, and not at all contrite about what had happened.

"What the fuck did you do?" hissed Apple as they climbed back into the taxi and headed back to Asmodeus' hotel.

Janie sat in stony silence.

"Well," said Apple.

"I'm processing," snapped Janie. "Give me a minute."

"This is—" said Apple, attempting to introduce her sister to Asmodeus, but Janie cut her off again.

"I'm not ready to meet new people," she said. "Just wait."

Once they had got back to the room, she seemed to have cleared her thoughts a little. As Asmodeus swiped the card on the door of his room, Janie turned to Apple. "I went to tell that bloody Fae character that she was completely out of line, and things got a bit weird."

"What kind of weird?"

"The police aren't the only ones who don't know how I got in that cell. One moment, I was throwing roast chicken carcasses and cheap bunches of flowers at people, and the next, everything went all swimmy, and I was in jail. Who's this?"

"This is Asmodeus," said Apple. "Asmodeus, this is my sister, Janie. She's processing things."

"It's alright. I've sorted my brain out now. He looks like a god."

Apple shook her head. "He's not a god, I promise."

"Correct, I'm a demon."

“Have you two had sex?” asked Janie. “He’s gorgeous.”

He nodded. “Yes, just before you rang for help.”

“Wait, are you the client in the flash hotel room?”

“Can we just stop, please?” asked Apple. “This is Asmodeus, and yes, he’s a client, but he’s also quite interesting and rich, and for some reason that I can’t quite put my finger on, I agreed to let him come and bail you out.”

He took Janie’s hand and pressed his lips against it. Delighted to make your acquaintance,” he said.

“Bloody hell,” said Janie. “You’re really gorgeous.”

She had walked into the room and was looking between the view and the man.

He smiled. “I do hear that from time to time.”

“Are you an actual demon?”

“I am, actually. Your sister is being very obstinate and not listening to me about the very important business that I need to get on with.”

“Since when do you believe in demons?” asked Apple.

“I believe in a lot of stuff, thank you very much.”

It’s good that one of you talks sense. I need to talk to your sister about Lilith and—”

“And I’ve told him I don’t know anyone called Lilith.”

“What, Lilith? Like the first wife of Adam?” said Janie.

“Yes!” Asmodeus struck his head with the palm of his hand. “Yes, thank you! One of you knows what I’m talking about. Yes, precisely.”

“And then she became a demon queen that ate babies.”

“Nope,” he said, “that bit was just propaganda. She was none of those things. But it’s a long story. Apparently, your sister has never heard of her.”

“Of course you have,” said Janie, wrapping the robe from Asmodeus’ bed around herself and settling back, her feet tucked under her. ‘How do you think I know about her? You were obsessed with her when you were seventeen. You didn’t talk about anything else. You had different pictures of her up on the wall, and you tried to learn Hebrew to read the original translation of The Alphabet of Ben Sirach."

"Really?" Apple and Asmodeus inquired at the same time.

"I can't believe you don't remember that," said Janie. "This is much better than my place, by the way. Can I stay here?"

"Sure," he said. "Knowing who Lilith is will make our conversation easier."

"I do remember a bit now that you mention it," said Apple. "But it's hazy. I have an awful memory of my childhood in general. I have years with maybe one or two core memories."

"You were going to get a tattoo. You had it planned out and everything. You were going to get a tattoo of Lilith the day you turned eighteen."

"Was I?" said Apple, staring off into space.

"And then one day you just dropped it. Moved on. Got a new fixation. You never mentioned her again."

Asmodeus looked grave. "It's just as well you forgot about it. Otherwise, it's possible that all of reality would have been rebooted, and you would have become completely different people. It's happened before, A lot, actually. And that leads me to my story."

"Not yet," said Apple, holding up her hand. "We need to talk to my sister about her shenanigans tonight first. Your story can wait."

"Can we get room service?" asked Janie. "I'm starving."

"Didn't they feed you in prison?"

"No. I didn't have a number allocated to me, so they couldn't spare any ham and cheese sandwiches. The boys were very nice about it all, though. I didn't get beaten or anything."

Asmodeus clicked on the display screen that showed the room service menu. "Order whatever you want."

"I got arrested because I went to talk to that Fae bitch, and she didn't like the fact that I was there."

Apple looked at her dubiously. "What, she just didn't like the fact you were there?"

"That's right."

"You were just standing in the street tapping gently on her front door, and she called the police, did she?"

Janie screwed up her face. "Things did kick off a little. There may have been some yelling and shouting and the like. And then I upended a large amount of garbage from a few wheelie bins onto her front doorstep. Then there was some more yelling. This annoying girl in a paisley dress had some opinions about things, and then I decided to get the neighbours involved, but the next thing I know, I was in a prison cell."

"So, you blacked out? Maybe someone did hit you."

"Listen to me, Apple," said Janie, enunciating clearly. "When I say the next thing, I know everything went swimmy, and I was in a jail cell and no time had passed, I mean that no time had passed. I'd just checked my phone, and it was the exact same time. There was no gap between standing on the street, considering pelting garbage at the women because they didn't seem as cross as I wanted them to be, and realising that I was surrounded by bars. It happened in a literal blink of an eye."

"Just out of interest," said Asmodeus, "does that kind of thing happen often here?"

"What, jumping through space but not time? No, it doesn't. Not that I recall anyway. Apple?"

"Nope, not as far as I know."

"I think it must have been paranormal," said Janie firmly. "There's literally no other explanation."

"It might well have been paranormal," said Asmodeus. "One question. Did you see anything flash through your head in the intervening moments?"

"Yeah, I did. I had what may have been a vision or something. It was a vision of me, but not me, like a different version of me with an actual job. And a mortgage. And a husband. Pretty depressing. I felt quite down after it."

"Yep." Asmodeus nodded. "That's what I thought. It was a dimensional dimorphal integrating maneuver. A bit of a party trick, but it gets the job done."

"A dimorphous what?" asked Apple and Janie at the same time.

A dimensional dimorphal integrating maneuver. It's a way of moving someone from one place to another as quickly as possible. Don't ask how it's done because I don't know, but some of the fae folk and other spectral beings on Earth were given the ability. They can do it to themselves or other people, but it comes with a vision of who you could have been if you really tried hard and worked on being the person you could have been.

"The person you were meant to be, you mean?"

"No, not meant to be. We're not meant to be anyone. There are just alternate paths."

"Really?" said Janie, looking crestfallen. "I find that a bit disappointing. I always thought we had a life path and a destiny."

"Can we just stop for a moment?" said Apple. "We're just accepting everything that this guy says as truth, are we? We're just accepting that he's a demon and that you got, what, teleported into a different place out of nowhere."

Janie shrugged. "But that's what happened. Look, mate, my sister isn't convinced. Is there a way you can convince her more, maybe? Something you could do. Any tricks?"

"I don't know," he said. "She seemed fairly satisfied earlier. Maybe you could call me… magic fingers."

"Euch, no, don't be tacky. Do something impressive."

So, he did.

EVE WEAVES A WEB

The house that Jared had organised for Eve to live in during her Earth sojourn was massive and majestic. Corinthian columns flanked the oak door. A turning circle, large enough to accommodate a semi-trailer, surrounded a water feature. It's mystic pools containing statues of frolicking, underdressed nymphs. As Eve peeked out of a crack in one of the gold blinds that covered the windows overlooking the drive, she saw Fae step out of a car and direct whoever was driving to park in the shade of a large palm tree.

She didn't plan to spend a lot of time in this house, but that had nothing to do with how utterly hideous she found it; she planned to be with Zeus whenever she had the chance. He'd fallen in love with her (again) within days, and the toxic ideas that had been pushing against his brain had fallen out of his head as easily as the love had flooded back in. They suspected it had been Adam, not God, who had implanted that dislike of women in Zeus on account of him not doing a very good job. So, it must definitely be Adam.

Eve saw Fae look around before she took her first steps toward the front door. She was tall and willowy in a way that Eve could never imagine being. Her black hair was cut in a sharp bob, and Eve thought that she looked stressed. Pinched.

Eve took a handful of her hair and pulled it over her shoulder nervously, letting the brown waves fall over her chest. *Come on, Eve*, she thought. Act naïve. Innocent. A little clueless.

She knew she could pull this off. The bronze satin wrap dress she had on was the one she and Zeus had bought in a boutique on Manly Beach last week. It hugged her generous curves, and she took a deep breath before throwing the door open with a huge, welcoming smile on her face.

Before Fae had a chance to take her hand down from where it was poised to knock, Eve threw her arms around her.

"Welcome, my friend. You're Fae, yes? I'm Eve, and I'm so thrilled to meet you. This is all a bit new to me. I was just transmogrified down here overnight, and here's me in this huge house, and I can go outside. Can you believe it? Outside? I was out there at 4.00 am waiting for the sun to rise, but I was a bit early, I think, so I wandered around the streets for a while, and then I had a snack and a nap. There was a note on the table in the kitchen telling me to expect you. My husband arranged this all. Do you know him? Have you met? Or did his man talk to you about me? Apparently, he has a man who arranges things. Jared?"

Eve saw Fae's cheeks flush red at the mention of Jared's name. She plunged on. "A man who fixes things! Sounds like a mafia movie, doesn't it? It's all quite a hoot. I'm having such fun already."

"You watch mafia movies?"

Fae seemed a little taken aback by the flood of information being thrown at her, so Eve decided to capitalize on this and keep going. "Sometimes. I like movies. I watch a lot of them. I like to see how the world works. But now I've been allowed down here, so I don't need to anymore! I can be part of things. I'm very excited. Can you tell?"

Fae opened her mouth and closed it again. "You seem very enthusiastic," she said after a moment.

"Come in! But could you please take those shoes off? I think this floor is marble, and I read on the internet that high heels can be damaging to marble floors. I love the internet. Are you familiar with it?"

Fae slipped off her shoes, and Eve pulled her by the arm, encouraging the woman who was at least a head taller than her to follow. A chandelier hung from the second floor over the open-plan room, and each tiny sphere of glass turned and glimmered in its own light. Prisms of colour reflected around the room in a heady swirl, giving Eve a moment of disorientation. Nervousness overtook her, and she sank her nails into her hand to steady herself as she led Fae into a formal dining room. She gestured to a chair, then tripped her way lightly down to the other end of the dining table and sat facing Fae, ten place settings between them. It was laid for a formal dinner, and Eve wondered how many people knew the number of friends they could happily share a meal with.

"It's lovely to meet you," said Fae. "Absolutely delightful, and of course, your reputation precedes you."

Eve smiled at her. "In what way?"

"Well, you're Eve. Mother of all mankind. Child of God. One who brought original sin into the world, too, if we're not putting too fine a point on that."

"Just between you and me," said Eve, "a lot of that is myth-making. There's a lot that people don't know. A lot I could tell. Can I trust you?"

"I wish you wouldn't," said Fae. "I don't want to sound rude, but I've got a lot on my plate at the moment, and I don't know if I can handle anything apart from showing you where the good coffee shops are. Pizza too, at a pinch. I can give you a vague hint of Sydney and hang out a bit, but workwise, I'm totally swamped. My job is proving to be more involved than I thought."

"But aren't I not part of your job now? I thought you'd been asked to look after me. On behalf of my family."

"Yes and no," said Fae. "You're on the list, but you're a long way down."

Eve took a deep breath. She hadn't known exactly what to expect, but this woman seemed rude. "I need someone to trust," she said. "I've been kept in a room away from everyone for so long that I don't know who I am or what I like. My husband and my father totally ignore me, and now they've finally let me free, but that's only because my husband is… I can't even talk about it; it's too upsetting."

Fae begrudgingly stood and walked toward Eve in her stockinged feet. She took a seat next to her. "How about I introduce you to my friend Wellingsley? She's a lovely person, about your age, I think, and she can help you."

Wellingsley, thought Eve with a little shiver of excitement. She was definitely one of them. She'd seen her name on a file. But she didn't want Fae just fobbing her off on someone else. She needed to stay close to her, too.

"Can I come with you? Please? I don't like this house. I'm scared." Eve placed her hand on Fae's arm and willed some tears to her eyes.

"Oh god, all right then. Come on."

A HUNKA HUNKA BURNING LOVE

The room wasn't literally on fire, but it certainly looked like it. Janie got down on her hands and knees and peered under the wall of flames that divided the lounge area from the exposed glass bathroom.

"It's not actually touching the ground," she said. "It's just burning in mid-air. Burning nothing. Is there a gas supply? It must be a flammable gas or something."

"It's got to be an optical illusion," said Apple, stretching her hand toward the flames but then pulling it back rapidly with a gasp.

"Obviously, it's hot. It's fire," said Asmodeus. "That was pretty stupid of you."

Apple crossed her arms, pressing her partially singed hand to her chest. "Fucking hilarious," she said. "Great trick." She could feel the skin of her fingers starting to blister.

Asmodeus noticed and gently pulled her hand toward him. He looked closely at it, turned it one way then the other, then he laid his other hand over it. After a moment of concentration, he let go and smiled at her. "That should do it."

Her hand felt completely fine.

She stretched out her fingers and twisted her wrist, looking at her unblemished skin. "I guess that's impressive," she said begrudgingly. "But given the fact you caused me to get hurt in the first place, it's no more than you owed me. But I still don't think this is evidence you're a demon."

He grinned at her. "Even after that amazing fucking?"

"Eh, I've had better," she said.

"Really," questioned Janie.

"Yeah, no. Actually, he was really good."

With a snap of his fingers, the flames disappeared, leaving seemingly no evidence of damage.

"Supposing, hypothetically, that we do believe you're a demon," said Apple.

"I do," said Janie, sticking her hand in the air. "Fire, healed hands, and what, you had four orgasms? Definitely a sex demon."

"If that's true," said Apple, "then why are you here? Why are we here? And why did you pay me for sex?"

"Firstly, I don't really understand your current social societal setup, so it seemed more ethical for me to pay for someone to sway the power dynamic."

"That doesn't sound very demonic," said Janie.

"Demonic is very much a misunderstood term. We get a lot of bad press, he said. "But yes, there is a reason why I'm here and why I chose you."

"Because of her fantastic rack," suggested Janie.

"I'm going to need you to shush for a moment," snapped Apple. "You're being tremendously unhelpful."

"I'm being the fun, light-hearted relief," she said. "You should try it sometime."

"Can I draw your attention back to when we were talking about Lilith?" he asked. "'mentioned this mythical figure of Lilith, and you said you didn't remember her, but then you actually did, and you were very interested in her once upon a time, but you seem to have buried that memory."

'Yes," said Apple.

There was a knock on the door as their food arrived.

"I swear there are some cosmic forces working to stop me getting to the actual main point," he grumbled through a mouthful of roasted lamb once they had all settled to eat.

"Lilith," he said, getting back on track. "So, Lilith was my true love. Is my true love. The most amazing and wonderful woman I have ever met. She is a whirlwind, an adventure, a deeply passionate, loving, wise, but impulsive creature. She is amazing."

"Doesn't stop you from having sex with other women, though," said Janie.

"Humans are weird. Monogamy is strange, you're all repressed," he said.

"So, where is she now?" asked Apple.

"God and Lilith had a falling out a long time ago."

"God. As in actual God?" Apple's expression was dubious.

"Yes, the current one, anyway. They had a heated, full, and frank exchange of views about a range of topics, and he took what I think was a pretty over-the-top action of—"

"Yes?"

"Fragmenting her throughout all space and time."

"Sounds messy," said Janie.

"Not her body," he said patiently. "Her soul. Bits of her. It broke into lots of different pieces and got thrown everywhere in an attempt to lessen her power."

"Isn't God all-loving and such?" asked Apple, puzzled.

"Occasionally. He's mellowed with time. He is getting wiser and more mature as he gets older. But still, he's a bit like an uncle who's had to get used to his nephew being trans and now tries to use inclusive language and not make gay jokes. He's doing his best, but it still gets slightly uncomfortable at times."

Apple looked over at her sister, who had now branched out to eating her raspberry coulis panna cotta. "You seem to be taking all this in your stride."

Janie shrugged. "Love it," she said. "Subverting the dominant paradigm. Mixing up what we think we know about life and the universe. Should be more of it. Big fan."

"So my true love got fragmented," he continued. "Her soul was divided up into an infinity of pieces, well, not an infinity, but a lot of pieces. They implanted these fragments in various people, and they took root. Lilith is powerful. Very powerful. The tiny parts of her kept making themselves known. But the people she was in, well, when they started to be aware of her, they would talk about it or verbalize it, and they would be discovered. I found some of them and tried to warn them ahead of time to be quiet. But for quite a large swathe of human history, God was totally focused on finding these people and then rebooting history, so they never existed."

"I beg your fucking pardon?" said Janie.

"Yep, literally rebooting time to get rid of her."

"She really got under his skin, didn't she? What did she do?"

"It's complicated," said Asmodeus. "There was a lot of background context, but the final straw was when she told Eve she should abort her first child. Eventually, and I was a bit out of the loop about all this because I drifted away from people in the know over time and found it harder and harder to see what was going on, but it was decided that things would be confined to one timeline and one location. So the bits of her that were left, the bits that made up the whole now, could be monitored more closely, and all the embers of Lilith were put on the one timeline."

"What is this ember of Lilith that you keep talking about?" asked Apple.

"As I said, Lilith is an incredibly powerful and visionary being. People these days call themselves change makers because they have the idea of putting chia seeds in a smoothie, but she was created to be the mother of humanity. She was created to be the woman to start a civilisation. Not from Adam's rib, as Eve was created, but as a fully formed powerhouse. The first real feminist."

"And she was destroyed. Bloody typical," said Janie.

"So, this bit of Lilith that's in some women…"

"They're oblivious to it, but it's there. It will be obvious in certain ways, the way they behave, the things they do, what they're interested in. Their strivings in life will point toward things that Lilith would want to do. And then, from what I've been able to tell, if they really come into their own and realise their full potential, they will realise Lilith is within them. And then if all these women embodying Lilith join up, then—"

"Yes?" The two women waited with bated breath.

"I'm not sure, but probably something pretty impressive. And I know she will eventually be back."

"How?" asked Apple.

"I don't know, okay? I don't know. I've got no idea. I've just been casting around history trying to find the one I love. As it turns out, pretty ineptly and uselessly. Every time I found her, time got rebooted, and now I don't even—"

"I have a bit of a problem with this," said Apple, rising off the bed where she had been lying, eating blue cheese dip with rice crackers. She placed her hands on her hips and tilted her head to the side. "Are you saying that women aren't feminists and strong and striving to be their most fulfilled and complete selves if they didn't get impregnated with this Lilith ember? Does this take away all their self-determination and ability to be amazing and powerful on their own? Because that sounds like patriarchal bullshit to me."

"When did I say that?" said Asmodeus, looking puzzled.

"You said that women who realise their full potential will have Lilith in them."

"I did not."

"Yes, you did. You mansplained women's empowerment to me."

"I most certainly did not," he snapped again. "Don't try to catch me by using buzzwords. I said that the women that Lilith is in will try to fully realise themselves, and if they do, she will be released."

"You're not even sure about that bit," said Apple.

"True, I don't know, but I feel like it makes sense. But no, I didn't say that *only* those women do."

"Maybe you should work out your spiel a bit more clearly before throwing it at people," said Apple, "because clarity around this is important."

"Do you believe it now, then?" said Janie, looking over to her sister.

Apple was standing in the middle of the room now, and she suddenly looked very alone. Her face was white, and she bit at the edge of one of her nails, a habit she had abandoned years ago.

"So, how does this involve me?" she asked haltingly.

"I know," said Janie, looking at her, her eyes suddenly bright. "It's obvious, isn't it? It's me. I have an ember of Lilith within me!"

THE HONEYMOON IS OVER

As they headed back to the office, the phone rang, and the name Tony lit up the screen. Fae had the momentary thought that she should make his individualized ring tone the sound of babies crying or something equally annoying, since that was what she felt every time she saw his name.

"Hi," she said, realising that letting it go to voicemail would just prolong the inevitable. "How are you going, chief?"

"Good," he said. "Great. I'm ringing to set up a meeting. For us to discuss our next moves. And a collaboration of some sort."

"That's wonderful," said Fae soothingly. "Great idea. That's just perfect. What I'll get you to do is just sit on that for a while until I've had a chance to free up Wellingsley and you two can—"

"Wellingsley, your girl?"

"Yes."

"I thought I'd be liaising with you."

"Well, yes, you're liaising with me, but I think that you and she would have much more in common. To talk about."

There was a pause, heavy breathing, and the crackling of what Fae assumed was fingers searching in a packet for potato chips.

"I don't know about that," he said. "My information isn't for everyone. I only want to deal with leaders, with people who..."

Fae held up an apologetic finger to Eve, who was sitting in the seat next to her. Eve knew Zeus was on the phone; she could hear his voice. This was part of the plan. He was supposed to be finding a way to connect up with all of them as soon as possible, and as far as Eve was aware, that was something Fae wanted too. But maybe not.

"I obviously don't want to pressure you to do anything you're not comfortable with, so I'll leave it with you. Let me know if you change your mind. But I understand if this doesn't work for you, and I wish you all the best." And she hung up.

"Who was that?" asked Eve casually. Her eyes were glued to the passing scenery, the cars and the roads and the traffic and the construction and the people and all the general palaver that the 2020s seemed to think made a country "civilised".

"An idiot," said Fae. "A complete imbecile. Don't worry about it."

Eve frowned and opened her mouth to protest, but realized, just in time, that would be a ridiculously foolhardy move.

Restarian pulled the car into a narrow street.

"If you see a large amount of garbage heaped in front of our building, it's not supposed to be there. It's an aberration. Just ignore it," said Fae.

A young woman was standing in the street, pushing at the pile of rubbish pathetically with a broom. Her dress was tied at the side to stop it falling into the mess, and her face looked red and sunburnt.

"Who's that?"

Fae was too busy trying to pointlessly explain to Restarian how to reverse the car without getting it scratched by upturned wheelie bins to notice the way she looked at Wellingsley.

"That's my assistant, Wellingsley. I'm going to let her set you up with whatever it is we talked about, and then I'll be able to get other things."

There was the smell of burning sulphur, and a figure appeared in the seat next to Restarian.

"What other things, Fae?" said Jared, swiveling his head toward her. His expression, Fae suspected, was like the last thing a multitude of baby gazelles saw as they bent their heads down to take a drink. From a croc-infested waterhole. "You seem to think you can tell me how I should do my job, so tell me, who exactly is in charge?"

Restarian decided that the spot he had awkwardly maneuvered the car into would do for now and leaped out as if the hounds of hell were after him, which they very well could have been. Sensing the vibe, Eve opened her door too and hurried behind him as he started to coach Wellingsley on rubbish removal.

Jared disappeared and reappeared in Eve's recently vacated seat. "Oh, nice," he said. "Still warm. I love the feeling of original sin. I asked, what is your business?" he repeated. "You keep saying you're not happy and you want to talk to me, and I get the impression that you're in charge. So, what is your business?"

Fae had never seen him like this. "Stop…v ibrating at me or whatever you're doing. I'm trying to do my best, okay? You asked me to keep the powers of several very headstrong and unpredictable women under control. My assistant is a boggart who never does what he's told. He makes things harder for me, do you know that? I have to try and make Zeus think he's a special and important manly man when even his voice makes my skin crawl, and now I've got to babysit the first woman, wife, and mother. I've got a bloody lot on my plate, and I'm finding it all overwhelming. So if you could give me a bit of a break, I'd appreciate it, all right?"

As she caught her breath, she was aware of Jared staring at her fixedly. "You want a break?"

She nodded. "If not a break, then a vague understanding that I have a lot of balls in the air, and while I do appreciate the trust you put in me in giving me this job, and while I know you must have seen something in me that I didn't even see in myself and wanted me to really grow and develop, there are some days when I don't wonder that those beliefs may have been a bit…"

"Yes?"

"Misplaced."

Silence hung in the car. Restarian had left the keys in the ignition, and an instrumental rendition of "La Guaracha" played on the radio.

"You have no fucking idea, do you? You have to get Zeus here with you. You've got Eve, which is a bloody miracle at this point. You need to start to make some bloody progress. Do you have any idea of the beings I have to deal with? Do you have any fucking comprehension of the stress I'm under? Or what's at stake? No, of course you don't because you're just not very bright."

She looked at him in shock.

"Of course, my belief in you is misplaced. You have to be the single most incompetent Fae I've ever met. I swear you've got no more of a brain than you did when I found you in that creation portal, all doe-eyed and stumbling. No, I chose you to do this because you would almost certainly fail. I have absolutely no faith you can keep these pieces of Lilith joining up. In fact, I think you most definitely won't. At this very moment, the demon Asmodeus is revealing to one of the subjects the truth of her origin."

"What?" said Fae, her face pinched and white. "Why are you doing this? Why set me up to fail? And why does…" She thought for a moment, trying to get all the pieces straight in her head.

He laughed, the sound rumbling in the confined space. "Sweetheart, I can practically hear your brains burning. Don't try so hard to think. You'll have an embolism. I honestly thought you'd find it funny. It is a bit funny, come on. And you're in on the joke now. I felt a little bad that I wasn't sharing it with you. Bad might be an overstatement, but it was… I thought about it, okay?

So yes, I got you the job. So that you would fail. I wanted this to go badly, okay? Don't take it personally, baby. You know, I think you're a delight, but you're not very good at things, are you? I needed someone to fuck this up, and you did. But no hard feelings." He dipped his head and peered out the window. "Look, Eve's chatting to Wellingsley. That's good. That's great, in fact. She's got a real vested interest in all this, but I suspect she'll tell you more about it as time goes on. She's a dark horse, that one."

He took her hand, kissed it, and with that, he was gone except for his fading, theatrical laugh that still reverberated around the leather interior of the town car.

"Why did you tell me that?" she said to the empty seat where he'd just been.

She had been selected for this job to fail. She had been chosen because of her innate ability to fuck up everything that she looked at.

She slipped out of the car and surveyed the rubbish. "Ring the council and tell them that one of their trucks did this. We shouldn't have to deal with it."

She realized she was yelling.

"What did he want?" said Restarian, looking at her warily. "He seemed… heightened."

"I have no idea what he wanted," said Fae, her snappish voice continuing. "I need to think," she said. "I need to get things straight in my head. There's too much going on, and I don't know what to do. Keep those two busy for me. I'm going for a drive."

LAST TWO STANDING

"Um," said Asmodeus, looking uncomfortable. "I mean, perhaps. It's not totally out of the question. But you're not necessarily the one that I…"

Apple sighed in exasperation and shook her head. "It's me, isn't it? It must be. I used to be obsessed with her, and now I'm a sex worker. It does feel pretty Lilith adjacent. And you and I did seem to have a bit of a spark between us, separate from the fact that we're two very attractive people who enjoy getting naked."

Asmodeus nodded. "Yes," he said. "It's you."

"How do you know, though?" she said. "Can you feel something about me? Can you feel that I have this dynamic within my very soul? Within my being? Did her soul cry out to you across the ages?"

He wrinkled his brow. "Not so much. I was given a list of names."

"You were given a list of names?"

"Of women in the greater Sydney area who have Lilith within them. Confining you all in a certain area makes it a lot easier to find you. Still don't understand why they decided to go with that plan."

"There's a bloody list?" said Apple. "That doesn't sound very mystical and otherworldly."

"I dunno what to tell you," he said with a shrug. "I was given a list with some names on it, and you were there. But to answer your question, yes, I can feel her. I can feel her existence. Even though she's not here as such, I can feel that she is somewhere. In a liminal space. And I know I can get her back."

"Can I see this list?" asked Apple.

"It can't hurt, I guess," said Asmodeus, crossing to a table. He moved bundles of money to the side and pulled out a piece of paper, looking at it for a moment before passing it to Apple. Janie looked over her shoulder, peering at the names.

"There you are," said Janie, pointing at the first name on the list. "I have to admit I'm surprised. I genuinely thought it was me."

"Why did you possibly think it was you?" said Apple. "I mean, I don't see how it's me either, but what about you would possibly make you think you have an ember of an ancient demonic goddess in you?"

"Not a demon," clarified Asmodeus.

Janie shrugged. "I don't know. I just feel like I'm destined for greatness. That I have an amazing potential within me, and I don't quite know what it is, and no one else sees it."

Asmodeus nodded kindly. "I see that. I get it."

"You do? You see that in me?"

"Oh no, I mean I see that you could think that, but I don't think you do."

Apple was frowning as she stared at the list. "What are the names that have been crossed off? There were originally eight, and now there are only two."

He sighed heavily and took the paper from her, stroking it gently. "Those are the ones we have lost, I'm afraid. The ones who are no longer—"

"Oh my god," gasped Apple, her hand flying to her chest. "You mean they're dead? They have been killed. Murdered? Or killed themselves? This is horrendous!"

"What, no," said Asmodeus, looking flustered. "What is wrong with you? Otherworldly beings don't just go around killing mortals. We're not supposed to, anyway. No, they're not dead. Their ember has just been snuffed out. Someone has been making sure that they don't reach the Lilith potential. I don't know the individual story of each of them, but… well, this is the way the list was given to me."

"There are only two names left," said Janie. "Does this mean that the eventual Lilith you're going to get back will be totally watered down? If there were… what, thousands to start with, and now there are two?"

"No," said Asmodeus, "I'm sure that's not the case, but—"

"That's not the point," said Apple, holding up her hand. "Just stop for a moment. It's all very well you telling me this and me discovering that there may, or may not, be the ember of a goddess inside me, but so what? Why are you even telling me?"

"It's obvious," said Janie, smiling beatifically at Asmodeus. "He wants to tell you. To give you a warning. To make sure that you never lose your ember. To make sure that no one ever tells you to… wait." Janie smacked her forehead with the heel of her hand. "It's Fae, isn't it? Fae Stephenson. She's the one who was sent to keep her small, to destroy her passion. See, I told you there was more to that bitch than meets the eye. This totally validates me dumping rubbish on her doorstop and also explains how I got… what was it?"

"Dimorphal dimensional—"

"Yes, see? We need to pay that woman another visit. I've still got my eye on her."

"Is that true?" said Apple.

"Which bit?" said Asmodeus, looking truly nervous for the first time.

She narrowed her eyes at him. "Why do you look evasive?"

"I haven't been told officially, but it makes sense. I don't know any other fae around here who would deliberately have gotten themselves involved in a mortal's business. She's definitely got something to do with the whole thing. I'm not quite sure how deep her involvement goes, but I can tell she's connected."

"And the other bit?"

"Do we want to order some more food, maybe?"

"Asmodeus," snapped Apple. "Answer the question. Are you here to encourage me to be my best self?"

He looked at her, his mouth open slightly as if about to speak. Then his eyes glazed over, and he closed it again. "I don't want to tell you," he said, and strode over to the window. He moodily stared out at the lights of the city. Dawn was breaking.

"What would happen to me?" said Apple. "What would happen to me if Lilith found herself?"

The back of Asmodeus's head seemed to shimmer a little with tension.

"What would happen," said Apple, her voice now pitchy with tension. "Why am I here? Why did you find me?"

"Don't you see?" he said, turning back to her, and the sisters could see the dark flash of an eternal fire in his eyes. "I didn't look for you; you came to me. You were the name that I found. Do you think I usually go around hiring women for sex? No, of course I don't. But I had the overwhelming feeling that in this situation, it was the right thing to do, and then it was you."

"It's a big coincidence," said Janie.

Asmodeus snorted. "Coincidence. It's an utter improbability. There's no way this would have happened by chance. You put an infinite number of monkeys in an infinite number of steam engines, and they wouldn't…"

"That's not quite how that goes," corrected Janie.

"It doesn't matter," he said, striding over to Apple and taking her arm. "This isn't a coincidence. This was meant to be. Someone is engineering this. Someone wants Lilith back, and I can only surmise that someone wants her and I back together."

"So if you find us both, she comes back, does she?" said Apple, wrenching her arm out of his grip. "If she comes out of me, then who am I? Where am I? Women throughout history have been utterly annihilated in the desperation to get rid of her, and now there are only what, two of us left? You think I'm going to stand around and wait to dissolve so this woman who pissed off God can come back and you can play happy families?"

She saw Janie quickly collecting up their belongings.

"Tell me the truth," she said. "What will happen to me?"

"I don't know," he said. "Honestly, I don't know. I don't think anyone does, to be honest. But I just thought that if we can get together, those of you who are left can get together, can talk, then maybe you will—"

"Have a sudden breakthrough? Has the answer to ultimate reality dawned on us?"

"No, don't be silly. No one knows that. But maybe have a clue. Maybe she'll just materialise. There's nothing to say that you'll be destroyed."

"Except all the other women who were destroyed. That's a bit of a bloody giveaway."

The first rays of the sun were sliding up over the horizon now, edging the tops of the buildings and infusing everything with a golden, ethereal glow. The room, specially designed to catch moments such as this, was suffused with light.

"I don't think you can be destroyed, though," he said. "She can't be, so that must mean that—"

"Nope," said Apple. "There are way too many maybes and musts here for my liking. You don't know. I'm just your means to an end."

She made a move for the door, and Janie pulled it open.

"You can't just leave,' he said. 'Just wait, please. I promise..."

He stopped, and the two women looked at him. "I was going to promise that no harm would come to you," he said with a wry smile, "but I can't make that pledge. But I can swear I'll do what I can to protect you and make sure finding Lilith will be as easy for you as it can. Look at it from Lilith's perspective. She's had everything taken away from her. Everything."

"And for that I'm supposed to give up everything in return?"

"I feel like you're being a little bit dramatic," said Janie to her sister. "There has literally been no talk of you giving up anything."

"There is a trail of dead women!" enunciated Apple with a yell. "A trail of dead women, Janie."

"And I've said that won't happen to you," said Asmodeus. "And no one has died. Literally, no one has died. Barely. Not lately, anyway. Well, when they did everything was rebooted so—"

"You've also said that you have no fucking idea what's going on. No, look. I'm not mad. I understand the position you're in, and it's very difficult. Hell, I understand the position of Lilith, too. It's an all-around shit sandwich. And I'm not saying that I won't help at all. I am about to storm out of that door, but before I do, I need you to know that if you can give me something a bit more concrete about how this is all going to work, and if it doesn't involve me losing major pieces of my essence or my psyche, then give me a call. Because, against my better judgment, I really like you, but I'm not entirely confident I won't wind up dead."

Janie removed her hand from the doorknob. "Are we storming out or what?"

"We are," said Apple. "I'm sorry, you seem to be a good and kind person. Demon. Whatever. But I didn't sign up for this, and I'm not willing to throw my life into disarray because you're following your heart or a random list or something. You don't even know if that list is reliable. This whole thing could be made up. I'm sorry, but I have to go."

She flung open the door, and she and Janie rushed toward the lift.

"Tell me you remember that other name," said Apple to her sister as they waited for the doors to open.

"Way ahead of you," said Janie, holding up her phone. "I'm Googling the other girl right now."

HOME TRUTHS

Adam was pacing back and forth. The wall of screens that displayed shifting scenes from the planet below flickered a roaming montage of disconnected occurrences.

He reached his hand toward the joystick that toggled between longitudinal coordinates and gently pushed it. One of the screens in front of him flicked to a view of a palatial faux McMansion monstrosity. While gazing around the room, trying to make it seem as if he was looking anywhere but the screen, one movement of his wrist zoomed the image in on the house, and he then flicked through each room.

He leaned forward, frowning, looking in each room, his eyes searching for the familiar figure.

Click.

Click.

Click.

Where *was* she?

He didn't think she could do much to screw up his plan. She had no real clue, no real power. But still, having her down on Earth made him nervous. He didn't know what she was up to, and he definitely didn't trust her. Getting Jared to oversee her was a sound move, but still. She was crafty. And he couldn't lose control of his wife. What kind of man would that make him? A living joke, that's what.

"Ah, you miss her," said a voice directly behind him.

He jumped, his hand skittering the view to a windswept scene somewhere on the 49th parallel, where he found himself staring at several morose moose staring down a car of tourists.

"Just browsing," he said, exuding guilt from every pore.

"Don't worry, I won't scold you if you're looking for Eve," God said. "Just because none of my relationships panned out doesn't mean that I don't understand the bonds of marriage." He lazily flicked through the screens the way that Adam had moments previously.

"Out probably," he said. "That's fine, though. She needs to explore things. Sepham has no doubt connected her with a new chum or some such."

A silence fell over the room, and God turned his head to peer at Adam. He moved his glasses down his nose somewhat—he didn't need glasses, strictly speaking, what with all the omnipotence and omniscience and all, but one of his new advisers had told him it would help with his image. "Are you all right?" he asked.

Adam shrugged but didn't answer.

"If I didn't know better, I'd think you were being petulant."

Adam crossed his arms, doing nothing to disprove the assertion.

"She's allowed to have some freedom, son." I don't know if we've done the right thing by her. We've kept her very sheltered. Very shut up. I don't think it's been the best for her growth."

"This current obsession with growth is taking us in a direction I'm not completely sure of," said Adam from between gritted teeth. "It's far better for her to have constraints. Not everyone has to grow and evolve into interesting and creative new versions of themselves, you know."

"Have to? No, they don't have to. But isn't it better that they do? That we do? I think that continually bettering ourselves and committing to a path to growth can only advance reality. Have I shown you the sketch of the new tattoo that I plan to—"

"Have you ever considered this from my perspective?" he said, a whine in his voice. "I've taken all my advice from you, all my mentoring from you, forever. You made me the man that I am."

"Literally."

"Quite."

"And now you're loud and proud, trying to be a better version of yourself? How do you think that makes me feel? What about me? Do I now have to question everything? Doubt everything? Completely reinvent myself? What kind of idiot does that make me look like?" said Adam.

With a wave of God's hand, all the screens faded to black. The flickering lights of the room dimmed, and even the gentle hum of the air reticulation system seemed to fade into the background. "My dear boy," said God, briefly pressing his hand over his mouth in dismay. "Is this what this is all about? Is this what the matter is? You've been out of sorts for a while."

Adam swung around and walked away. "I'm fine. It's not a big deal."

"I want to apologise if I've done anything that might impinge on your ability to be your full and most completely potentiated self."

"Please stop," said Adam. "This is making me uncomfortable."

"Ah, yes, consent. This is something that we do now. Consent. Fine, fine, I'll leave you be. But you, in turn, have to let Eve be."

"What if she gets involved in our business?" he hissed.

"What business?"

"You know." He glanced around furtively. "Lilith."

"Ah, yes, Lilith." God shook his head sadly. "So many mistakes. So many mistakes there. Not my finest hour. Not my finest millennium." He shook his head again, and a look of grave regret suffused his whole being. "I shouldn't have reacted as I did.

I made a mistake. I shouldn't have let you and your youthful enthusiasm influence my actions. Oh!" He smiled widely, looking at Adam. "That's growth, isn't it? Saying that I did something wrong? That's very good! I like that. Just wait a moment…"

He pressed a button. "Sepham, if you're around, could you just pop into the main hub? I have an insight for you."

Sepham appeared in the room, a slow glow that grew in solidity until he was fully formed.

"Sorry," said the angel. "I was in a bubble universe down the corridor. It would have taken me a literal infinity to walk."

"Hi there, Adam," he said, not making eye contact.

Adam made a noncommittal noise of acknowledgment. If God noticed that anything was wrong, he ignored it. The two could not stand each other but tried to maintain a cordial demeanor as much as possible.

"So, big news," said God, opening his arms expansively. "I've just had some clarity and self-realization!"

"Well done, sir," said Sepham, clapping his hands together enthusiastically. "That's wonderful. Really top notch. What was it surrounding? Something that we've been discussing? Anything that we were targeting with your homework?"

"In a manner of speaking," said God, gesturing to a seat. Sepham sat and tucked his robes around his legs. "Adam, do you think you could get us a drink, please?" asked God, beaming with excitement. "I'll have a lemon lime and bitters. Sepham?"

"Ooh, lovely. I'll have one of those too. Maybe with a straw? One of those twisty ones? Would that be too much to ask?"

Adam narrowed his eyes. "Am I to assume," he said to Sepham, "that you are the one who had been filling his head with all these new ideas?"

Sepham glanced at God nervously. "He's asked me to mentor him, in a manner of speaking."

"Mentor God?" said Adam. "How is someone supposed to mentor God? He's God. He's perfect!"

The angel and the old man chucked at the same time. “Oh, I can assure you most definitely that we have realized I’m not,” said God. “But we might get there eventually, mightn’t we?”

Sepham nodded sagely. “It’s possible. You’re making amazing progress.”

“This is ridiculous,” snapped Adam, stalking off to the bar fridge in the next room. He muttered to himself as he made their drinks, and words such as “bloody liberties” and “new age claptrap” could be heard above the clink of deliberately slammed down bottles and cutlery. When he returned with the two drinks, they were still deep in conversation.

“I need to make some amends,” said God, looking up at him as he took the drink.

“Have you been crying?” snapped Adam.

“This is emotional business,” said Sepham. “Great things are afoot, and they will have an impact on the development of reality. Tears are warranted.”

“I find this interesting, that’s all,” said Adam, hands on his hips. “I find it interesting that you, Sepham, who have had no problems at all in dabbling in what I’ll charitably call ‘grey areas’ in the past, now seem to be the end-all and be-all when it comes to wisdom.”

“What do you mean?” said God.

“I mean,” said Adam, “that Sepham here is no better than he should be.”

“I don’t even know what that means,” said Sepham, but the look of nervousness on his face was unmistakable.

Suddenly, the screens in front of them sprang to life. Several of them displayed scenes of destruction, falling buildings, huge waves, and general mayhem. God leaned forward and pressed a few buttons, then peered at the screens. “Wait, what am I seeing here? Victor, what am I seeing?”

A voice blared from a speaker next to the screens. “Earthquake in an ocean somewhere. Wasn’t scheduled, but you know, tectonic plates can be absolute buggers. Going to be quite a large loss of life."

God sprang up, threw back the last of his drink. "Lucky this is non-alcoholic. I must have known something was going to kick off."

"Yes, there are going to be a lot of prayers incoming, and the call centre will probably appreciate you dropping in to give them a pep talk. Wait… yes, they're coming in thick and fast. Also, from what I can tell, we're going to have a lot of incoming souls in the next few days, so take that into account too."

"Mavis, God called into thin air.

A disembodied voice answered. "On it already. I'm getting makeshift dorms ready. We weren't aware of this one. We had a plane come down in Australia because some woman didn't put airplane mode on, but this was unexpected. If we all scramble through, we can get something arranged."

God put his hands on his hips. "See," he said. "This is why I need a good team around me. Thanks to everyone, you two especially. My backbones. My life rafts. I couldn't do any of this without you. I should throw a party. An appreciation party. To let everyone know how much I really appreciate the support and assistance everyone has given me as I find my feet. And I could…" A look of insight suffused his face.

Adam tilted his head to the side. "Do you really want everyone to know just how much you have been struggling?"

"Struggling is a big word, don't you think? Certainly, finding my feet would be an accurate description, but struggling, maybe not."

The voice in the air sounded again. "Sir? Anytime you're ready would be fabulous."

"Of course, of course. Okay, you two, I'll probably be needing you as the day progresses. Adam, can you take care of things here for me?"

"Off you go," said Adam with a flick of his fingers. "You go off and do what it is you do, and we'll be fine."

"He really is more of a figurehead role than anyone realized when everything was set up, isn't he?" said Sepham as the bustling figure left the room.

"Don't try and get me involved in chatty, friendly discussions," said Adam. "I've got a bone to pick with you. I don't like these new ideas you've been putting in his head."

"I am simply his adviser," snapped Sepham, glancing around furtively. "Don't think that everyone doesn't know you're visibly keeping yourself above any activities that could call your image into question. And don't think there haven't been questions asked about that, mark my words."

"What do you mean?" asked Adam.

"I mean," said Sepham, leaning forward and looking him square in the eye, "that some people think you might be setting yourself up for a takeover."

"Oh, don't be ridiculous," blustered Adam. "Don't be so patently, fully, and entirely ridiculous. God, do you mean? The job of God? There's no way I'd want to do that."

"All right," said Sepham, raising his hands in mock defeat. "As I said, it's not me saying it. I've just heard word of it."

"You're helping him be better now, are you?"

"I'm trying," said Sepham magnanimously. "I'm doing my best to help God. I don't understand why you're annoyed at me. Equality and everyone having a fair go."

"You sound like one of those bloody communists," snapped Adam.

"Would that be so bad?"

Adam glared at him. "You've gone mad. I don't think you should be anywhere near my father. If he's listening to your stupid ideas, then maybe he shouldn't be in charge anymore."

"See," said Sepham, pointing his finger at Adam. "That. That is exactly what people are talking about. You need to be careful, son."

Adam was about to lurch into a rant about the appropriate addressing of superiors when he noticed the screen behind Sepham had flicked off the carnage and now showed a suburban street with several people moving about. He recognized one of the figures and peered closer. He moved the controllers, and the picture blurred completely before coming into sharp focus on his wife's face. The coordinates showed that she was nowhere near the house she had been given to live in.

What is she up to?

He scanned the surrounding area and saw several other women, one he recognized but whose name he couldn't quite bring to mind. How did he know her? Being acquainted with human females was not something he spent time doing, so there must be some way that he knew her…

Suddenly, it dawned on him. She was one of the women with Lilith implanted in her. He could hear Sepham still talking behind him, but everything else had shrunk to black, and he could hear a high-pitched ringing begin to thrum in his ears.

His wife was talking to one of the Lilith embers. She was smiling at her. Enjoying herself. How had they found each other? Had she formulated some plan? Decided to double-cross him?

He had to get down there.

EXPLODING BOGGARTS

Eve kept the bright and enthusiastic smile on her face as they walked into the cool of the building. "This is your office, is it? We have offices at home, but they're much bigger than this. My new house is huge. Too big for just one person. Would you like to move in with me? My husband and my father gave it to me because I was bored, and I didn't know what to do with myself. It's got pillars. It's very fancy. I might need some new clothes. Would you like to go shopping? We haven't been properly introduced, but I know all about you. You're Wellingsley, yes? I've seen photos of you." She kept up the barrage of peppy conversation and was, at this stage, thoroughly sick of the sound of her own voice.

Wellingsley, who looked a little rattled, turned and looked at her. "Photos of me? Where?"

"The main office. My husband has a book full of photos of women, and you're one of them, said Eve. Just enough to interest her but not give too much away. "He likes paying attention to other women. It's kind of his thing."

"That's unfortunate," said Wellingsley, who was moving a pile of papers from a chair to a table. "And awkward. I'm sorry."

"It's fine," said Eve. "It's great, even. It's absolutely going to work for good. I have a plan."

"Really?" said Wellingsley. "Well, good on you. That's great. What a fantastic can-do attitude. I'm impressed."

Eve nodded. "I am," she said. "It's going to work out really well. It's going to be empowering. For women everywhere. My plan, that it." She stared at Wellingsley closely, trying to see if she could detect any note of understanding or awareness. Was there any Lilith there she could connect with?

"Great," said Wellingsley, dropping eye contact.

"It looks nice in here," said Eve, realising she might be being a little too intense. "I'm a bit of an interior designer myself, you know. I've worked on lots of different rooms. Well, room. The same one redone a lot of times."

"Wait," said Wellingsley, "I do need to ask more about this. Can we just go back a minute? Your husband has a photo of me?"

"Yes."

"In his office?"

"Yes. In a folder. Or a file."

"And you're going to deal with it?"

"I'm going to deal with several things, but him having photos of you is one of them."

Wellingsley glanced around nervously. "Okay. Well, I should just let you know that I've never been in a relationship with a married man. And I've decided to become celibate again anyway."

"Oh", said Eve, "that's funny. I was practically a virgin for ages. But now I reject the whole notion of virginity. As if someone having sex with you can define things that much. I'm very into feminism, you know."

"I might not be a fan, actually. I'm mulling it over at the moment. But you understand that I am not involved with your husband, right?"

Eve stared at her.

Wellingsley stared back.

"Do you feel anything?" asked Eve with a whisper. "Any connection between us? Or anyone else?"

"No," whispered Wellingsley, stepping back. "I don't. I think I need to go and find Fae."

The room filled with a deep silence.

Wellingsley didn't breathe.

Eve giggled, a huge grin spreading across her face. "It's okay, don't worry. I just thought you might have a clue, but it doesn't matter if you don't. You'll understand soon enough. At this stage, you're just a… what's the word? Pawn, yes, you're just a pawn."

"I don't like that much either," said Wellingsley, feeling suddenly self-conscious. "I don't know you or your husband from Adam."

"Oh, that was very good," she said. "That was excellent. Was that on purpose? You're very funny. I'm serious about you coming to stay with me, though. I need a friend. Or two. There's someone else I want to meet today. A woman called Apple. She's also in the photos. I thought we could all get together and have a sleepover or something. That sounds like something that girly girls would do."

"Apple?" said Wellingsley, eyes widening. "Apple the sex worker?'

Eve shrugged. "I don't know. Red hair." She pulled a piece of paper from her pocket and read the address. "This woman here. She needs to become our friend. You and Apple need to become friends, and I need to be there, too. To oversee things. We'll be a trio."

Wellingsley shook her head vehemently. "No, we won't. She's awful. She sells her body for sex, you know. And she's…well, there's all sorts of vectors of disease stuff that Fae could tell you about if you're interested. It's pretty unpleasant. Fae absolutely wouldn't want you to mix with her."

"The whole point of me being here is so I don't have people controlling who I see and what I do," said Eve, "and I'm pretty sure they aren't going to be watching me all the time, so I should be safe."

Wellingsley frowned. "What do you mean by watching you?"

"No, I said they *won't* be watching me," stressed Eve. "They won't be. They've got cameras everywhere, but I think I guilt-tripped Dad enough to make sure he'll be leaving me alone for a while. My husband is another story. He'll want to see everything I do." She looked at the walls of the room. "I feel like they only have cameras outside, but I could be wrong. I still have a lot I need to get my head around."

"Look," said Wellingsley. "I don't know your personal situation, but I'm sorry if you and your husband are having struggles. I don't think that wandering around Sydney looking for new people is our best course of action, but why don't you help me with planning the Ladies Academy?"

Eve wrinkled her nose. "The what?"

"The Ladies Academy. It's Fae's brainchild. She's a visionary, you know. An ideas woman. She's setting up an academy to teach women how to be ladies, to help them to fulfil their feminine destiny. To give them other choices in a world of rampant feminism."

Eve crossed her arms and looked at her, head tilted slightly to the side. "You're really not what I expected," she said.

Wellingsley smiled uncertainly. "What do you mean?"

"You're just not what I expected. Not what I thought I'd find when I—"

"I wasn't aware you expected anything of me, considering we just met."

"Well, I kind of knew about you. I'd heard some stuff. And I made some assumptions. But you're not at all like her."

"Like who?"

"I thought I'd feel something," said Eve. "I thought there would be some kind of connection. We used to know each other. We were practically best friends. But it's like we're total strangers.'

Eve signed and perched on the edge of a chair. 'But I'll work something out soon, don't worry."

"Right," said Wellingsley briskly. "Will you please just excuse me for a moment?"

"Wait," said Eve, holding up one hand. "Can you hear yelling?"

There was definitely a kerfuffle coming from the other end of the house. Wellingsley headed down the dark corridor toward the noise, and Eve followed her. At the end of the hall, there was a small kitchenette, and the door was open just enough to see two figures who were engaged in a full and frank exchange of views.

"Who are they?" whispered Eve.

"It's Restarian, Fae's assistant, but I don't know the handsome man in the suit."

"She says you're no use at all, so what am I paying you for?" said the suited man aggressively.

"I am useful," blustered Restarian. "Who's doing all the driving? Who's clearing all the garbage? Me."

The man in the suit shook his head. "No," he said. "She said you're not being helpful, so that's that. I have a certain loyalty to her, you know. And if she wants you gone, you're gone."

"Oh, you bloody well do not have loyalty to her. You're a manipulative arsehole, Jared. I think this whole thing sounds very fishy, if you ask me. Choosing your little tame Fae to do an important job for the Upper Realms? That's patently bullshit. She's a dear, but she can't do this kind of thing."

There was silence for a moment.

"Do you have any idea who I'm working for?" said Jared.

"Adam and God," said Restarian. "That's who you're working for. You're working for them to keep the Lilith embers apart."

"That's right," whispered Eve. "That's what he's doing. That's what I'm here about, too," she added as an aside to Wellingsley.

Wellingsley's confused expression deepened.

"Wrong," said Jared. "I am working for far more powerful

beings. And if I'm pissed at you, they're pissed at you. And you're not useful anymore."

Restarian looked up into the air as if he could hear something coming from a great distance, and in front of Wellingsley's eyes, his form began to change from a man into a black, scaly, squat creature.

He glanced up into the air around him, a haunted look on his face.

Jared crossed his arms and shook his head sadly. "The Eons want a word with you," he said, and the creature that had been Restarian seemed to answer a voice that only he could hear.

"No, I was just," he said. "Yes, I know, but…"

Then he disappeared as if he were being sucked into a huge cosmic tube. There may have been screaming. Jared flicked some dust from the lapels of his jacket, and then he too disappeared.

Eve and Wellingsley stared into the space that had been vacated.

"That was unpleasant," said Eve. "The poor boggert. They get such a rough end of the stick. Now he'll have to start his whole progression again as a whelk or something. It will take ages to work his way up to boggert level again.

"Fae," said Wellingsley, her face blanching. "I need Fae." She grabbed her phone and pressed Fae's name.

"No, you don't," said Eve, firmly taking the phone from her ear. "Fae is not who you need at the moment, although the fact that she's being exploited too adds a different dimension to this whole debacle. I'm going to go now, though. You should come with me. I know what I'm doing, I promise."

Wellingsley stared at her, her face still white.

"Are you all right?" asked Eve with concern. "I know this is all new and strange to you," she said, "but I need you to believe me."

The tears spilled down Wellingsley's face. 'Restarian was just here, and then he turned into a monster, and then he disappeared into the air like he was being pulled into another realm. Did you hear him screaming?"

Eve sucked air in through her teeth. "I know," she said. "Very nasty. Not hugely unusual, but nasty, nonetheless."

"But what does it mean?" asked Wellingsley. "What's happening? And why does your voice sound different? It's not all high and girly now."

"What this means is that things are starting to happen. I'm not completely sure of everyone involved at this stage and what their stakes are. I've been working on this for a long time, and we're getting close, but there are still some bits I need to work out."

Wellingsley stared at her. She seemed totally different to the girl she had met a few hours ago. She stood taller, her smile wasn't as scarily expansive, and her hands were placed easily on her hips instead of hovering around her mouth and hair.

"Who… who are you exactly?" asked Wellingsley.

Eve grinned and held out her hand. "I'm Eve. Mother of humankind. And I'm here to rewrite history. Do you have a pair of scissors?"

FEDORAS AND BEST FRIENDS

Eve attacked her thick, long hair with a pair of kitchen scissors she'd found lying on the bench. "Wait," protested Wellingsley with horror. "You can't just cut it all…"

But it was too late. Eve held out great swathes, hacking at it with the scissors, and soon, there were tufts of fuzz sticking up in disarray around her determined face and a pile of hair around her feet.

"You shouldn't have done that," said Wellingsley after a moment.

"Why?" snapped Eve, the rush of adrenaline still bursting through her. "Because hair is your crowning glory? Because the patriarchy has told you that to be a real woman, you have to have long luxurious locks to signify your femininity andmanhood?"

"Er, no," said Wellingsley. "It's just that there's a hairdresser next door who is really nice, and he could have done a much better job than you've just done. You could have gone all waifish and adorable. It would have really suited you. As it is now, people are going to stare. You look like you've just had an emotional breakdown."

Eve pursed her lips and lifted her chin. "I don't care. This is a symbol of my freedom and of my turning my back on the conventional beauty standards of the world." There was a pause. "Do you have a mirror?"

Wellingsley grimaced. "I really wouldn't."

"It doesn't matter anyway," said Eve, shaking her head and steeling herself. "I'm here for important business, and my personal appearance is the absolute least of our concerns. Important events are unfolding, and you, Wellingsley, are an integral yet currently utterly oblivious piece of the puzzle."

"I wish people would stop calling me naïve and oblivious," grumbled Wellingsley. "It's doing nothing for my self-esteem."

"I thought it was what you wanted. I thought that playing dumb was part of this whole vibe you've signed up for. This whole trad fem cosplay you've been enjoying. I mean, I get it. I've been playing dumb and naïve for ages. I was for a while, admittedly, but even after I started to get a brain, I had to pretend."

"It's got nothing to do with being dumb," snapped Wellingsley. "Choosing to turn your back on feminism and the way women are being forced into new and possibly unwelcomed roles is not dumb."

"I didn't say being dumb, I said acting dumb, which is worse. Now that I come to think of it, you try to be forced into that role, the role of being subservient and having no choices and being totally controlled by the men in your life. Try that, with no choice, and then decide how fun it is to dress up in an apron and wait till your man comes in for a visit, and for that to be the only conversation you have all day. Find out what it's like to live with that and then see how fun it is be role play being oppressed. To know that with just a little bit more power, a man could lock you up for the rest of eternity."

"Look, I don't know your background. I don't know anything about you. I am aware that there's something very strange going on here, yes, but I don't think that your bad marriage is a reason to attack me and my choices. How I live my life is not your business."

"No, no," said Eve, covering her mouth with her hands. "I didn't mean to be so rude. It's just that my husband is angry and controlling, and I'm scared of what he might do. We're supposed to be friends. I'm sorry, all right. I have some issues around this whole submissive thing that I clearly need to work through on my own, and it's not your fault."

"Apology accepted," said Wellingsley. "Thank you for that. I appreciate it."

"However," said Eve.

"Ah, not an actual apology then."

"No, it was an apology, but I'm getting back to the original point that you don't know what's going on. Can I at least have you concede that?"

Wellingsley nodded. "Yes."

"And there are otherworldly things going on."

"There is the slight chance that I might not have a complete idea of the actual nature of reality."

"So, you're open to that possibility?" asked Eve. She didn't want to overwhelm the young woman any more than was totally necessary.

"I think I have to be, don't I? It's been a very weird day. I'm either having a mental breakdown, or things might be radically different from how I imagined things to be. And given I'm not the one who just hacked all my hair off, I think I'll have to go with the latter."

Eve's hand went to the top of her head. "Is it very awful?"

"Yes," said Wellingsley, nodding. "It's an absolute fright. Do you want a hat?"

"Probably best," said Eve. "We need to go now."

Wellingsley disappeared into a dark room and came out holding a dark green fedora. "I knew I'd seen this lying around somewhere. No idea where it came from."

Eve took it and placed it on her head at what she hoped was a jaunty angle. "Better?"

"No. Bad in an entirely different way now."

Eve took Wellingsley's hands. "I need you to listen carefully, okay?"

The idea Eve had was enough to count as a plan, she was sure of it. But it was a little rudimentary, and people really needed to listen and do what they were told and not knock her train of thought off its slightly tenuous rails.

"I can do that," said Wellingsley, and Eve smiled with relief.

"And I need you to trust me."

"Why?"

"Because I'm going to ask you to believe some very hard to wrap your head around things very soon, and if we're utter ride or die best friends who have each other's backs entirely and trust each other implicitly, then it'll be easier."

"Just out of interest," said Wellingsley, "have you ever had a best friend?"

"A best friend? No."

"Or… any friends at all?"

"I've lived in an expansive bubble of reality that terraforms for me whenever I want it to change, watched over with eagle eyes by my father and husband who I have a kind of brother dynamic with. There hasn't been a lot of opportunity to make many friends."

"That explains a lot," said Wellingsley. "You've really been kept a prisoner?"

Eve shrugged. "I've had everything I could ever want. I've had clothes and jewels and books and food. I can't really complain. But yes, I essentially was. And I'm terrified that it will happen again, only worse."

"Are you really Eve? Like, Adam and Eve?"

Eve nodded. "But what you know down here and what reality is are two different things. It's not up to all the hype, I promise you."

"What, so the Bible isn't true?"

Eve looked aghast. "You didn't think it's true, did you?"

"Who me? No, not at all. I'm not a Christian. But a lot of other people do. And even those who don't identify as a Christian know all about it."

"Do you believe I'm who I say I am?"

"Why not? At this stage, I can either believe what people tell me or go mad, and quite honestly, I couldn't afford the psych bills now that Dad found out I've dropped out of law and has cancelled my allowance."

"Oh, look, we're both disappointing our fathers massively," said Eve. "Maybe we really are destined to be best friends."

"Look, about that Eve thing. Did you really cause original sin to take over?"

"I thought you didn't believe in it all?"

"No, no, I don't, but I'd be interested to know how much of what Western society believes in has a basis in reality."

"Well, I don't feel like we really have time for a deep dive, but technically, kind of, yes. I ate the fruit, but there is context. Lots of context. But what I can say is that very little of this was my fault. I was manipulated and taken advantage of. There's a whole story."

"Yes," said Wellingsley, "the snake, right? It all came down to the snake."

"No," exclaimed Eve. "Absolutely not the snake. See, this is the whole issue! This is why I'm here! It's got nothing to do with the snake. Nothing at all. Well, that's not quite nothing. She was very naughty for a while, I must admit, but if I hear any talk of 'asking for it', then we will have big problems. Massive issues. I won't hear a word of that. But it wasn't the snake, all right."

Wellingsley stared, taken aback for a moment at the passion in Eve's eyes. "Okay, not the snake. Got it. I was kind of joking, though. I didn't think there would be an actual snake."

"Oh, don't misunderstand me. There was one. A snake, that is. A woman who was a goddess who was also a snake. And that's what I need to talk to you about and try to fix. I've got to repair all the damage that was done. She's amazing. You'll love her. And that's why I need your help."

"All right." Wellingsley took Eve's hands in hers. "All right. I'll help you."

Eve threw her arms around Wellingsley's neck. "Thank you," she said. "This will make everything so much easier. And what I need you to remember is that I was a very good daughter. And a passable mother of all mankind, but I didn't really ask for any of those jobs, so any deficiencies are probably down to a lack of passion. But I want you to know that I am, and always have been, an excellent and committed wife to my husband."

Wellingsley nodded. "Sure, of course. I've got no reason to think otherwise."

"Exactly," said Eve. "Until things were irrevocably broken."

"Ah," said Wellingsley. "I've heard that before. Mainly with my parents."

"Good," said Eve. "You've got some context. Now. Let's go. We need to go and find Apple, and then I want you to meet my boyfriend."

THE WHEELS ARE FALLING OFF

"I need updates," snarled Adam as soon as he saw Jared materialize in front of him.

"Just wait, man," said Jared. "My legs aren't solid yet. I can't talk with bits of myself missing."

Adam was pacing, and by the look on his face, he had been for some time.

"Why are you all sweaty?" said Jared as he took a seat in the one recently vacated by God.

"Don't sit there," snapped Adam. "That's not your place. Move."

Jared stood and wandered over to the panel of screens that were flickering desultorily between different earth-bound scenes.

"Everything under control down there?" he asked, looking out at Adam from under his long fringe, his eyes dark and inscrutable. "Nothing dramatic happened in the last day or so?"

"No, it's fucking not under control. Eve is talking to bloody Wellingsley! How do you not know that? I'd think you'd have a better idea than I would. You're the one who spends all your time down there. What are you doing on Earth anyway? What's your real motivation?" His eyes were wild.

Jared shrugged. "It's more entertaining. Humans are batshit crazy. Really ridiculous. And when you bring together humans and the Upper Realms." He brought his hands together, linking his fingers, before tearing them apart with a "whoosh" noise. "It's chaos. Really, a great deal of death and destruction."

"And that's fun for you, is it?"

"It keeps me busy. Whiles away the long, endless millennia of pointlessness. Gives me something to do. Anyway, I wouldn't want to hear any judgment from you. You're in absolutely no position to criticize me for getting involved in human business. You're an absolute bugger for it. You and your dad. Continually getting involved in shenanigans that you don't need to. And I wouldn't worry about the Wellingsley and Eve thing."

Adam took a deep breath. "I've brought you here for a reason."

"I'd hope so," said Jared. "As I said, you're all sweaty, and you're pacing around like a maniac. What's the matter?"

Adam placed his hand over his mouth and muttered something very low and very muffled.

"What?" said Jared, frowning and walking toward him. "Speak up. I can't hear you."

Adam glanced around, a hunted look on his face. "We might be overheard," he said. "I don't know who might be listening."

"Well, this was a bloody stupid place to bring me, wasn't it? Why didn't you find somewhere we could have had some privacy?"

"My wife is down there," snapped Adam, "and I'm not happy about it."

"Surely that's your issue?" replied Jared.

"And she's with Wellingsley," he said.

Jared was absolutely delighted by this situation, but kept it to himself. "How do you know they're together?" he asked.

"I saw them on the camera. Together. She's just supposed to be buying shoes and watching movies and eating avocado toast. Not meeting up with Lilith embers! This is not okay. My wife knows

Lilith. Knew Lilith. If there's any part of her that's conscious in this Wellingsley character, then who knows what will happen. They might… call to each other or something."

"Don't be delusional," soothed Jared. "Nothing's going to happen. You're catastrophizing. They would have just run into each other by coincidence and—"

"I didn't employ you for commentary. I employed you for action."

"As I said at the beginning of this," said Jared, "there are a lot of moving pieces. There are a lot of competing parties, and nothing is easy."

"So, what you're saying is, the situation isn't over yet."

"Yes. No. Not yet." He shrugged. "You're a businessman. A leader. You know what it's like to have people working under you. Mad as a pack of cats. Or like herding cats."

"So you don't think that Eve trapsing around Sydney, fraternizing with your targets, is an issue."

"It is such a non-issue that it barely warrants talking about. It is zero percent of a problem. I mean, what it says about your marriage is a whole other kettle of fish, but as for the Lilith situation, it's fine. Fae will do her job admirably. She's a consummate professional."

"Maybe I should go down there," said Adam.

"Euch, no, terrible idea," said Jared emphatically. "You'd hate it, and you'd just get in the way. There are too many Upper Realm characters down there as it is."

"Who else?" asked Adam suspiciously. "I'm finding it very strange that all of a sudden it's like a fucking Lilith convention down there."

"There have been some wildcards come into play," said Jared. "Some competing interests. I can't control everything, you know. Remember Asmodeus?"

"Oh, him," spat Adam. "He's such a weirdo. Those bloody red leather pants he used to wear. Such a loser. Total poser."

"That's as may be, but he's down there too."

"What?" gasped Adam, the blood dropping from his face, fear replacing colour. "What's he doing there? I definitely don't want to run into him. He's the number one Lilith fan. Idiot."

"As I said, a lot of moving pieces."

Adam started pacing again, one hand rubbing furiously at his forehead. "But he'd be wanting to make her whole again, wouldn't he? How… how has this happened?"

Jared sighed and shook his head, reaching out to pat Adam comfortingly on the shoulder as he paced past. "Look, I wouldn't worry too much about it. He's a demon, right? Probably incompetent. I wouldn't pay it any mind."

"This is a disaster," said Adam. "Do you have any other bombshells for me?"

Jared scrunched up his face as if in deep thought. "There's Fae. There's Asmodeus. There's the normal rabble who live down there but don't have much to do with important business. Can't think of anyone else off the top of my head."

"The whole point of you," blustered Adam, "Is that you know exactly what is going on."

"What I do know is that you're not needed down there."

Adam steered fixedly off into the distance. "I don't like where this is heading," he said. "There are way too many people involved. We should have kept everything far apart. This was a terrible idea. Of yours."

"Trust me," said Jared again, but he was increasingly worried that his words were falling on deaf ears.

"And I'm very uncomfortable with my wife being anywhere near this. Everyone thinks she's so sweet, but she's a crafty little cow who needs controlling."

"You shouldn't speak about your wife like that," Jared said mildly. "She's in a big house, and she's just going to go shopping and buy shoes and watch TV and that womanly kind of stuff."

"But she's not," shrieked Adam. "She's patently not! She's becoming involved!"

"Adam," said Jared, taking hold of the man's arms and looking into his eyes. "You're too good for all of this. You've got bigger things to worry about. Remember? You're going to test the waters to see if Daddy will step aside. And take over by force if need be. I've still got lots of irons in the fire concerning that, remember? You shouldn't be concerning yourself with all this women's business. It's below you."

"But," said Adam through gritted teeth, "if Lilith forms again, then she will stop me from doing everything I want to do. She hates me and always assumes the worst."

"You think she's the only thing standing in your way, do you?" said Jared, doubtfully.

"Absolutely."

"Well, you need to trust me then."

"Do you know," said Adam, "that the more you tell me to trust you, the more emphatically I do not."

"I am a trickster," said Jared, shrugging his shoulders. "You knew this at the outset. It's not as if it's a big reveal. But I do think that you should spend more time plotting the takeover rather than thinking about what's happening down on that godforsaken little rock. You have an expansive mind, and I think you need to put it where it can be best used."

And the more Jared encouraged him to stay where he was, the more Adam realized he needed to get down to Earth.

MEDITATIONS ON THE NAMING OF FISH

"I think I should go down to Earth," said Adam as he strode into the small, usually unused room.

God was wrestling with a swathe of green, sequined fabric, holding it against a puce background, with his head thoughtfully cocked to one side.

"It would only be a super quick trip I'd need to take," said Adam, trying to sound breezy and casual and not like every fibre of his being was screaming at the importance of what he was saying.

God didn't reply. He had leaned the ream of fabric against a large mirror ball and was admiring the effect of the sequins reflecting in the hundreds of tiny mirrors.

"I just..." Adam's attention was suddenly focused on something else entirely. "What's been happening in here? What on earth are you doing?"

"Welcome to the Party Action Planning Room, or PAPR, as your dad insists on calling it," came a voice from somewhere in front of him.

He wrinkled his nose in distaste and looked around. "What's that smell?"

"Urine," said Sepham, appearing from behind a cabinet containing self-applying wrapping paper. "Some creatures hid in here recently when they were being chased by a Siberian tiger, and nobody noticed, so they sort of made it their own, I'm afraid. As you can see, they've made a dreadful mess. We need to get someone on to clearing it."

"Eve did all of that," said God. "Well, she oversaw the staff, anyway. I'm noticing her absence more and more each day. Can you reallocate that role to someone else, Sepham?"

The angel smiled. "Consider it done."

A pile of old magazines toppled over as something brown and quadrupedal scurried away.

"This place is turning into a bloody zoo," grumbled Adam. "You can't walk five paces without kicking something small and furry. It's getting ridiculous."

"I know, I know. I'm working on it," said God. 'I've got a committee on to making a pocket reality for recently extinct animals, but it's on the rapidly growing to-do list that I'm trying to wrangle. I could really do with some more help around here."

"Speaking of that," said Adam. "That reminds me. I think I should go down to Earth. To check on Eve. Yes. I should go down to Earth to check on Eve."

God and Sepham were now flicking through a deluxe helium balloon catalogue and not listening to him in any convincing way.

Adam waited for a moment. "Well?" he prompted eventually.

"Eve? She's doing fine. She'd let us know if she wasn't. She's happy with her big house and her shopping. You know what she's like—a simple girl. Bless."

"Bless," agreed Sepham benignly.

"Still," said Adam. "I feel like I should check on her. Go to Earth and check on her. Now."

"She's fine," said God again, giving Adam attention for the first time. He peered over his glasses. "Do you doubt that I know what I'm talking about? She's fine. She's having a bit of a break from… all this."

"Yes, and the place appears to now be covered in piss."

"Covered is an exaggeration," protested Sepham. "More of a sprinkling, I'd say. Definitely not covered."

"She needs time to herself," said God firmly. "She doesn't need checking on. And I could turn the cameras on to her if I needed to, but we are giving her some privacy."

"But she's my wife," snapped Adam.

"Yes, she is. And she needs some time to herself and some space."

"A husband and wife shouldn't need space from each other."

"Haven't you been living in separate quarters for the past five hundred years?" asked Sepham innocently.

"Exactly, good point," agreed God. "Privacy and space are essential in a healthy relationship. There needs to be a bit of mystery. I've been reading about codependency, you know."

"You've changed," grumbled Adam under his breath.

"Yes, and not before time," agreed God.

"I need to go down to Earth," Adam repeated.

"Eve is fine," said God firmly.

"Yes, but…" Adam found his plan slipping away and cast around furiously for a legitimate reason as to why he should be allowed to go down to Earth. "I think that I should—"

"Wait," said Sepham. "You hate Earth. You said you'd never go down there again. You swore off it in no uncertain terms."

He saw another furry head disappear beneath a pile of velour bean bags and had a sudden bolt of inspiration. "Sorry, did I say Eve? I meant animals. I've been thinking that I should oversee the animals. The ones that are going extinct. You know, do some reconnaissance. You yourself said you need some help with jobs, and at the rate that humans are killing animals, there won't be any left if we wait much longer. Well, it's not very respectful of you and your creation if we let that happen. I could do some investigation. See what's going on."

God frowned and looked over his glasses again. "Animals? You have absolutely no interest in animals. I've never once heard you express an interest in them."

"If you could just cast your mind back," said Adam, changing to a slightly haughty tone, "I was in fact the one who named them all in the first place. Remember? I've been invested from the beginning. I have been integral in their overall development and have, may I go so far as to say, had a kind of benign overseeing role with them over time."

"Oh, yes," said Sepham wryly. "The Tasselled Wobbegong and the Sarcastic Fringehead. You did an amazing job with the naming of the fish, especially. Really covered yourself with glory there."

"There were a lot of fish to get around," hissed Adam. "Do you have any idea how many names I had to come up with? It's a bloody miracle I didn't just number them all and call it good enough."

"No, that's true," said God, a thoughtful look on his face. "You did name the animals. You really have been there for them from the beginning. You took your job very seriously. I shouldn't discount that."

"The Wrinkled Scrod," Sepham said under his breath.

"Exactly," said Adam. "Just because I don't relentlessly babble on about my interests all the time like some people, it doesn't mean I don't have a deep and passionate regard for the whole animal kingdom."

"Spiny Lumpfish," Sepham continued.

"So, what's your plan, then?" asked God. "I'll need something a bit more concrete before I agree to this, you know. I'd rather not have you down there running around willy-nilly, especially given that I've temporarily lost Eve, too."

"I'm thinking just some basic reconnaissance," Adam said.

"See what's going on. Check the lay of the land." He cast around for some more amorphous expressions he could use.

"Wahoo," said Sepham into his hors d'oeuvre catalogue. "You called one of God's magnificent creations a Wahoo."

"Why are you reeling off stupid animal names?" God finally asked.

"I think," said Adam, "he's trying to use it as proof that I don't know what I'm doing when it comes to animals."

"How strange," said God, frowning at Sepham. "Do you think you two could benefit from some couples counselling, or the like? I don't enjoy seeing you two, who are both so important to me, not getting along."

"We're not a couple," snapped Sepham.

"You know what I mean. You're a couple adjacent. You do spend a lot of time in proximity to each other."

"Anyway," said Adam, "the sooner I get down there and start overseeing, the sooner I can stop them all getting killed. Or whatever it is that happens to them. Eaten. Do they still eat them?"

"Don't go and talk to Eve, though," said God. "Leave her alone. She needs time to herself."

"No, of course not. Nothing could be further from my mind."

"You're sure you don't want to help plan the party?" enquired God.

"No, really. That's never been my idea of fun."

"Whereas I," said Sepham gleefully, "am a big fan. This is all super fun, and I think it's going to be a great event."

"You will come back for it, of course," said God, and it was more of an order than a request. "Everyone is going to be here. It's a big thank you to everyone for being part of my development over the past few millennia. A way of giving something back. Nothing says thank you more than taco stations and balloon animals."

"I'll leave the whole thing in your capable hands and drop in for a Bellini," said Adam.

"And can you please liaise with Sepham on the animal front? Let him know how it's going."

"The balloon animals?" asked Adam uncertainly, forgetting for a moment the whole basis of his cunning plan.

"No, the extinct ones. The hopefully not extinct ones, I mean. The whole point of you going to Earth."

"Oh, yes, of course, of course. I'm already thinking about it. Action plans and all that."

God frowned at him, an uncharacteristically perceptive look on his face. "Adam, is there something that you want to tell me? Is everything all right?"

"Yep, all good. Just… getting on task. Looking for a way forward. Saving the animals and all that. I'll definitely be back for the party."

ADAM IS VERY UNPOPULAR

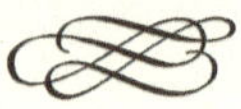

"Were you a horse girl?" Wellingsley asked Eve as she followed her down the busy street.

"What do you mean, a horse girl?" Eve was squinting up at the tall buildings that surrounded them, blocking the light and creating unpleasant wind tunnels that the city planners had clearly decided weren't worth worrying about. She had a vague idea where she was going, but she was still a little worried.

"Did you ride horses when you were a girl?" asked Wellingsley.

"I was never a girl," said Eve, looking around at the storefronts and irritating people who were trying to get around her while she dawdled. "I was created like this. Physically like this, I mean."

"Ah, okay. There's just a weird power about short women who rode horses when they were younger. They feel like they can take on the world."

Eve felt a surge of delight. "I've done a lot of work. A lot. I used to defer to everyone all the time. Then I decided I didn't want to do that anymore, but I still had to act all sweet and deferential. I was playing the long game, you see."

Wellingsley nodded. "Yes, I get that. I understand. Did you have really overpowering parents?"

Eve smiled. "In a manner of speaking, yes. One, really, but yes. Big shoes to fill." She glanced around. "I think this is where we need to be. Around here somewhere."

Wellingsley grabbed Eve's arm and pointed to a figure leaving a building across the road. She was a tall, striking red-headed woman, arm in arm with a shorter woman. They were deep in conversation, and the red-headed woman was glancing around nervously as if looking for someone. "That's her. That's Apple. And the one with her is Garbage Girl."

Eve pulled Wellingsley into the street and ignored the honks that rose around them.

"Apple," yelled Eve in a surprisingly loud voice as the two sisters hurried away down the street. "Apple, I need to talk to you."

The women looked around, eyes widening in surprise when they alighted on Wellingsley.

"Oh, shit, she's recognised me. They're going to think this has something to do with Fae. They probably think we're here to accost them about sex work."

"We're not here to accost you about sex work," called out Eve, deciding that they didn't have time to play games as the crowds around them were now parting far more rapidly than they had previously.

"In fact, I'm a big fan. Of sexual empowerment. Keen to hear more about it at some stage if you have time."

The two women had stopped, and they quickly caught up to them.

"Hi," said Eve, smiling broadly. "Hi there. I'm Eve, and this is Wellingsley."

"We've met,' Janie said firmly, glaring at Wellingsley.

"Have we, though?" said Wellingsley. "I feel like met is an overstatement. I mean, I was there, but etiquette was thin on the ground."

Eve squeezed her arm. "Let's not get sidetracked." She stepped toward Apple and took her hand. The taller woman didn't pull away.

"I need to talk to you," said Eve. "It's of huge significance, and I need to tell you something very important."

"She's probably going to ask you to trust her in a moment," said Wellingsley wryly, "and against your better judgment, you will. She's very—"

"Authentic," said Janie, frowning and looking back and forth between the two women.

"Yes, that's it. Oddly authentic. Good description."

"I think we're in the way," said Janie, noticing that the people having to step off the path to pass them were glaring and muttering.

"Is this anything about Lilith?" asked Apple. "Me being Lilith. Or Asmodeus. Do any of those two names mean anything to you?"

Eve looked shocked. "You already know?"

"I've just had some random demon tell me I've got bits of some dead goddess latched onto me. I don't know what, or who, I'm part of, but I can assure you that not only do I not know everything, I have no idea what's going on."

"Wait, is your name Wellingsley?" asked Janie.

"Yes. I'm sorry about all the Fae stuff. I kind of got swept along with all the—" started Wellingsley.

Apple held up a piece of paper with two names on it. "We were looking for you. We wanted to find you. And we did." Apple frowned. "That was disturbingly easy."

"Of course it was," said Eve. "It's all happening, see? We're meant to be doing this. I'm meant to be doing this. Lilith is finding her way. Everything is going to be all right."

Eve grabbed Apple and Wellingsley's hands and pulled them closer, as well as moving them against the wall of a shop and out of the foot traffic. "We need to go somewhere safe. He wants to find you, and if he does, then I don't know what will happen. I need to keep you safe so that we can bring her back. Do you understand?"

There was a wobble in the air, and across the street, a man popped into existence. Most of the people around him seemed not to notice, as if a random man manifesting in the middle of the street were a daily occurrence, but Eve's grip on Apple and Wellingsley tightened.

"He's here," she hissed, her eyes locked on the back of the man's head. He glanced around before beginning to walk down the street. A chill ran through her as he looked around. "Damn it all," she said. "We've got less time than I thought. I don't know how he convinced Dad to let him down here, but he's going to be looking for you two, and we can't let him find you."

"Who?" asked Apple, standing on her tiptoes and peering across the road to get a closer look at him. "Who's that? And why does he want us? What's this got to do with Fae?"

"Listen," hissed Eve. "Yes, Fae has got something to do with this, but not in the way you think. That, over there, is my husband. It's Adam. As in, yes, Adam and Eve. He's looking for you two, and we can't let him find you. He's a dreadful, horrible person, and he is very, very dangerous."

Apple placed her hand on her chest and swayed a little.

"Are you all right?" asked Eve, a look of concern on her face. "What's the matter?"

"I believe you," said Apple softly. "I feel very strange. As if bits of me are floating off. And I feel a deep revulsion toward that man."

"Yes," said Eve eagerly. "You know it's true, don't you?"

"Can you feel that?" she said, turning her head to look at Wellingsley. "Something is happening."

Wellingsley frowned and glanced back and forth between Eve and Apple. "No," she said. "I don't feel anything. What are you talking about?"

"Don't worry," said Eve, dismissing her. "You will later. But we need to move. Now."

"We could go upstairs to the hotel," said Janie suddenly. "Asmodeus is still there."

"No, not him," said Eve. "I didn't even know he was here, dammit."

"Do you know him too?"

"I know of him," she clarified, "and he has his own motivations too. I don't want it to be him; I want it to be me. He shouldn't get to do such a special thing. Not a man. No, we need to get to my boyfriend's place. He's the one who will help us bring all this together. He's been here for a while, undercover. Getting things organized."

"Your boyfriend," said Janie, looking at Eve with something approaching respect for the first time. "Your husband has just disappeared down George Street, and now we're off to find your boyfriend? Nice. I quite like you. I vote that we go. Apple?"

Apple nodded, clearly finding it difficult to form a coherent sentence.

"Let's go," said Eve. "Can someone get me a taxi?"

Wellingsley's phone rang. Mum sprang up on the screen.

She declined the call.

They bundled into a taxi, Eve taking the front seat, everyone else squashing, fairly illegally, into the back.

They sat in silence.

Wellingsley's phone rang again.

Eve gazed over her shoulder. "You should answer it. It's your mum."

Wellingsley declined again.

"She'll just be growling at me about something. I don't have the capacity for all of this right now."

It rang again. This time, Fae flashed on the screen.

"Fuck me, you're popular," said Apple. "Just turn it off. Unless you want us all to hear your conversations when you eventually give in and answer."

Wellingsley turned it off.

A MATTER OF BUNKERS

The man opened the door a crack, as if to check who it was before throwing it wide open and ushering the four women inside. As soon as the door was shut behind them, he grabbed Eve in a crushing embrace, and she wrapped her arms around him. The next thirty seconds were very awkward for everyone involved.

Apparently, except for them.

"I love you," he murmured into her newly cropped hair. "This looks amazing. You're so beautiful. This short hair is stunning. So choppy. So risky. You're an absolute style icon, and I adore you. I'm so glad we found each other again in all the impossibilities."

"My love," she said, her hand reaching to cup his cheek and rubbing her thumb over his lips. "I'm here now. Everything is okay. Are any new memories coming back?"

"Some," he said. "More. But not everything."

They kissed deeply.

Apple cleared her throat. "While I am a big fan of whatever is happening here, I can't help but feel we should be somewhere else."

"Yes, of course," said the man, breaking away reluctantly from

Eve's lips. "The bunker, you're absolutely right. Everything is prepared for you."

"Actually, my first thought wasn't bunker, my first thought was you two having the private moment that you so clearly need, but okay, keep talking."

"A bunker," said Janie eagerly. "We love a bunker."

"Really?" said Wellingsley, confused. "Why do you both love a bunker?"

"What's not to love?" said Janie. "Safe, secure, hermetically sealed. You can withstand the apocalypse and head back up when everything has died down."

"Rows and rows of tinned food, pumped air, maybe some of those plants that grow in water. Fabulous," continued Apple.

"You two are very odd, has anyone ever told you that?" said Wellingsley.

"Oh, god, yes," they both said together. "Many times."

"You're not twins, are you?" asked Wellingsley.

Eve's face registered a look of shock.

"Twins? What?"

"Calm down. We're not twins. Don't be ridiculous. She's six years older than me. Do we look like twins?"

Wellingsley shrugged noncommittally.

"Why would that be a problem, though?" asked Apple, looking to Eve, who had pulled herself out of her boyfriend's clutches.

"I don't know, she admitted. "I don't know if Lilith being in just one of you would be a problem or not. It just sounded like something extra I don't want to have to deal with."

Zeus stepped forward and locked the door. "Let's get them safe and sound downstairs."

Wellingsley's phone rang, and she looked at it in surprise.

"I thought you turned that off," snapped Eve.

"I did," said Wellingsley, seeing Mum flash on the screen yet again. "That's weird, it just spontaneously turned itself on."

"Just answer it, for god's sake," said Janie. "Then we can go and explore this bunker I've heard so much about."

"Have you?" said Zeus uncertainly. "I hope you haven't built up too much excitement about it."

"It's just an expression," snapped Janie. "Wellingsley, answer the bloody phone."

"Mum probably turned it on with the force of her will," muttered Wellingsley before answering it.

"Hi, Mum. Yes. No, I'm fine. No, nothing happened. I was just out of range. What? You did? Are you all right? Do you think you should go to the hospital then? Do you think you might… No, that's fine. I'll keep my phone on."

"She okay? "asked Apple.

"She just had a funny turn about fifteen minutes ago. Felt like she was out of her body or something. She wanted to make sure it wasn't anything to do with me, which is strange and out of character for her to even ask. Maybe she's menopausal, finally."

"Come on," said Zeus, leading them down the corridor. "This way."

They walked down a corridor that led to some stairs that took them down a narrow passageway, which became smaller and more metal-looking as they progressed. Janie tapped the wall. "Nice," she said. "Is this fibre cement?"

"Yes," said Zeus, turning around and looking at her appreciatively. "It is. You know your cladding."

"I do," she nodded in agreement. "Apple and I spent many happy hours planning and designing our own bunkers when we were kids."

"Nice," said Zeus. "I appreciate that."

"You two are so weird," said Wellingsley.

"Oh, sorry, Little House on the Prairie," snapped Apple. "You were more busy focussing on destroying two hundred years of female empowerment, I suppose. No time for bunker planning."

"If we could just," said Zeus uncertainly as they stopped in front of a heavy metal door, "maybe stop the bickering. I didn't think they'd be like this with each other," he said, looking to Eve.

"Like what with each other?" snapped Apple.

"Well, hate each other."

"We don't hate each other; we just have some radically divergent views on some fundamental topics. I'm sure we could have some middle ground if we tried."

"How did you think we would be with each other?" asked Apple, frowning. "In fact, why are you thinking about us at all?"

"I don't know. I just felt there might be a certain bond. A certain basic understanding between the two of you."

"It's Fae's fault," said Eve wryly. "There probably would have been a bond before Fae got to them. She sewed discontent and sprinkled ill will and division."

"She does that," said Apple and Janie together. "That's exactly what she does."

"She does not," protested Wellingsley. "She lets people be exactly who they want to be without preconceptions or expectations to behave in a certain way. She's a real feminist."

Zeus finally managed to unlock the door, and he ushered them inside as it swung open. Janie and Apple exchanged a brief, thrilled expression.

"Please don't think I'm complaining," said Apple. "But why do you have a bunker? What's the whole point of this?"

"Apart from the basic fact that it's incredibly cool and fabulous," said Janie hurriedly. "Take that as a given. Love this polished reinforced concrete. Very Cold War chic."

"It's for you," he said. "For you and Wellingsley, that is. And… well, it was going to be for some others too, but unfortunately, Fae has had her way with them, so they're no longer part of this. Now it's just… It's just you two."

"What?" said Apple, her face ashen. "What has Fae done?'

"I knew there was something deeply wrong with her," said Janie. "What has she been doing?"

"What? God no," protested Zeus. "She's not killing people. Stop saying that. She's—"

"She's killing their ember of Lilith," clarified Eve.

"She is extinguishing the embers of Lilith. She's letting loose the ember of Lilith, and…" he saw the look of absolute confusion on their faces. "Okay, sit down," he said, gesturing to a sofa and several dining chairs. "Let's start from the basics. Eve, would you like to tell them the whole story?"

She nodded earnestly, and Apple and Janie made themselves comfortable. "Yes, I think it's my place to do so. It's time."

So, she told them. Of Lilith. And of Adam. Of herself. The Garden of Eden. And of how God disembodied Lilith and attached her ember onto women throughout time and Earth. Of how he then rebooted history. Until finally all the pieces ended up here and now. And Fae was dulling their light. But Fae wasn't exactly the bad guy here—it was Adam who wanted all this to happen. But she wasn't precisely the good guy either, Eve clarified.

"Yes," said Apple, clapping her hands and jumping to her feet when that final piece was put into place. "I knew that there was something up with her! And I knew it was personal!"

"Yes," said Eve. "She was trying to stop the Lilith part of you from growing. The sex part, I assume."

"Hang on," said Apple. "My sexual expression is a deep and integral part of who I am. It's the core of me. Are you trying to tell me I'm only a sex worker because this ancient demoness thing glommed onto me back in the day? Because I'm going to have a big problem with that. What about free will?"

"I don't know," said Eve, a note of exasperation in her voice. "I don't know how all of it works. I don't even know if my dad knows, to be honest."

"And what about me? asked Wellingsley, who had been quiet up to this point. "What was she doing with me?"

"The fact that you were happy becoming a lawyer and all of a sudden she's trying to get you to be a 1920s housewife," said Janie. "Pretty effectively, from what I can tell."

"But I always wanted that," said Wellingsley. "I just never felt brave enough to say it before. She made me brave. She helped me be who I really am."

"I don't know, I feel like she was manipulating you. But maybe this is what you really wanted. I'm not in your brain. I'm sorry," said Janie, turning to Zeus and Eve. "I can't get the image of trying to scrape dog shit off your shoe on the footpath out of my head. Is that what getting rid of Lilith part is like? Knocking a dog turd off your shoe? Because I'm a very visual thinker, and that's all I can see."

"So we don't die when the ember goes?" asked Apple. "Can I just confirm that, please?"

"No, you don't die," said Zeus. "Nobody is dying."

"Anyway, this is where you're safe. No one can sense you, or find you, or see you in here. None of the beings looking for you will find you."

"What do you mean by 'beings'? How many are there, for fuck's sake?" snapped Apple.

"Adam and Asmodeus and Fae. Possibly some others," clarified Zeus.

Eve sat, slid her hands between her knees, and clasped them together. She looked young and lost. But only for a moment. "I'm going to be totally honest here. Really very honest and upfront. I made this whole mess."

She waved away the room's loud protests.

"No, I did. I'm the one who told them that Lilith was there watching in the garden that day. I turned my back on her when she needed me. I keep thinking that maybe if she and I had stood up to them, to Dad and Adam together, that maybe things could have been different. Maybe the whole of human history could have been different. And now she's the only one who can stop Adam making me a prisoner."

Apple and Janie glanced at each other awkwardly. There was silence. Finally, Apple was the one to step forward and place her hand on Eve's knee. "While I do appreciate, of course, that you are incredibly significant in the, like, entirety of civilisation and the Western tradition and, I guess, the Bible, and all that, I really don't think you could have done a lot about this. You were up against God, you know."

"But I told them she was there! I let her down! The last thing she would have known was that it was me who betrayed her."

"That bit is true," said Wellingsley. "You have to concede that that bit is probably true."

Zeus glared at her.

"Exactly," said Eve. "So, I need to fix this. I need to get Lilith back to wholeness. For her sake, and my sake, and because I think she's the only one who can control Adam. I need to find a way to bring her back together. You two… back together."

"And you promise that we won't die?" asked Wellingsley, and Apple nodded approvingly.

"You won't die," said Zeus. He took out his phone and scrolled through his Instagram feed. "Look at all these women."

Apple took his phone, and Wellingsley and Janie peered over her shoulder as she scrolled.

"Eve, do you know that your boyfriend follows exclusively women?"

The three women turned and glared at him.

"You're like an actual walking red flag," snapped Janie.

"Just keep scrolling," said Zeus, not even trying to keep the note of exasperation out of his voice.

"Yes, I'm scrolling," said Apple. "There are a lot of women here."

"Oh, that one's quite old," said Wellingsley.

"And that one."

"So, he has eclectic tastes."

They glared at him again.

"These," said Eve, snatching the phone out of Apple's hands, "are the women Fae has taken Lilith away from. They're all women who were going to be something inspired by Lilith, but Fae put out their embers, okay? Look, they're all living their lives perfectly happily. Some aren't even any different, not in a way anyone noticed. Maybe a little less opinionated and with some inexplicable memory loss, but still themselves. You will still be yourselves. We'll just have Lilith back here, too."

Apple and Wellingsley looked at each other. "I feel like we need to talk," Apple said. "I feel like we should discuss it before coming to a decision."

"You want to discuss something with me?" said Wellingsley. "You want my opinion? But you don't like me."

"I don't *not* like you," said Apple. "But even if I didn't, I need to hear what you think about this. It's serious. Of course I'd want to hear your opinion about it."

"First thought, are you sure it's just us?" asked Apple, turning to Eve. "We're the only ones who still have the Lilith poop attached to our collective shoes?"

"As far as we can tell," said Eve, "you're the final two carrying the last of Lilith. You're the final hope. If we can't combine them, and the embers get snuffed out, then she'll just… float around in space forever or something. I don't know, but I'm pretty sure that the only way I can get Lilith standing in front of me so I can apologise to her is by getting you two to work together to do it, okay? And trust me, the other person looking for you isn't going to be asking for consent."

"Who, Asmodeus? No, he's lovely," said Janie.

"No, not him," said Eve. "I'm sure he's doing his best, but he's kind of useless."

"Hot but useless," added Zeus.

"Exactly," conceded Eve. "Hot but useless. It's Adam you need to be worried about."

"Why?"

"He'll do anything to stop Lilith. And he wants to take over from Dad."

"How does God feel about that?" asked Apple.

Eve sighed and thought about this for a moment. "I mean, I think he's kind of been imagining that Adam would take over from him one day, but he'd have to offer it. As far as I can tell, Adam wants to muscle in and take over and recalibrate everything. Lilith can manage him, though. She's the only one who can kick his arse."

Wellingsley nodded. "So I can see she's needed. But will we be safe? I think that's the main question here."

"Look, once again, we don't totally know, okay? And until you two decide whether you're going to do this, it's all hypothetical anyway."

Wellingsley stepped over to Apple and took her hand awkwardly. "I think we do it. It's an important thing, and even though I'm scared, I think we should."

"Are you sure,' said Apple. "I don't want you to feel like we've pushed you into this. And you really do like Fae, for some reason."

Wellingsley looked at the people surrounding her. "This is the right thing to do," she said. "And you all listen to me. You want to hear what I have to say. You have no idea how much that means to me."

Apple squeezed the other woman's fingers. "Of course, we listen to you. That shouldn't be the reason why you do something, though. That's the bare minimum for friendship. You need to get better boundaries; we'll discuss that after all this is over."

"But we should bring her back. It's the right thing to do," said Wellingsley firmly. "Whatever the consequences."

TOO MANY CARJACKINGS

Fae had been driving for hours. She'd had to fill up with petrol twice and grab frozen Cokes from drive-throughs for sustenance and to replenish moisture.

She had been crying.

A lot.

She was thinking about her life. Her choices.

Jared was the love of her life. Her only one. How could this have happened?

Eventually, she found herself driving in the CBD. She had just followed where lights and roads had led her, and while the middle of Sydney wasn't most people's idea of a relaxing drive, she was past caring.

She had been both sweet-talked and played by a trickster who she thought loved her. Played by that same man who had promised her the world and been willing and able to deliver… nothing.

As she stopped at some lights, the passenger door opened.

Adam slipped in.

"What the actual fuck," she said.

"Hi," he replied, fastening the seat belt around his chest. "You should lock your doors. You could get carjacked."

"I think I just was."

She turned on her indicator and made a move to pull over.

"No," he said. "Keep driving. I want to move. And talk."

He looked over at her.

"Are you going to kill me?" she asked.

"No, I'm not. I'm not a carjacker. I'm Adam."

"Adam?" she repeated uncertainly.

"Adam, that's right. Your employer."

"Oh," she said.

"That's right. Oh, and you're Fae, Lady of the Lake in a previous incarnation. And mercenary extraordinaire to whoever will pay the highest amount of money."

"That's not true," she said. "I'm not getting paid anything at all."

"Yes, you are."

"I'm not," she said firmly.

"I've paid fifty million dollars into an account for you."

"I haven't seen hide nor hair of it."

"Bloody Jared," they both said at once.

"But you've been doing the job, though."

She nodded. "I wanted to help Jared, but he's betrayed me."

"What happened?"

She didn't answer.

"Fae," he prompted.

"He set me up for failure," she said. "He wanted me to fail. I thought I was supposed to be dulling the light of all these Liliths, and I thought I was chosen to do a good job, but as it turns out, he chose me because he thought I'd be bad at it."

"What?" said Adam, a note of steel in his voice. "That's not true."

"It is," she sobbed, and Adam grabbed hold of the wheel as she scrabbled around next to the seat for something to wipe her nose with. "He told me. He wants Lilith to form again, so he chose me to try and keep her apart because he thinks I'm incompetent and knew I'd do a bad job."

"That fucking arsehole. That absolute bastard," spat Adam.

"Thank you! I know! I can't believe he'd do this to me," hiccupped Fae.

"What do you mean you can't believe he would do this to you?" Adam didn't try to keep the tone of disbelief out of his voice. "What possible action has he ever taken throughout the entirety of history that would make you think any of this is in any way out of character for him? He's a total and complete arsehole, and now he's fucked both of us over."

"You don't know him like I do," she sobbed.

"Right, pull over," he said. "Find a space and pull over."

She did as she was told, and he took off his seat belt and turned to stare at her.

"We're in love," she said. "We're in love, and you don't know him like I do. I don't know what's the matter with him lately. This cruelty is very out of character."

"This isn't out of character," blithered Adam, unable to believe the words he was hearing. "There has never been someone who acts so consistently in character for 100% of the time. He is a literal trickster. No one even knows where he came from. He can't be trusted to ever keep his word, or ever to anything that could vaguely be described as ethical or correct, and I can't believe I ever put my trust in him."

"He told me he loved me," she said.

"When?"

"About 1500 years ago, based on our current timeline."

"Right. 1500 years ago. He said he loved you once, 1500 years ago."

"Oh, don't be stupid," she said, her voice taking on an element of determination for the first time. "Of course, it wasn't just once. Do you think I'd be in this state if he'd only ever told me he loved me once, 1500 years ago?"

He raised his eyebrows at her.

"It was three times, and there was a fifty-year gap between each proclamation, so if you don't think that's a fairly serious and committed relationship, then I feel sorry for your wife."

"He does not love you. I know for a fact that he has had relationships with about eighty different beings personally known to me in the last hundred years, and that's just the ones I know about. Yes, you've been played. We've both been played, but I'm the one who is now going to do something about it."

Her lip quivered.

"Sorry, but aren't you meant to be a kick arse boss bitch kind of person?"

"It's not my fault," she spat. "I'm anxiously attached. I spend hours at a time questioning why he used a certain emoji or why he hasn't messaged back, or whether I came on too strong four hundred years ago when I breezily asked if we could catch up sometime in the next century if he didn't have any better offers. It's not my fault; it's the way I am."

"He doesn't love you, okay?"

"I think he still might if I just—"

"You're not very bright, are you?"

"Why does everyone keep saying that? I'M JUST VERY DISTRACTED!"

"Your job was supposed to be to keep her apart, and now my wife is here tramping around with all the pieces, bonding and who knows what else. Lilith cannot form again. She just can't. This whole 'one timeline and one place' was clearly a giant ruse, and I was stupid enough to fall for it." He smacked his hand against the dashboard, and a shock jock blared into life on the radio, talking about the current influx of homophobic migratory seabirds or some such.

"It was pretty stupid to fall for it," said Fae, brightening a little. "What were you thinking? Obviously, this was going to fail."

"But you weren't able to discern that, were you?" he shot back.

"I think we've already established that I'm not very bright, and I'm being exploited by everyone I've ever met, and I'm a complete mess."

"I'm going to have to do this myself," said Adam, an idea dawning on him. "I'm going to have to take steps. I can lock them away somewhere. That's it. I can lock them all in pocket universes, and she'll never be able to form again. And put Eve in one for good measure. I should have done this from the start. Tell me where the women are," he said. "Tell me where the women are, and I'll deal with this myself."

"I bloody well will not tell you," said Fae. "Don't even have a dog in this fight. I was just trying to make Jared happy, but that failed spectacularly, so now maybe what I should be doing is making women friends rather than pitting them against each other. And you can't just lock up your wife."

"Tell me where they are," he snarled.

"I don't know where they are. I've resigned."

"You can't resign," she said. "I've paid you good money to do this."

"No, you haven't. You've paid my ex-boyfriend money to do this, and I've, as far as I can tell, been left with absolutely nothing to show for the last several thousand years. I was the Lady of the Lake," she said, tilting the rearview mirror down and looking at her face. "I was the fucking lady of the lake! What happened to me? What did I become?"

"Don't get all empowered now," he said. "I need to find these women and stop a disaster from happening."

"Screw it," she said, opening the door and grabbing her handbag as she left. "I had a fucking mint job. I was the Lady of the Lake. I was friends with really important people. And a mediocre man made me forget all of that. A mediocre man with no appreciation for wine and an overbite. I lost my damn head for that. Fuck me."

She slammed the door, and he could see her yelling something while she stood on the footpath.

He rolled down the window.

"Why don't you go and find Jared," Fae was yelling, "and ask him where they are. Keep going with your stupid plan. The one that was reliant on my incompetence. Well, guess what? Looks like I'm not so incompetent at all, doesn't it? So good luck in finding everyone, and I really hope that you two don't die in a fiery accident somewhere."

"What fiery accident?" yelled Adam out the window as she stomped away. "What fiery accident? That was very specific? What have you been planning?"

She didn't look back.

"I don't know how to drive," he snapped, to no one in particular.

He was sitting with his forehead on the wheel, eyes closed, and had been for quite some time, when there was a tap on the window. He had slid over to the driver's side in an attempt to turn off the radio, but had been unable to work out how to do that, and the talking had made way for the best hits of the 2000s, which had made him start to strongly feel that he would ask his father if it might be time for another flood.

Tap tap.

He didn't bother to turn his head.

Tap tap.

"Go away."

Tap tap. More forcefully this time.

"Fuck off!" he yelled into the steering wheel.

The door clicked open.

"You can't be here," said a voice.

He turned his head to see a short woman in a brown overcoat standing in the doorway. She had a beige hat jammed down on her head, and tan laced shoes on her feet. She gave off an overwhelming brown aura, and even her face looked like a little shrivelled-up apple.

"You'll need to go," she said. "There have been reports."

Adam sat back, rubbing at the imprint of the steering wheel that he could feel on his forehead. He plastered a smile on his face. "I'll just be a moment," he said. "I just need a… moment."

"You've had several moments," she said. "I've been watching you for an hour. It's time to go."

"It's not my car," he said apologetically. "It's my… It's my secretary's. She parked it here. I guess I'll have to deal with her mess. As usual."

The woman glared at him. "I know," she said. "As I said, I've been watching you for an hour."

He glanced around nervously. An hour? Where had that time gone? "That's not good," he said. "I need to get moving. I need to find them." He put his hand on the key in the ignition, started the engine, and attempted to pull the door shut. "You're right, I shouldn't park here. I'll just—"

An arm darted through the open window, and a vice-like grip grabbed his fingers and pried them off the key. The engine shut off abruptly. "I didn't say anything about parking," she said, and her fingers remained tightly clamped around his. "I said you need to go. From here. You need to leave them alone, leave this whole Lilith thing alone, and leave. Go back to your father. You're not wanted here."

His chest tightened. "Who are you?" he said between ashen lips.

She stared into his eyes. "I'm the one who is telling you to fly off whichever fluffy cloud you want to sit around and play harps on. You are not of the earth. This is not your domain. So, fuck off and leave my women alone."

"Your women," he spat. "Who do you think you are? How dare you speak to me with such profanities? How dare you speak to me at all? I don't know who you think you are, but—"

There was a sudden sharp pain in his shin. He instinctively grabbed at his leg, but then it was his fingers that burst into pain as she lifted her leg to kick them too.

"What?" he yelped. "Stop kicking me. What do you think you're doing? Stop it. You're going to get hit by a car or something. Get out of the bloody street."

She had drawn back and was using her brogue-encased feet to kick him repeatedly. She had to lift her leg quite a long way to do this, but was managing to get quite some power behind it, and he could feel bruises start to blossom under his skin.

"Stop it!" he yelped again, sliding over the middle console and into the passenger seat. "Stop it! This is assault. You can't just go around kicking people. What's the matter with you?"

For a short chunky person, she slid surprisingly deftly into the driver's seat and slammed the door shut. "Thanks," she said. "I hadn't planned on this bit, but I feel like it flows quite well, actually. Good plan." She started the car and pulled out into the Sydney traffic like she'd been driving for her entire life. The fact that she could barely see over the steering wheel seemed to pose no issue for her at all.

"Wait, stop," he said. "You can't do this. You can't carjack me." He heard the locks click, and he looked around desperately for a way out.

"You're a liability, Adam. You're a liability, and you're in the way, so I'm going to take you somewhere where you can't bother anyone."

"This is not happening," he said. "I have not been abducted by an octogenarian with no fashion sense. This definitely isn't happening."

"You must always reduce women to what they're wearing, mustn't you," she mused. "Have you noticed how you do that?"

"How would you know what I do?"

"I told you. I've been watching you. And I hear things."

He stared out the window as identical shopping centres after identical shopping centres passed by.

"Who are you?"

"No one really," she said. "I mean, you can call me Cally, but I'm a mere frippery. I'm like the wind. Ephemeral. You don't need to think about me at all."

"Would you stop talking in riddles, you ridiculous wrinkled old prune. I can't help but think about you because you are quite literally abducting me." He knocked on the window, trying to catch the attention of anyone in the street, but they were in the middle lane now, and, anyway, no one would have taken any notice. The old woman had picked up quite a bit of speed.

"I'm not abducting you. You're such a drama queen. You always have been, you know. It's ridiculous, especially since you've always been the golden child. No, we're just going for a drive. I need to go and grab someone else, and then our group will be complete."

"What group?" asked Adam.

"Just wait and see," she said, and accelerated onto the highway.

A TRULY TERRIBLE IDEA

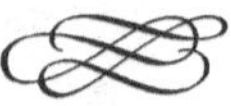

"I wish Adam were around," said God. "Is there any improvement in all the animals not being extinct down there? He's very odd at the moment, don't you think? He's acting very strangely and unpredictably. I need his help."

God, Sepham, and Mavis were standing in the middle of a huge room, with a low stage at one end and particle board on the floor. It was enormously echoey and bare, with plaster walls, and it looked as if it were a low-budget, shoddily made scout hall. Various beings were walking past carrying potted plants, strings of lantern lights, and great masses of balloons that would form, eventually, words and phrases highlighting particularly witty or succinct things God had said throughout his life.

Sepham and Mavis walked along behind God when he began pacing around, pointing out what he wanted where, and where he thought the step and repeat would be best placed.

"Not sure how the animals are," said Sepham. "Last I heard, Adam was in Borneo or some such. Bali? Possibly Burundi. You know how I am with geography. He seems fine, though."

"Good. That's good. As long as he's happy, right? That's all we want for our children. For them to be happy. Yes? Except I don't think he's that happy at the moment. I spend a disproportionate amount of my time worried about him. Parenting is extraordinarily difficult."

Sepham smiled tightly. "Well, I wouldn't know. I'm an angel. We can't have children. You didn't give us that ability."

"I didn't," said God, stopping to look at Sepham quizzically. "Are you sure?"

"Well, yes," said Sepham. "Fairly sure. We're not gendered. It would be tricky."

"Why do I always call you he then?"

"You've just always assumed my gender, sir. I've never bothered to mention it."

"But..." God handed the fake pineapple he was holding to Mavis, who tried, unsuccessfully, to juggle it and the stuffed capybara she was already holding.

"Are you sure? I thought I gave angels the ability to have babies? No, I'm sure I did. It's called... parthenogenesis. Yes, parthenogenesis. I was a big fan for a while. I'm sure I made it so the angels could reproduce that way. Reproduction without all that messy mucking about. Cuts down a lot of wasted time in washing sheets, so I'm told."

"Yes, I'm aware of the process," said Sepham.

"Of course."

"Fairly sure it's not us, though. Aphids, maybe. Could you be thinking of aphids?"

"Aphids," clarified God.

Sepham nodded.

"So, not angels?"

"No."

"Whoops," said God with a laugh. "Oh, well, not to worry. Parenthood is highly fraught. You've seen how much mine aged me. You're better off without it. Where was I? Ah, yes, we just want our children to be happy."

He looked around the room. "This will come together nicely. It will be a fabulous party. And both my children will be here. They will need to be back here, of course. I'll need you to go down and fetch them. I want everyone I love to be here."

"Really," said Sepham. "Me? Couldn't we get someone else to go down and get them? I've been flitting back and forth so much lately that I think I'm developing vertigo. It's playing havoc with my sinuses."

"Of course you. I don't trust anyone else. Adam needs to be brought up here right as the party starts, and I want you to be the one responsible for that. He's the..." God looked around and pulled Sepham by the robe into the corner.

"Go and check on something," he said to Mavis, noticing that she was following them. "Maybe go and see if that delivery of artisanal cheeses has arrived yet."

She headed off, searching for somewhere to offload the pineapple and the capybara.

"You see," he said to Sepham, glancing around to see if anyone was listening, "I'm wondering if maybe it's time to officially bring Adam and Eve in on the leadership. Well, mainly Adam. He's been helping so much."

Sepham boggled at him for a few moments. "By *all this,* you mean the lantern string lights and the potted ferns, right? Right?"

God shook his head, a smile spreading across his face. "No, not just this. Well, yes, this, but not just this. I mean everything! The entirety of all space and time. Or at least the bits of space and time that I've got dominion over, which, just between you and I, is getting smaller and smaller by the day."

"But you've been doing so well!" said Sepham desperately. "All the work that you and I have been doing. All the new ideas you've taken on board. And taken on board so well. I'm your fiercest, most passionate advocate. I'm immensely proud of you."

"Thank you," said God, his face flushing with embarrassed pride. "I have been doing my best."

"Exactly! And your best has been stupendous. Why give all of that up now? Just when you're really hitting your stride. Why dilute your power and risk getting rid of all the new ideas you're bringing in?"

"Adam would keep my legacy safe."

"Have you asked him about your legacy? Or his feelings about your 'wokeness' as he calls it? Because he's not a fan. And you're doing so very well."

"Do you think I am though? Really?"

"Oh, sir, absolutely I do. I do. You've barely made a misstep for years. Hardly any smiting at all, and well, acts of God have been reclassified these days anyway, so you never have to take the fall for them anymore. And you've been getting some really good press in general. Heaps of people don't even believe in you at all anymore, so you're well and truly off the hook with that demographic. I feel like you have the potential to make some amazing progress over the next few millennia. Some very high-level and benign ruling. I mean, it practically takes care of itself these days anyway. It's passive income at this stage."

God shook his head. "You're very kind, and I do appreciate the fact that you've noticed how far I've come, but I don't think I don't. But don't you think this is the right thing to do? Pass it on to the kids. Adam in particular. You know him as well as I do. He's absolutely up for the job. He's wise, he's strong, he's a leader. Truly giving and kind."

"I'm sorry, but are we talking about Adam? Your Adam?"

"And this is where the announcement could be made," said God, veering off topic. He had wandered to the area at the front of the room and was gesturing to the stage. "I will have everyone gathered here. All the people who have been important to me over the years. And yes, some who knew me when I was not considered the benign leader that I am now. We can have some cocktails and cheesy nibbles, and then I'll make this big announcement that I'll be handing the whole thing over to my children. It will be huge. A wonderful night. And they, of course, will be massively grateful.

Then I'll head off for a holiday somewhere. Valhalla is lovely this time of year. Catch up with my boy, Odin."

Sepham sighed and looked around at the flurry of activity that was going on around him. "I think it's time I told you something. About Adam. Something important. I have strong suspicions that—"

"Very good," said God, not listening at all. "Here comes Mavis with a tasting plate. How exciting! And remember, not a word to Adam. We'll keep him down there until things are ready to kick off here."

"Which will be?" enquired Sepham with exasperation.

"Oh, I'd say about tomorrow our time."

ZEUS AND THE MATTER OF PERSONAL GROWTH

"To be honest," said Eve, flicking on one of the filtration units that circulated air in the bunker, "I did somewhat hope that you two would just stand together and something would happen."

"Like a chemical reaction?" suggested Janie.

"Yes, yes, that's right! Like a chemical reaction. The proximity between you would cause something amazing to happen. Have you two hugged?"

Apple and Wellingsley looked at each other as if the other had just grown an extra head. "Have we what?"

Eve made a lackluster gesture with her arms. "Have you… hugged. I don't know. Maybe that will get things moving."

"We're not hugging," pronounced Apple carefully. "If this whole thing needs hugging to make it happen, then it's a hard pass."

"It's a good idea, my love," said Zeus, squeezing Eve's hand, "but I think that we might need to think outside the box with this one. Obviously, proximity isn't doing it. Does anyone have any other ideas?"

"Calling for Lilith?" suggested Janie hopefully.

"What, like actually out loud?" asked Eve.

"Yes."

"Like she's a puppy?" asked Apple, an eyebrow raised.

Eve cleared her throat and said, "Lilith? Hello, Lilith? Are you there?"

The women glanced around nervously as if expecting her to jump out of one of the reinforced walls.

They listened, the silence pressing around them. The lack of city sounds, the total absence of noise except the gurgling of someone's stomach and Apple's halting breathing filled the room.

Nothing happened.

"I thought—" started Janie, but Eve held up her hand.

"Wait," Eve hissed. "What was that?" They all stepped up their degree of listening another few notches, straining their ears. "Nothing," said Eve after a moment. "Sorry."

"I did rather think," continued Janie, more forcefully this time, "that you would have planned this a bit more. You went to all the effort of getting us here."

"You're using the word *us* a bit fast and loose," Eve snapped. "You're not even part of this."

"She's my emotional support sister," said Apple. "I'm here, so she's here."

"You have to understand," said Eve, "that we're finding our way in the dark for the most part. We are trying to right the wrongs of the past with no road map. A terrible thing was done to Lilith many years ago, primarily at my hands, and I've been trying to make it better. But…" Tears sprang to her eyes. "That doesn't mean I know what I'm doing or that I've got a clear idea."

"What about you?" said Apple to Zeus. "Why don't you have an idea of what's happening? And… actually, as it seems like we've got a minute to talk about it, what have you got to do with any of this anyway?"

"Because Eve wants me involved," he said simply. "And she is the love of my life."

Eve placed her hand on his arm. "He knows what it's like to make mistakes," she said. "He had several millennia when he, and I know he won't mind me saying this because he owns it, acted like an absolute dickhead."

"It's true," he said. "For a long time, I embraced toxic masculinity. But when I met Eve, I realized there was another way of being. She brought a new light to my life, and I've basked in its shine ever since. But then I forgot about her for a while, but now we're back on track."

He and Eve locked eyes and became lost in each other.

"Gross," said Janie. "I think I prefer toxic masculinity to whatever that is."

"The fact is," said Eve after a moment, "he has been helping me try and bring all of this together, but we don't have access to how to fix things. There's no recipe or road map. My husband was the one who fragmented her. Well, no, it was Dad, but Adam manipulated him into doing it. In fact, Adam has manipulated him into most things."

"Wait, God can be manipulated?" asked Janie.

"Not by everyone," said Eve. "Adam is his son. He has no clarity around him."

"What about you, though?" asked Wellingsley. "You're his daughter. Doesn't he listen to you, too?"

Eve smiled and shook her head. "He loves me, but he would never listen to me the way he does Adam. I'm a woman, you see."

"And there we have it," grumbled Janie.

"Adam is scared of Lilith. And he hates her. He's terrified she'll come back and stand in his way. I think she's the only one he really fears.

"And would she stand in his way?" asked Apple.

"Absolutely. She'd snap him in half. Absolute carnage. People would write songs about the appalling consequences."

"They're more likely to live stream it these days," said Apple, "but I get your point."

"Could you two at least hold hands again?" asked Zeus, attempting to get back to the main point. "See if anything happens?"

"Oh, for goodness sake," said Apple, and grabbed hold of Wellingsley's hand, linking their fingers together. "There, see? Nothing."

"You don't feel anything at all?" asked Zeus.

"Absolutely nothing. Nothing at all."

"Not even a little bit of electricity? A frisson?"

"Dude, let it go," said Janie. "There's no frisson."

"Maybe it's here that's the problem," said Eve, looking about the bunker. "Maybe it's something to do with location. Maybe she can't get in because of all the reinforcement and the bombproofing and all that."

"What do you mean by 'get in'? Is she outside? Existing somewhere? I thought that she was in us?" questioned Wellingsley.

"Attached to us," continued Apple. "In our heart or our soul or something."

Zeus and Eve glanced at each other awkwardly, in a move that they seemed close to perfecting.

"Once again, our intel surrounding that is a bit limited," said Eve. "We're pretty sure she doesn't exist outside of you as such because, as we said, she was discombobulated throughout space and time, which would imply she doesn't have existence, or even consciousness, outside of whoever she's attached to."

"But you don't know?" asked Apple.

Eve shook her head. "Our best guess was to get you together and the parts would…"

"Look, this is a bit embarrassing, but yes, we thought that all the people who have her connected to them still would get together, and all the pieces would just reconnect like a magnet," admitted Zeus.

"Did you have any actual reason to think that?" asked Janie.

"No," she said. "It just felt like it would make sense. To me."

"So you might be right?" Janie continued.

"In what way?"

"Maybe this bunker is stopping the chemical reaction or chain reaction or whatever the heck it is from being able to happen? Maybe having us locked up in here is the problem."

Zeus looked alarmed. "You're not strictly locked up. It's for your own good."

"Oh, honey, no, that's not a great line. Never say that to a woman again," said Eve, patting his arm.

"We're in here for a reason, though, right?" asked Apple. "It's to protect us?"

"From hordes," said Zeus. "Absolute hordes. All after you two."

"Hordes?" queried Apple. "Hordes of what? And why haven't we seen them yet?"

"They're very stealthy," he said mysteriously.

"Could we just have a moment, please?" said Eve to Zeus suddenly. "For some girl talk?"

"Of course," he said. "Shall I make tea?"

Once he left, Eve turned to the girls. "All right, let me explain the whole Zeus situation. He and I fell in love and began to conduct an illicit and passionate affair. Whenever I could sneak away, we started creating a new life down here on Earth. But then Adam suspected that I liked him and wiped Zeus's memory and made him a terrible person."

"Suspected that you liked him?" questioned Apple. "But he didn't know about the whole affair thing?"

"Crickey, no," said Eve. "Can you imagine? But I found Zeus again, and we fell in love again because we're soulmates and we're destined to be together forever."

"Nice," said Apple. "I approve of the whole passionate love thing. But what about the hordes?

"When we were setting up the house, before we were discovered, Zeus was very keen to be involved in helping me in my quest to find Lilith again. I didn't really know how the whole thing was going to play out, but making a bunker seemed to get him excited and gave him a job. Before I got a chance to come down to Earth, he had quite a lot of time down here without me, you see, and communication was limited, and there may have been some… mistranslation."

Apple frowned. "Mistranslation? How so?"

"It's a bit embarrassing," said Eve, her face flushing.

"Excellent, said Apple, rubbing her hands together. "I love an embarrassing anecdote."

"Well, given that I am Eve, daughter of God, mother of the entire human race, and kept in very exacting circumstances, it was hard to keep the connection we wanted. When I wasn't actually down here with him, I could sometimes call him quickly when the 5G signals actually worked without too much static and interference. Communication was difficult."

"I'm impressed you've been able to maintain a relationship at all," said Wellingsley.

"If you know you know," said Eve, a smile lighting up her face. "I've been in a loveless, sexually unfulfilling, neglectful relationship for four thousand years. When I found someone who thinks I'm the most amazing, clever, funny, sexy woman in existence, then you better believe that I'm going to make it work."

"Bunker story," urged Janie. "Enough of the romance. I'm committed to the whole bunker arc."

"We were just talking about our future together and the things we wanted to do some day, and I said I wanted to go and get a burger at Manly with him one day, and he thought I said I wanted to live in a bunker when I get down to Earth, and he took that and ran with it and before I knew it I had this state of the art bunker that he'd built for me. So I needed to make up a back story about why I might need it, and keeping you safe was the best thing I could come up with."

Janie giggled.

"The best thing I could come up with on short notice," she stressed.

Apple started laughing too.

"Oh, stop," said Eve, a smile beginning to spread across her face. "He was so proud of himself. You should have seen all the spreadsheets and everything. He was loving having a project so much, and I didn't have the heart to tell him all I'd wanted was a burger with some egg and beetroot and some good chunky chips."

"Don't," she giggled. "He's Zeus, for goodness sake. He's had an absolute bugger of a time, and I know you would have heard what an absolute egotistical arsehole he used to be. But I yelled at him about it for a while, and he came to his senses. That's the problem with that whole Greek pantheon. They just don't give their gods a good talking to."

"I feel like Hera did," said Apple.

"Well, that doesn't matter," said Eve, brushing that aside. "He's mine now, and I am his, and he shows me he loves me every day."

Apple grinned. "By building you a bunker."

"I mean, it is a very good bunker," said Janie.

"No, don't get me wrong; it's first class. And we love a bunker."

"We do," said Janie. "We do love a bunker."

"There," said Eve. "So, no harm done. You got to see a really first-class, state-of-the-art bunker, and he got to feel useful and think he's protecting you. Or something. And here he is, back with the tea," said Eve, raising her voice as he pushed back through the door.

"Look what I just found in my pocket," he said, drawing out a large, blue velvet embossed piece of card. "It just appeared there."

"What is it?" asked Eve.

He held it out, and they read it. "It's an invitation. God's having a party," he said.

Eve suddenly felt something pushing against her and pulled one out, too. "Oh," she said, "I've got one too. Fun."

Apple squirmed and drew a piece of card from her underpants. "That's a bit bloody invasive, isn't it?"

She looked at Janie. "Your turn."

Janie patted her pockets, her bra, and her legs, but nothing seemed to have appeared on her.

"Give it a minute," said Apple. "I'm sure you'll get one too."

"We're all connected to God in some way. Maybe Apple got an invite because of the whole Lilith thing," said Eve hopefully.

"Oh," said Janie, her face falling. "If that's the case, then I won't get one. I'm just a hanger-on."

"Don't worry. I'll bring you as a plus one," said Apple.

Wellingsley was looking in her handbag eagerly, digging around in the detritus. "Mine must be here somewhere," she said, but after a moment she stopped looking, her lips a thin line.

Apple cleared her throat. "Also, I have an idea. Clearly, we're at a bit of a dead end here, but I think there's someone who might be able to help us. Someone who knows Lilith better than any of us. Someone who is even more invested in her reestablishing herself than the rest of us. It's that whole love thing, Eve."

"Who?" asked Eve.

"Of course," said Janie. "Of course! Well done."

"Yes," said Apple. "We need to find Asmodeus."

ABDUCTED BY A MAD OLD BAT

They drove for a long time. Not being familiar with the city, once the Opera House and the bridge had passed them by, Adam had no idea where they were going. He slumped in his seat and crossed his arms, feeling powerless and annoyed and irritated and a little bit scared. He didn't like this combination of emotions, so he decided to make it the old woman's problem.

"You're going to pay for this," he said. "You have no idea what you've unleashed by abducting me. You've made a very bad mistake. Do you have any idea who my friends are? And what am I supposed to be doing?"

"I know what you're going to do. You're going to lock women up in a pocket universe, and I've got no time for those sorts of shenanigans," said the old lady, and she turned up the music.

He seethed. "Don't make me yell," he said more loudly this time. "You won't like me if I yell."

She turned the music down. "I'm only doing this because I need to concentrate at this intersection up ahead," she said. "Don't think that I want to hear your rantings."

"My father," he said, more loudly than he needed to, "is God.

You know, ruler of the entire universe, and I don't think he will be very happy when—"

"Ruler of the *known* universe," she said.

"What?"

"He's the ruler of the known universe."

"Well, obviously. Which is all of it."

"Which is patently not all of it," she said, "otherwise why would it be called the known universe? Why have that distinction if there isn't an unknown universe? And," she said, getting on a roll, "known universe specifies a particular group of people, too. The people who are in the unknown part, well, for them it's part of the known universe, isn't it? So really, you're talking about someone who isn't actually in charge of very much, when it comes down to it."

"Are you mad?" Adam asked after a beat.

"I'm just saying," stated the old woman, indicating to go around a lorry that seemed intent on pushing a mini into the median strip, "that saying that 'my dad is God' is not quite the flex you think it is."

"I've been abducted by a mad woman," he muttered.

"Anyway, I know your dad, and nothing about him makes me think I have anything to be scared of."

"I'm sorry, but you will excuse me if I find that very hard to believe."

"I am monumentally uninterested in what you choose or do not choose to believe. Your reality, or even your perception of reality, has little to do with how things actually are, so listening to you blather on about the carnage that your father will inflict on me when I still have the photos of him and I on a particularly debauched evening operating the guillotine during the French Revolution has little impact on me. Your father and I go way back, and once upon a time, he came to me for advice, so you'd best keep that in mind before you threaten me again. You're an absolute disgrace, boy."

There was a long stretch of silence, and they seemed to be heading to a rundown suburb on the outskirts of the city. The lawns of the houses were dry and overgrown, and unpainted weatherboard houses with cardboard pressed against the inside of the windows sat at the end of cracked concrete driveways.

"Where are we going?" he demanded.

"We're going to have a chat," Cally said. "About your life and your choices. And the massive disappointment that you've turned out to be. I decided that my place would be the best option."

"I do not have time for this," he snapped. "I have a very important job to do, and it's time sensitive. I need to find some old friends before my father—" he stressed the words, "calls me home. He's having a huge party, and I'll need to be back for that."

The woman took one hand off the steering wheel and rustled around in the woven bag that rested against her chest. She pulled out a bag of yarn, a laptop computer, and some kind of bottle with a small plastic nib before finding what she was looking for.

"Is this it?" she said, waving a rectangle of card at him. It was about as long as her hand, gold, with blue sequins and velvet tassels adorning the edges.

He took it out of her hand and read:

You are Invited to a CELEBRATION of REGRETS, SUCCESSES, and NEW BEGINNINGS.

Please come dressed for a party and celebrate into the wee hours with me and my nearest and dearest.

Bring a plate.

Tomorrow, My pad. You will be summoned at the appropriate time.

Hugs, G daddy

"Looks like I'm invited," she said. "I told you I know him."

"Not to be offensive," he said, "but he's invited everyone he's ever met, by the sounds of it."

The old woman was pulling the car into one of the cracked concrete driveways between a rusted chain-link fence. It ran up through a dead, yellow lawn, past the side of a weatherboard house and a tall grey timber fence that may once have been newly painted but had lost any glimmer of newness many years ago. The car stopped with no room for Adam to open his door.

"Here," she said, "this is my place. Come in and have a cuppa."

He opened the door, or at least tried to open it. It was jammed up against the fence.

"Oh, sorry, love," said Cally. "Just climb over and come out my side."

She left the car and walked to the door, which was along the side of the house, as he clambered over the middle console, nearly doing himself a damage on the handbrake.

"I want you to know that I'm not consenting to this," he said. "You've abducted me against my will."

"Oh, calm down. I'll have you back in time for the party. In fact, you can be my escort. Would you like that? I can be a… what do they call it? A cougar."

Adam couldn't accurately describe how unpleasant he found that concept.

Once they were inside, the old woman opened the curtains and let some light into the small sunroom. The cracked vinyl floor was faded, like the rest of the room, and the hospital green walls glinted in the sun that now flooded the room.

"Sit down," she said, gesturing to the red sofa bed that ran under a window. "Sit down, and I'll put the jug on."

"You know I could just leave," he said.

"Yes, of course you could. You can. You could have before. You could have jumped out at any number of lights or intersections. You could have run down the driveway and out into the street the moment I parked, but, to be fair, there's a good chance you would have been mugged the moment you went out there. But anyway, you didn't."

"I couldn't really," he said awkwardly. "You had me prisoner."

She barked out a laugh and thrust a cup of International Roast into his hand. "Look at these wrists. You could have snapped them like a twig. Look at me. A gust of wind could knock me over. I'm in my life's autumn, you know. You could have gotten away at any time, but you didn't. I wonder why."

Adam considered leaving at that moment, just on principle, but she was right. He had no idea where to go, and there was no way he would survive on the streets. He was way too pretty.

"We need to talk," she said. "And you know it. You sense it. You felt something between the two of us when we first met, didn't you?"

"Is this that cougar thing again? Please don't do that. It makes me very uncomfortable."

"Do you think your upbringing was everything you wanted it to be?"

He sipped his coffee as a way of avoiding this question, but rapidly realized that he didn't know which was worse.

"My father did the best he could."

"Yes, he did," she said. "He did. But despite that, he raised a selfish, headstrong, self-centred brat who's used to taking what he wants and using people for his own needs. And who has manipulated his father to the nth degree and now, from what I hear, is about to make some very stupid decisions."

"Rubbish," he said. "That's just ridiculous. I'm a people person. Not just that, I'm a people pleaser. Everything I do is to help other people. To make them happy. I give too much, that's my problem."

"And the worst thing is," she said, interrupting him, "that I think you believe your own rubbish."

"It's not rubbish."

"Lilith," she yelled, her voice suddenly strong and vibrant.

"You caused Lilith to be thrown to all the winds because you didn't like the way she—"

"Because she threatened to kill my child."

"Oh, rubbish. She did no such thing. She suggested a way to conveniently get rid of it, and after the way things panned out with Abel, maybe that wouldn't have been such a bad idea."

"That's funny," muttered Adam. "That's exactly what Eve said."

"You got offended because your fragile masculinity was threatened, and you started a vendetta against her that's absolutely disproportionate to what happened. And you're still scared of her."

Adam pursed his lips.

"That's true, yes? That's why you're careering around Sydney coming up with harebrained schemes and fraternising with trickster demons, yes? Just because a woman once got the better of you, you want to make sure that every piece of her stays oppressed."

"You don't know what you're talking about," he muttered, at a loss for any other scathing or witty comeback.

"I'm disappointed," said Cally. "I'm disappointed, that's all I can say. I'm not going to fall into the trap of saying that this is my fault because I refuse to buy into that paradigm, but I can certainly see some ways where you could have been pointed along a different route during your timeline, but you weren't. Oh, I suppose I could have popped in from time to time, redirected you, given you some sage advice or wisdom along the way, but would you have listened to me?"

"Would I have listened to a crazy old woman yelling at me and feeding me foul coffee? No, no, I wouldn't."

"So here you are, looking for the pieces of a woman that you broke in the first place, thinking that she would even want you when she sees you."

"Of course, she would want me. I have so much to offer her. I have everything to offer her."

"Oh, really? Why don't we get a closer opinion then?"

NO HORDES. NO HORDES AT ALL

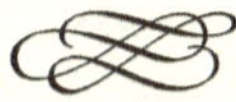

"I've met him," said Apple.

Eve stared at her uncertainly. "What? What do you mean you've met him?"

"Met him," said Janie, using air quotes.

"He's down here looking for the Lilith ember people, too," said Apple. "Didn't you know? I feel like you'd be all over that kind of thing. He found me. Kind of. But, yes, he's here."

"How would I know?" said Zeus. "I've been in a bloody bunker for six months solid with my memory wiped; how would I know he's here?"

"Well, he definitely is, and he's trying to find us. In fact, he's the one who gave me Wellingsley's name. He wants Lilith back, too, and he tried to persuade me to go along with him on the search. Of course, at that stage I didn't know anything about it and thought I might explode or something, so I wasn't as receptive to the idea as I am now."

"I don't feel like anyone has absolutely and positively ruled out exploding," said Janie.

"There will be no exploding," said Eve. "I'm serious. Humans are special creations, and I'm literally the progenitor of the human race. We might not know exactly how to get her back, but I can assure you that humans dying to get Lilith complete would be against the rules."

"There are rules?" asked Wellingsley doubtfully.

"I feel like rules are decidedly thin on the ground," muttered Apple.

"You have no idea," said Eve, rolling her eyes. "So many stupid rules. But to be fair, some are quite useful, such as the one that I know will guarantee that neither of you will die to get Lilith back."

"That's a comfort," said Wellingsley. "I think I can speak for both of us when I say that." She looked to Apple, who nodded.

"Look at you two all bonding," said Eve with a smile.

"So, Asmodeus is here, is he? On the planet?" asked Zeus.

"In Sydney, if you want to be very specific," said Apple.

"This is great," said Eve. "I'm sure he can help us."

"I'm not sure that he had much of a clue," said Apple.

Eve brushed this comment away with a wave of her hand. "It will all fall into place; I know it will. If only we had a way of finding him."

Apple held up her phone. "Would his number help?"

"Probably, yes. There's just one problem," said Zeus.

"Oh, I can assure you that there are many more than one problem," said Apple. "There are multitudes, which are increasing exponentially as far as I can see."

"If you leave this bunker, then disastrous things might happen. We'll have to find a way to get him here. And I can't be morally responsible if the untold hordes—"

"Darling," said Eve, placing her hand on his arm. "I think that the terrible disaster they might face was overestimated slightly."

"What do you mean?" he asked, looking puzzled. "There are hordes."

"There aren't, strictly speaking, hordes."

"Why did you tell me that there were hordes then?"

She wrinkled her brow and looked to the other women for help, but they quickly dropped eye contact. You've made your bed, you lie in it, the gesture said.

"You were so excited about making the bunker," she said, "and you'd put so much effort into it, and I wanted to make you think there was a need for it, a reason that you went to all this effort. I invented hordes and disastrous consequences. And out of all the things that's sprung back into your memory, the hordes are one of them." Eve shrugged. "I would have preferred you remember the peach pebble ring you were going to propose to me with, but we can work on that."

"Anyway," said Janie, taking Apple and Wellingsley by the hand and pulling them toward the door, "you two clearly have a lot to talk about, so we might just pop upstairs where there's better reception and call Apple's fella."

"He's not my fella."

"God, I wish he were. Have you seen him, Wellingsley? Fucking gorgeous."

They headed upstairs, and behind them, they could hear the sound of Zeus saying something along the lines of how he truly appreciated the fact that Eve was trying to save his feelings and how loved how she held his emotions close to her heart, but…

"How is it," hissed Janie, "that what looks like the most functional relationship in any of our lives is between a married mother of the human race and a previously lying, abusive misogynistic arsehole?"

"You know what they say," said Wellingsley. "There's a lid for every pot."

Apple was on the phone.

"He says he'll meet us in the plaza in ten minutes. Also, that he's thrilled we've found each other, and he knows exactly what to do next."

INVISIBLE FLOATING NUMBERS

Asmodeus greeted first Apple and then Janie with a polite peck on the cheek as they met in the Plaza. "Good to see you both," he said. "Safe and all. Have you had a good day?"

"Yes, thanks," said Apple. "How is your delicious hotel room?"

"Ah," he said with a wink, "less with the lack of you in it."

"We have news. This," gestured Janie with a flourish, "is Wellingsley."

"Hi," said Asmodeus, smiling pleasantly and enveloping her hand in his. "Lovely to meet you."

He looked around as if searching for someone else.

"Wellingsley," enunciated Apple clearly. "As in, woman on your list. We found her. Well, Fae found her, and then Eve found her, but... tada! So, here we all are, and you can get you, girl, back together, and we can make magic happen and change history or whatever."

Asmodeus looked at Wellingsley closely. He stared. He drew very close and looked into her eyes. She took a step back, feeling awkward. Her cheeks reddened.

"No," said Asmodeus. "She's not one of them."

"What do you mean she's not one of them?"

"There's no Lilith in her," he said.

"But she was on the list," said Apple. "Of course, there's some Lilith in her."

Asmodeus shook his head apologetically.

"Could there be another Wellingsley Baxter?" suggested Janie.

"Don't be stupid," said Wellingsley. "Of course, there wouldn't be. This isn't about me. I was never meant to be here at all. I'm part of a bloody clerical error or something."

"Don't say that," said Janie, resting her hand on the woman's arm. "You are part of it. Of course, this involves you, too. Otherwise, why would Fae have taken you on? Scooped you up like she did?"

Asmodeus cleared his throat. "I'm sorry, but I have to agree. I think this might be a simple admin error. I got my list from the same man who gave Fae the job in the first place, so maybe it was just a matter of someone reading the wrong name on the register or something."

"What?" said Apple, her voice sharp. "You mean we don't even have the right person? We've been wasting all our time? No offence, Wellingsley."

"None taken," said the young woman.

"What's that?" said Apple, peering at the air just above Janie's head.

"What?" said Janie.

"There's a number there."

Janie turned and looked up into the air. "Where?"

"There. That massive glowing number."

"No, there's not."

Asmodeus followed her line of sight. "Oh, shit. That's the countdown. We've only got a few minutes to go. He's being a bit cocky with assuming none of us want to get changed, isn't he? He's lost all concept of time. Just quickly though, Apple, I'm glad to see you're on board finally."

"You bet I'm on board," said Apple. "This is huge. This is being part of something really big, important, and spectacular. And it's my career backup plan." She waved her invitation in the air. "I'm invited to God's big shindig, for fuck's sake. Once again, no offence, Wellingsley."

She didn't bother to reply this time.

Asmodeus pulled a now familiar piece of card from his bag. "Snap," he said. "Did you get one, Janie?"

"She's my plus one," said Apple. "Maybe you could take Wellingsley."

"Don't bother," snapped Wellingsley. "I didn't even want to go anyway. I know where I'm not wanted."

"I don't think you're not wanted, specifically," said Asmodeus in a vain attempt to smooth the waters. "I think it's more that no one knows about your existence."

Janie glared at him,

"No," he protested. "She's not unwanted as such. She's simply a triviality in the scheme of things. That's what I mean."

Wellingsley's phone rang, and she pulled it from her purse, wiping tears from her eyes. "Yes, I'm in the plaza," she said to her mother. "How did you know? Can you see me?" She gazed around, looking for Gloria. "I can't see you."

"I can see you, don't worry," said Gloria into her ear. "You're under a new light installation. Almost on top of it, by the looks of it. I'll come to you. I'm behind you. I've got something funny to show you. Well, funny odd, not funny ha-ha. A woman with very peppy short hair and a delightfully Rubenesque figure just gave it to me and told me I'm going to be a guest of honour, and I'm wondering if Rupert is trying to butter up support from the rival stations, but even he hasn't taken to calling himself God, so…"

Several things happened at once then. She saw her mother waving with one hand and holding the phone with the other. Seeing that Wellingsley was looking at someone beyond them, the group turned in that direction.

"Everyone," said Wellingsley, "this is my mother, Gloria. Mum, these are my friends."

At the same time, Asmodeus let out a shout and almost leaped forward with a look that somehow mixed astonishment, shock, and complete recognition.

The timer reached single digits. Apple and Asmodeus heard a low resonant bonging sound as the numbers decreased. Her mother, oblivious to the look on Asmodeus's face, reached out to give her daughter a kiss on the cheek and said something that seemed lost in the movement of Asmodeus grabbing Apple's arm and thrusting her toward Gloria.

Wellingsley started to protest, sure that he wouldn't have pushed Apple deliberately, but powerless to come up with any other explanation. Janie too staggered backward, nearly falling, but putting her arms out at the last minute to steady herself.

Almost as two separate occurrences, the numbers reached zero, and an explosion of confetti burst into the air. There was a massive flash of light, which put Wellingsley in the mind of the footage she had seen of atomic bombs exploding over the Pacific Ocean. There was no other way to conceptualize the blinding whiteness that spread over the plaza, seemingly originating from within the spot where Gloria and Apple were standing, but then dispersing out from them like a wave. A low, roaring sound was in their ears, and then, quite suddenly, as if it had been the world's quickest and most hallucinogenic fever dream, it was all gone, and there remained just Wellingsley and Janie standing in the plaza on their own.

CURRIED EGGS IN TUPPERWARE

Cally looked toward a door on the other side of the room. It lay beneath the reach of sunlight, shrouded in darkness, as if some kind of force field prohibited the light from reaching it. The door was the same off-green as the rest of the room, but the cheap plastic doorknob was crooked and discoloured from many decades of constant use.

Adam was on his feet, staring at the door, his breath in his throat.

"Ask her," he croaked. 'What do you mean? Is it—"

She laughed. "No, not Lilith, clearly. I mean, ask Fae. She's the expert, after all."

The door opened gently, and Fae appeared, but a very different Fae from the one the world had previously seen. Gone was the sharp suit, the heels, the crisp collar. Instead, she wore an off-white gown, and her hair fell down her back in shiny waves. She was barefoot and had an unworried and peaceful expression.

"Fae," said Adam uncertainly. "What are you doing here?"

She walked over and placed her hand on the old woman's shoulder. "I've resigned," she said. "I'm not part of any of your agendas any longer."

"Yet here you are," he spat.

"Careful," warned Cally sharply. "You were very rude to her in the car. You owe her an apology."

"Don't let her convince you she's a helping woman, or that she's on your side," he said. "She was trying to keep Lilith down on my behalf. She was being an anti-feminist."

"Because I was stupid," she said. "Because I was trying to make someone love me."

"You ruined the lives of women to make someone love you," he said. "That's pathetic. And you did ruin lives, you know."

She raised her chin defiantly. "I didn't. I really didn't. You inflicting Lilith on them was the real change. I freed them from what they should never have been, if anything."

"Yes," said Adam, "because most women don't want to be like Lilith. Most women don't want to be leaders or visionaries. You're all weak and—"

"No," said the old woman. "You're totally wrong. They can be whatever they want to be. It's just that most of the women Lilith was affixed to weren't of that variety. Not everyone has to be a CEO or a lawyer or a human rights advocate. Some women don't want to have opinions. Some are quite happy to be elderly hags running halfway houses for fae who have got themselves in trouble."

"Women need leadership," said Adam, enunciating each word. "They need to be shown how to behave. Take my wife, for example—"

"You stupid boy." The old woman laughed, her chuckles giving way to the barks of a raspy cough.

Fae went to the tap in the small kitchen attached to the sunroom and ran herself a glass of water.

"You've built up a totally delusional idea in your head, haven't you? I told your father that he needed to involve stronger women in your upbringing. That in the absence of a present mother, you would need someone around to show you which way is up. Especially…" she stopped and sipped the water.

Fae looked at her with concern, and Adam scowled at Fae. "How did you get here anyway?" he asked, ignoring the old woman's words. "You left me in the middle of the street. Illegally parked, if you don't mind. Anything could have happened to me."

"Of course, look around for someone to blame, you stupid boy. You have no idea, do you?" said Cally.

"About what?"

"About who I am."

"You're a mad old bat who saves useless fae from dealing with the consequences of their incompetency, from what I can tell. I'm your mother, you fool," the old woman snapped. "Your mother. I didn't want the responsibility of bringing up a child. Your father wanted to perpetuate some 'coming from the dirt' myth to see how gullible people were, and I had no reason to think he wouldn't make a perfectly passable father."

"What?" Adam's face was ashen. "Don't be stupid. I don't have a mother. I wasn't conceived. I was an original creation. I am the father of all mankind. Dad breathed air into me after creating me from dirt, and then we made Eve from my rib. It was a whole plan. He mapped the entire thing."

"Give me strength," said the old woman. "You have a belly button, you idiot. Why would you have a belly button if you were created from dirt? What possible reason would there be for that?"

Suddenly, the room darkened, and a light blared into visibility in the air in front of them. Large, blue 3D numbers illuminated their faces with a ghostly light. Five blinked a few times before the numbers changed and counted down to 4:59 and then 4:58.

"Oh, cripes, it's the countdown," Cally said. "Five minutes until we're going to be particulated up for the party. I need to get my good handbag and my going-out plastic pearls. You look gorgeous, Fae. Don't change a thing." She cast a judgmental eye over Adam. "You're wearing that, are you?"

"All my clothes are up there," he said. "I haven't had a chance to get changed. Bugger. I've missed the window now. You bloody meddling fools. Not only am I terrified that Lilith is going to pop up out of nowhere and yell at me, but I've now also got a mother, apparently, and I'm wearing fucking jeans and boat shoes. This is not the vision I had when I went through all of it in my head."

"Ah," she said. "That's your problem. Having expectations. That's where you went awry, I'd say."

The numbers hit 4:00 and continued to decrease.

"I can't do this now," Adam said in a shrill voice. "I'm not ready. My clothes are barely smart casual, and this is a party. Dress to celebrate! I was considering making a big announcement. This is going to be a terrible evening; I just know it! This was supposed to be an amazing night."

"Calm down," said Cally. "Get Fae to take you and find you some clothes. There's plenty in there. I told you, it's a halfway house. I've had more through here than you could imagine. I've got to go and get the curried eggs out of the fridge and put them in the good Tupperware."

Adam looked between the women with an expression of anger, annoyance, and a little despair.

"Go on," said Cally. "Fae will show you. Dress up for your dad. He hasn't had a really big shindig in years. The last one was when you and Eve were safely ensconced in the Garden of Eden. You weren't even invited, but look how far you've come. Now, pop off and find some dress shoes."

A VERY FLASH AFFAIR

Sepham looked around, annoyed to find Jared leaning against a wall, eating a pig in a blanket.

"Stop eating the hors d'oeuvre," he snapped. "We're not going to have enough if people who didn't bring a plate start to help themself before things even start." He peered at the other man closely. "I am right in assuming you didn't bring a plate, aren't I?"

Jared rolled his eyes and didn't even deign this question with an answer.

There was a flash and a fizzle in the air as a small group of beings, dressed to the nines and clutching a platter of what looked like bovine feet wrapped in more bovine, appeared in the corner of the room.

Sepham sighed. "Great. We're going to have every species particular form of pigs in a blanket by the looks of it. I knew God should have allocated food groups. I bet we end up with five hundred potato salads and no oysters."

The room was much improved from the way it had looked eighteen hours previously, but it still, at its bones, was utterly recognizable as a scout hall. A huge scout hall in a pocket universe, one that was licensed to provide service for thousands of beings, but a scout hall nonetheless. Wall hangings showing different stages of God's life had been displayed throughout the room, and the floor was covered in fake grass. "A lovely, outdoorsy vibe," God had said, but to Sepham it looked as if someone had put a roof over several football ovals.

Another small group appeared in a distant spot, too far away for Sepham to see what they were carrying.

"Do you think people will have the sense to take everything to the tables against the far wall?" he said to Jared, rhetorically. "Do you think I can assume that people will think for themselves?" He watched them all milling about for a moment and then pursed his lips. "No, of course I can't." He thrust a clipboard into Jared's hands. "Look after this and take any food off people who arrive," he ordered. "But don't eat it," he called over his shoulder.

Jared looked around idly, then glanced down at the clipboard. It seemed to be a rundown of times and events, based loosely around something the party planner had devised before he had resigned in a fit of pique the previous week. It seemed centred around the arrival of God, the star of the show, and another event about twenty minutes after that was simply labelled as "climax".

There was a frisson in the air next to him, and three figures appeared—an old woman wearing a brown overcoat, a younger woman wearing a flowing white gown, and a man of indeterminate age wearing an ill-fitted pair of blue pants and beige shoes.

"Nice shoes," he said.

"Fuck off, Jared," said Adam. "I am not in the mood. You totally screwed me over, and you're on my bloody list now. Once I get all this sorted out, you will not know what hit you." As soon as he had gained his balance, he stalked out of a nearby door.

"Fae," Jared said, smiling at her and pulling her hand up to his mouth. "I see you've taken on your old form. Stunning. I always loved the whole Lady of the Lake get-up, all ephemeral and wispy."

She kept her eyes fixed on a distant point and didn't smile.

Cally smacked at his hand, breaking the connection. "Fuck off, Jared," she said. "Leave her alone. You've done enough damage."

"Is everyone going to be telling me to fuck off all night?"

"It's not his fault," said Fae. "It's not your fault I fell in love with you. I imprinted on you like a duckling. But I'm over you now."

The old woman thrust her curried eggs into Jared's hand and pulled Fae away. "Be careful. You're still not right in the head as far as he's concerned. Put those eggs out somewhere," she snapped over her shoulder as she bustled the young woman away.

"I don't know about anyone else," said Jared out loud to no one in particular, "but this whole thing seems to be going swimmingly well."

A tremor ran up through Jared's feet, and he staggered a little. He thought it might be the impact of his third gin fizz, but he saw that other people were staggering too. A dark space had begun to occupy the area in front of the stage, at first a tiny speck, then growing to the size of a basketball.

People in the nearby vicinity quickly grabbed their belongings and moved out of the way as the deep black nothingness grew until it was the size of a bus. Then the nothingness became opaque, and a group of beings could be seen within it, taking their seats at a table that they seemed to have brought with them.

"It's the Eons from Beyond the Void!" cried Jared joyfully. "Finally! Lads! So good to see you! You are going to *love* what I've got planned for you. Look, I've got snacks!" He made his way into their carefully curated movable void.

Nearby, another group swam into visibility. They seemed to be talking as soon as they arrived.

"Why the fuck did you push me?" Apple snapped at Asmodeus. "I don't even know this woman."

"Apple, meet Gloria. Gloria, meet Apple," said Asmodeus. "Now, you do."

"Where are we?" asked Gloria, looking around.

"God's Big Party. That's what the invitation was for," clarified Asmodeus. "I know, it's a shock. You've become involved against your will."

"Ah," said Gloria. "That does make more sense than Rupert inviting me to one of his parties after our last run-in, I must say. And why am I here?"

"Could be any number of reasons. Have you done any work for God? Or met him?"

Gloria shrugged. "Not that I'm aware of, but I've helped a lot of people. Makes sense that I'd be invited. I feel a bit rude that I didn't bring a plate as the invitation specified. Is God around so I can apologize to him personally?"

"He's probably a bit busy at the moment," said Asmodeus after a moment.

"Not to worry," said Gloria. "I'll catch up with him later. I might just go and work the room for a bit. Anything I should know? Anyone I should make sure I meet?"

"Probably," said Asmodeus in bemusement. "I guess just… go and chat? You're not at all bothered? Surprised?"

"Discombobulated?" finished Apple.

"No, not really," said Gloria. "I've been around a bit. Seen things."

A server passed by carrying eight plates of various patisserie, and she deftly swept one off their fourth arm.

"There we go," she said. "Now I come with a plate." And with that, she disappeared into the crowd.

"Fuck me," said Apple. "She's an absolute weapon. No wonder Wellingsley has always lived in her shadow."

It was at that moment that Sepham coughed loudly and tapped the microphone, blaring feedback into the room.

"Jesus," gasped Apple.

"Actually, I wonder where he's gone to," said Asmodeus, looking around the crowded room.

"If we could make a start," said the angel, and the room fell silent.

THE PLOT THICKENS

"First," said God, wrestling the microphone off Sepham, who couldn't manage to stop himself holding it too close to the speakers and causing terrible feedback, "I want to welcome you here on this very auspicious occasion." He smiled and waved, pointing at a few special people in the audience.

"And a big welcome to the Eons who have dropped in from Beyond the Void. I know you lot don't always like to spend time here, in our frightfully limited dimensions, but I really appreciate you squeezing yourselves into seven dimensions for an hour or two, and I've been reliably informed that the pate you brought is first class, so make sure you get a taste of that before it's all gone! Now, I know many of you are wondering why I've called you all here today."

"To get drunk," called an already inebriated but seemingly happy member of the crowd.

"Yes, that too," laughed God, who seemed to be in his element. "To get drunk, to party, to catch up with old friends, and to thank you all for the help, love, and assistance you have given me over the years. Even those who didn't know they were helping me have helped me in so many ways. And for that, I want to thank you. You're all amazing."

There was a round of applause, as much for themselves as for him, and the rooms thrummed with a happy, convivial vibe.

"There's bloody Fae," said Apple, catching sight of the lady of the lake. "I've a good mind to go and talk to her. Clear this all up once and for all. Find out what her problem is." She pushed her drink into Asmodeus's hand and set off with determination.

Asmodeus turned to see Jared, somewhat unsteadily, sidle up to him. "Up to shenanigans I see," he said, shaking the man's hand. "How did you score an invite? I thought they would have paid someone to tie you up and put you in a car boot for the duration."

"You know me," said Jared. "They can't live with me and can't live without me." His eyes darted shiftily around the room.

"I don't know how you do it," said Asmodeus, shaking his head in awe. "You're an absolute arsehole. You fuck up lives, you do exactly what you want, but you always land on your feet. How do you do it, you old dog?"

Jared swept the long, dark fringe out of his shining eyes. "But am I really? An arsehole?"

"Yes," said Asmodeus. "Yes, of course you are."

He shrugged. "Okay," he said. "You continue to align with that whole paradigm, and I won't challenge your belief. You just believe whatever you want to believe about yourself."

They stood together for a while, enjoying their drinks, watching the crowd. Jared edgily moved back and forth on his feet and automatically took a drink from any waiter who walked past. There was now a slide show being projected on a big screen at the front of the room, and the crowd was craning their appendages, trying to catch a glimpse of whether they'd made an appearance. It went on for quite a while.

"Oh, help," said Jared as he noticed two women barreling toward him. It was Apple pulling Fae by the hand.

"Jared," said Apple, "Fae has something to say to you."

Jared tried to hide behind Asmodeus, who stepped deftly out of the way.

"You are a manipulative arsehole," said Fae, looking him straight in the eye. "You used the fact I had a crush on you to manipulate me to do things I had no business participating in. I do realise that I had the power to say no and did not, but I also think that you exploited my feelings."

"I did," said Jared. "I absolutely did. I knew you were in love with me, and I used that to get what I wanted. Happy?" He held out his mostly empty glass. "If you get a drink, we can do a cheers and move on."

"What's going on?" asked Asmodeus, looking back and forth between the two women.

"We've had a chat," said Apple, "and I've realized it wasn't really Fae's fault, so now we're friends."

"You're Apple, are you?" said Jared.

"Yes, how did you know that?"

"I hear things. I know things." He winked at her.

"Don't try to charm me," she said. "I'm on Fae's side."

"My dear," he said, taking another drink, "I am a trickster. I keep telling people this. I have never pretended to be anything more. I never pretended anything else. Did I Fae?"

"A little bit. A little bit you did."

"Do you blame a snake for biting?" he asked Apple, a look of earnest explanation on his face. "Do you blame a tiger for eating a sweet baby gazelle? A vegan for mercilessly attacking an innocent packet of tofu? No, no, you don't. So why does anyone ever feel that I should act in any way other than the one I do? In fact," he said, "I think that I'm the most authentic being in the entire room. Possibly, the universe. I'm utterly, unashamedly myself, and I never pretend to be anything else. Can you say that about yourselves?"

Apple, Fae, and Asmodeus glanced at each other uncomfortably.

"Exactly," he said, passing each of them a glass from a waiter who'd walked by, then clinking each of their glasses in turn. "So, whatever happens as the night progresses, I want you to remember this conversation. Everything that happens should be viewed in light of that. Now, let's listen. I think he's about to get to the good bit."

The slide show had finished, and God had stepped up to the mike again. He had been talking to someone out of the audience's line of sight, and a look of concern had crossed his face. He was shaking his head and looking at his watch, his brow furrowed and his beard tremoring a little.

"As you know, I want you all here to thank you. And a vitally important part of that is thanking my amazing children. We're just having a bit of trouble tracking them down, but please take a moment to help yourself to some of the delightful crispy offal bites that Nesferatu brought along, and we will be back with you in just a moment."

"I don't know where she is," hissed Sepham. "She got the invitation, of course. She should have been brought up here at the same time as everyone else. I don't know why that didn't happen."

"Find her," hissed God, making sure the smile stayed on his face as he spoke. "I don't want to continue without her, and I can't keep all these people here indefinitely. They'll get bored. And we'll run out of food."

"And oxygen," offered Sepham.

"We've got Adam, though, right?" asked God.

"We've got him. He's in a terrible mood, but he's here."

"Dad," said Adam, gesturing at his father from behind the curtains that edged the stage, raised just enough off the floor for people to be able to see what was happening, but not enough to give too much of an aura of superiority or patriarchal dominance. "Dad, they won't let me go back in to get changed, and I do not like this outfit."

"You look wonderful, my boy," said God, taking his son's hands. "Do you have a report ready for the party?"

"A report?" asked Adam uncertainly.

"Yes, on the extinction event you've been working to prevent. To show your leadership ability and willingness to step up."

Adam looked at him blankly.

"The reason why you've been down on Earth. Remember, I said I'd need a report for you to present when it's all over."

Adam shook his head as if shaking away an annoying fly. "No, I haven't, and quite honestly, I don't know why you're obsessing about that. No one cares."

"But I gave you the specific job to do," he said.

"Yes, yes," replied Adam. "I'll do it next time. Next week. I'll put out a PowerPoint, and we can email it to anyone who cares. I need to go and put on some other clothes; these make me look like a poor person."

"Adam," said God, looking aghast. "You can't say that."

Adam rolled his eyes. "Alright, they make me look like a fiscally challenged person. Either way, I'm not going out there looking like this. Just because you want to pretend to care about pathetic losers doesn't mean that I need to join you."

"This is a party partly in your honour. And Eve's. So, I expect you to—"

"I didn't ask for it," said Adam. "I didn't ask for a party, did I? So maybe you should just do it all on your own. I didn't ask to be born either. Neither of my parents consulted me."

God stared after him aghast. "Why is he acting like this?" he said to no one in particular.

Sepham, who had been hovering around God's elbow, couldn't help but become engaged. "Acting like what?"

"So rude. So entitled. So uncaring of his responsibilities."

Sepham tilted his head to the side, contemplating how to say this in a way that wouldn't get him smited. "And that's different from usual, is it?"

"Of course it is." God's face looked horrified. "He's usually so understanding. So good at giving advice. So supportive of me."

Sepham pursed his lips. "Permission to speak honestly without you banishing me to some peripheral dimension where everyone is shaped like a hexagonal prism."

"Permission granted."

"This is how he always behaves when he doesn't get what he wants or when he's under stress."

"No, it's not," said God. "He never acts like this."

"That is true," said Sepham carefully. "He doesn't act like this very often. Around you, that is."

"Wait," said God.

I'll give him a minute, thought Sepham.

"Is that because…"

"Yes. Because there have been exceedingly few occasions in his life where he has had anything withheld from him, or when he has been under real stress. Character-building stress, anyway. You have always given him everything he wanted. Always."

God rubbed his head. "This changes everything," he whispered.

"I did try to tell you," said Sepham unnecessarily. "Many times."

"And Eve?" he said. "Is she like this, too?"

"No, but I suspect she's not here because she doesn't want to be," he said. "She's not here because she's made a new life for herself, and from what I can tell, she wants it to be lived separately from you and Adam."

"I'm a failure," said God. "This is all a failure. I wanted to tell everyone publicly how amazing they both are and ask if they wanted to take on a leadership role."

"You were really leaning into that idea?"

"Yes. Eventually, I was going to retire. And learn how to put those ships in little bottles. Maybe start up a food truck selling tacos. It's all planned. I was going to call it 'Not Just for

Tuesdays'. I think I'd be great at that. But now, what am I going to do?"

"In that case, I need to tell you something," said Sepham.

God eyed him uneasily.

"Adam was planning on taking over. Not tonight specifically, but he was planning on…wresting power from you, or some such."

"Wresting?" said God in bemusement. "But he wouldn't have had to. I was going to offer my position to him."

"Well, he didn't know that. He wanted to take it by force. And one of the reasons he was so obsessed with keeping Lilith away was because he worried she might stop him. Because she's the only one powerful enough to ever stop him. And also because he loathes her to an unreasonable and troubling degree."

"Excuse me," blustered God. "I'm actually God. I would absolutely have been able to stop him from taking over."

"But would you?" said Sepham. "You've always given him everything he wanted. I assume he just thought he could demand it from you and you'd cave. You've never set boundaries."

God's face fell.

"And he doesn't agree with your new character development. Doesn't like the whole woke pacifist equality vibe. He thinks you're weak."

God's tired eyes looked at Sepham pleadingly. "Why didn't you tell me this earlier?"

"I tried to…"

All of a sudden, a voice cut across the babble of the crowd, and a figure pushed their way through the curtain. "Where is he?" asked the woman.

"Just when I thought my day couldn't get any worse," said God in a weak voice as he saw Cally descending on him. "Please don't tell me all my exes have been invited?"

"I feel I should tell you that the boy now knows I'm his mother," she said, standing before him and barely coming up to his chin. "And he's none too happy about it."

"How does he know? I've successfully kept that from him his whole life."

"It was time he knew," she said sternly.

"That would explain his mood. It's all your fault."

"Bullshit," she barked. "He's got an appalling attitude, and he acts like an entitled brat. I'm pretty sure that the thirty minutes I've spent with him didn't make that happen. That's ingrained, that is. Ingrained entitlement. I'm just disappointed, is all I'll say."

God grabbed her hands, a look of desperation on his face. "I was going to hand over the leadership to them tonight. I was going to let them become co-rulers, but now I can't because I've just realized it's too much responsibility for them. I haven't trained them. But Adam was going to try to take over by force or something."

"He's more likely to try to take over by sulking, from what I've seen of him. What about the girl?" she asked. "Could she do it on her own?"

"No, she's been gadding about on the planet buying shoes and trying to find herself. And she's…well, she's a girl. She's flighty. She can't do it on her own. What am I going to do?"

"Don't ask me," said Cally. "I'm off to try the finger food. There's some good stuff down there. But not the offal, steer well clear. That poor animal had a long and fraught life."

"But they're waiting for me," he hissed, casting around for Sepham. "I'm expecting to make a speech at any moment, but I don't know what to say now. I—"

"I can do it," said the old woman. "Do you want me to have a go?"

"Of course I don't want you to make a bloody speech at my own party," he snapped. "What possible reason would you have for thinking I'd ever want that?"

"I'm just offering to help," she said innocently. "You're so touchy these days. You need a holiday."

"I'm trying to take a holiday," he said between gritted teeth. "I am trying to find someone who is capable enough to look after things while I'm gone, but, as you can see, I can't even rely on my children to attend a simple party appropriately, so there's very little chance that I'll be able to."

"Ah," said the old woman. "Nepotism. Nice."

"Don't you talk to me about nepotism," he snapped. "Don't you even dare. You wouldn't even have that—"

"Oh, shut up, you decrepit old has-been. Everything I have I got from my own hustle, so don't think for a moment that you have had anything to do with my run-down weatherboard house and guttering that needs a complete overhaul."

"Your guttering needs an overhaul, does it?" said Jared, sidling up to them. "I think I know a good joke along those lines."

"Who are you?" asked God. "Who even is this? I don't have time for autographs at the moment, sorry, son. I'm in the middle of things."

"Just wanted to thank you for the invite," he said. "Much obliged. I've been doing quite a lot of work for you lately, and I wanted to let you know that I'm a big fan. Huge. Been chatting to some of your work colleagues too. They say hi." Jared waved toward the area that the Eons were occupying.

"They wanted to say that they hope you get everything you deserve tonight. They're mutual work colleagues of both of us, I suppose you could say."

"Sir, you're going to need to make your big speech now. This running sheet didn't create itself, you know," said Sepham, gently pushing Jared out of the way.

"Sorry," said God, peering at Jared. "Which colleagues?"

"The Eons," said Jared. He waved into the crowd again.

God glanced at Sepham nervously. "I'm beginning to think it may have been a mistake to invite them. They're so unpredictable."

"Well, you did business with them. It was the right thing to do.

You can't go around leaving out major donors. Especially not them."

"Quite right," said Jared. "You wouldn't want to annoy them more than they already are."

"I'm beginning to think," said Sepham, "that you have quite a close relationship with everyone."

"An especially close relationship with the Eons from Beyond the Void," Jared said.

"Very good," said God, his attention now firmly on his speech. "Someone has to, I suppose."

"You used to have a good relationship with them, too, didn't you?" he said, looking at God pointedly. "You had an excellent relationship with them. When they could give you what you needed. Remember that? Remember when they used to do jobs for you?"

"Er, yes," said God. "They did, I suppose. I don't really remember…"

Sepham pulled at Jared's arm. "Come on," he said. "You're being weird. More weird than usual, and I don't have the capacity to deal with it at the moment, so you're going to have to rejoin the party. Where's my clipboard?"

"No idea," said Jared. "I'm getting quite drunk, you know."

"I would have expected nothing less. If you want to make yourself useful, go and find Adam."

A TOUCH OF GUILT

Fae couldn't help but watch Jared as he worked the room, her attention unable to settle on Apple's chatter in her ear. He was magnetic. His three-piece suit shimmered, but in the way that only very expensive material shimmers.

He seemed to know everyone, chat to everyone, and be friends with everyone. There were calls to him from one corner, and as soon as he'd gone and engaged in hearty pattings on the back, he'd be called over to another group. She loved to watch him; he was so smooth, so handsome, so…

"Stop it," barked the old woman as she sat down next to her. "Stop looking at him. It won't do you any good. You're not going to get over him if you're all doolally at him, schmoozing people and being all debonaire. Leave it alone. I think there are bigger things for you to focus on tonight."

"Like what?" she said. "What am I going to do now? I've got no man. I've got no job. I've got no lake anymore."

The old woman stared at her to the point that Fae felt awkward and looked away.

"Do you feel anything… strange? Anything at all? Anything a bit odd?"

"No," said Fae. "Why have you been asking me that so much?"

The old woman shrugged. "I just thought you might, that's all."

"But what am I going to *do*?"

"Never mind about that. We'll find you something. A hobby. Look, you've been invited to this nice party. That's a good start, isn't it? Getting out from under yourself. Why don't we find you someone new to talk to while we're here? There are a lot of new people. Look, there's Asmodeus. He's lovely." She waved and gestured him over.

"This is a motley crew, isn't it?" he said by way of greeting.

"I can't believe some of the people who have turned up. Are there any chairs around? Let's make a little enclave here." He cast around, and soon there was a small cluster of chairs where he, Cally, Fae, and Apple sat.

"How about Wellingsley's mother?" he asked. "Does she want to join us?"

Apple peered around. "She's still working the room. She's giving out business cards, if you can believe it. It's amazing. I don't know if people genuinely want them or if they're just too scared to say no."

"Oh, wait up," said Asmodeus, noting a hush come over the crowd, which was parting in waves.

"What's happening?" asked Cally, a look of displeasure on her face that something potentially dramatic was happening without her prior awareness.

Hand in hand, two people were walking toward the stage area. A short, voluptuous woman with an ugly green hat pulled over her head, and a man who was only slightly taller than her, dark and tubby.

Whispers began to scatter through the crowd that had fallen silent at their entrance. Whispers of Eve and Zeus could be heard darting around the room.

"Oooooooh," said Cally, grasping her drink and sitting back as a huge grin spread across her face. "I'd heard talk of this, but I didn't know it had really happened. I am *loving* this. They're going to write songs about this night, I can tell you right now." She reached for another mini meringue.

"What?" said Apple, leaning in toward her conspiratorially. "What's going on?"

The old woman grabbed her hand. "See, that's Eve. You know, Garden of Eden?"

"Yes, lovely girl."

"I think she's about to stand up for herself finally. There's some ancestral healing business going on in here, let me tell you."

Eve held Zeus's hand more firmly as they stepped up onto the stage. She had moved quickly to get the invitation to Gloria and then get here herself, but there was one thing she still wasn't sure of, a stubborn piece of the puzzle she hadn't been able to work out. But as the Guardian of the Library had said, trust. So she did. Or tried to. She embraced God, who was looking slightly shellshocked, and gave what the entire audience could see was a withering glare at Adam, who seemed to shrink a little in the face of it.

She looked away from him and took the microphone. "Good evening, everyone," she said, and her voice was strong and clear. She looked down at the crowd, and her eyes lit on her former assistant, Petalyn. She was holding a sandwich in one hand, and with the other, she gave Eve an enthusiastic thumbs-up.

"I am absolutely delighted at whatever is about to happen," muttered an old woman next to her, just loud enough for Eve to hear. The woman propped her feet up on an empty chair. "This is definitely going to be the second-best bit of the evening." The people around shushed her, and Eve carried on.

"Good evening," she said again. "I don't know if any of you know this, but my name is Eve, and I'm…" She faltered. "I'm God's daughter." She glanced back at her father, who had sat in a plush red chair specially designed for the occasion, making eye contact with him for a moment.

Here, the crowd broke out into applause in the strange way that groups of people sometimes do. The same way that an announcement that a couple has been married for thirty years causes people to spontaneously clap, although it's not clear whether that's because of genuine appreciation or absolute pity.

"This gathering today was arranged by my father, and from what I know, everyone who is important or significant to him in some way is here."

A few people clapped again, and she felt Zeus slide his hand comfortingly onto the small of her back.

"So, yes," she said again. "My name is Eve, and I'm here to speak my truth. Once upon a time," she said, "I was young and stupid. Young, stupid, newly married, and I loved a man. Because of this, I made mistakes. I betrayed the best friend I'd ever had. The only person who was brave enough, who was strong enough, to tell me the truth. I betrayed her, and in doing so, helped kickstart the patriarchy."

Here, there was a clear division in the crowd. Some started to fidget edgily, avoid eye contact, and pass their drinks from one hand to the other. Some smiled broadly and looked around, meeting the eyes of people across the room in a way that said, "Here we go. This is going to be good."

"I'm here to atone for my mistakes."

"Very Old Testament," she heard a woman in the crowd say. "Nice one. I appreciate it."

"I caused a good woman, an amazing woman, to be destroyed. Well, there was an attempt to destroy her. Because of my actions, I allowed my husband and father to fragment her off into every corner of the universe."

Behind her, she heard her father saying something about how it wasn't her fault, and she shouldn't be blaming herself, but she carried on.

"With the help of the love of my life, I pledged to do everything I could to get her back together, to make her whole again, and to be my friend. But on that note, I want to introduce the most amazing man I have ever known. Zeus."

He waved bashfully from beside her but refused the microphone when she offered it.

"My marriage to Adam is, and always was, a lie," she said. "And I need it to be known in front of my community, in front of all of you, that I can't live this lie anymore. He is a cruel, unloving husband who wants to control me. And by the end of the night, if I can do what I hope I can do, we'll all get the chance to see my friend Lilith again."

She handed the microphone to her father and embraced Zeus.

"Well done," he muttered into her hair. "You were magnificent. But do you have an exact plan, as such? Because I feel like there's going to be a lot of people watching you from now on."

"You stupid cow," growled Adam from behind her, where he had been standing, glowering, watching. "You stupid cow. How dare you make a fool of me?"

Eve turned her head slightly so that no one in the audience could read her lips. "You're the only one making a fool of yourself," she said. "You're a relic from a dying age, and everyone's laughing at you. Now shut up while our father talks."

"Well," said God, "if that's going to happen, and forgive me for being honest, but I'd be quite delighted if we could make that work. Eve and I have been in accord about our regrets surrounding that for some time. But, if we're expecting something exciting later, then I'd better get on with the rest of it. Truth be told, the actual aim of this party has been a bit of a moving feast over the past few hours, but I am nothing if not flexible! It's true that I've made many mistakes during my long and blessed life. In the early days, I made decisions that I wasn't proud of. To those people who have stayed with me over the years, who have stayed by me, loved me, and yes, mentored me, I say, thank you. Firstly, to my progeny, Adam and Eve. Yes, I know you both said you don't want your names associated anymore, but forgive me this last indulgence, my dears. To my loyal, steadfast Sepham, who has not only done my bidding but also guided me in areas that I needed to work on, to…"

He continued to list names. "And now for my mistakes," he said.

The crowd was growing restless.

"This is getting a bit self-indulgent," said Apple. "I don't know any of these people. Some of these mistakes are pretty boring and not juicy at all."

In the middle of the room, Jared moved away from the table where the Eons were sitting. He was looking for someone, or several someones.

"Look out," said Asmodeus. "Here he comes."

He approached them, smiling. Fae's face lit up automatically before she had a chance to fix it into its new position, but he walked right past her, approached Apple, and put his hand out. "May I have the pleasure of your company, my dear?" he asked. "I know you don't like me, but indulge me in my little frippery for a moment, will you?"

Apple shrugged, stood, and linked her arm in his, rolling her eyes at Fae as if in apology.

Arm in arm, they disappeared into the crowd.

Cally took Fae's hand, but she slapped it away. "If you ask me how I'm feeling again, I will not be responsible for my actions."

CHAMPAGNE COMEDY

In the crowd, Eve saw Jared take Apple by the arm and lead her away. She stepped backward behind Zeus, hoping that her father wouldn't notice her disappearance, and left the stage. As she stepped into the crowd, she could hear his voice continue.

"So, the reason I have you all here tonight can be divided into two parts," said God. "First, to apologise to everyone I have wronged. I hope, over the next few millennia, to apologise to each of you individually. But also, I want to start looking to the future. Forward planning. Looking at the best management structure going forward. I did consider making Adam leader, but I've decided he isn't quite ready."

Eve glanced up at the stage and saw Adam's face blanch first white, then flush red.

"I've decided that I'm here at the helm for a reason, and let's be frank…"

"Hi, Frank," called the wag from the audience.

"No one else can do it as well as I can do it. I'm pretty good."

An appreciative titter rang through the crowd as Eve continued to look for Jared.

"I've learned so much over time that I've decided to commit to another four thousand years of rulership. Imagine what we can get done with that kind of continuity!"

Jared appeared from the crowd with Apple still on his arm, passing by close enough to touch.

"Apple, stay here," hissed Eve. "Wait for me. I'm not quite ready, yet." But Apple didn't hear her.

"May I have a moment at the microphone when you're done?" Jared called out as he neared the stage. "Why don't you try an open mike thing? That would be a good touch."

God stared into the crowd, trying to identify who had called to him. "Oh, it's that popular chap. Yes, maybe some standup might be fun? Would you like to start? And you have some assistants with you. Is it a magic show? What do you think?" He looked to Sepham, who seemed to think that Jared having the microphone was a terrible idea.

"Come on up," he said to Jared.

Eve waved at her father, trying to get his attention, but he didn't seem to see her.

"You do seem to have quite a magnetic personality, don't you? Maybe you could step in and do some entertaining for me. Let's give him some space, everyone."

"Right. Is this thing on? Hi there, I'm Jared." He waved and smiled. "Some of you know me. Some of you, better than others." He winked and pointed at a few people in the crowd. "Okay, a lot of you know me. I've been around for a while. And today, I want us to work together to solve a mystery."

"Oooooh." As if on cue, the crowd around Eve gasped theatrically, already putty in his hands.

"That's right. I want to solve a mystery. A conundrum. A challenge if you like. You see, I like puzzles. Tricks. Riddles. Love them. And I'm very good at them. And some of my people know that, right?" He pointed toward the Eons from Beyond the Void. "Now, they're my people. My boys. My girls. We've had some good times together. And I love a bet. And if you know anything, you know how those absolute scallywags from Beyond the Void love a flutter! And whoo-hoo, what they've promised me! Now, a bit of context. The elephant in the room? It's Lilith, right? She's taken on this mythological status because, yes, she had a fight with God and Adam, and they turned her into the biggest puzzle in the history of the universe."

There was an uneasy hum in the room now. Some beings were still smiling broadly, some were glancing around nervously, and one or two had decided it would be a good time to leave the venue entirely.

"Literally, she's a jigsaw, right?" continued Jared, draining the last drops of a glass he had found on the podium. "And my word, the attention she's been getting. You'd think she was the only thing happening at the moment. Adam hates her on a really dysfunctional level. Eve is trying to assuage her personal guilt. Asmodeus wants to play Happy Families. I know, right? How good do you have to be to make a sex demon pledge to be monogamous?"

He shaded his eyes and peered out into the audience. "Who knew her? Hands up, who had partied with Lilith? And by partied, you know I mean…" He made an ambiguous movement with his eyebrows that most people were able to correctly interpret. "She was fun. A party girl. But the myths that have grown up about her, good and bad, they've taken on a life of their own. You either think she's plotting the downfall of civilization, or you see her as the first female president of everything. Which is weird because she's been a bunch of discombobulated molecules for thousands of years. Because God fucked it all up, didn't he," he said, his voice getting louder now, his eyes wilder. "I know that you all know. It's the universe's worst-kept secret. They had a fight, and she got fragmented. But," he continued, holding up a slightly unsteady finger, "there's another bit here we need to get to. A good bit."

He took the microphone off its stand and held it as if he was going to launch into a song like an old crooner. “There’s some stuff you don’t know. Do I need to tell you? Do you want to know?”

“Yes!” cried the more disreputable members of the crown.

“About me! Let’s talk about me. Where did I come from? No one knows that, do they?”

Eve felt a presence behind her and turned to see the old woman who had been making the interjections earlier. “You know what you’re doing, don’t you?” she said.

Eve nodded. “Yes, I do.”

“Good.” The woman took hold of her hand and patted it. “You’re very impressive, you know. Very impressive. I’m here if you need me.”

Eve could see God watching Jared carefully. His eyes seemed sharper than usual, his face impassive. He had one leg comfortably crossed over the other, and he jigged his foot while his arms rested on the plush sides of his chair. He sipped his wine.

“So, I arrived on the scene, a wunderkind, a bolt of lightning. Kazam!” He made shooting motions in the air with his fingers. “But that lot,” he pointed down to the Eons beyond the Void, “that lot, well, notice any similarities? Maybe not. I’ve got fewer holes in my head than they do. And only two penises. But apart from that, yeah, that’s my bros. My homies. I left a long time ago. But they didn’t forget me, did they?”

“Yes, we did!” yelled one of them, and the crowd laughed, somewhat relieved.

“They remembered me. And when I said I wanted to go back, they set me a puzzle. Now, how many of you have been to Beyond the Void? Yes? None of you. Well, let me tell you, it’s amazing. Even the water has an alcohol content of 60%. Where was I? Ah, yes, the puzzle. Solve the puzzle, win the prize. And what’s the prize?” He tapped the side of his nose. ‘That’s for me to know. But the puzzle, I can tell you that bit. The puzzle is Lilith!’ He peered into the crowd. “Did we talk about Lilith? Asmodeus, she’s your woman, right? How come you haven't been doing a better job finding her?"

"Be fair. I've been trying," Asmodeus called back.

"Barely," said Jared. "You've all been useless. Not like me. I've been making connections, working it out. The Eons said that if I solve the puzzle, I get to be the winner! And of course, they wanted to piss off God. Will you be pissed off, God? When she comes back?"

God waggled his hand noncommittally and muttered something about letting bygones be bygones. There was a pulse of unrelenting darkness from the Void's table, and Jared glanced at them a little nervously.

"That's a little disappointing," he said. "I think they were expecting you to be irritated. Some old fire and brimstone, maybe. We didn't expect character development on your end. Never mind, I'll plug on. Who's your first choice for the ones with an ember of Lilith?" he asked Asmodeus.

Asmodeus pointed up to the stage.

"Apple, right? Ding, ding, ding, yes, we have a winner."

"You," he said, swinging around and pointing at Adam. "How about you? Where do you think she was?"

"There was a girl," he said. "Wellingsley."

"Nope," Jared said, cutting through the air with his hand like a knife. " You're totally wrong."

"But you're the one who told us who she was in," said Asmodeus, who had made his way to the foot of the stairs. "You're the one who gave us the bloody list!"

"Why must people keep listening to me?" he barked. "Why do people believe a single thing I ever say? I'm a trickster. I make shit up. I was still trying to work out who she was in. I was hardly going to be able to give you a complete list, was I? While I was still trying to find all the pieces? But it was… drumroll, please… Cally!"

The old woman next to Eve let out a bark of laughter. "Oh, he's gone doolally this time," she said.

"Yes, Cally, she's down there with Eve... see?" He waved down at her, and she shook her head as she made her way up to the stage, pulling Eve along with her.

"I've got my fingers in a lot of pies," yelled Cally to the audience, "but this isn't one of them."

The crowd laughed, loving her immediately.

"You didn't think I'm a Lilith ember, did you?" she whispered into Eve's ear, "because if you do, we're fucked."

"No offense," replied Eve, "but I don't even know who you are."

"Excellent. Play those cards close to your chest until it's your moment."

"But there's one more thing," said Jared, causing the microphone to pop unpleasantly. He positioned Apple next to Cally and moved Eve to stand behind them. "One main piece. These are just embers. There's one huge whack of Lilith still unaccounted for. The crucial piece. The keystone, if you like. This one took me a while, I'll be honest with you. The first ones were easy, but this one took ages. But there are no coincidences, are there? And she was already intimately involved! But I had a last-minute hunch, and today, my hunch will be validated."

"Fae," he called. "Oh, Fae, my gorgeous girl, can you come up here please, light of my life?"

Fae made her way to the stage.

"Do any of you know Fae? She's lovely. Gorgeous girl. I'm quite in love with her."

He smiled and stroked her face with his hand cupping her chin.

"Gorgeous girl," he repeated. He reached out and took Cally's hand, placing it in one of hers.

"It's you," he said to Fae. "It was always you."

He took Apple's hand in his, placed it in Fae's, and then...

THE VORTEX CLEANS UP

Nothing happened.

"Fuck," said Jared mildly. "That's all I had. Damn it."

"I did tell you," said Cally. "Maybe give Eve a go now."

Eve stepped up and put her hands on her hips. "So typical," she said, "that you think you're right when you've actually got no idea what you're doing. You think you can just waltz in here with a shoddily written list and clean up?" She shook her head in disgust. "It's not Cally, it's Gloria. Gloria, can you come up here, please?"

The impeccably dressed woman who had been working the room and had already brokered several deals between her news station and the Upper Realms gave her a wave and stepped forward. "Of course," she said. "Delighted. This is such a fascinating, dynamic crowd. I'm quite in awe of you all."

Jared, pale-faced and grumpy, had left the stage and now sat next to Adam, the two of them mainlining a particularly virulent beetroot-infused vodka.

"Two of the three women needed to bring Lilith back are Apple and Fae," said Eve, "that's correct, but it's also Gloria. You were close with Wellingsley, but it was actually her mother. How you ever thought a conservative wannabee housewife would be an ember of Lilith when her mother has made the list of the top fifty women in business for fifteen years running and is one of the most iconic lesbians in the country is beyond me, but okay."

"Hurry up," heckled Jared sullenly. "I'm bored. If you're so great, then bring Lilith back. At least give us something to look at."

Eve took Fae's hand and placed it once again in Apple's, and Gloria took both their hands. There was an audible sigh as if the universe had let out a breath it had been holding for eternity, and all of a sudden, a tall, naked woman appeared in front of them. Her olive skin glowed, and her hair cascaded down around her shoulders. She looked about her, her eyes wide and a look of aghast bemusement on her face. She seemed to be standing for a moment, but then realized that gravity existed and collapsed to the ground.

"Oh, come on," yelled Jared, leaping to his feet. "That was all my work. Two out of four ain't bad, surely. Come on. I should get some credit for that." He stood with his hands up in the air, but no one was paying any attention to him. Everyone was focused on the collapsed woman, who was now surrounded by Fae, Apple, Gloria, Eve, and Cally, who had made her way onto the stage.

A hushed murmur ran over the crowd. They weren't sure whether this was real or an elaborate piece of performance art, but either way, they hoped it wouldn't impact the open bar.

God strode forward and spoke powerfully into the microphone. "Well, that's the magic show done. Now, may the party commence. Music please! Music!"

And a reggae version of "Bat out of Hell" blared through the speakers.

He kneeled next to the unconscious woman. "Is she all right, do you think?" he asked softly.

Cally had her hand on her forehead. "What do you think, you bloody fool? She's just been brought back from the liminal spaces. She hasn't even felt her body in several millennia. She's been a disembodied consciousness floating around directionless. How the bloody hell do you think she is?"

"She's breathing," said Fae. "Just."

Cally closed her eyes and concentrated for a moment. "She's not all there," she said.

"You're not all there," muttered God.

"I mean, she's not all here. Some of her ember isn't here yet. There's a part of her still missing."

"How do you know so much about this? She's not conscious, that much is pretty bloody obvious," said Eve.

"We've been communicating. I've been having seances with her. I know what she wants. She's going to change things for women."

"But she wasn't dead," said Apple. "How can you have seances with someone who isn't dead?"

"She was hardly bloody well alive, was she? She was a disembodied consciousness floating around reality. How many times do I have to tell you this?"

"What have I done?" said God, pulling at his beard anxiously.

"This is a physical manifestation of your shenanigans over history," snapped Cally. "This is what you do, and you've always done except usually you don't see it. You need a poor woman collapsing at your party to really understand it, do you?"

"Yes. I did solve the puzzle." Jared's voice came to them from below the stage. "She's there. It's solved. It's a whole...jigsaw. Look, two legs, a head, and an appropriate number of breasts. I have done exactly what you challenged me to do. I completed the mission successfully!"

"What's happening?" said Cally to Asmodeus, who was hanging back and watching the women surround Lilith.

"The Eons won't fulfil their side of the bargain because they say Jared didn't complete the task properly. They're saying that just because her body is there, it doesn't mean she is."

"They don't even care," snapped Cally. "They're just shit

stirrers who like mischief. If you hadn't stiffed them in your business dealings, we could all be dancing the Pride of Erin right now, you know that, don't you?" she said to God.

Fae was ignoring everything around her. "What have I done?" she sobbed softly. "I was trying to keep her fragmented all this time, but I was part of her? There was an ember of her in me? Why didn't I know? Why didn't anyone tell me?"

"No one knew, not for sure," said Cally. "And historically, when people did discover it, reality was rebooted. Then, after Old Mate here kicked the Eons off the job, any discovery meant their memory was wiped."

Adam broke into the circle and pushed Fae and Cally away. "I'll take over from here. She was created for me at the beginning of history, so I'm going to take her away for the appropriate medical care."

"Don't be ridiculous," said Cally. "She doesn't need medical care. She's just a shell. You can't—"

"I'll make sure she gets the medical care she needs to keep her in this state. She's the perfect woman now, isn't she? Totally silent."

"No," hissed Fae, pushing him away roughly. "No, you can fuck off. She's ours now. Don't you dare even touch her."

He stumbled back, taken by surprise at her sudden burst of strength.

The argument between Jared and the Eons was becoming more heated now, and a swirling vortex was stirring as their voices rose. There seemed to be a lot of accusations being hurled back and forth about deals made and deals done, and who owed who and the lack of entertainment that had been promised. The color of the membrane that surrounded the Eon's table, which had been almost completely translucent during the more pleasant nibbles and drinks part of the evening, was darkening rapidly, and the vortex at the centre of it began to spiral wildly. Jared leaned forward and demanded that they meet him halfway, but various beings within the net could be seen stuffing bread rolls and miniature doughnuts into their bags as a precursor to leaving.

"They're off," muttered Cally. "And none too soon."

As Adam staggered backward, he fell from to stage directly into the space occupied by the Eons table, and at the precise moment that he met the dark vortex, there was a muffled pop, leaving a pitch-black, yet also completely nonexistent void, in the space that their table had occupied.

Both the Eons from Beyond the Void, Jared, and Adam had disappeared.

"I suppose that solves that problem then," said Cally, and God met her eye and gave a tiny, almost imperceptible nod.

"We need to move away from here," said Asmodeus, pushing between them all. He knelt and lifted Lilith's still body in his arms, pulling her toward his powerful chest. He closed his eyes for a moment and rested his head against hers before looking to God. "Can't we go somewhere else?" he said. "Away from all this ridiculousness?"

"Certainty, certainly, ah, Sepham," beckoned God. "Can we pop into another room? Is there a little dimensional vortex here we can use?"

"Yes, of course. But do you really think you should leave? I mean, it's your party, and the dance floor does seem to be taking off now."

"Quite right, quite right. And I have been practicing the Nutbush. I just feel a trifle responsible."

"We don't need you," said Cally. "This is women's business now."

"Yes of course, of course." He took Zeus by the arm. "Let's leave them. I guess I need to get to know my new son-in-law."

Sepham ushered them into a small room off the main stage, which was filled, inexplicably, with papier mâché.

"One of us must know what to do," said Eve. "We just need to make all the connections. She's waiting for us. She's waiting to come back and take her rightful place."

"I feel so helpless," sobbed Fae. "I wish I knew what we could do to help her."

Minutes went by. Lilith was breathing, her face perfect, her body still, but they all unmistakably knew there was no soul within her.

Eve chewed her lip. "I wonder," she said. "If maybe…" And she disappeared toward the door. "I'll be back in a minute," she called over her shoulder.

"It's hardly the time for dancing," muttered Asmodeus.

They sat, listening to the thumping bass from the other room, and waited for something to happen.

Eve returned a few minutes later, pulling a bemused-looking Wellingsley and Janie by the hand.

"We're invited now, are we? said Janie a little haughtily. 'Who's this then?"

"This is Lilith," said Apple. "She's the future of all womankind, from what I can tell. I'm not sure if all the details have been worked out, though. A lot has happened; I'll fill you in later. Eve, what are they doing here?"

Asmodeus cradled Lilith's head in his lap, brushing her hair back from her face.

"It must be her," said Fae. "I can't have been that wrong, can I? There must be part of her in Wellingsley. I'm sure. I felt it. When we were at the panel, I felt this strange connection. Yes, it was mostly her mother, but I think there was still a piece of Lilith in you, Wellingsley, even if no one else knows about it. You're still involved. You're still important to this. Together, we can call her back to fulfil her destiny."

Wellingsley sank to her knees, reached out her hand, and took Lilith's cold fingers in hers.

Nothing happened for a moment, and then with the tiniest sigh as if creation took a breath but didn't want to disturb the air at all, Lilith opened her eyes.

SOMEONE DIDN'T READ THE SCRIPT

"Amazing, thanks," Lilith said, pulling herself up to a sitting position. She ran her fingers through her shining hair and stretched her back, pressing the palms of her hands into it. She smiled broadly at Asmodeus and stroked his cheek. "Hey, handsome," she said.

"You're back." He smiled, and their lips met.

The women who sat in a circle surrounding her sat back, giving them some space, smiling beatifically.

After about thirty seconds with neither Lilith nor Asmodeus coming up for air, the women began to look down at the ground or pick at their nails.

After two minutes, Cally cleared her throat. "Welcome, Lilith," she said. "We have waited for this moment for a long time. My name is Cally. Your coming was prophesied."

Lilith removed herself from Asmodeus and looked at the old woman.

"And I'm honoured to meet you," Cally continued.

"Prophesized, you say." Lilith looked around as if noticing the other women for the first time. "Oh my, look at you all. Are you… Are you the ones I was attached to?"

They nodded or mumbled agreement or just smiled. “We are,” said Apple. ‘We’ve been carrying pieces of you.”

“Thanks,” said Lilith brightly. “I appreciate it. And you all managed to find each other, too. Eventually, so thanks for that. Took you a while, though.”

“You were aware of it?” asked Apple. “Of us?”

“Kind of,” she said, scrunching up her face as if to demonstrate her tenuous understanding of things. “I had some vague idea. I’d get a flash every now and then, and someone would communicate with me every once in a while to fill me in, but it’s all a bit hazy.”

“That was me,” said Cally. “We were in communication.”

“I feel like communication is a bit of a stretch. I didn’t have a huge idea what was going on.”

There was an awkward silence.

“But thanks though.”

Eve cleared her throat. “Lilith,” she said softly. “I want to apologise for betraying you. For causing all this in the first place.”

Lilith looked at her and pulled herself to her feet. The rest of the group followed suit until they were all standing around like they were guests at an exceedingly uncomfortable cocktail party where the host had forgotten to put on any clothes.

“Eve,” she said. “You’re looking well. You’ve put on quite a bit of weight.”

Apple and Janie frowned and glanced at each other. Asmodeus put his arms around Lilith’s waist and nuzzled her neck. “Everyone has been so excited to meet you,” he said. “They’ve worked hard to get you back to yourself.”

“It’s only fitting,” she said. “It kind of was your fault, wasn’t it, Eve?”

Eve bit her lip and looked uncertain. “Yes, yes, it was. And I’m sorry.”

Lilith shrugged. “Whatever. It’s done now, I suppose. I have a lot to catch up on.” She winked at Asmodeus and ran her hand down his chest. “Can we go? Where are we living now? I want to have a lot of sex and then maybe go swimming. In the tropics."

"Um," Cally stepped forward. "I think that we were…"

"Yes?" Lilith looked down at her.

"I think we were expecting you to… I don't know. Go out and talk to God? Maybe address all the women? You're kind of…" The old woman's voice was uncharacteristically uncertain.

"A leader," said Fae. "You're kind of our leader."

"And my best friend," said Eve.

"I was going to get a tattoo of you," said Apple.

"Why?" said Lilith simply.

"Why get a tattoo?" asked Apple.

"No, why am I your leader?"

There was some uncomfortable shuffling of feet.

"Well, because," said Wellingsley, "you've been part of a lot of women over history. Part of… part of us. We're together because of you."

"You've helped make us who we are," said Apple. "For better or for worse."

"You're part of us," said Gloria. "Apparently. I've only just found out about it all tough so I might not have everything clear."

"You want me to lead you?" said Lilith.

Fae bit her lip. "Now I say it aloud, it sounds a bit…"

"Odd," said Apple.

"Maybe not lead exactly," said Eve. "Mentor perhaps."

"Support possibly?" said Cally.

The women all looked at each other.

"That doesn't sound like something I want to do," said Lilith.

"But hang on," said Cally. "You're part of mythology. Of folklore. You have a role to play. Word of you has spread. People know of you."

Lilith tilted her head on one side and looked at the old woman, not unkindly. "Not to be rude," she said, "but this really does feel like a 'you' problem. Or at least, not a 'me' problem."

The music continued to pump from the other room, and she looked to the door. “What’s happening in there?” she asked.

“There’s a big party,” said Asmodeus, his hands still around her waist possessively. “God is throwing it.”

“Oh, him,” she said, rolling her eyes. “Even more reason to head out right now.”

“I think he’d quite like to see you. He feels bad,” said Eve. “Once again,” she said, “I feel like I’m being asked to deal with a lot of things that are quite dramatically not my problem. Please don’t tell me I’ve appeared thousands of years in the future, and women are still supposed to be dealing with everything, whether they want to or not. I didn’t buy into any of this then, and I’m not now.”

She grasped Asmodeus’s hand firmly and looked up at him. “Let’s go.”

And he led her away.

LET'S DANCE

The women looked at each other. Eve had her hands on her hips and was frowning.

"Is this embarrassing?" asked Apple. "I feel like we should be embarrassed."

"How can she not care about us?" said Fae, tears in her eyes. "After all of this, and she just walks away. After everything we've been through. And now I don't even have a boyfriend. What am I going to do?"

Cally's lips were pressed so tightly together that they almost disappeared in her weathered brown face. "It's true, though," she said. "The girl never committed to anything. She never claimed to be anything." She shook her head sadly. "But surely she would have realized how important she is to us."

Eve finally spoke. "This was the whole point, though. To make whole again. To help her become herself again after what was done to her in the past."

"Well, yes," said Fae.

"Yes," agreed Apple.

"Of course," said Cally. "But I think I speak for all of us when I say that she owes us some—"

"She doesn't owe us anything, don't you understand?" Eve's voice was strong. "We're just as bad as the men if we attach expectations of what she'll do for us to her."

Gloria stepped forward and broke into the conversation for the first time. "Allow me to give my outside perspective," she said, "seeing as I'm part of this, apparently, but have had to do some very quick reconnaissance and decipher what's happening on the fly."

The women looked at her.

"This Lilith woman, the one who just left with the swarthy gentleman, hasn't actually seen or heard or known anything for several thousands years, right?"

"Sort of right," said Cally. "We'd had chats."

"It sounds like she didn't have a huge awareness of them, though," continued Gloria. "And while she has been away, myths and stories and traditions have grown up."

"Yes," said Eve. "Lots."

The women again nodded.

"And it seems like that God character, who I fully intend to network with soon, and that Adam and Jared, who have had discombobulating experiences of their own, have built up a pretty negative narrative, and some of you, and other women, have built up a positive one."

"Exactly," said Apple. "Positive. We're positive."

"But that doesn't matter," said Gloria. "It doesn't matter if it was positive or negative. She didn't ask for any of this. And now she's back, and she's gone off to have what I hope is a lot of wild sex with that man of hers. Which she is allowed to do."

"But—" said Apple.

"No, she's right," said Eve. "Listen to her. It makes sense."

"She's allowed to do whatever she wants, and it's got nothing to do with you," continued Gloria. "Or, I suppose, us. I was part of her, too. Or am. Goodness, I don't know." She shook her head and rubbed the bridge of he nose. "I don't know. No, actually, I do know. I'm pretty convinced that I'm right about this. You forcing her into a narrative of saving women or whatever is just as bad as what was being done to her."

There was silence for a moment.

"She's right," said Wellingsley, and Eve smiled at her and squeezed her hand.

Gloria looked at her in amusement. "I don't think you've ever said that before."

"I don't think I've ever thought it before," Wellingsley replied, and smiled at her mother. "But you are right. She can do what she wants to do. But so can we. We have some Lilith in us, don't we? Or we did. Or something."

"I'm just a plus one," said Janie, "but that's okay. Saves me an existential crisis."

"What do we do now?" asked Fae. "This has been my whole life for a while now. Admittedly, I've swapped sides a bit, but still. There's been a lot of Lilith."

"Well," said Gloria. "I'm pretty sure I can arrange a meeting with the Boss in here." She pulled a bottle of vodka from her handbag. "I took this from the bar, and if I can get him in a corner for twenty minutes, I'm almost entirely sure I can convince him to go off and take on this dreadful taco idea that he seems set on and leave the running of things to me. Anyone else in? Eve, what about you? This is your legacy, after all."

Eve beamed at her and looked at the women standing around. "I don't want to be in charge," she said. "I wanted to help Lilith and be free of Adam and stop him from ruining any more lives, and I've done that. *We've* done that. Now I want to have friends, read books, and spend time with my true love."

"Sounds awful," said Gloria. "But your choice. It's all about choice, isn't it?"

Eve wrapped her arms around the older woman's neck. "I really like you, you know. I really like all of you."

"We really like you, too," said Apple. "You're kind of the mother of all women, you know. You brought us together."

"I suppose so," said Eve. "And now for a reason I can be proud of."

"Do you think you can convince God to leave you in charge?" asked Janie, turning to Gloria.

"I don't think, I know," said Gloria.

Wellingsley nodded. "She can. She will. She's amazing."

"Anyone else in?" asked Gloria.

"What, taking charge of everything?" replied Apple.

Gloria nodded.

"Fuck yes," said Apple.

"Let's do it," said Fae.

"I could give it a go," said Cally with a thoughtful nod.

Eve laughed and shook her head. "Too much excitement for me. I'm not really a boss babe. But I could do with a good dance. Let's tear up that dance floor until someone asks us to leave."

So, they did.

ABOUT THE AUTHOR

Eva Leppard grew up in the 70s and 80s on a steady diet of BBC comedy and Douglas Adams books. Having spent most of her early years prowling through the bush with a pocketknife and a cat, she had plenty of time to start creating her own fantasy worlds. She still lives in the Australian bush, but now dreams of a penthouse in a big city with fewer spiders and more coffee shops.

Her debut novel, *The Pitfalls of Being a Goddess*, was published in 2023, and her second, *Mother Trouble* released in 2025.

www.ingramcontent.com/pod-product-compliance
Lightning Source LLC
LaVergne TN
LVHW050925080826
845145LV00001B/219

* 9 7 8 1 9 6 4 8 8 5 6 0 5 *